A NOTE TO PARENTS

When your children are ready to "step into reading," giving them the right books—and lots of them—is as crucial as giving them the right food to eat. **Step into Reading Books** present exciting stories and information reinforced with lively, colorful illustrations that make learning to read fun, satisfying, and worthwhile. They are priced so that acquiring an entire library of them is affordable. And they are beginning readers with an important difference—they're written on four levels.

Step 1 Books, with their very large type and extremely simple vocabulary, have been created for the very youngest readers. **Step 2 Books** are both longer and slightly more difficult. **Step 3 Books,** written to mid-second-grade reading levels, are for the child who has acquired even greater reading skills. **Step 4 Books** offer exciting nonfiction for the increasingly proficient reader.

Children develop at different ages. **Step into Reading Books,** with their four levels of reading, are designed to help children become good—and interested—readers *faster*. The grade levels assigned to the four steps—preschool through grade 1 for Step 1, grades 1 through 3 for Step 2, grades 2 and 3 for Step 3, and grades 2 through 4 for Step 4—are intended only as guides. Some children move through all four steps very rapidly; others climb the steps over a period of several years. These books will help your child "step into reading" in style!

Foreword

After decades of relative neglect, followed by a period during which some historians treated it as little more than a passing fad, the study of women's history emerged to take its place as one of the more fruitful fields of scholarly inquiry. Within this broad area of exploration, more narrowly focused efforts to shed light on the role of women in early America proved particularly productive and exciting. Since 1970 well over sixty books and articles, along with numerous reviews, have drawn attention to the conduct and circumstances of women living during the colonial and revolutionary eras, and through our increased understanding of the lives they led we have gained additional insight into the nature of seventeenth- and eighteenth-century America. Such scholars as Mary Beth Norton, Linda K. Kerber, Joan Hoff-Wilson, John Demos, Suzanne Lebsock, Laurel Thatcher Ulrich, Lyle Koehler, Lois Green Carr, and Lorena Walsh (to name only a few) have expanded both the knowledge and the perspective of their profession and given the history of early American women an importance far greater than the status generally accorded them by the male-dominated society in which they lived.[1]

As one might expect, this veritable explosion of scholarship gave rise to considerable debate, for new works produced new insights, which in turn forced revisions of assumptions previously held. And in research such as this, where so much was new, where the energy and intensity was so great, revisions came rapidly and what was orthodoxy one day was repudiated at the next symposium. Fortunately these new interpretations proved so provocative, and those advancing them were so skillful, that what might have confused has instead confirmed that women's history is indeed worthy of more than cursory consideration and that those who ignore these findings do so at their intellectual peril. What has been accomplished in this field of study in such a short time is nothing less than remarkable.

Although early American women, like their later counterparts, suffered from a lack of scholarly attention prior to 1970, the little that was written about them painted a not altogether disagreeable picture of the female condition in Britain's North American colonies. The so-called "golden age" hypothesis, advanced earlier by Elisabeth Anthony Dexter, Richard B. Morris, Herbert Moller, and Mary Ritter Beard, contended that in this era American women were few and their labor was critical to the survival of the family unit; thus they enjoyed greater social esteem and personal independence than their descendants who lived in the nineteenth century. What brought this age to an end was industrialism, which took many women out of the home—that special province that gave their lives meaning—and put them in the factory as workers without a status of their own. Meanwhile other women, mostly those in the middle class, suffered a different, yet equally debasing fate as they were absorbed into the "cult of domesticity" that made them little more than ornaments in the home that once sustained them.[2]

As interest in the evolution of the status of women increased, the idea of a "golden age" came under attack. Mary Beth Norton led the way as she argued convincingly that the colonial era was hardly what previous scholars made it seem; rather it was a male-dominated society where opportunities for female self-expression outside the home were few and even there the life of the colonial wife was hardly "golden." It was a world where what a woman was, and hoped to be, was linked first to marriage and after that to her husband, a world where the "feminine sphere" was narrowly defined and constantly trivialized by the men in her life, and where what was or was not accepted behavior was so thoroughly internalized by most women that to do otherwise was unthinkable. Bound and restricted by rituals of domestic training, courtship, marriage, and the demands of a family, early American women followed predictable patterns broken only rarely, and then at the danger of being branded "unfeminine." Though things may have been worse in the following century, the 1700s were hardly halcyon days.[3]

As the "golden age" hypothesis crumbled before this scholarly assault, Norton and other historians began to wonder whether the question of lost status between the seventeenth and the nineteenth centuries was really relevant to what modern scholarship should be seeking to accomplish. The whole argument, according to Lee Ann Caldwell, "seems premature, for much research still must be done to determine the status of women within their own society before valid comparisons can be made."[4] Along these same lines Norton suggested that women's studies might best be served if scholars concentrated on "the identification of the major changes and continuities in women's lives during the colonial and revolutionary periods," a course that was already revealing "a far more complicated picture, one in which definitions of gender roles, the nature of the colonial economy, demographic patterns, religion, the law, household organization, ideas and behavior brought from the Old World (especially England), and the colonists' attitudes toward themselves and their society all contributed to defining the circumstances of women's lives."[5]

Efforts to do what Norton and Caldwell suggested led historians to consider what impact the American Revolution had on those women who lived through it, and this set off yet another round of debates. Joan Hoff-Wilson's investigations led her to conclude, in a manner revealing that the "golden age" thesis has not been entirely rejected, that the struggle for independence "retarded those societal conditions that had given colonial women their unique function and status in society, while it promoted those that were leading toward the gradual 'embourgeoisement' of late eighteenth-century women." Thus, she argued, "The American Revolution produced no significant benefits for American women," but instead "the end result was increased loss of function and authentic status."[6] Norton and Linda K. Kerber, on the other hand, found that the Revolution was a transforming event during which "the boundaries of the feminine sphere itself began to change" as women assumed attitudes and engaged in activities far different from those of their mothers and grandmothers. This latter argument, which at present appears more widely accepted, holds that though they were still restrained by conventional views of sex roles these "daughters of liberty" found they could operate farms and businesses for absent husbands, make decisions for the welfare of their families without male advice, engage in political discussions (albeit in private), aid in the war effort, and in general contribute to the society of which they were part in ways unheard-of then and unappreciated until now. It was a time when many women learned to appreciate their own capacities, which for most proved a rewarding, liberating experience.[7]

Differences as to just what impact the Revolution had on the lives and status of colonial women led to debate on the nature of the postwar feminine sphere. Some scholars continued to explore the relationship between pre- and postwar conditions and though most rejected, or greatly modified, the "golden age" concept, they nevertheless found that the struggle for liberty proved a disappointment for women expecting their status to change appreciably for the better. Others, led by Kerber and Norton, looked at the broader issues involved and in the process sought to better understand why women's lot was as it was and to assess the implications of that condition. Obviously women benefited little politically from independence. New Jersey's brief flirtation with women's suffrage notwithstanding, American men chose to ignore Abigail Adams's plea to her husband, John, to "remember the ladies" when drafting laws for the new nation. Still, women did find a somewhat more exalted place in the American republic, and this condition revealed not only the foundation of the emerging social order but also helped clarify how the nineteenth-century "cult of domesticity" came about.[8]

After independence, wartime experiences combined with republican ideology not only to alter the view men held of women but more importantly to change women's view of themselves. Fundamental to this new attitude was a shift that occurred in the relationship between husband and wife. In the home, which had been (and remained) the center of the feminine sphere, the once patriarchal arrangement increasingly gave way to a mutual understanding that, while not directly challenging traditional beliefs concerning a woman's destiny, nevertheless elevated the role she played in the private society of the family to equal in importance that role which her husband played in public. What emerged from this was the image of the "Republican Mother," guardian of those virtues on which the new nation depended and transmitter of those values to her children, especially her sons. Given such responsibilities, it was no longer possible to trivialize the feminine sphere as colonial men so often had done, and with this change in status American women as a group took their first halting steps toward true equality.[9]

To date, most studies of eighteenth-century women have been largely exercises in collective biography. Few subjects left the records on which to base an individual account, so scholars have resorted to the time-honored practice of gathering together scattered material and unifying it to form a meaningful whole. Until emerging assumptions are applied to specific lives, however, much of the humanity that is so critical to history is missing. Fortunately John and Janet Stegeman's *Caty* provides scholars and laymen alike a unique opportunity to make just such an application. Self-described "amateur history-seekers," the Stegemans have produced a well-researched, clearly written biography that is an example of popular history at its best. And like so much of this genre, it is uncluttered by the interpretive intrusions of academic historiography. This allows the reader to follow the life of Caty Greene for its own sake or, if one wishes, to use it as an aid in drawing one's own conclusions about the validity of generalizations made by modern scholars.

Since Caty was born late in the colonial era, her early years offer scant opportunity to assess the "golden age" thesis, although as a member of a well-to-do family her childhood did have its ideal qualities. However, evidence suggests that, despite the existence of a well-defined feminine sphere, women in her family were taking charge of their own lives in ways still not fully appreciated. Caty's mother, six months pregnant when she went to the altar, was one of a significant number of women whose similar condition at marriage has been cited to prove that the patriarchal rules of propriety designed to keep girls in place, intact, and thus more appealing to marriageable men, were breaking down. More importantly, the future Mrs. Littlefield's role in this attack on the code was anything but passive, nor did it make her unacceptable to her future husband. Caty inherited much of her mother's independence in sexual matters, though less of her imprudence; thus through the daughter contemporary readers can see and appreciate how, even then, the "double-standard" was perceived and violated. [10]

The death of her mother when Caty was six threw her into a circle of women relations who assumed the responsibility for her education and her introduction into the society that would shape her expectations and occupy her time. Here, as so often happens when generalizations are applied to specific cases, one finds contradictions as well as confirmations. Obviously yearning for an education beyond that given most young ladies, Caty was forced to accept male dictates in this regard; nevertheless, through the influence of her "independent" Aunt Catherine, she developed a self-confidence uncharacteristic of colonial women in general, an attitude some scholars find emerging with the Revolution, but less evident in the years before. Despite this self-confidence, Caty Littlefield accepted, indeed sought, the fate of most of her counterparts: marriage and an identity linked to that of her husband (further evidence of the few options open to colonial women no matter what their rank, and of how they had internalized their condition). Following a traditional courtship in which the rules of propriety and collective family decision making were observed, Caty married Nathanael and the two settled down for what promised to be the life of a typical colonial family.[11]

Marriage was considered the critical event in the life of the early American woman. It determined her fate, for a good match promised happiness while a bad one doomed the bride to a lifetime of physical and mental hardship. Furthermore, marriage elevated women in the eyes of both sexes, and gave them a status considered superior to their single sisters, which, in a male-dominated society, meant an identity recognized and appreciated by those in control. Legally, however, it only moved her from one sort of dependence to another—from dependence on the males in her family to dependence on her husband, although in the latter case she had at least some say in selecting her master. Still, as a *feme covert* (by law part of her husband), her status was legal, which, if the match was good, further enhanced her position. But if the match proved bad, it compounded the tragedy.[12]

If all this concerned Caty Greene she left no mention of it. Instead she settled down to be the mistress of the household and companion of her husband, the common desire of upper-class colonial women. What made her life different from that of the women of her rank who preceded her was the American Revolution, and even more than that, her husband's involvement in it. Exposed to political discussions, and in many cases able (indeed encouraged) to take part, she found her feminine sphere expanding even before the conflict began. Then, when Nathanael left home, she truly began to appreciate the impact that events would have on the lives of women like herself. Without a male figure to define and direct, women were forced to assume responsibilities usually reserved for husbands, brothers, or fathers—duties often considered inappropriate for someone of their gender and at times improper for members of their class. Poorly trained in domestic arts (Aunt Catherine had other interests), Caty was all the more ill-prepared to take over the administration of a household. This lack of preparation was compounded and complicated by periodic pregnancies, a condition both longed for and feared by colonial women. Pregnancy further reduced her administrative effectiveness as it increased her realization of how she was being denied the emotional and psychological rewards of normal family life.

Caty's experiences during the Revolution both confirm and offer exceptions to the general trends identified by modern scholars. Unquestionably the war was for her a liberating event, but not one to which she was entirely receptive. Forced to take on tasks for which she was unprepared, and in many cases which might have been denied her in more normal times, she nevertheless struggled to retain some semblance of that way of life the war prevented her from enjoying, even though such efforts generally confirmed her prewar feminine role. Visits to the army, not just to see Nathanael but also to be part of the social whirl that accompanied the officer corps, became a highlight of her existence. Comfortable in the company of men, she became the subject of gossip (indeed almost scandal) as she bent the rules of propriety that governed the lives of women nearly to the breaking point. Caty Greene was expanding the feminine sphere, but one suspects she would have done the same had there been no war.

But of course there was a conflict and it could not be ignored. Necessity demanded the reorganization of tasks and responsibilities, and Caty's efforts to cope with these reinforce many of the assumptions currently in vogue. Her relations with those outside the military, especially with other women, reveal that others of her sex were making adjustments and venturing into areas heretofore considered outside their domain or beyond their abilities. Difficult as it is to say if Caty was beginning to see herself as something other than the wife of General Nathanael Greene, or that she was creating for herself an identity she would later wish to retain, it is clear that in the light of what followed the Revolution, the training provided her proved critical. [13]

With victory Caty Greene assumed she would settle down to the life of a respected, well-to-do eighteenth-century gentleman's wife. Here one can see how, despite her recent experiences, Caty's postwar circumstances were still defined by prerevolutionary standards. Although she had successfully coped with the pressures war, and the politics of war, had placed on the family, Caty now deferred to her husband, who took charge and apparently kept her ignorant of how the politics of peace threatened the prosperity she expected. Of course she knew something of their financial condition from Nathanael's occasional warnings not to spend so much, but it was not until their dismal prospects forced them to move to Georgia that she understood the full extent of their plight. In this attitude Nathanael Greene acted much as his colonial predecessors, and Caty's response seemed to confirm his position. Since he "burdened" her with money matters usually when he asked her to confine her material and social circumstances, any protest made her appear little more than a self-indulgent child, too irresponsible to act as an equal partner in affairs of such importance. It was, however, an arrangement acceptable to both, for Caty showed as little interest in invading the male sphere as Nathanael did the female. They understood each other well, loved each other deeply, and sought only to live as they perceived people of their station should. [14]

Liberation for Caty came not with the Revolution but with widowhood. Nathanael Greene died in June of 1786 at Mulberry Grove, the Savannah River plantation on which he hoped to recoup his fortunes. His death confirmed how little Caty knew about family finances, and the rest of her long life provides the modern reader a unique opportunity to witness an eighteenth-century woman trying to make her way in the economically destitute, politically corrupt state of Georgia. In this regard her career also confirms that postwar America was still a man's world, and women were subject to their rules and regulations. Men settled the Greene estate, oversaw the education of the eldest son, advised the widow, and in general governed Caty's affairs on her behalf, as if she were not capable of doing so herself. But rather than rebel against these conditions, Caty Greene learned to use them, and in the end found a degree of self-realization that would have been impossible had she been married, which may explain why she kept her single status so long. As a widow she became involved in financial affairs and politics in ways that would have been inappropriate, if not impossible, if her husband had been alive. Yet these activities, which were clearly in the male domain, continued to be conducted with the help and support of men. It was a man's world. Caty Greene knew it and made do as best she could. [15]

At the same time Caty continued to function in the traditional feminine sphere, although some elements of "republican motherhood" are evident in her conduct. Concern for her daughters' education beyond customary domestic requirements revealed that the female bonding of mothers and daughters was broadening to encourage the latter not only to prepare themselves to be good wives but also to take on the more challenging, though as yet unspecified, responsibilities of republican marriage. In this and other ways Caty Greene came to represent what Mary Beth Norton described as "the Americans' vision of the ideal woman—an independent thinker and patriot, a virtuous wife, competent household manager, and knowledgeable mother." Her eventual marriage to Phineas Miller had most of the trappings of mutual understanding and respect that the new view of such a union and the woman's role in it encompassed. What freedoms she had gained she valued, and though still a child of the eighteenth century, Caty saw a better era coming and wanted to be sure that she and her daughters were ready for it. [16]

So it is that the experiences of Catharine Littlefield Greene highlight not only the changes through which American women went during the latter half of the eighteenth century but also emphasize so much of what remained the same. In many instances Caty rejected those attitudes about self and status internalized by so many of her counterparts and made what use she could of the liberating forces at work in her life. And yet, despite the many ways her career confirms assertions and generalizations advanced by modern scholars regarding the impact of revolution and republicanism on the colonial feminine sphere, one cannot escape the feeling that she would have happily given it all up just to be the wife of General Nathanael Greene, or at least given up most of it, for one is also left with the distinct impression that as such she would have been one of the most "liberated" wives of her generation. Such speculation aside, how Caty coped with the challenges she faced, and the nature of the world she sought to create for herself and her family, provides an instructive example for those readers seeking to understand what the American Revolution and its aftermath meant to a segment of society that is finally recognized as a significant part of the colonial population.

But Caty's story is important beyond its value to the study of the female experience during and after the Revolution. She witnessed, and at times participated in, some of the most far-reaching events in American and Georgia history: the end of British rule, the postwar political maneuvering that left her husband and others like him wondering if the right revolutionaries won after all, the Yazoo fraud and its consequences, and the invention of the cotton gin. She knew, indeed was intimate, with some of the most important people of her day, including Anthony Wayne, Eli Whitney, George and Martha Washington, Alexander Hamilton, and of course, Nathanael Greene. These events and personalities come alive through Caty, thanks to her careful and sensitive resurrection by John and Janet Stegeman. What we have here is an exciting, informative book that will both entertain and enlighten its readers, and for it we should be grateful.

HARVEY H. JACKSON

Notes

I wish to express my appreciation to Ann Ellis of Kennesaw College and Virginia Shadron of the Georgia Department of Archives and History for reading this Foreword and offering helpful observations on the current state of women's studies.

1. For a representative sample of the current work on early American women, see Mary Beth Norton, *Liberty's Daughters: The Revolutionary Experience of American Women, 1750–1800* (Boston, 1980), and "The Evolution of White Woman's Experience in Early America," *American Historical Review* (June 1984): 593–619; Linda K. Kerber, *Women of the Republic: Intellect and Ideology in Revolutionary America* (Chapel Hill, 1980); Joan Hoff-Wilson, "The Illusion of Change: Women and the American Revolution," in Alfred F. Young, ed., *The American Revolution: Explorations in the History of American Radicalism* (DeKalb, Illinois, 1976); John Putnam Demos, *Entertaining Satan: Witchcraft and the Culture of Early New England* (New York, 1982); Suzanne Lebsock, *The Free Women of Petersburg: Status and Culture in a Southern Town, 1784–1860* (New York, 1984); Laurel Thatcher Ulrich, *Good Wives: Image and Reality in the Lives of Women in Northern New England, 1650–1750* (New York, 1982); Lyle Koehler, *A Search for Power: The "Weaker Sex" in Seventeenth-Century New England* (Urbana, Illinois, 1980); and Lois Green Carr and Lorena Walsh, "The Planter's Wife: The Experience of White Women in Seventeenth-Century Maryland," *William and Mary Quarterly* (October 1977): 542–71.

2. The "golden age" hypothesis may be found in Elisabeth Anthony Dexter, *Colonial Women of Affairs* (Boston, 1924); Richard B. Morris, *Studies in the History of American Law, with Special Reference to the Seventeenth and Eighteenth Centuries* (New York, 1930); Herbert Moller, "Sex Composition and Correlated Culture Patterns of Colonial America," *William and Mary Quarterly* (January 1945): 113–53; and Mary Ritter Beard, *Woman as Force in History* (New York, 1946).

3. A fine general explanation of the weaknesses of the "golden age" hypothesis may be found in the preface to Norton's *Liberty's Daughters* and in her article "The Evolution of White Women's Experience."

4. Lee Ann Caldwell, "Women Landholders of Colonial Georgia," in Harvey H. Jackson and Phinizy Spalding, eds., *Forty Years of Diversity: Essays on Colonial Georgia* (Athens, 1984), p. 184.

5. Norton, "The Evolution of White Women's Experience," p. 595.

6. Hoff-Wilson, "The Illusion of Change," pp. 387, 430, 431. See also Julia Cherry Spruill, *Women's Life and Work in the Southern Colonies* (1938; reprint New York, 1972).

7. Kerber, *Women of the Republic*, p. xi; Norton, *Liberty's Daughters*, p. 156. See also Robert A. Gross's review of these two books in the *William and Mary Quarterly* (January 1982): 231–38.

8. Kerber, *Women of the Republic*, pp. 81–82; Norton, *Liberty's Daughters*, pp. 191–93.

9. Republican motherhood is explained in Kerber, *Women of the Republic*, pp. 265–88. See also Carl Degler, *At Odds: Women and the Family in America from the Revolution to the Present* (New York, 1980).

10. The best, easily available assessment of colonial courtship is in Norton, *Liberty's Daughters*, pp. 51–61. See especially pp. 51–52, 55–56.

11. Norton, *Liberty's Daughters*, pp. 40–70. Readers wishing to assess *Caty* in the light of contemporary scholarship should begin with this book. In addition to *Liberty's Daughters* and the other studies cited above, one might also consult Norton's "'What an Alarming Crisis Is This': Southern Women and the American Revolution," in Jeffrey J. Crow and Larry E. Tise, eds., *The Southern Experience in the American Revolution* (Chapel Hill, 1978); Robert V. Wells, *Revolutions in Americans' Lives: A Demographic Perspective on the History of Americans, Their Families, and Their Society* (Westport, Connecticut, 1982); the January 1982 issue of the *William and Mary Quarterly*, which is devoted to articles and essays on women and the family; Nancy Woloch, *Women and the American Experience* (New York, 1984), pp. 1–96; Carol Ruth Berkin and Mary Beth Norton, eds., *Women of America: A History* (Boston, 1979), pp. 3–150; as well as *Signs: Journal of Women in Culture and Society*, which is the leading scholarly journal devoted to the subject.

12. On the legal status of American women and its implications, see Norton, *Liberty's Daughters*, pp. 40–70; Morris, *Studies in the History of American Law*, chapters 3 and 4; Kerber, *Women of the Republic*, pp. 139–55; and Caldwell, "Women Landholders of Colonial Georgia."

13. For a discussion of women during the revolution itself, see Norton, *Liberty's Daughters*, pp. 155–227; and Hoff-Wilson, "The Illusion of Change."

14. How colonial women were kept isolated from family financial affairs is described in Norton, *Liberty's Daughters*, pp. 4–9.

15. For the impact of widowhood, see Norton, *Liberty's Daughters*, pp. 132–47; and Kerber, *Women of the Republic*, pp. 141–47.

16. Norton, *Liberty's Daughters*, p. 256. Norton also provides insight into the relationship between mothers and daughters (pp. 100–109), the concept of "republican marriage" (pp. 234–38), the education of women in postwar America (pp. 256–94), and the idea of "republican motherhood" (pp. 242–55). See also Kerber, *Women of the Republic*, pp. 185–288.

Preface

Over a span of six years, while reconstructing the life story of Caty Greene, we followed her footsteps from the place of her birth on precipitous Block Island off the coast of New England, to the flat, marshy Georgia sea island of Cumberland. Our journeys took us to the eleven states (of the original thirteen) in which Caty lived and traveled, and, while tracking down her letters two centuries after she had written them, to parts of the country that had been only western wilderness in her day.

Purely amateur history-seekers, and armed with a single credential—a letter from W. Porter Kellam, the Director of Libraries at the University of Georgia—we set off in 1970 on our search for information. We had some timid reservations at first but our trepidations were shortlived. Everywhere we went the story was the same. People opened their vast historical treasures to us without question and did everything at their command to help us along with our project.

We think the fact that we were novices helped our cause. Sensing our inexperience, directors of libraries and historical societies put themselves at our service, personally guiding us to the archives we sought, giving us *carte blanche* use of their facilities and, not content with that, helping arrange our accommodations and even taking us out to meals. Owners of private collections were equally gracious, and those whose property once belonged to Caty and her family took hours out of their day to show us the grounds, even furnishing our transportation when the distance was great. Along the way other new acquaintances and correspondents who possessed information we sought never once objected to our inquisitiveness or turned down our requests.

Perhaps our first big thrill during our examination of manuscripts was seeing Caty's handwriting for the first time. But our first disappointment was in realizing that her letters to her husband, General Nathanael Greene, had all been destroyed. Even the Rhode Island Historical Society in its recent exhaustive search for Greene documents could not find a single one. The editors surmise that Caty burned the letters because she did not want her poor spelling and grammar on display. We think there was another reason as well: since she wrote honestly and candidly, her personal comments may have embarrassed her in retrospect.

The absence of Caty's letters to her husband are a great loss, for we miss the amusingly descriptive style that characterized her later correspondence. Fortunately, General Greene was most specific in his replies, often repeating his wife's questions and complaints before answering them. From this we were able to make accurate conclusions as to what she wrote but not in her own delicious language.

In other areas, too, we faced the task of filling in missing pieces. We backed away from the type of "biographer's license" that allows the author to guess and then write, as fact, the exact words his character spoke, or the precise action he took, in a given circumstance. As far as possible we based our story on first-hand information, drawn from hundreds of original documents. When blank spots appeared, we depended heavily upon secondary sources, but, determined not to perpetuate some myth originated by a fanciful author, we gathered our impressions from the aggregate of as many such sources as we could find. Sometimes we were forced to piece together our narrative from tiny scraps of information, but without the necessity of fabricating from whole cloth.

We think the lady we present to our readers comes close to being the real Caty Greene.

Now for our roll of honor:

First of all our gratitude goes to Glenn W. LaFantasie, publications director of the Rhode Island Bicentennial Commission/ Foundation and our principal editor and advisor. His counsel, encouragement and friendship far exceeded the call of an editor's duty. He was succeeded as director by Paul Campbell, who carried out on our behalf the fine work of his predecessor and made final arrangements for the book's publication.

Our special thanks go to the following for their hospitality and assistance at the sites of Caty's dwelling and stopping places: at Block Island, R.I.: Mrs. William O. Ball, Sr., Mrs. Harold Dodge, and Captain Oswald Littlefield; at East Greenwich, R.I.: Mrs. Thomas Casey Greene, Thomas Casey Greene, Jr., and Mrs. William Greene Roelker; at Coventry, R.I.: William Nourse; at West Point, N.Y.: Captain and Mrs. Robert Guy and Curtis Esposito; at Savannah, Ga.: Mr. and Mrs. Arthur Solomon, Jr., Mr. and

Mrs. Malcolm Bell, Jr., and Mr. and Mrs. Huguenon Thomas; at Cumberland Island, Ga.: Mr. and Mrs. Rick Ferguson and Mrs. Lucy Ferguson.

Our principal manuscript work was done at the following libraries and historical societies where we were given every assistance by those named, to whom we are indeed grateful: William L. Clements Library, University of Michigan: Howard H. Peckham and William S. Ewing; Yale University Library: Judith Schiff; South Caroliniana Library, University of South Carolina: E. L. Inabinett; University of Georgia Library: W. Porter Kellam, John Bonner, Susan Frances Tate and Mary Beth Brown; Georgia Historical Society: Lilla Hawes; Rhode Island Historical Society: Richard K. Showman, Margaret Cobb, Albert T. Klyberg, Nathaniel Shipton and Virginia Catton.

The following were most cooperative in making manuscripts available to us: Gertrude D. Hess at the American Philosophical Society; John D. Kilbourne and Nicholas B. Wainwright at the Historical Society of Pennsylvania; Stephen T. Riley and Ross Urquhart at the Massachusetts Historical Society; Doris E. Cook at the Connecticut Historical Society; John M. Jennings at the Virginia Historical Society; Kenneth A. Lohf at the Columbia University Libraries; John P. Baker at the New York Public Library; Agnes Sherman and Ira M. Simet at the Princeton University Library; James M. Coleman, Jr. at the Morristown National Historical Park; and Alexander V. J. Gaudieri at the Telfair Academy of Arts and Sciences.

Correspondents who contributed valuable information on Caty's life, or who criticized early drafts of this book, include Elizabeth Evans, Theodore Thayer, Clara G. Roe, Mrs. Hugh W. Loney, Mrs. Stahle Linn, Jr., Bernard Nightingale, Patricia A. Duffy, Elizabeth L. Mullins, Dr. Benjamin Tefft and Edward Bowen.

Our appreciation extends also to many persons at home and nearby who were indispensable to our undertaking. They include our faithful and tireless family editor and encourager, Dorothea W. Stegeman; our excellent typist, Mrs. Joan Burns; and a number of those who helped us in a hundred ways, including Merton Coulter, Richard K. Murdoch, Phinizy Spalding, Marion S. Hodgson, Joanna Traylor, Mary Claire Warren, Sarah Maret, JoAnn DeZoort, Billie Newton, Martha Miller, Susie Hicks and Nancy Andrews.

John Foster Stegeman
Janet Allais Stegeman

CATY

**A Biography of
Catharine Littlefield Greene**

1 A Colonial Childhood

In May 1761, Catharine Littlefield stood with her relatives on a high hill that faced the sea and overlooked the meadows and pastures of Block Island. A network of stone fences rose and dipped across the face of the craggy terrain. Though barely six, little Caty was old enough to understand the meaning of the solemn gathering. A burial party lowered into the ground the coffin of her mother, who at the age of twenty-eight left behind a husband and five children.

Ten years before, the wedding of Caty's mother and father had been an important social occasion, uniting the best-known families on the island. Whether any commotion was made over the bride's advanced state of pregnancy is not recorded. Documents show only that John Littlefield made an "honest woman" of Phebe Ray with four months to spare. The baby was a boy.

On February 17, 1755, Caty, the third child, was born. She was named for her mother's sister, Catharine Ray, a beautiful dark-haired woman whom Caty later was said to resemble even more than she did her own mother. It was Aunt Catharine who was to adopt Caty after her mother's death and to become a dominant influence during her growing years.

Caty's life on Block Island was sheltered and secluded. The tiny isle, lying isolated in the Atlantic twelve miles off the Rhode Island coast, with its fifty white families and a number of friendly Indians and free blacks, was her world. Her family home stood near an inland pond protected from the ocean by a high ridge. Here, as on any part of the island, there was a constant awareness of the majesty of the sea. On a clear day, standing atop a cliff, Caty could see up and down the coast of the mainland across the sky-blue sound. When the sun would disappear, the water would turn gray, the fog or windswept rain would roll in to enshroud the landscape, and the island would become her prison.

A sense of timelessness pervaded the isle. There was little to separate one day from another, few reasons to quicken one's pace, and seldom any need to ask the hour of the day. There were no schools to hurry to before the bell rang and no markets to visit before closing time. A single meeting hall was the only public gathering place and here the subject discussed was usually politics—a topic not likely to interest a young girl.

Except for oxcarts there were no conveyances upon the island, and the only roads were oxpaths. Because of the absence of streets and avenues, the wooden dwellings stood here and there as if placed haphazardly, connected by the criss-crossing paths leading from each house to a number of others. The few trees that grew on the island were stunted and dwarfed by the fierceness of the winds.

Everyone rode horseback and the women wore riding breeches so they could straddle their mounts as men did—a habit that was shocking to visitors from the mainland. Like the other children on the island, Caty learned horsemanship early and became familiar with every trail, field, and fence in the area. There were wonders to be seen at the edge of the ocean and the sound—the colors of the stones on the rugged beach and the tenacious strands of bright green moss clinging to the pilings in the clear water. Wrecks that littered the shore were constant reminders of the awesome power of the sea.

Caty's ancestors had lived on Block Island since the earliest days of the settlement in the 1660s. The isle had been acquired from the Indians by the colony of Massachusetts Bay in the usual manner of the white man—partly by negotiation but mostly by force. It was then sold by the colony to a private syndicate of men from Braintree, all of whom had their own reasons for wanting to seek new freedoms. Like Adriaen Block, the Dutch explorer who had given the island his name, they were sea-faring men who had long been fascinated by the isolated isle whose sheer cliffs rose vertically from the sea.

One of the original company was Simon Ray, a great-grandfather of Caty Littlefield on her mother's side. He became the patriarch of the settlement, administering its affairs with the firmness and justness that distinguished his character, and which, many years later, became traits that Caty's children would recognize in their mother. As an English lad of sixteen, Ray had migrated with his father to America and was among the earliest settlers to land at Plymouth. A man of immense strength and moral fiber, he lived to be 101. Retaining his mental abilities to the last, Ray could recite much of the Old Testament from memory though he had been blind for years. Caty knew well the story of his early days on Block Island. He and his large family had shared a single cow with two other families, subsisting on milk pudding at daybreak and the day's catch of mackerel at sundown, with a full day of fishing and clearing the land in between.

Much of the island's character could be traced to Ray and his followers. The island settlers had come because they had tired of Massachusetts dogma; and, having won their new liberties at great sacrifice, they guarded them as priceless possessions. Detached and independent, cut off from the outside world, they were answerable only to their own neighbors, thinking, speaking, and worshipping—or not worshipping—as they pleased. This freedom of spirit made a lasting impression on Caty.

Some of the early settlers had brought a number of Scotsmen with them to the island to help work the soil. As soldiers of Charles II during the English Civil War, these Scots had been captured by Cromwell at the Battle of Worcester. Parliament, not knowing what to do with the prisoners, had sold them as servants to English colonists in the New World. One of them, William Tosh, a cavalryman who had been unhorsed during a charge at Worcester, was another of Caty's forebears.

The character of these hardy Scots was passed on to their island descendants. Along with the other settlers they persevered, making their livings by tending their fisheries, flocks, and herds, or by building sailing ships, including the sturdiest little coastal vessels known to the American colonies.

Caty's mother was the daughter of Simon Ray, Jr., who had inherited all of his father's landed property and had added abundantly to his family's fortune by investing in shipping interests at Newport. He had four remarkable and beautiful daughters by his second wife, who was a direct descendant of Roger Williams. They attracted men of great stature on both sides of the sound.

Of the four, Caty's mother Phebe was the only one who married an islander. Caty's Aunt Judith and Aunt Anna had already married at the time of her infancy, Judith to the nephew of Benjamin Franklin and Anna to a future governor of Rhode Island. Aunt Catharine, Caty's namesake, was not yet married. She later became the wife of another Rhode Island governor but was being wooed by Benjamin Franklin himself—married and much older than she.

John Littlefield, Caty's father, was distinguished in his own right. The best known of the Littlefields who had populated the island since the earliest days of the settlement, he was a landed man through inheritance and a deputy to the General Assembly of Rhode Island. To Caty he was a man of love, warmth, and fun, who liked to cuddle little children in his lap and tell them stories. She listened tirelessly as he recounted anecdotes of the island and of her kinsmen. One story concerned two of her father's uncles who were both named Ephraim Littlefield even though they were brothers. The older, an apprentice seaman in the British Navy, had been lost at sea. The younger was given the name of the departed brother by the mourning family. Many years later the younger Ephraim, having settled in New England, met an old man of the same name, who resembled himself. He was in fact the lost brother who had not gone down with the ship after all.

There also were harrowing tales about the earlier days of the island. Alone and unprotected, it had often fallen prey to pirates and other marauders. Once it had been seized and held for days by a party of French privateers. During this time Caty's Great-grandfather Ray, who refused to divulge where he had hidden a trunk, was tied to a tree, beaten, and left for dead. The island's cliffs had also provided a hiding place for William Kidd, and Caty had heard that some of his treasures were still buried there.

Caty's endless days on the isle were occasionally relieved by family trips to Newport, thirty miles across the sound, in "double-enders." These were the sailing vessels for which the island was famous. Built so they could be launched from beaches and equipped for both sailing and rowing, the boats were shaped like cow-horns, their keels angling abruptly upward at both bow and stern. The masts were bare poles, flexible enough to bend sharply in the wind without snapping. The seaworthiness of these small but durable craft was demonstrated over and over again in Block Island sound, for there are few places off the American coast where winds are more capricious or currents more treacherous.

Caty and her family might set out for Newport on a calm day, only to have the weather change abruptly, with shrieking winds buffeting the little boat while it plunged through the mountains and troughs of huge waves. Caty hated these gales, and never lost her consuming fear of a stormy sea. But always the hardy little craft would ride out the storm, even at times when larger vessels could not.

For Caty there were few thrills that compared to the joy of entering Newport harbor, New England's richest port and second only to Boston in size. Many of the ships that she saw lining the docks were manned by adventurers, with pirated goods stored below the decks. Other vessels were engaged in the "triangular service"—rum was shipped to Africa and traded for slaves, the blacks were then transported to the West Indies and traded for sugar and molasses, and these goods were brought back home and made into rum. On each leg of the voyage the ships' captains reaped huge profits for themselves and their investors, one of whom was Caty's Grandfather Ray. Speculating in such commerce was considered a perfectly respectable means of livelihood in Caty's day, and her family was very much at home within the circles of Newport society.

For Caty and the other children of Block Island, learning came through conversation with their elders, whose knowledge also was limited by their isolation. There was little on which a darting, vibrant imagination could feed. Many of the answers to Caty's questions about the wonders of nature, if offered at all, were clouded by superstition. No tutors were available, even to a Ray or a Littlefield, and this deficiency showed up consistently in the correspondence of the families, who, in spite of possessing rich vocabularies, were wretched spellers.

Caty's father recognized the potential of her mind and longed to have her educated. An opportunity came two years after the death of her mother in 1761. Her Aunt Catharine, by then the wife of William Greene Jr., a Rhode Island political leader, offered to take Caty into her fine home on the mainland. She lived in the town of East Greenwich, where excellent tutors were available.

The invitation was accepted, and at the age of eight, Caty collected her belongings, left her island home, and embarked upon her new adventure. She was unaware of the rumblings of a slowly-developing tempest that was already casting ominous shadows across the land.

The home where she lived on the mainland stands today, its parlor still warmed by a huge fireplace, its exterior surrounded by beautiful grounds. It occupies a slope near the top of a ridge, with a western view of the green valley below. On the opposite slope, beyond a brow of the hill to the east with an inlet of Narragansett Bay beyond, lies the quaint Rhode Island village of East Greenwich. Here the world opened up for Caty Littlefield. She became the close companion of her Aunt Catharine and was accepted into the household just as lovingly by her "Uncle Greene."

The Boston Post Road passed only a block away from the house and the family's carriage was often on it for a short shopping trip to sprouting Providence, or for an all-day jaunt to Boston itself. The passage to Newport from East Greenwich was a lark, the blue waters of Narragansett Bay as placid as a lake compared to the turbulence of Block Island sound. There were also occasional visits back to Caty's island home for reunions with her family.

She began her studies under Greenwich tutors, who were impressed by her enthusiasm and native intelligence. But she never learned to spell—a deficiency shared by her Aunt Catharine, whose errors were as frequent as Caty's and very similar.

Caty knew that her aunt corresponded regularly with Benjamin Franklin, but never knew how close their attachment had once been. Prior to her marriage, Catharine Ray had met Franklin at the Boston home of her sister Judith, wife of Franklin's nephew. The year before, the great inventor and philosopher had published his first papers on his experiments with electricity, and Catharine was fascinated by his discourse. He in turn was charmed by the beauty and vivacity of his lovely new acquaintance.

On his return to Philadelphia, Franklin was accompanied as far as Rhode Island by his young friend. Along the way the travellers became lost on several occasions, requiring an overnight stay in a tavern. At Newport they tarried several days together before proceeding to Westerly, where they separated. By this time, notwithstanding the fact that Franklin was a husband and father and twice his companion's age, the two were very much in love.

The letters that followed, which still enliven the yellowed papers of the Franklin collections, make it clear that the couple reached only the brink of the precipice, much to Franklin's surprised annoyance. In his first letter after reaching home, he complained of Catharine's "virgin innocence" and compared her bosom to a storm that raged outside his window—"as white as the snowy fleeces—and as cold."[1] He later approved of her "prudent Resolutions in the Article of granting Favours to Lovers"— but only when they pertained to someone other than himself.[2]

Catharine's first letters were lost or destroyed. "Excues my writeing," she said in a later message, ". . . for Suerly I have wrote too much and . . . have Said a thousand things that nothing Shoud have tempted me to [have] Said to any body else. . . . For give me & love me one thousandth Part so well as I do you and then I will be Contented and Promise an amendment."[3]

A long separation had its cooling effect. The longings subsided, the letters matured, and the friendship pursued a platonic course. After Catharine married William Greene, Franklin twice visited the couple in their East Greenwich home. The correspondence continued, and sometimes Caty's adventures were mentioned in the letters.

In spring and summer Caty and Aunt Catharine went on rides and picnics along the banks of swift-running streams and on the shores of the sparkling bay. In winter, cozy gatherings took place around the parlor fireplace in the comfortable house on the side of the hill. Caty's Uncle Greene was a popular leader of Rhode Island Whigs in their persistent resistance to Toryism. The company that came to visit his home included those whose names would become household words throughout New England. As time went on, a watchful eye was kept on the house by Loyalists who considered these young men patriots of the most radical bent.

The chief topics under discussion around Uncle Greene's fireside were the relentless determination of the British in extracting revenue from the colonists and the various means by which these efforts could be thwarted. In 1765, the year after Caty came to live in East Greenwich, she began hearing about the Stamp Act, which meant little to a child her age. But at dinnertime she would get a political education whether she wanted it or not. She came to know the contempt her family and their friends had for the law that required the records of virtually all business transactions to be printed on paper stamped and taxed by the Crown. The following year, word came that the Stamp Act had been repealed, and Caty saw the happy side of politics. Victory was in the air. Grim faces brightened, men slapped other men on the back, and people danced in the streets.

The Stamp Act repeal, however, was followed by other

obnoxious tax laws that soon brought back the living room grumblings, sometimes punctuated by shouts, and always accompanied by the smell of cigar smoke that Caty came to identify with the politics of rebellion. Among such surroundings her character began to take form. As her body underwent the miracles of the teens her personality also burgeoned into bloom. Some of the young men of East Greenwich and surrounding towns now came to the Greene home not to discuss politics but to visit their hosts' pretty niece.

One that came often from Westerly with his father was Sammy Ward, Caty's favorite cousin. Like herself an offspring of one of the dazzling Ray sisters of Block Island, he was Caty's male counterpart, good-looking, rollicking, and with a look of mischief in his eye. Sammy was the son of Aunt Anna and her husband, Samuel Ward Sr., twice governor of the colony of Rhode Island and a popular champion of colonial rights. Young Sammy possessed a sailor's vocabulary of oaths that annoyed his father as much as it amused Caty.

Another visitor who frequently called on her uncle was Nathanael Greene, a distant kinsman of his. Anchorsmith, merchant, and staunch believer in the patriots' cause, Nathanael had known Caty for several years through her cousin, Sammy Ward, with whom he had a special friendship even though the boy was much younger than he. Now suddenly little Caty had grown up under his nose. Her "merry laugh . . . and lively wit"[4] were quite a solace to a man trying to recover from a lost love. His long romance with Sammy's sister, Nancy Ward, had recently been broken off for the simple but crushing reason that she no longer loved him.

Nathanael, twelve years older than Caty, was approaching thirty when he realized that he might be falling in love again. When he looked into Caty's luminous eyes he was reminded of Nancy. Could his new emotion have been inspired by this resemblance? Nathanael wasn't quite sure at first and he wanted to think it over.

He had been born and reared at Potowomut, a tiny community near East Greenwich occupying a strip of land that projected into Narragansett Bay. He still lived in the family home when Caty moved to Greenwich, and she frequently passed his house as she rode to a favorite picnic site near the tip of the peninsula. It was during one of these rides that Nathanael first admired her young figure as she passed by on horseback.

The fourth of eight sons of a Quaker preacher who owned a farm and several forges and grist mills, Nathanael recalled his childhood as interminable days of Bible study and hard work, broken occasionally in the summertime by dives into the cool stream that flowed near his home. His one great pleasure was being allowed to go into town when the General Assembly met at East Greenwich, and he never forgot those early scenes—the bustling about of innkeepers, the tapping of cider-barrels, the baking of apple pies in huge outdoor ovens, the setting of long tables with bowls of suet-pudding and dumplings and gravy, the rushing to-and-fro of the busy, and the loitering of the idle. Nathanael walked among the scurrying men, studying expressions, trying to distinguish the important from the unimportant, and thoroughly losing himself in his pleasure.

His father saw to it that he was taught to read, but Nathanael's early education was confined to Bible study. The truth could be found only in the Scriptures, his father said; other literary pursuits led to the raising of doubts. As Nathanael grew older, his strict parent relented under great pressure from his son, and a tutor was hired. Soon his father's worst fears were realized. After a discussion of philosophy between Nathanael and a Yale collegian, the younger Greene's days of unquestioning faith came to an end.

During this period dancing became Nathanael's favorite weakness and often led to beatings when he returned home. Once a thrashing was frustrated when he stuffed shingles in the seat of his breeches. Another time he and his brothers promised their father that they would plow to a certain stone before quitting for the day. They moved the stone halfway across the field, plowed to it in no time, and all went dancing at a neighboring farm.

Their pious preacher-father was also a shrewd businessman who accumulated a modest fortune from his forges and mills. After his father's death, Nathanael and his seven brothers operated the plants and farm. They also owned a merchant ship engaged in the Caribbean trade. This vessel would soon become entangled in a serious encounter with British authorities.

In 1770, when he was twenty-eight, Nathanael built a home in Coventry. His new house was in an isolated area close to his family's forge, located on the banks of the Pawtuxet River. Here he developed his skills as an anchorsmith and merchant of moderate means. Caught up in the spreading spirit of rebellion, young

Nathanael frequently rode the ten miles back to Greenwich to join the political gatherings at the William Greene home. In time he was making even more trips as he came under the spell of Caty Littlefield, or "Kitty," as he knew her then.

Just under six feet tall, Nathanael was strongly built but had a slight limp in his gait from an old knee infection. "He is a rather large man," it was said of him, "with a face indicating fire and firmness, tempered by the innate goodness which looks out of his clear, quiet eyes."[5] Though probably less handsome than some of his younger rivals, there was a twinkle to his expression that endeared him to his friends. Being twelve years older than Caty made him even more attractive to her. His maturity, thoughtfulness, and articulateness were all in his favor.

The Caty that Nathanael saw then, though still in her teens, was already comfortable in the society of men. Friendly and cheerful, she had at the same time an aura of mystery and excitement; "her power of fascination was absolutely irresistible."[6] Few men ever failed to notice her when she walked into a room. Her enchantment was sometimes seen by other women as a form of female guile. To men her appeal, like that of her Aunt Catharine, was not simply a matter of flirtation that fed their masculine vanities; deep emotions were touched as well. Men drawn close to her were men of substance, and the bonds could be strong and durable.

There are no known existing portraits of the young Caty, but word-pictures by those who knew her are plentiful. "She was a small brunette with high color, a vivacious expression, and a snapping pair of dark eyes." She possessed a "form light and agile." "Flossy black hair, brilliant violet eyes, clear-cut features, transparent complexion . . . united to make her lovely."[7] Few descriptions failed to contain the word "lovely."

Caty did not expend as much of Nathanael's time as she would have liked, and she often found him annoyingly preoccupied. Like Uncle Greene, he was constantly irritated by the high-handedness of the Crown and by the spineless acquiescence of the colony's General Assembly. In 1772, during the early days of his friendship with Caty, he was involved in a lawsuit that demanded much of his time and energy. During February of that year the merchant vessel he owned with his brothers was seized by the *Gaspee,* a royal schooner that patrolled Rhode Island waters to help enforce the revenue acts, and a large cargo of rum and sugar was confiscated. On June 9, while chasing another merchantman, the *Gaspee* was lured into shallow water, running aground on Namquit Point just below the town of Pawtuxet. Word of the incident passed along the shore. That night a group of civilians rowed out to the schooner, boarded her, and burned her to the water-line. The commander of the *Gaspee*, Lieutenant William Dudingston, was critically wounded in the process and a great cry was raised by the Loyalists. For the first time in the American colonies a violent act of rebellion had taken place, and British blood had been shed.

The *Gaspee* episode dominated conversations for months. Caty heard that Nathanael was one of the accused, but he established his innocence without going to court and threatened to "let the sun shine through" his accuser. He then struck a counterblow that had all New England buzzing. He brought a lawsuit against Lieutenant Dudingston, claiming illegal seizure of his merchant ship and cargo, and won the judgment. Young Greene was well known in the colonies after that.

Nathanael's victory, however, did not mean that Caty would no longer have to share him with public events. One crisis after another occupied his attention, and the courtship had to be squeezed into any time that was left over. Social evenings became political ones. Small talk turned into heated discussions, with Nathanael's face turned away from hers to argue a point with someone else. What was the best way to protest the tax on tea? Should the leaves be dumped in the harbors, or burned along with the proclamations of Lord North? What could be done to help the people of Boston, whose harbor was closed by an act of British Parliament? How defiant could the people be without provoking open war? She tired of such talk, and sometimes slipped silently out of the room.

Once she got her own way by taking Nathanael to Block Island, far from the scene of dissension, where she could talk to him about books and parties and clothes. And here she could dance with him to her heart's content, far from the eyes of his Quaker family. She introduced him to her father, who had remarried some years before and was busy raising a second family. One of the daughters never forgot the picture of her older half-sister organizing an evening's frolic, dancing and laughing through the night, always at the precise center of fun.

On July 10, 1774, Nathanael wrote to Sammy Ward in Westerly:

Friend Samuel

Please to deliver the inclosed Cards to your sisters—
On the 20th this instant I expect to be married to Miss
Kitty Littlefield at your Uncle Greene's—as a Relative of
hers and friend of mine, your company is desird upon the
occasion. The company will be small consisting of only a
few Choice Spirits—As she is not married at her fathers
house she declined giveing any an invitation but a few of
her nearest relations and most intimate friends. There will
be my brothers & their wives, Mr. [James M.] Varnum &
his wife . . , Christopher & Griffin Greene [Nathanael's
first cousins] and their Wives, and who from Block Island
I dont know, and Mr. Thomas Arnold,—those are all except
your family.

. . . believe me to be your sincere friend
Nath Greene[8]

Ten days later, in the fine house on the East Greenwich hillside
where she had reached maturity, and in the same room from
which Benjamin Franklin had often admired the green valley below, Caty became Mrs. Nathanael Greene.

Nathanael drove his bride to her new home in Coventry. The
pleasant but bumpy country road was lined by forests of walnut,
oak, and cedar, crossing pretty brooks and ascending high ridges
that gave glimpses of the shining waters and green islands of
Narragansett Bay. The dwelling to which they drove, still standing
on the elevated plain overlooking the narrow Pawtuxet River,
was then far removed from the nearest neighbor. The grounds
were barren of trees and shrubs, but Nathanael, who had long
cursed the infertility of the soil around the house, was sure that
his new wife would apply a magic touch of green. To have this
home surrounded by lush gardens and majestic trees was a dream
never to be realized, but this was a small matter for two people
in love.

The neat, square house was snug, the ceilings low, the rooms
small compared to those in Aunt Catharine's home. The two main
floors each had four rooms, divided by a wide hall. On the third
floor was a garret. Eagerly exploring the first floor, Caty found,
to her delight, Nathanael's library, a room at the rear overlooking
the slope above the river. Her husband was proud of the nearly
300 volumes he had carefully collected over the years, and she
found the books a warm and pleasing decoration for the room

and a challenge to her eager mind. She had visions of long winter evenings before the fireplace where they could read to each other as long into the night as they wished.

From the library window, she could see and hear Nathanael's forge, its whir the only sound of civilization. Above and below, cool waters of the river rushed over rocky shoals. It was a promising, peaceful spot to begin a marriage. But the lovers were living in the wrong times and in the wrong part of the world to be blessed with a life of tranquility. The happy days they shared at Coventry were numbered, and the number was cruelly small.

2 Life With a Besieging Army

Darkness had for some hours settled over the village of Coventry after the peaceful spring day of April 19, 1775. It must have been near bedtime for Nathanael and Caty Greene when they heard approaching hoofbeats in the distance—a sound that would be heard throughout the length and breadth of New England before that night was over. A lone horseman dismounted near the door of the dwelling and within an instant he was in animated conversation with Nathanael, while Caty listened in fear.

During the afternoon urgent news reached Providence from Massachusetts and was quickly disseminated throughout the Rhode Island countryside by messengers passing the word from house to house. At dawn that same day, British regulars, marching out of Boston to destroy military stores at Concord, had been challenged on the Lexington green by a group of militiamen; shots were fired and men were killed. After the volley, the King's soldiers had marched ahead in the direction of Concord. The time for armed resistance was now at hand.

Caty knew that Nathanael must go at once, with only time for a hasty goodbye. As she watched her husband bridle and saddle their fastest horse her only comfort was his hurried promise to return at the first opportunity to arrange for her care. But she knew that if war broke out in earnest it was a promise he might not be able to keep. As his form dissolved in the darkness, she felt that pang known to every soldier's wife at the first awful moment of being left alone. It was good that she could not then have known what was to become apparent a few weeks later— she was with child.

Two anxious days passed, then suddenly Nathanael was at home again, holding her in his arms, assuring her that the danger was over for the moment. He told her how he had ridden to East Greenwich, shouldered a musket, and marched off as a soldier in the ranks of the Kentish Guards, a neighborhood militia company he had joined a few months before. The unit was halted at the Massachusetts border by an order from Rhode Island's Tory governor, Joseph Wanton. Ignoring the order, Nathanael and three others secured horses and rode deep into Massachusetts before learning of the British retreat back to Boston. War was certain, Nathanael told Caty, but at least there would be time to provide for her security.

She approved the plans Nathanael presented. While he was away on military duty, his older brother Jacob would operate the Coventry forge and, with his wife, Peggy, move into the house to help care for Caty. She would be free to stay in Coventry under their wing or to move in with the rest of his family at Potowomut. She knew she would be welcome there; Nathanael's brothers adored her, and the unmarried ones regarded her as their special pet.

These plans agreed upon, Caty saw her husband off again, this time to answer an urgent summons by the General Assembly sitting at Providence. When he returned he brought with him his commission as a brigadier general in command of the Rhode Island Brigade. Caty was flabbergasted; a few days before he had been a private. Nathanael explained his remarkable jump in rank. The assembly had authorized the raising of a brigade of 1,500 men as an "army of observation" to cooperate with similar forces from other New England colonies for the common defense of the provinces. Two colonels of militia had been offered the command, but had turned it down. Nathanael, the private and the Quaker, was amazed when he was offered the post, but he accepted on the spot.

Caty examined her husband's commission. "You are," read the document, "hereby in his Majesty's Name George the Third, by the Grace of God, King of Great Britain, &c, authorized empowered and commissioned to have, take, and exercise the office of Brigadier General . . . to preserve the interest of His Majesty and His good Subjects in these Parts. . . ." What strange words these were with which to charge an officer committed to rebellion. Commissioned by the King? Nathanael explained the inconsistency to her. His duty as a soldier was to protect the constitutional rights of the people, and he could obtain the right to perform this duty only through the constitutional head of government. There was no other authority by which a citizen, Loyalist or patriot, could obtain a commission.

Nathanael told Caty that Boston was the object of the colonials' mobilization. On a map in his library he showed her a plat of the city and traced the events to date. The port had been closed to all but British shipping and Thomas Gage, acting governor of Massachusetts, was imposing restrictions that essentially deprived the citizens of their common rights. They could not leave the city or be out on the streets at night without a pass. Their homes and food stores were subject to seizure for the comfort of the British soldiers. Patriots who had been involved in tea protests were blacklisted and their property condemned.

Caty was appalled to hear of the indignities and hardships being suffered by the Boston Whigs—which included her particular friends and relatives living there—and of the veil of mistrust and fear that had descended over the port city she had loved visiting with Aunt Catharine. She winced at Nathanael's words that Boston had become a city of hate. She kept the map of the city handy in the library where she could pinpoint events as they arose.

The politics that had bored her as a child at Uncle Greene's now took on new meaning. Through Nathanael's careful tutelage, which would continue by mail when he left home, and through the pages of the *Providence Gazette,* brought weekly to Coventry by an express rider, Caty followed the course of the colonial campaign. By late spring she learned that the New England provincial brigades had collected at Cambridge, a college town separated from Boston by the Charles River and its broad mouth. Here they were joined by brigades from the middle and southern colonies, setting the stage to drive the British out of their stronghold.

She knew by now that the siege of the city was not all that the leaders of the rebellion had in mind. Much more than the recovery of Boston was at stake. The port had become the emblem of resistance to tyranny and the fragile seedbed of liberty. If Bostonians could be made to submit, so could Americans everywhere. If the city could be relieved of its shackles, so eventually could the colonies. It was the great testing ground. Would patriots really fight to the death to relieve their countrymen? Would the Ministry risk total war against the King's subjects to enforce its laws? Which standard would the masses rally around? The people of the world awaited the answers but no one with more personal anxiety than Caty.

Besides the political news, the *Gazette* was the source of other articles and notices of interest to Caty. She read of the coming and going of sailing vessels, of the arrival of silks, woolens, and gowns at a favorite shop near the Great Bridge of Providence, of searches for runaway slaves, of the opening of smallpox inoculation centers, and of "infallible" cures for cancer. And there was the delightful account of how a Mr. Coggeshall expressed his personal rebellion to the Crown by walking out on Newport's Long Wharf and turning his backside toward the British bomb brig in the harbor. The brig retaliated by firing two four-pound shot at him, but Coggeshall lived through it and became an instant hero.

When Nathanael left for Providence to confer with civil officials, Caty expected him to return home before he set off for Cambridge. But he wrote that he did not have time to get back to Coventry and would have to tell her good-bye by letter. She was taken aback by some of his remarks. Was he having second thoughts about entrusting her to his brothers? "I have recommended you to their care," he wrote, ". . . unless they should so far forget their affection for me as to request anything unworthy of you to comply with. In that case maintain your independence until my return . . . [and] if Providence allows, I will see justice done you."[1]

With her husband gone, Caty realized immediately that she would not be content to remain in Coventry. Almost certain now that she was pregnant she took a shopping trip to Providence, buying dresses she hoped would mask her changing contours. On returning home she announced to her surprised in-laws that she was going to join Nathanael at his headquarters near Jamaica Plains, just west of Boston. Accompanied by an officer on his way to camp, she made the all-day drive in her carriage.

She found Nathanael and his staff comfortably situated in a fine house near his brigade's camp. Close by, other Rhode Island

officers were quartered in a formerly Tory-owned mansion surrounded by sixty acres of beautifully kept grounds, where the
soldiers pitched their tents. Caty found that the mansion's hot-
house had been turned into a powder magazine; otherwise there
was little to suggest that the teeming, noisy Rhode Islanders had
hostile intent.

To her, the country boys of Rhode Island were a totally disor-
ganized bunch. They seemed completely unprepared for military
life; talking and laughing, they paid little heed to their officers'
command. They sulked when reprimanded and threatened to go
back home. At the dress parades they often appeared without
their shoes and stockings and made no effort to keep in step or
maintain straight lines.

Caty saw her husband for the first time as a stern master of
command who worked endlessly trying to make soldiers of his
raw undisciplined men. Although it upset her to see soldiers receiving their punishments in full view, absorbing their thirty-nine
stripes or riding the wooden horse with guns tied at their feet,
she knew it was necessary. She was also concerned because many
of the officers, afraid of offending their men, refused to enforce
proper punishments and Nathanael had to see that the full penalties were carried out. She could see the strain this put on him.

Ever the patient instructor, Nathanael explained to her the
colonial plan for forcing the enemy out of Boston. The British
base was within the city proper which occupied a peninsula jutting
out into Boston Harbor, connected to the mainland by a narrow
pedicle, the neck, at the southern end. By controlling the neck,
and by occupying the harbor's outer shore, where artillery pieces
could command the waterway, the colonials could eventually
starve the British out of the city.

To Caty it all seemed simple enough at first glance, but Nathanael explained that there were major problems to be overcome
before the plan could succeed. There was practically no American
navy to oppose British transports, gunships, and cargo vessels,
or to prevent the enemy from shuttling soldiers by water from
Boston to any point along the harbor's perimeter. Moreover the
enemy had sufficient cannon within the city to dominate the neck
and many points along the outer shore. Finally, even if these
obstacles were overcome, the British soldiers could not be starved
out without causing severe hardship to the citizens, who were
prevented from leaving Boston on pain of death.

In mid-June Caty drove back to Coventry with Nathanael, who

had been ordered to return to Rhode Island to muster supplies. In their own home once more, surrounded by the peaceful countryside, they could pretend that there was no war. But on their second evening at home an urgent message came from Cambridge—fighting had broken out north of Boston and the general was needed at once. Full of dread and disappointment, Caty was left behind at her doorstep once more as her husband galloped off for an all-night ride to the American lines.

After what seemed to her an eternity, a message came back from Nathanael that told the story. Arriving at Cambridge in the early morning following his long journey, he paused only for a brief rest before riding on to Charlestown. Here he found the village "all burnt to ashes" and the battle over.[2] Two nights before, under cover of darkness, a colonial force had slipped over to the Charlestown peninsula, north of Boston, to fortify a hill—on the property of a farmer named Bunker—that commanded the bay and dominated British positions near Charlestown. In the confusion of darkness the Americans placed their guns on the wrong hill, called Breed's, but the effect was the same. Soldiers in the British garrison on the peninsula woke up to find American cannon trained on them from the high ground.

Royal reinforcements in Boston boarded transports and were rowed across the harbor, setting fires in Charlestown (where patriots shot at them from the windows of their homes) before attacking the hill itself. Nathanael spoke with pride of the American resistance at "Bunker's Hill." Provincial troops heroically held fast until their powder ran out and inflicted staggering losses on the enemy.

Although his letters meant everything to her, without her husband's actual presence and reassurance in the face of all the mounting developments he described, Caty became insecure. Tracing his activities on the map as she read his reports no longer was enough. She was lonely and miserable, and her little world at Coventry seemed to be falling apart.

She was not by inclination or training a domestic person. Although Aunt Catharine had carefully begun the broadening of her mind through tutors, she had neglected to cultivate in Caty the feminine arts of weaving, sewing, gardening, and other endeavors that ladies of her time pursued. Caty could not even knit. She had been taught some stitchery and this she employed half-heartedly and with no enthusiasm on some baby clothes. Bored with that, she combed Nathanael's library for topics of interest to her. When reading no longer appealed to her, she found little to occupy herself.

Her house-mates, Jacob and Peggy Greene, had at first been helpful, but now Caty found them irritating. Jacob's constant gloomy outlook was in direct opposition to Caty's natural cheerfulness. She was bombarded by worries Jacob did not try to conceal about the forge, the household, and the state of war. Already trying to suppress her fear for Nathanael's safety, she found her outlook becoming as clouded as her brother-in-law's and she became depressed and nervous. Besides Jacob's intrusive pessimism, Peggy presented another frustration. Caty, the bride, found she was being displaced as queen in her own home. Because Jacob became master in Nathanael's absence, Peggy slipped into the role of mistress. Competent and efficient, the more experienced housewife grew impatient with the bride's bumbling and often wasteful efforts in the kitchen. She found it easier to do things about the house herself rather than wait for Caty, who hated regimentation and schedules. Peggy took on the chores that should have been Caty's and which would have occupied her hands and mind.

Caty felt shoved aside. Her displeasure turned to resentment and she felt stifled by negativism and uselessness. She began to have neurotic symptoms that increased her unhappiness. She was frightened by her pregnancy and all the little ills it brought. She was totally unprepared for and unfamiliar with her condition. She was sure everything was going wrong. Caty became obsessed with concern for herself and Nathanael's safety until she was convinced she was sick and needed a doctor.

She decided to spend most of her time in Potowomut where she could be cared for by Mother Greene, Nathanael's stepmother, and the wives of his other brothers. At the same time she could be near the doctors of East Greenwich. She soon had a regular collection of physicians who were personal friends as well, and always at her beck and call, comforting her, assuring her that her many complaints were of a purely nervous origin, the result not only of her pregnancy, but of the stresses of the disarranged life imposed upon her by the war. Otherwise they found her perfectly healthy and told her so.

In July Nathanael wrote Caty from Cambridge that George Washington of Virginia, recently appointed commander in chief of all provincial forces by the Continental Congress, had arrived in the American camp. Nathanael told of meeting the general, of the universal admiration everyone felt, and of the surge of confidence that spread through the camp the moment he arrived. Meanwhile, Nathanael wrote, he had changed his own headquarters to Prospect Hill, two miles from Cambridge, where the Rhode Island troops had been ordered to occupy the left, or northern extremity of the American line.

The summer wore on for Caty, shuttling between Potowomut and Coventry. She sometimes feuded with her in-laws, her squabbles usually involving the women in the family, almost never the men. Nathanael always took her side in his letters. He sometimes, however, expressed mild irritation himself when she was slow in forwarding books or clothing that he had sent for weeks before.

Caty was particularly delighted by visits from Colonel James Varnum, an old East Greenwich friend who had attended her wedding. Six years older than she, Varnum was a graduate of Rhode Island College, and had been Nathanael's lawyer in several litigations, including the *Gaspee* affair. Visiting Caty on leaves from the camp of his Rhode Island regiment near Cambridge, he liked to tease her about her school-girl French, and often tossed French phrases at her to interpret. During a visit from him in the late summer, she saw at once that he bore bad news. Augustus Mumford, Varnum's adjutant and a mutual East Greenwich friend, had been decapitated by a British cannon ball that came crashing into the American lines. It was Caty's first message of death and it intensified her awareness of something she had not let herself think about—Nathanael was now exposed to the dangers of a real shooting war.

Colonel Varnum brought along a note from Nathanael. "My dear angel," it began, "the anxiety that you must feel at the unhappy fate of Mr. Mumford, the tender sympathy for the distress of his poor lady [and] the fears and apprehensions for my safety, under your present debilitated state, must be a weight too great for you to support. . . . Stifle your grief, my sweet creature. . . ." He asked that she call on the widow of the dead officer, express her sympathy, and then dismiss the subject from her mind.[3] Visiting a dead soldier's family was a duty, as a general's wife, that she had dreaded. And she did not know how she could ever dismiss so ugly an event from her mind.

In September Caty heard from Nathanael that her cousin Sammy Ward, now a captain, had departed the line at Cambridge to join Benedict Arnold's expedition to Canada. It promised to be a perilous journey, but Sammy had gone off merrily with his regiment, which was under the command of Colonel Christopher Greene, Nathanael's cousin. Nathanael had advised Sammy against the venture but he was determined to go, much to the distress of Caty when she got the letter.

As days grew shorter and cold weather approached, Caty was relieved to learn that cannonading along the lines had largely stopped as the opposing armies began to bed down in their winter quarters. In November, when she heard that Mrs. Washington was going to camp for a visit, she immediately began to think about the possibility of doing the same. Nathanael had invited her to come in mid-winter after the baby came, but she was fully aware that there were excellent physicians in the army near Cambridge. Why couldn't she be under their care at headquarters and perhaps even have her baby there?

There is no record of Nathanael's arguments on the subject, but if he objected he did so without firmly saying "no." This was all the encouragement Caty ever needed. She went on a shopping trip, an activity she depended on more and more to lift her spirits and bolster her morale. Then, packing her carriage with a new wardrobe and a trunkful of baby clothes, she and her driver made the long trip to Cambridge. Here she found the village surrounded by earthworks, well prepared for war. The streets were crowded with soldiers, the Common was a parade ground, and the buildings on the Harvard campus had been converted into barracks. The students were gone, having been sent home or to other schools months before.

The Rhode Island soldiers at Nathanael's Prospect Hill camp presented a much more favorable appearance than those Caty had seen at Jamaica Plains. They had undergone the rudiments of basic drill and were showing more respect for their officers. Accustomed to the inclement elements, they presented a healthy though weatherbeaten appearance and were obviously well fed. Their rations included corned beef and pork four days weekly, salt fish one day, and fresh beef on the other two, with a daily allotment of a pound of flour, butter, fresh vegetables, and a quart of spruce beer. Equipped with a motley assortment of muskets that they had furnished themselves, the Rhode Island troops wore broad-brimmed headpieces bent into cocked hats, homespun shirts, variously colored coats and waistcoats, breeches that came to just below the knee, long stockings, and cowhide shoes with large buckles.

From the top of Prospect Hill near Nathanael's headquarters, where Caty had moved in with her husband, she could see the enemy's garrisons on nearby Bunker's and Breed's hills and the stark chimneys of burned-out Charlestown. With her spyglass she could see, across the water two miles away, the fine buildings of Boston and the scurrying about of the "lobster-backs," the red-coated troops of the King. As she watched the soldiers and civilians tearing down wharves to make firewood, she was concerned for her Boston kinsmen and wondered how many had managed to escape.

A smallpox epidemic was known to have broken out in Boston and there was danger that the disease might spread to the colonial soldiers besieging the city. Nathanael, hearing that British officials were purposely sending out infected emissaries into the American lines, urged his soldiers to be inoculated and required it of his officers. Since live virus from infected persons was used in the inoculation process, many recipients became quite ill, and all had to be quarantined. Nathanael turned his headquarters dwelling into a hospital for members of his staff who were going through the quarantine period. Since Caty had been inoculated earlier in Providence her exposure presented no hazard. She was hampered in her efforts as a nurse because of her late pregnancy, but her cheerful presence helped buoy the morale of the half-sick, incarcerated officers.

She also began to make social visits. One of her first was to the John Vassal home, which now served as General Washington's headquarters in Cambridge. She was received by Lady Washington in the paneled parlor just across the hall from the general's office. Thus began a lifetime friendship. Martha Washington was a short, plump, almost plain woman of forty-three years—twice Caty's age—but a thoroughly good and gracious lady.

After a brief talk, she took Caty across the hall to meet the general, who rose from his desk to greet them. There he stood, straight as an Indian, muscular, broad-shouldered, with penetrating eyes under heavy brows, a few marks from a recent bout of smallpox visible on his nose. He received Caty cordially, putting her immediately at ease by teasing her about her "Quaker-preacher" husband. She in turn promised she would name her baby for him if she were lucky enough to have a boy.

The Greenes became frequent dinner guests at the Washingtons' along with the other high ranking officers and their wives, including the Horatio Gateses, the Thomas Mifflins and, later in the winter, the Henry Knoxes. Some of the bachelor officers

were often on hand. Washington let his wife do most of the entertaining while he relaxed, listening to the chatter of the ladies,
drinking toasts, or cracking nuts.

The generals' wives came to the understanding that they would
remain for the winter, inspiring the joke around camp that their
husbands agreed to the plan because of the cold nights and the
scarcity of firewood. Each couple entertained the others in turn,
and camp-life took on a social glow. Caty thrived in such surroundings. Friends observed that "there never lived a more joyous,
frolicsome creature."[4] She came to know the generals well, and
was warmly responsive to some, while indifferent to others.

One of Caty's favorites was General Israel Putnam, almost
sixty, a recent hero of Bunker Hill. Bearing a large facial scar
from a tomahawk wound of earlier days, he told stories by the
hour of incredible adventures and miraculous escapes. Caty added
the stories to her own collection of anecdotes and in later years
often charmed audiences with talks about the general long after
he was dead: how he had once crawled, unarmed, to the extremity
of a cave to ferret out a snarling she-wolf; how, tied to a stake
by savages, with a fire lit under him, he had been saved by a
sudden shower of rain; and how he had been the only survivor
of a shipwreck off Cuba, floating to land on a piece of debris.
With each campaign that followed, the general would have more
tales for Caty to add to her list and somehow his storytelling
made the war seem less frightening.

On the first of January, 1776, Prospect Hill was the scene of
a stirring event. It was the date of the inception of the Continental
army that succeeded the first hastily organized body, which was
now disbanded. A great crowd of soldiers and civilians gathered
on the parade, a stone's throw from Nathanael's and Caty's quarters, to celebrate the occasion. As cannon roared, the first flag
of the American union was raised atop the hill, within sight of
the British garrisons in Boston and Charlestown. Caught by a
stiff wind, the huge banner opened up to reveal its thirteen alter-
nating red and white stripes, with the united crosses of St. George
and St. Thomas on a dark blue canton, waving defiantly in the
very faces of His Majesty's troops.

In early winter Caty's baby boy, George Washington Greene,
was born but the place of birth and exact date are not known.
Whether Caty remained at headquarters for the delivery, or returned to Rhode Island, is not recorded. She was so mobile, with
or without child, that it is difficult even to hazard a guess.

In February she and the baby were in East Greenwich when an urgent message came for her to return to headquarters. Nathanael was ill with jaundice and needed her at his side. "I am yellow as a saffron," he wrote, "my appetite all gone and my flesh too. I am so weak I can scarcely walk across the room. . . . I am grievously mortified at my confinement as this is the critical period of the American war." Should Boston fall, he continued, "I intend to be there if I am able to sit on horseback."[5]

Caty at once made plans to return to her husband, delaying just long enough to make a quick shopping trip to Providence. She then set out with her baby to Prospect Hill and nursed Nathanael through his illness. Though he recovered rapidly and was soon in the field again at the head of his troops, Caty decided to remain at headquarters until the campaign was over.

During this time she met young Colonel Henry Knox and his wife Lucy, who rivaled her husband in portliness. Lucy was going through a frantic period. Her father, royal secretary to the province of Massachusetts, had disapproved of her courtship with the Boston bookseller and outspoken patriot, Henry Knox. When she married him and accepted his politics she became estranged from her entire family. As the Continentals tightened the loop around Boston, Lucy's parents were still within the city that was being heavily shelled by her husband's artillery.

Colonel Knox had recently returned to the American lines from an expedition to Ticonderoga. In an amazing wintertime feat, he had brought back with him much-needed artillery pieces that had been lying idle in northern New York. Knox immediately renewed his friendship with Nathanael, who in earlier years had come into his Boston bookshop to discuss military tactics and politics. Now, meeting Caty, Knox did not at first know how to react to her perpetual light-heartedness. The two measured each other. Caty initially found Knox unattractive, not because of his obesity and crippled left hand, but because of his negative reaction to her.

Colonel Knox's early judgement of Caty, which would later change completely, was not an unusual one. Often during her life she would leave an impression of superficiality with those whose friendships were casual. Only such a brief bit of herself did she offer to those she did not know well or admire. But to those she truly loved she gave her heart completely and would accept nothing less in return. Some historians have made the most of this theme. Biographers of Caty's male acquaintances, in attempting to read her character through their subjects' eyes, have sometimes portrayed a passionate vamp who was ever ready to lure their heroes into love affairs.

Caty always preferred men's company to that of ladies, a fact that became apparent at Cambridge and led to the first whispering campaign against her. She was only twenty-one, still a mere girl (as Nathanael put it) with a limited education and little experience in the ways of the world. When she attended parties at the headquarters of other generals, whose ladies were present, she often fell into silence rather than to compete with trained intellects. But in her own dwelling, surrounded by her husband's aides-de-camp, her natural charm and beauty carried her through.

The staff at Prospect Hill was an intimate group that was always referred to as "the family." The officers were either bachelors or were without their wives. When Caty was present at headquarters, her privilege as a general's wife, she was naturally the center of attraction. Her pregnancy in earlier days at camp in no way detracted from her appeal. Then when she returned later with her baby to nurse her sick husband, though her days were filled with cares, the evenings belonged to her.

There was no need for the amenities of the genteel hostess or for stilted proprieties she felt were unnatural. She was most comfortable when just being herself, a self that reflected a spontaneous response to admiring gentlemen. As the glow from crackling fires lit up the living room, she laughed, danced, sipped Madeira wine and played cards and parlor games. She engaged in repartee that was fun for both herself and her companions, with perhaps a burst of unladylike glee at a slip of the tongue or a *double entendre* that would have horrified her female counterparts but delighted their husbands.

In time some of the young aides became smitten. Caty, with her love of approbation, did little to discourage them. Always the total female, she knew how to employ the word, the glance, or the smile that was most likely to appeal. Nathanael was well aware of the little game being played and was delighted by it. Not only did he love to see his wife sparkle but it comforted him to see the grim faces of his aides light up. For them Caty's playfulness was a needed respite from the cheerless task of making war.

When the young officers came to know their general better, they no longer tried to conceal from him their feelings for Caty, and they often took affectionate liberties with her in his plain view, confident of the good natured indulgence of both of them. This was enough for the whisperers; what more could they ask? That none of the general's aides ever intended to press his advantage beyond the light-hearted level, and that Caty would never have permitted them to do so, were possibilities the gossips did not choose to pursue.

Another trait in Caty's character certain to loosen tongues was her indifference to religion. On Block Island she had been brought up to go to church as a privileged option rather than as a requirement, and she saw no reason to change her attitude on the mainland. When it was observed that Nathanael seldom went to services when Caty was in camp, she got the blame. Nathanael was distressed. "If the true reason should be enquired after," he told her, "you would escape the charge."[6] Three years before, Nathanael had been "read out" of his own Quaker meeting at East Greenwich after having been seen watching a military parade in Connecticut. Now that he was in the army, his life was totally inconsistent with the principles of the Quaker faith.

By late winter the Americans were in possession of much of Boston Harbor's outer shore, and now needed only to place batteries on the heights nearest the city to bring British ships within easy artillery range. On the night of March 2, to divert attention of the enemy from the movement to the high ground on the opposite side of the city, the colonials cannonaded Boston from the north and west. As huge guns roared atop Prospect Hill, timbers shook and windows rattled in the Greene home. The British returned the fire and the thundering roar of the artillery duel lasted all night. For Caty sleep was out of the question,. and she kept an anxious eye on the baby. Amazingly enough he slumbered peacefully through most of the din.

Late that night a tremendous explosion rocked the house as a shell from a thirteen-inch gun burst near the dwelling. Caty, rushing to little George, found that though he had awakened, he remained quiet. An hour later an anxious message of inquiry came from Lady Washington, who, lying tense in her bed in Cambridge, had heard the ominous sound. Caty, though terrified by the blast, found her own nervousness less acute in the face of true danger than it had been when, pregnant and far away from Nathanael, she had been consumed with imagined fears. Holding close the warm bundle of her infant son, she sent back a relatively calm note of reassurance to Lady Washington.

During the height of the bombardment, a colonial battery

slipped undetected to the summit of a hill just south of the city overlooking Boston's docks. If the provincials could maintain this position, the British were doomed. The final trap was set.

Thirteen days later, from high ground near her dwelling, Caty trained her glass on Boston to watch the activity there. Dozens of transports and other vessels were loading at the wharves, under cover of artillery fire, and a hundred more lay at anchor in the harbor, awaiting their turn. Would the British send their troops by water to attack the heights as they had done at Bunker Hill, or were they preparing to evacuate?

The answer finally came. The enemy ships moved away from the docks and proceeded due east toward the harbor exit. Doubt no longer remained—the British were quitting Boston. After an eternity of sitting at anchor in the outer harbor, the fleet finally sailed for the open sea.

3 The British Wedge

Boston, the hub of New England, was liberated from British military rule. Nathanael rode to the city on horseback at the head of his Rhode Island Brigade, leaving Caty with little George at Prospect Hill. Their good-byes had been happy ones, their hearts lighter than at any time since hostilities had begun almost a year before.

Two days later Caty was sent for by Nathanael. Leaving her baby with a nurse she drove into Boston with one of the general's aides, anxious to join the celebrations. But as the carriage passed through the city gate a depressing sight met her eyes. Boston bore little resemblance to the city she had remembered. Buildings were unpainted. Houses, fences, and even churches had been pulled down to make firewood. Gardens were overgrown. The Common was scarred by trenches.

There was little merry-making in the streets. The inhabitants, though thankful for their deliverance, were too worn-out to frolic; their haunted faces reflected their long-standing misery. Most of the city's Tories had fled with the British fleet and those who stayed in Boston, risking the wrath of their neighbors, remained behind closed doors.

John Rowe, a merchant who had been forced to stay in Boston during the entire siege, invited the Greenes to a victory supper, serving them the best meal to be set on his table for many months. The occasion was a cheerful one, but Caty noted that her host wore the same drawn and solemn expression that she had seen throughout the city.

After driving back to Prospect Hill, Caty packed her belongings and those of little George in readiness for their trip back to Coventry. Upon Nathanael's return he showed Caty his new orders. They directed him to march his troops to New London, Connecticut, where they would embark for New York City, thought to be the eventual destination of the British fleet and army. Since the line of march was through Rhode Island, this gave him the opportunity of accompanying his little family to Coventry along the same roads that his soldiers walked. The spring thaw had set in, causing long delays in the journey over muddy roads.

The march was barely underway when an urgent message arrived reporting that the British fleet was off Newport. Caty felt pangs of anxiety for her family and friends there and on Block Island. She was soon relieved, for within hours a second message came refuting the first. British ships were nowhere to be seen. The men who had sounded the alarm had, in their apprehension, mistaken the undulations of the fog for sails of a mighty fleet.

Nathanael spent only one night at Coventry, then was off with his troops for New York. Several anxious days passed before Caty had word of his arrival. The brigade, after leaving New London, had run into a frightful snowstorm, a gale that had separated the transports and for a few harrowing hours threatened the entire expedition. Safely landed in New York, the troops were assigned to a camp near Brooklyn, and Nathanael was placed in command of the defense of Long Island.

Tied down by her baby son, Caty's life in Coventry was more restricted than ever. All was not happy for her when she visited Potowomut either. The strict Quaker household forbade even the playing of cards, and she was constantly reminded that her ways were not their ways. She had a spat with Sally, the wife of Griffin Greene, one of Nathanael's cousins, and received instructions from her husband to mend the situation. This she dutifully tried to do by inviting Sally to visit her, but the invitation was not accepted. She was glad that Nathanael did not expect her to go further than this in an attempt at reconciliation.

Her relationship with Aunt Catharine was also beginning to

deteriorate. The whispering campaign against Caty had reached East Greenwich and the ears of her aunt. Catharine Greene was well aware of the reckless nature of her niece, and although she understood her restlessness she could not condone the immaturity and lack of judgment she felt Caty exhibited. She, herself, had been subjected to temptations in her youth, but breeding and training had brought her through unscathed. Now she felt that Caty was giving in to circumstances. She was not only disappointed in her beautiful namesake, but felt that some of the reputation Caty was gaining as a self-serving, irresponsible woman was rubbing off on her. She resented this. She had done all she could to try to restrain the headstrong spirit of the young girl she had taken on at the time of Caty's mother's death, and now the fondness she felt was turning to hostility. She had even tried to turn Caty's father against her.

Nathanael stood squarely by his wife's side. Earlier, when he thought there was a chance of reconciliation, he had written his brother "Kitt" about the matter. He had admired Aunt Catharine and appreciated her earlier attempts at educating Caty. But now he could see no excuse for exposing her faults to family and friends instead of trying to correct them. Writing Caty too, he urged her not to go more than halfway in her effort to patch up the relationship.

In late spring, 1776, when Caty heard that several of the generals' wives were in New York City, she immediately made her own plans to visit her husband. There were two routes of travel open to her, each carrying its own hazards. She could sail through Long Island sound, patrolled by British ships, or go by carriage through the country, which might subject her to delays during bad weather. Also, she knew that the approaches to Manhattan Island were teeming with Tories who made travel miserable for anyone who did not openly agree with their brand of politics.

Caty chose the sea route. Leaving her baby with Nathanael's family, she boarded a schooner at Newport and sailed along the coast, through the treacherous Hell Gate passage, and down the East River to a dock in lower Manhattan. Though the trip was uneventful in the eyes of most of the passengers, Caty, hating water travel even under the best of circumstances, was relieved to step safely off the vessel. Upon landing she was driven to the headquarters-residence of Henry and Lucy Knox, at the foot of Broadway, adjacent to the Bowling Green and close to the Battery and heart of the city. Here she was joined by her husband who had crossed over on the ferry from Brooklyn. His joy at seeing Caty was tempered by his anxiety; the British fleet, known to be in Halifax, was expected to sail for New York at any hour. This thought was put aside for the moment as Caty and Nathanael enjoyed their visit together in the handsome three-story mansion overlooking the harbor.

Nathanael spent most of his time with his troops on Long Island, completing the fortifications on Brooklyn Heights, shuttling back and forth across the river for visits with his wife. While he was away Caty "did the town" with Lucy Knox, who became her close but often jealous friend. Lucy could not help comparing her own great bulk with the figure of her tiny, animated companion. As jolly as her husband, Lucy managed to conceal the heartbreak she had suffered in Boston. When the Americans entered the city after the British evacuation they found that her parents had fled with the enemy fleet. She had heard nothing from them since, nor would she ever again.

The New York that Caty and Lucy saw was a city of 20,000 inhabitants with wide streets, large public buildings, and handsome homes. From the Knox residence a grassy lane called Broadway stretched to the north, lined by shade trees and fine town houses. Toward the East River were block after block of shops, coffee-houses, taverns, churches, and markets backing up to the wharves at the end of each parallel street. West of Broadway, toward the Hudson, there was mostly open country with scattered private homes.

Caty and Lucy found the city braced for the invasion. Some streets were barricaded, and the rivers were lined with forts and redoubts. But the bustle of the town went on, augmented by the tempestuous happenings of that June of '76. The city's Whigs, long tormented by the Tories, seized the upper hand with the coming of Washington's army and made the most of their new advantage. Caty and Lucy were witnesses to several "Tory rides" in which the victims, often tarred and feathered, were carried through the streets on rails. Public drunkenness was common and prostitutes roamed the streets, boldly plying their trade among the soldiers. Military policemen regularly dragged harlots and their soldier-companions to the provost dungeon. Caty and Lucy, who had never been exposed to such scenes in New England, looked on in startled fascination.

From the Knox home they frequently made the two-mile ride northward to Richmond Hill where the Washingtons were quartered in a fine home overlooking the Hudson and the Jersey shore beyond. As guests of Lady Washington at midday meals, they renewed acquaintances with the generals' wives they had met in Cambridge. Here, with the other ladies, they received repeated lectures from the officers on the dangers of remaining in New York.

Caty visited Nathanael at his Brooklyn camp, crossing the tricky currents of the East River. She traveled on a flat-bottomed ferry equipped with a sail and oars, a voyage that required more than two hours. She found Brooklyn a sprawling country village with its inhabitants completely preoccupied with the imminent invasion and, in most cases, eagerly looking forward to it. The area was truly Tory country, with the Loyalists outnumbering the patriots by over five to one. The pro-British sentiment caused multiple annoyances for Nathanael and his staff.

The Tories made no secret of their intentions. They openly carried arms to the southern tip of the island, and along the shores of the Narrows, at the entrance to New York Harbor, where British landings were certain to be made. The army commanders rounded up many of the Loyalists, and Caty saw some of them brought in to headquarters, weeping like children. Nathanael found that they were mostly ignorant country boys, unacquainted with public matters, and their sympathy for the Tory cause betrayed the strong influence of their mothers and grandmothers. There were dangerous Loyalists on the island, he said, but they were smart enough to escape detection; those brought in were of such dull wits that they were of questionable value to the enemy.

Caty was accustomed to seeing troops in various states of undiscipline, and Long Island was no exception. Some of the soldierly pranks that Nathanael officially condemned were privately sources of amusement to him and his wife. When the weather got hot, for example, soldiers would strip and swim in full view of the neighborhood. Without bothering to dress, they would run naked down the road to their quarters, shrieking like Indians.

Before the end of June a message came that little George was sick in Rhode Island, and Caty was immediately put on board ship to return home. Arriving in East Greenwich, she found her son recovered and wrote Nathanael that she was preparing to return to New York. In spite of her husband's letter of protest, in which he stated that British vessels had already been sighted off Sandy Hook near the harbor entrance, Caty returned to Manhattan in early July.

This time she traveled by carriage, accompanied by a driver. The trip through Connecticut was tedious, requiring two days, but the roads and accommodations were moderately good. Reaching New York, the travelers stopped to eat at a tavern near Kings Bridge. Here they were exposed to the politics of the gruff Tory proprietor who rudely told them to leave when they refused to support his views.

Driving on to lower Broadway, Caty surprised Nathanael during dinner at General Knox's headquarters. As she was ushered into the dining room she received, instead of the warm welcome she had expected, a stony stare of disbelief. After a speechless moment Nathanael explained the reason for his alarm over her return. British landings had already been made on Staten Island and only the day before a British gunboat had moved at full sail past the Battery and up the Hudson River. General Knox had seen the spectacle himself, while at breakfast, and within an hour had shipped his own wife to Connecticut.

The return of Caty caused embarrassment to General Knox. Lucy asked her husband, in a stormy letter of protest, why Caty had been allowed to visit headquarters when she herself had been sent away? "Mrs. Greene's return was a vast surprise to us," General Knox wrote back. "I am much mistaken if [General Greene] hadn't have rather lost his arm than to have seen her here at this time. He was over here at the time she arrived and would not believe she was coming until he saw her."[1]

Even General Putnam gave Caty a gentle reprimand, but to no avail; having just arrived she had no intention of going back home. Within a few days, despite hurt feelings, she had reason to be glad that she had stayed. While strolling with Nathanael on the Bowling Green adjacent to the Knox home, she was introduced to Alexander Hamilton, a handsome artillery captain, who henceforth would be a valued friend.

July 9 was a special day for Caty—a day she would never forget. A brigade of Continentals was drawn up on the green and was quickly surrounded by a large crowd of civilians. Both soldiers and citizens listened to the reading of a declaration that had been ratified by the Continental Congress in Philadelphia five days before: "When, in the course of human events, it becomes necessary for one people to dissolve the political bands which have connected them with another. . . ." The assemblage listened silently until the last paragraph was read, then issued a mighty and sustained roar of approval. When the troops were dismissed the crowd moved noisily to the equestrian statue of George III that stood on the green, threw ropes around it, and pulled it crashing to the ground. Independence had been declared—now the time had come for it to be won.

With no navy to oppose them and with fixed batteries on the bluffs representing little hazard, British warships began to sail up and down the Hudson River at will. At the same time, their forces on Staten Island, with easy access to Long Island across the narrow channel at the south end of the harbor, were swarming over without opposition. Even Caty realized she simply could not remain any longer in New York, and she was sent home until the battle for the city was over.

She settled down at Coventry once more, but none too happily, and soon she realized that she was pregnant again. On top of this discovery word came that Nathanael was ill and had to be brought over to Manhattan on the eve of the British attack on Long Island. This time Caty was ordered to stay home while Nathanael's brother, Kitt, was sent to care for him at a Broadway dwelling that had been converted into a hospital. Here the brothers could hear the guns roaring on distant Long Island where the armies met head on in one of the bloodiest battles ever fought on the American continent.

From Kitt news was relayed back to Caty at Coventry. In late August came word that the Long Island defenses were overrun and Nathanael's troops defeated. The surviving army of 9,000 men was pinned down near Brooklyn with its back to the East River and all hope abandoned. When Caty heard that Nathanael, still in his sickbed, had broken down and cried at the news, she also wept.

Suddenly, the earlier dismal reports of retreat and surrender were tempered with news that the army was saved, but it was not until many days later that Caty got the thrilling details. On August 29 an incredible feat had taken place. Up and down the shores of the East River every conceivable type of boat was commandeered and sent to the ferry slip at Brooklyn to remove the trapped Americans to Manhattan. The boats were manned by the Marblehead brigade of Massachusetts and by regiments from the vicinity of Salem, consisting of seafaring men, many of whom had made their living by fishing for cod off the banks of Newfoundland.

Only such men as these could have handled the vessels, operating without lights, in the treacherous currents of the East River.

During the night when the winds became unfavorable, the sailors bent to their oars in flatboats, making crossing after crossing to pick up the soldiers. By dawn the following day several thousand men remained on Long Island, but a merciful fog allowed the shuttle to continue. Within a few hours the entire army had been put safely ashore on Manhattan without the loss of a man during the passage.

Caty's relief at the survival of Nathanael's troops was short-lived. His next letter stated that the army's position in New York was as untenable as the British situation had been at Boston several months earlier. Moreover, the Americans had scarcely a gunboat to oppose the enemy's movements. The British could send transports up either the Hudson or East River, land troops at any point, and cut off the supply lines from the mainland.

Caty ached over the news from Manhattan. Nathanael's health had returned but his command, in common with all the military units, was in distress. Militiamen were quitting in droves as their enlistments ran out, and if replacements were found they were men with no army experience. Leadership deteriorated as sectional jealousies developed among the officers. Hospital facilities were inadequate, medical personnel poor, and many regimental surgeons were dishonest, often granting sick leave upon the payment of a fee.

Weeks passed before Caty heard from Nathanael again. While reading of the American retreat from Manhattan Island her concern for her husband turned to agony. She had no idea of his whereabouts until a letter came from him in October, written from Fort Lee on the Jersey side of the Hudson. He told of how, after the withdrawal from Manhattan Island, his troops had crossed the river upstream and had then doubled back down the Jersey shore to the palisades opposite Harlem Heights. Just across from Nathanael's new position stood Fort Washington, the only post on Manhattan Island remaining in the hands of the Americans. (Today the George Washington Bridge connects the sites of the two forts.)

Nathanael's description of life at Fort Lee made Caty yearn to come for a visit. The general had most of his old headquarters "family" around him, as well as her cousin, Sammy Ward, who had returned from the ill-fated invasion of Canada. Sammy had harrowing stories to tell. As a nineteen-year-old captain in Benedict Arnold's division, he had made the bitter march to Quebec by way of the wild rivers and portages of the Maine woods, shuffling through the December snow, on the last leg of the trip, with only pieces of his shoes strapped to his feet. At one point of the march, his company, to keep from starving, subsisted on a stew made from the carcass of a dog. Captured during the unsuccessful assault on Quebec, Sammy was imprisoned—and treated well by the Canadian civilians and British command—until his exchange.

The merry William Blodgett, an old friend from Providence, and Thomas Paine, a scribe who had gained a name for himself through his "Common Sense" essay, were among Nathanael's aides-de-camp, as was Billy Littlefield, Caty's younger brother. Caty's hopes of rejoining her husband soared as she read messages from his staff, sent through him, urging her to make the journey westward. They explained that she could go on safely to Philadelphia in case of attack. Nathanael conceded that her radiant smile and effervescent personality were sorely missed. "Colonel Bedford lodges with me and wants you to come," he wrote. "Col Biddle . . . is continually urging me to send for you to go to [Philadelphia] and spend some weeks with his Lady. . . . But as you are at home in Peace I cannot recommend your coming to this troublesome part of America. . . . Billy is captain of my Guard. I have recommended him to the assembly for a lieutenancy in the new army. He has got hearty and well again, and is desirous of continuing in the Service. Major Blodget is quite fat and laughs all day. Common Sense and Col Snarl or Cornwell are perpetually wrangling over mathematical problems."[2]

Caty begged to come, even suggesting a route to New Jersey that would pass far enough north of occupied New York City to avoid great risk. But her husband was firm in his insistence that she stay home. It was well that she was not foolhardy. Bad news soon followed: Fort Washington, with all its men and a great supply of military stores, fell to the enemy within plain and painful view of Nathanael and his staff on the opposite shore of the river. This made their own fort untenable, and Nathanael withdrew his troops to Hackensack, where they joined General Washington's division.

There was a long wait for Caty before further news came, and when it came it was not good. Nathanael was depressed over the fall of Fort Washington since it had been largely at his insistance that it be defended to the last; otherwise the men and supplies might well have been withdrawn weeks before. Most distressing of all was the news beginning to filter back from New York concerning the treatment of the captured soldiers. Packed into stifling dungeon-like jails, abused by their vindictive captors, and essentially ignored by the Tory-dominated citizenry, the anguished men were allowed to rot in their own filth.

In early December, Caty received a letter from her husband written at Trenton, New Jersey.

> Trenttown, Decemb 4, 1776
>
> . . . The enemy have pressed us very hard from place to place. The time for which our troops were engaged expired, and they went off by whole brigades, notwithstanding the enemy lay within two or three hours march of us, and our forces remaining not half equal to theirs. The virtue of the Americans is put to a tryal; if they turn out with spirit, all will go on well; but if the militia refuses their aid, the people must submit to the servitude they will deserve. But I think it is impossible that the Americans can behave so poltroonish. The militia of Pennsylvania, and particularly of Philadelphia, are coming in by the thousands. In a day or two I hope to advance upon the enemy, and drive them back as fast as they drove us in. . . . Their footsteps are marked by destruction wherever they go. There is no difference made between the Whigs and Tories; all fare alike. They take the clothes off the people's back. The distress they spread wherever they go exceeds all description. I hope to God you have not set out for this place. . . . Continue at home, my dear, if you wish to enjoy the least share of happiness. . . .Be of good courage. Don't be disturbed— all things will turn out for the best. I wish you abundant happiness and am affectionately yours
>
> N Greene[3]

Caty was now in the last half of her pregnancy and had moved back into Nathanael's family home in Potowomut. She was at peace with her in-laws and, for a short time, was not consumed by personal anxieties. The handsome dwelling (built by Nathanael's great-grandfather and still in possession of the Greene family today) was a fine home in which to bring up a child. Caty played with little George on the terrace overlooking the stream below and in the pleasant fields where Nathanael had plowed as a boy. When her son slept she had time to read books and study her French. But her heart, never truly free of apprehension, was now seized by a new terror.

In early December, while Nathanael and his troops were backed up against the Delaware, Caty was told of the sighting of a British fleet in Narragansett Bay. As the ships sailed up the western passage they were in full view of panicky citizens along the shore of the mainland who had no idea where the landings would be made. Finally the fleet turned southeastward and anchored off Middletown, a few miles north of Newport. On December 7 the main body of troops, largely Hessians under command of General Henry Clinton, were put ashore and bivouacked in farm houses about the island, pillaging wherever they went. Clinton then marched on Newport and captured it without opposition.

Caty, not trusting the untested Rhode Island militia, felt that East Greenwich now lay completely at the mercy of enemy troops. An attack seemed inevitable. She knew that the Greene residence at Potowcmut, as the home of a rebel general, would be high on the list of buildings marked for destruction. So would the Coventry house, for the same reason, as well as the home of Uncle Greene, who was known to the British as a leading revolutionary. Caty had nowhere to go, and was terrified.

At the time of her greatest apprehension, she received a letter from Nathanael telling of the atrocities by the enemy in New Jersey. "The Tories are the cursedest rascals amongst us," said her husband. "They lead the relentless [Hessians] to the houses of their neighbors and strip the poor women and children of everything they have to eat or wear; and after plundering them in this sort, the brutes often ravish the mothers and daughters and compel the fathers and sons to behold their brutality."[4]

That very month Caty had read the words of Nathanael's aide, Tom Paine, who wrote: "These are the times that try men's souls." Now her own soul was on trial. Living within a stone's throw of a garrison of the relentless enemy, and feeling a frightful responsibility for her son and unborn child, whom she had no means of protecting, she fought hard against giving way to fear and despair.

Word came from Nathanael that the Continentals had retreated across the Delaware into Pennsylvania. The colonial soldiers, with no tents, many without shoes and blankets, kept themselves alive by eating their "firecakes," made by baking raw flour on stones around their campfires. A later letter gave further discouraging news:

> . . . The troops under the command of general [Charles] Lee we expect to join us today, but without the General,

who had the misfortune to be made a prisoner on Friday
last by a party of light-horse. The General, by some strange
infatuation, was led from the army four miles; the Tories
gave information of his situation, and a party of light-horse
came 18 miles and seized and carried him off. Fortune
seems to frown upon the cause of freedom. However, I
hope this is the dark part of the night which generally is
just before day. . . .

I hear a fleet and army have made their landing in Rhode
Island. God forbid that they should penetrate into the country with you as with us. . . . The eastern delegates applied
to his Excellency George Washington to permit me to go
to New England to take command there, but the General
would not permit me to go. . . . We are fortifying the
city of Philadelphia and doubt not that we shall be able
to keep the enemy out this winter. The city is under martial
law; the Quakers horridly frighted for fear the city should
be burnt. . . . I have no hope of coming to New England
this winter. . . .[5]

Just as Caty's spirits had reached their lowest ebb, the tide
changed. Despair and loneliness were dissolved by sensational
news from Trenton. On Christmas night Nathanael, in command
of one of three divisions on the Pennsylvania side of the Delaware,
had orders to counterattack by recrossing the frigid river into
New Jersey. As he was rowed across the ice-choked waterway in
a "Durham boat" at McKonkee's Ferry, he had the honor of having
General Washington at his side. Arriving safely on the Jersey
shore after a harrowing crossing at four in the morning, he and
the other commanders began collecting their men who were
landed up and down the river by the same Marblehead sailors
that had saved the army at Long Island. Then during a violent
blizzard the columns marched down a slushy road to Trenton,
where a large and unsuspecting Hessian force occupying the town
slept through the bitter night. Caty read again and again Nathanael's description of the events that followed:

We . . . attacked the town by storm [at seven] in the morning. It rained, hailed and snowed. . . . The storm of nature
and the storm of the town exhibited a scene that filled
the mind during the action with passions easier conceived
than described. The action lasted about three quarters of
an hour. We killed, wounded, and took prisoners of the

enemy between eleven and twelve hundred. Our troops
behaved with great spirit.

. . . Should we get possession of the Jerseys, perhaps
I may get liberty to come and see you. I pity your situation
exceedingly; your distress and anxiety must be very great.
Put on a good stock of fortitude. By the blessing of God
I hope to meet [you] again in the pleasure of Wedlocke.
Adieu my love.[6]

In January, 1777, Caty had another heartening letter from
her husband. The Continentals, instead of withdrawing to Philadelphia for the winter, as everyone expected them to do, had
again struck a blow that caught the enemy by complete surprise.
Marching around the enemy flank into the heart of New Jersey,
they had attacked the enemy garrison at Princeton, winning a
complete victory and flushing the last of the redcoats from Nassau
Hall, the stone-walled building that housed the college. Now
boasting two stunning victories, the Continentals were settling
down for the winter on the high ground of Morristown.

Caty prayed that the happy turn of events would allow Nathanael time for his wife and child. It seemed she never loved
him more than when he was least attainable to her. She missed,
almost unbearably, his warmth and strength. And faced now with
another confinement, she longed for his nearness. She hoped
the parable in one of his letters had been prophetic; surely the
blackest part of the night was over. Surely he would be coming
home to her soon.

4 New Jersey: A Brief Reunion

Nathanael could not get his leave to come home, but Caty's mind was more at peace. Tensions began to ease a bit in Rhode Island during the early days of 1777. The British, apparently content to remain at Newport, made only an occasonal raid on the mainland to ferret out patriots who fired on their shipping from various points along the shore.

A letter came from Nathanael assuring Caty that the Continental army could hold its own if challenged by General Howe in New Jersey. But the attitude of the people left him chagrined. "O that the Americans were but spirited and resolute," he wrote, "how easy [would be] the attempt to rout those miscreants. But their foolish delays and internal disputes I fear will prolong the War to a much greater length than is necessary to complete the work. I am sure Americans will be victorious finally, but her sufferings for want of union and public spirit may be great first. There is no people on earth that ever had so fair an opportunity to establish their freedom at so easy a rate. . . ."[1]

In another letter, Nathanael described one of the dwellings serving as his New Jersey headquarters and suggested it would make a comfortable resting place for her after the baby came.

His room was located in the home of Lord Stirling, near Basking Ridge, several miles south of the army's encampment at Morristown. It was the showplace of New Jersey, surrounded by lawns, gardens, vineyards, and a fruit orchard; nearby were stables of fine horses and even a park stocked with deer. Like all homes in the neighborhood, it provided shelter for members of displaced Whig families from New York and eastern New Jersey who had fled during the British invasion and flocked for protection in the vicinity of the Continental army.

Caty knew that Nathanael's host, "Lord Stirling," was actually a native American named William Alexander who earlier, during a residency in England, had laid claim to ancestral land and petitioned Parliament for the title of Earl of Stirling. He had been turned down, but upon returning to America he assumed the appellation of lord nonetheless. With befitting ostentation, he rode around the countryside in four- and six-horse coaches with coats-of-arms engraved on the panels. Though he was a bona fide general in the Continental service, he was known in the army by his pretended title.

Lady Stirling and her daughter, Kitty, both much admired by Nathanael, lived at the headquarters-mansion. So did several other young lady refugees from the family of William Livingston, first state governor of New Jersey, who had been forced to leave occupied Elizabeth. All the women of the residence sent messages to Caty through Nathanael urging her to come for a visit as soon after the birth of her baby as circumstances would allow.

Caty wished with all her heart that she was there. The last stage of her pregnancy was a difficult one and all her old fears returned to complicate her state even more. The Greene family was concerned for her, recognizing a valid complaint instead of the imaginary ones they had grown impatient with before. Her condition required the services of several medical men. Her chief attendant was Dr. Joseph Joslyn, a famed Scottish physician, much sought after not only in medical circles, but also in the society of East Greenwich where conviviality sometimes got the better of him. Caty often teased him about an incident that had occurred earlier in his career. While hunting ducks on the bay, the doctor, with a drink or two under his belt, had accidentally shot himself. With no medical aid at hand he kept himself from bleeding to death by stuffing a wad of chewing tobacco in his wound.

Caty was also visited by a consultant from Newport, Dr. Isaac Senter, chief surgeon of Rhode Island's state hospitals and a close friend of Nathanael's. As a professional man, he was given a pass by British authorities in occupied Newport to travel back and forth between that city and the mainland. Tall, genial, and popular, Senter was twenty-three, the same age as Caty, and already a veteran of the war. Like Sammy Ward he had been a member of Colonel Benedict Arnold's doomed expedition to Quebec, and as chief surgeon had removed the ball that had shattered Arnold's leg in the first hours of the attack upon the city. Returning home with a remnant of the broken army, the young surgeon had resigned his commission to resume his civilian practice.

Nathanael's relatives and Caty's doctors did all they could to make Caty comfortable and to reassure her. She wanted the ordeal to be over with, yet she dreaded the delivery. She found little to take her mind off herself. Little George was shunted from one family member to another and not allowed to visit his mother. She longed to hold him, but found the active youngster too much for her strength and nerves.

At last, in March, the baby came, a girl named for Martha Washington. A relieved Kitt Greene wrote the joyful news to his brother. "Thank God for your safe delivery," Nathanael wrote back to Caty. "When I shall see the poor little [one] God only knows. I am exceedingly happy at your being in Potowomut, and rejoice to find the brothers so kind and attentive to your wants. How shall you or I ever repay their kindness? We must leave that to some after day. . . . Mrs. Washington and Mrs. Bland from Virginia are at camp. . . . Mrs. Washington is extremely fond of the General, and he of her; they are very happy in each other. . . . Pray, my dear, are you determined to suckle your baby or not? On that depends your liberty."[2]

Caty, although unusually weak, was determined to go to Nathanael. She tried to mask the fact that she was coming down with a cold, but when her cough became alarmingly worse her doctors were called in again. She had pneumonia and was forbidden to think about a trip. Crushed with disappointment and feeling very ill, she asked only to be given something to snap her back to health so that she could make plans to go to the Stirlings' home.

Her doctors prescribed four grains of mercury, but when she failed to improve they ordered her to bed for a month and placed her on a strict diet. Too weak to write, she was bombarded by letters from Nathanael in concerned and finally angry tones, demanding to know what was the matter. "Nothing is more painful than a state of suspense," he wrote. "Pray, my dear, let me know the worst. . . ."[3] Caty had assumed in her hazy, fevered condition that his family had written him of her illness. Now she found from his letter that it had been over a month since he had received a line from anyone. Pulling herself together she got a message off to him explaining the circumstances of her illness.

She had an immediate response from her husband, saying he was "almost thunderstruck" at the receipt of her letter. He had long looked forward to being with her, he wrote, and his heart mourned her absence. "If Doctor Joslin attends you," he added, "let him know if he don't make a radical cure in a fortnight, at most, he shall have more holes in his hide to fill with tow wads."[4]

During her illness Caty had been harrassed by an impressing officer of the Rhode Island militia who persisted in seizing whatever of her personal property he chose. She was frantic and furious and felt completely impotent, too weak to fight back. When two horses were taken she wrote Nathanael that the seizure was nothing short of robbery and that the officer's action was prompted more by malice than by military necessity.

Nathanael's reply typified the aching frustration of a man unable to protect and provide for his family. To know that Caty was ill and being so tormented wrung his heart. He promised her that it would not have happened if he had been there, and begged her to be patient. "I pray almighty God may restore your health and comfort again," he wrote. "Nothing would give me greater pleasure than to come and see you but . . . the general [Washington] will not permit me to go. . . . I feel a blank in my Heart which nothing but your presence can fill up. There is not a day or night, nay not an hour, but I wish to fold you to my heart."[5]

Her convalescence was slow. With Nathanael's last message Caty gave up hope that he could come to her, so she began to make plans once more for a trip to his New Jersey camp. At first he discouraged her from leaving home but later, seeing how strongly she felt and giving in to his own loneliness, he began to relent. "If you think your health and strength will endure the journey," he wrote, "my heart will leap for joy to meet you."[6] He told her to come equipped with everything necessary and to spare no expense. "If you are in want of anything from Boston write to Mrs. Knox," he advised. "But remember when you write to [her] you write to a good scholar, therefore mind and spell well. You are defective in this matter, my love; a little attention will soon correct it. . . . People are often laughed at for not spelling well. . . . Nothing but the affection and regard I feel for you makes me wish to have you appear an accomplished lady in every point of view."[7]

Caty read the first part of his letter with enthusiasm, but the rebuke offended and hurt her. She had laughed with Nathanael about her spelling in earlier days, but on this occasion he spoke in serious terms. In healthier, happier days she might have ignored the remarks or soon forgotten them, but now, just out of a sickbed and suffering from depression that followed her pregnancy and illness, she could not dismiss them. Staring up at her coldly from the page, the words would not go away. They seemed to imply that culturally she was inferior to Lucy Knox and that Nathanael was ashamed of her. Caty wrote nothing of her feelings at the time, but she was only waiting for a better opportunity to express herself.

In July General Howe, despairing of trapping the Continentals, had abandoned New Jersey altogether, retiring his troops to Staten Island and then embarking them on an expedition to parts unknown. This left the way clear for Caty to make her long-planned trip to Nathanael's headquarters, now located at "Beverwyck," a private dwelling nine miles from Morristown occupied by the in-laws of one of his aides.

She already knew much of this home through Nathanael's letters, and had yearned to join her husband there many weeks before she was able to make the trip. Nathanael had written that his hosts, Mr. and Mrs. Abraham Lott, refugees from New York City, were as merry as children though much older than he. They had several well-educated daughters with whom Caty could study music and French in her spare hours. Lady Stirling, Kitty Stirling, and the Livingston girls would be nearby. All the ladies of Basking Ridge looked forward to meeting Caty and eagerly awaited her arrival.

Although she was not up to it, and in spite of the strong disapproval of her in-laws, Caty went shopping before setting out for New Jersey. Her "battle attire" was always a new wardrobe. Before joining Nathanael at his headquarters she always went on a shopping spree, buying garments that were as important to her as muskets were to the men. When she was pregnant she needed the reassurance of new outfits that flattered her condition. After delivery she found she could not go immediately into her old wardrobe. By the time the clothes she had on hand could be worn, she had tired of wearing them and felt they no longer were in style. Now, in the face of Nathanael's criticism of her, and because she was thin and wan after her ordeal, she felt the need for reinforcements strongly. Not only did she shop for herself but she spent lavishly on the children, too. Admittedly weakened by the exertion, but somehow buoyed up by the hope that her looks would be improved by the purchases, she completed her travel plans.

Accompanied by her son, baby daughter, and one of Nathanael's aides, Caty made the trip overland. Using a circuitous route through the back country she was careful to avoid New York City and the worst of Tory country. It was the first of many jostling, interminable carriage-rides she would make as she passed back and forth between Rhode Island and the New Jersey camps. Ill-kept, unmarked byways and dusty paths often turned to quagmire after a sudden shower of rain. Few streams were bridged, some were fordable only in dry weather, and it might be miles to the nearest ferry, often operated only at the whim of the owner. In New York state and beyond, roadside inns were frequently little more than hovels, presided over by rude and suspicious proprietors who were more interested in airing their politics than in seeing to their guests' comfort. As time went on, Caty made friends along the way, but on this first trip to New Jersey she found none beyond New England.

One respite for the weary travelers was the crossing of the Hudson River on the ferry near Fishkill, some fifty miles north of New York City. (Ruins of the old ferry slip can still be seen at the water's edge in Beacon.) Only a short distance downstream, fortifications were being erected on the heights of West Point, but this feverish activity was beyond the view of Caty and her party, who enjoyed one of the most beautiful views in America. The scene, in its serenity, was far removed from the constant struggle between the opposing armies to win control of the waterway.

The four-day trip proved too much for Caty. She became ill. She thought the journey would never end. Tossed about in the carriage, her splitting head once more feverish, she was grateful that the children were as good as they were. Finally the little party arrived at headquarters with Caty looking pale and fragile. But she forced herself to appear as gay as ever. At the Lotts' she and Nathanael fell into each other's arms for the first time in twelve months, and their little differences and hurt feelings were temporarily set aside.

An exhausted Caty found that she and Nathanael were to be jammed into a bedroom with their children and other young people in the crowded household. They were together thus for only three nights before Nathanael was ordered south toward Philadelphia. He immediately sent word from his new headquarters for Caty to join him for a few days, leaving the children in care of the Lotts. Caty read the message wearily. "Our accommodations are not good," it said, "but you will sleep in a room with only myself and I hope you'll have no objection to that. . . . My heart pants to see you."[8]

Caty, however, did not rejoin Nathanael. She was indisposed again, this time with "camp distemper," and by the time she recovered, Nathanael and his troops were busily engaged in Pennsylvania. It was now known that General Howe's troops, aboard transports accompanying the British fleet, were in Chesapeake Bay, and that Philadelphia, the capital of the rebellion, was their obvious destination. The Continental soldiers, 11,000 strong, had passed through the city on their way to meet the enemy, marching twelve abreast down the streets before the cheering populace, each man wearing a green sprig in his hat as an emblem of hope.

A message from Nathanael, dated September 10, 1777, the day before the great battle on the banks of Brandywine Creek, gave Caty a vivid picture of the activity there as the Continentals stationed themselves between Philadelphia and the advancing enemy. He described the distressing scenes of the inhabitants leaving their homes with their furniture, driving their cattle before them, the women and children traveling by foot. Caty's heart was wrung when she read, "The country all resounds with the cries of the people." Nathanael told her how tired he was, having sat on his horse for over thirty hours, going without sleep for over forty. When he did finally get a bed it was so dusty that he was plagued with asthma all night.[9]

Dreadful news followed shortly. The Continental lines along the Brandywine had been flanked by General Howe's forces, and the Americans were routed. Nathanael, placed in command of a brigade of valiant Virginians, helped avert complete disaster that might have wiped out the army, but the tide of defeat was too strong to turn back. Philadelphia now lay exposed, and members of Congress fled in confusion, leaving the city to the British just a month after the American forces had so merrily jaunted through the streets.

Caty, who had been confident of the army's ability to hold the British at bay, had looked forward to joining Nathanael in comfortable quarters in Philadelphia. Now she was at a loss, not knowing which way to move. The thought of the horrible trip back to Coventry and another dismal season there made up her mind. She decided to stay on with the Lotts at Basking Ridge, and remained there for most of the fall.

Nathanael anticipated her despondency over the defeat at the Brandywine and tried his best to cheer her. He wrote her that General Howe, after the battle, had scoured the countryside to enlist country doctors to assist his surgeons. "There must have been a terrible carnage among his troops" Nathanael wrote. "I suspect the next action to ruin Mr. Howe totally. . . . Pray how does all my good friends do at Mr. Lotts—I suppose you have all long faces and fearful apprehensions. Tell them to cheer up and fear not, all things will go well. . . . We are gathering about [Howe] like a mighty cloud charged with destruction and by the blessing of God I hope its execution will be dreadful. Many reinforcements are coming in and Mr. Howe will find that another victory purchased at the price of so much blood might inevitably ruin him. . . . O my sweet angel how I wish—how I long to return to your soft embrace. The endearing prospect is my greatest comfort amidst all the fatigues of the campaign."[10]

In October came more disappointment: word of another defeat, this time at Germantown. The British, with no further hindrances, were free to reduce the forts on the Delaware River before settling down in comfortable quarters in Philadelphia as guests of the jubilant Tories. The Americans, on the other hand, deprived of any semblance of a permanent post, faced a miserable, exposed winter with only the countryside to support them.

Caty, abandoning hope of seeing her husband again soon, made the most of her stay in Basking Ridge. The war dragged on, but her health had returned and she was tired of living in a state of perpetual gloom. Dancing parties were arranged at the Lotts' home and a Colonel Cary became her partner. When word got back to Lucy Knox in New England of the good times enjoyed by Caty near Morristown, she became furious with her husband once more for not having been allowed to stay on herself.[11]

Nathanael heard of Caty's parties through her dancing partner, Colonel Cary, when that officer reported to headquarters. "I am happy to hear you are so agreeably employed," he wrote his wife. "I wish the campaign was over that I might come and partake of your diversions. But we must first give Mr. Howe a stinging, and then for a joyous winter of pleasant tales. . . . In the neighborhood of my quarters there are several sweet pretty Quaker girls. If the spirit should move and love invite who can be accountable for the consequences? I know this wont alarm you because you have such an high opinion of my virtue. It is very well you have. You remember the prayer of that saint—Tempt me not above what I am able to bear. But I promise you to be as honest as ever I can."[12]

Caty found the letter enigmatic. Did she, for the first time, detect a threatening tone? Was Nathanael angry that she had frolicked while he fought? She did not fully understand the intent of the letter although she read it many times. If it was an effort to tease her, she did not find it amusing.

Reluctant to leave the gaiety at the Lotts', where she once more had found herself the center of attraction, and living in dread of another pregnancy, she had previously expressed doubts about coming to Nathanael's camp. His letter decided the issue. First she must get the children back to Rhode Island. Then she would go to her husband for the winter, wherever his headquarters might be.

5 Valley of Distress—and Hope

In February, 1778, Caty, entrusting her babies to her in-laws in Rhode Island, set out to join Nathanael at his camp in Pennsylvania. She made the hard trip in freezing weather in her carriage, accompanied by an aide. The new winter quarters of the Continental army lay upon the west bank of the Schuylkill River, twenty miles from Philadelphia, in a deep valley surrounded by a semicircle of high ridges. Nearby was the iron plant that gave the area its name—Valley Forge.

When Caty arrived at the snow-covered camp, she beheld a scene she would never forget. The army was in tatters, many of the men without hats, coats, shirts, or shoes. Some of them stood guard covered by ragged blankets or dressing gowns to keep from freezing. Others were so literally naked that they refused to come out of their tents or huts. There had been no meat for days, commissaries were practically empty, and the rawboned men subsisted on hand-to-mouth provisions brought back from forages into a countryside already depleted by the raids of the enemy.

The enlisted soldiers were building a village of log huts, arranged along regular streets. Each cabin measured fourteen by sixteen feet and housed twelve men under a low roof sloped sharply to shed the snow. On the street side were a single door and window, with a fireplace on the opposite end topped by a clay-and-wood chimney. To the rear of the soldiers' huts lay those of the officers, a little larger, and each with two windows. Even the general officers occupied the tiny log cabins at the time of Caty's arrival. She and Nathanael made one of them their home.

Soldiers not busy with construction were scattered about in every direction, and their captains had little idea of the number of enlisted men under their orders or their whereabouts. Their muskets were covered with rust, and many could not be fired. Morale was at rock-bottom, and the naked, starving men were close to open mutiny. They had received no money for three months and had heard only a few vague rumors that they might get their December pay in March. Many of them scavenged on their own, forming roving bands that plundered the surrounding countryside. Some of the soldiers, not satisfied with stealing from the farmers, stole from each other or simply walked out of camp and went over to the enemy.

To prevent marauding, desertion, and mutiny, officers were forced to impose severe penalties. Caty bore witness to several soldiers being drummed out of camp, astride their horses backwards, without saddles, their coats turned inside out, their hands tied behind their backs. Men caught stealing were whipped with as many as 200 lashes, "well laid on," with a surgeon standing by to halt the proceedings when a victim had absorbed as much punishment as his body could stand. For out-and-out treason, soldiers were put to death.

Nathanael was one of the camp's chief foraging officers, taking large numbers of troops on expeditions through the country to commandeer provisions for the army. Even farmers sympathetic to the American cause, however, looked on the foragers as if they were locusts. Fearing Continental currency offered by the soldiers would be worthless by spring, they hid their foodstores and even their livestock. Caty often saw the disheartening sight of the wagons returning to camp with pitifully small supplies, just enough to keep the army from perishing for a few days, until another foraging party could be sent out.

She settled into her cabin as best she could. Although there was precious little space to put her things, she shook out and hung up the few good gowns she had brought in her trunk. At first they seemed inappropriate even to her, but as the harsh winter wore on she would be glad she had them. So would all who came to count on her beautiful and cheerful presence to raise their spirits.

Martha Washington, Lucy Knox, and Lady and Kitty Stirling were in camp, as well as a number of friends among Nathanael's aides, including her own favorite cousin, Captain Sammy Ward. One of her physician friends, Dr. Peter Turner of East Greenwich, a post surgeon and brother-in-law of Mrs. James Varnum, was near at hand and was often consulted by Caty. General Varnum's headquarters-home, a snug dwelling that still stands above the parade ground, was a popular gathering place for Caty and her Rhode Island acquaintances. The women visited back and forth, hoisting their skirts above the slush and snow, making their little temporary quarters as homey and attractive as they could.

In late winter, Caty and Nathanael moved three miles down the Pottstown Road into the comfortable quarters of "Moore Hall." This was the home of the gentle family of a patriot named William Moore, who had long been tormented by neighbors in the Tory-ridden countryside and by marauding soldiers from the camp. The Moores were delighted to have the general and his wife—and their military guard—as guests of the household to help protect them from their own countrymen.

Caty's unfailing vivacity was a boon to the morale of the officers, and Moore Hall was often packed with visitors. She had studied French during the previous spring and now found her knowledge of the language a pleasant and practical way of communicating with foreign officers in camp—men such as Lafayette, duPortail, Pulaski, Steuben, and Kosciusko.

One of the more frequent visitors to the Greene dwelling was the Marquis de Lafayette. Tall and thin, with reddish brown hair, receding brow, and large nose, he was anything but handsome, but his popularity increased with every day he spent at camp. He had been commissioned a major general in the Continental army the year before, at the age of nineteen, and had distinguished himself at Brandywine, where he had been wounded. Extremely wealthy, Lafayette was serving at his own expense as a volunteer on Washington's staff, having left behind a beautiful wife, a young son, and a brilliant social life among young courtiers in Versailles, to fight for a cause he believed in. Lonely for his family, he talked endlessly of them to Caty and listened in turn to accounts of her own little ones in Rhode Island.

"Baron" von Steuben, another frequent visitor, was a forty-six-year-old German bachelor. Upon reaching America the former

Prussian captain had presented himself to Congress as a high-ranking officer and received a commission as major general from the gullible governing body. Brought to Valley Forge as drillmaster, he was soon performing miracles. He first trained a guard for General Washington, then using his unit as a model, was able to transform his entire division, within weeks, into an effective command.

The Baron rose at three in the morning, smoked a pipe while his valet dressed his hair, drank a cup of coffee, and was on horseback at the parade ground at sunrise. He possessed a long torso and short legs; Caty thought he looked quite tall astride a horse, and was always surprised how short he was when he dismounted. She was also highly amused by his fits of profanity and loved to imitate him. He would swear first in German, then in French, and realizing that his oaths were not understood by his men, would end up with a great "Gott damn!"

The bleak camp became a challenging stage for the charming warmth of Caty Greene, and she was a radiant glow in the gloom of Valley Forge. Although there were no dancing parties or formal soirees, evenings were spent in congenial groups over a cup of tea or coffee. The greatest amusement of the officers and their ladies was singing. Caty raised her untrained but enthusiastic voice with the rest, and took her turn with the others when called on for a "solo."

Her presence captured the attention of seventeen-year-old Pierre Duponceau, an aide to Steuben. After the war he recalled the indelible impression Caty had made on him at the time. "In the middle of our distress," he wrote in his memoirs, "there were some bright sides to the picture which Valley Forge exhibited. . . . The lady of General Greene is a handsome, elegant, and accomplished woman [who] spoke the French language and was well versed in French literature. . . ."[1]

Caty, however, felt less accomplished than the young Frenchman supposed. There was the matter of Lady and Kitty Stirling. Try as she would, Caty could not escape the fact that Nathanael found them not only attractive but polished in a way she knew she was not. She was uncomfortable with them and on her guard not to appear less than they were. She was secretly pricked by little darts of jealousy and she did not like it.

Among the friends Caty made at Valley Forge were men who would play major parts in her future life. One was Brigadier General Anthony Wayne, who had helped save the army from starvation by rounding up cattle on foraging expeditions and bringing back to the valley large supplies of beef on the hoof. He was married, but his pious wife, who lived only a few miles away, never came to camp. At thirty-two, the handsome, debonaire general was eight years older than Caty, and though a hard-bitten commander in the army, he was comfortable in the society of ladies.

As a young Pennsylvanian he had left the taverns, the racing stables, the billiard games, and other diversions he was addicted to, and set forth to Nova Scotia as a colonizing agent and surveyor for a land speculation syndicate that included Benjamin Franklin among the investors. Here the inexperienced twenty-year-old Wayne thought he had found a veritable paradise and rainbow's end. He returned to the family farm, Waynesborough, with glowing reports, certain that he was on the way to a tremendous fortune.

It was at this time that Wayne first discovered women. Previously a man's man who had preferred taproom talk to genteel society, the hazel-eyed, strong-jawed, ruddy young man met Polly Penrose, a friend of his sister's and daughter of one of Philadelphia's most prominent shipbuilding families. After a brief courtship, Polly and Anthony were married, and two weeks later the young husband took his innocent bride to Nova Scotia—an adventure which probably sealed the doom of their relationship as husband and wife. Enduring hardships she could never have imagined, Polly was miserably homesick, and when at last she returned to Waynesborough she vowed that she would never leave home again. And she never did, even after her husband joined the army and often camped only a short distance away. Seldom did Anthony come back to her, and when he did he quickly became restless and bored with domestic life. The dashing Wayne remained an incurable ladies' man, always eager to renew his attachments with the many other women he had met and found attractive and responsive.

At Valley Forge, Anthony met Caty Greene and saw in her the prototype of all he had held desirable in his other loves. An affable, voluble companion, understanding his loneliness, she was willing to have him seek her out when his spirits were low. She in turn was stimulated by the company of this charming man, completely unconcerned that the whisperers might find in this liaison substance on which to feed. She had been through all of that before. Confident that Nathanael saw such female tactics for what they were—gossip, no more—she continued to enjoy the friendships that were open to her in her own free way.

Other friendships formed by Caty during the early weeks of 1778 were developed under rather ominous circumstances that would have a direct bearing on the course of her life. In February, during the valley's bleakest days, General Washington was in despair. The collapse of his quartermaster and commissary departments had brought his army to the brink of destruction. The previous quartermaster general had abandoned his post without offering his resignation, and Washington recommended to Congress that Nathanael be appointed to the position. When the offer came, Nathanael accepted because of his wish to please Washington, but only with great reluctance and with the understanding that he maintain his command in the field and be allowed to pick his own assistants in his new post.

For his subordinate quartermasters, Nathanael selected John Cox, an affluent Philadelphia merchant, and Charles Pettit, secretary to Governor Livingston of New Jersey. For his commissary general he appointed the extremely wealthy Connecticut businessman, Jeremiah Wadsworth, whose monetary credit was good all over America, and who came to be considered one of the chief financiers of the Revolution. Strongly built and handsome as well, Wadsworth was exceedingly attractive to the ladies in camp, and Nathanael often teased him about the fact.

Nathanael went into private partnerships with his assistants, one with Cox and Pettit, the other with Wadsworth, thus overlapping his official duties with those of private enterprise. Such a combination, whereby public responsibilities and personal interests might well conflict, much frowned upon by modern governments, was entirely consistent with the customs of the times. The partners bought interests in a number of ships in the name of Jacob Greene, Nathanael's oldest brother, and several of these vessels were engaged in the business of privateering. Such commerce was not only an acceptable way of life in the Revolutionary era but was the most popular form of speculation; even the incorruptible General Washington, the most respected man of his day, wanted to buy a quarter interest in a privateer.

Nathanael's enterprises, however, were condemned by members of Congress because they had been secretly conceived without knowledge or permission of the governing body, which felt it should be apprised of the financial transactions of all officials in its employ. The affair brought much anguish to Nathanael and

Caty; nevertheless these private companies helped maintain the army at a critical time and very likely saved it from ruin. Under the system, when stores were dangerously low and could not be replenished through channels of a near-bankrupt government, the quartermaster general was able to fill his warehouses from his own private resources.

All three of Nathanael's new associates, now members of his official family, became exposed to Caty's charms. They adored her, brought her presents at every opportunity, and placed themselves and their departments at her service. The friendship Cox and Pettit established with her was on a light-hearted basis, pursued over a cup of tea or glass of wine. The affection Wadsworth felt, however, was anything but casual. At some time early in the course of what would be a long acquaintance, perhaps the first time he met her at Valley Forge, and notwithstanding the fact that he had a wife in Connecticut, he found himself inextricably attracted to the lady of his chief.

Caty, in turn, was conscious of Wadsworth's appeal. He evoked a response in her that she examined closely and decided to guard carefully. She felt a distinct difference in this man's company from that of the other officers. The warmth of their mutual attraction was banked at Valley Forge, but she was highly conscious of it.

As spring unfolded there was a new surge of confidence in the army. The reorganization of the quartermaster department under General Greene, the magic of Baron von Steuben on the drillfield, and the coming of warm weather all had their happy effects. The army began to look more like a military force and less like an armed horde. Talk no longer dwelled on mere survival but on the coming campaign to drive the enemy out of Philadelphia.

Spectacular events began to occur in rapid succession. In April General Charles Lee, for months a British captive, returned to his command at Valley Forge following his exchange. Word was then received that France and Spain had officially recognized the independence of the United States and that the French government had entered into an alliance with the new nation. In early May, during the great celebration to honor the events, Caty rode to the parade ground in a carriage with Martha Washington, followed by Lady Stirling and her daughter, an order of procession immensely satisfying to Caty. The brigades were drawn together, prayers were offered, and a sermon of thanksgiving delivered. General Steuben, his hair powdered and dressed, inspected the troops, after which, to the music of fife, bugle, and drum, they marched past the reviewing stand where the commander in chief and the other generals received and returned their salutes. After the review the ladies joined their husbands at the banquet tables, where wine flowed freely throughout the sumptuous meal.

Although the British outposts lay less than twenty miles away, little was seen or heard of the enemy. There was even a rumor afloat that His Majesty's troops might evacuate Philadelphia without a fight. War seemed far away and a spirit of merriment prevailed in the American camp. Members of the various staffs produced plays that were enjoyed by the generals and their ladies, and when Nathanael was too busy to attend, Caty accompanied the Washingtons and the Stirlings to the performances.

Among Caty's various acquaintances in camp, Lady Washington was her only close female friend. The small, dumpy middle aged woman did not feel the threat to her position that the other officers' wives felt. Martha was secure in her place in her husband's heart. Although she knew that the general looked at the beautiful Caty with deep male appreciation, she found no cause for disapproval. Caty was like a daughter to them both. She was accepted for what she was—a young woman of uncommonly good looks and high spirits who brought a breath of fresh air wherever she appeared. Her pluck and endurance were admired by both Washingtons who looked on her as a boon in a troubled era.

With the approach of summer, Caty's residence at Valley Forge drew to a close. Her final days, though gay on the surface, were not happy ones. Her association with the Moore children at headquarters made her yearn for her little ones at home. "Poor girl," Nathanael wrote William Greene. "She is constantly separated from her husband or children, and sometimes from both."[2] Letters from East Greenwich had brought word of little Martha's illness. "Dr. Senter is giving her medicine for the Ricketts," read a note from Nathanael's cousin, Griffin Greene, "and thinks she shall soon be able to have the better of the disorder. His little Excellencey [George] is well and hearty and grows finely."[3]

Feeling wretched, Caty consulted Dr. Turner and found out what she had dreaded—she was pregnant again. But her real distress was one of the spirit, the gnawing, haunting doubt that had crept into her soul. Was her husband's regard for her as high as it had once been? Did she measure up, in his esteem, to Lady and Kitty Stirling? He spoke so often of *their* culture and refinement. Did he prefer their company to hers?

She was not quite ready to pose the questions to Nathanael. But they weighed heavily upon her as she said good-bye and hurried off in her carriage for the long trip home.

6 War Comes to Rhode Island

Anxious to get back to her children and away from the eyes of the camp during the miserable months of her pregnancy, and plagued by a shattering state of uncertainty, Caty made the trip from Pennsylvania with only an occasional stop for rest and food. Nathanael had provided a driver and arranged for her first night's lodging at the home of a friend, but she paused only for supper, then drove straight on through the night. When Nathanael heard of it he scolded her in his first letter: "What was your hurry? Why did you expose yourself unnecessarily and risk any disagreeable consequences that might follow?"[1]

Caty found Rhode Island once more in a state of alarm. British soldiers had launched an expedition from Newport to break up a gathering of state troops. On their way back to their garrison they entered homes in Warren and Bristol, robbing the inhabitants and burning their houses to the ground.

Martha Varnum was in Warren when the raiders came through and she told Caty of her experiences. While baking a cake for a wedding party in the home of a relative, she heard the alarm: "The British! The British!" The wife of a rebel general, she could not risk detection for fear of being taken hostage. She hid in a cornfield while other ladies in the household, flying in another direction, heard British soldiers cry out, "Fire high at the women." All escaped physical harm but when the white-faced ladies reassembled following the departure of the raiders the wedding celebration was forgotten.

Caty picked up her children at Potowomut and returned with them to Coventry. Letters from Nathanael kept her informed of events at Valley Forge and of the friends she had left so recently. He complained of his lonesomeness. "There is no Mrs. Greene to retire to and spend an agreeable hour with," he wrote. "Mr. Mo[o]re and the family all inquire after you with great affection and respect. . . . Mrs. Washington and the other ladies at camp are daily asking about you. . . . Mrs. Knox professes great regard for you, and often inquires how and where you are. You will judge of the regard from former circumstances. . . . Mr. Lebrune . . . does want to see Mrs. Greene very much. He thinks he loves her very well."[2]

Soon the remoteness of Coventry and the lack of interesting companionship began to play on Caty's nerves and she wrote Nathanael of her wish to live elsewhere. She did not want to impose further on her in-laws in Potowomut, where she often felt oppressed by Quaker austerity, and she felt increasingly distant from her friends in East Greenwich. At her husband's suggestion, she and the children traveled to Westerly, on the coast near the Connecticut border, and moved into a comfortable farmhouse owned by Nathanael. She described her life there in a letter to Dr. Peter Turner, who had been her physician at Valley Forge.

> Liberty Hall, Westerly June 9, 1778
>
> Dear Doctor,
>
> There have been so few adventures in my journey here and my time so idly spent since my arrival, that I think it not worth while to give you a relation of either nor know of no subject worth writing upon—I can however tell you my health is much better than when I left Greenwich, which I flatter my self is a little interesting to you—I am (contrary to my own expectations) extreamly pleased with my situation here. The house is pleasantly situated. . . . We have fine fish in a bundance good butter milk—and I can tell you I have been visited by the finest circle of ladies I have seen for a long time and have had two invitations to dine out one of which the rain prevented my acceptance of—I

have one good neighbour and what I call my second blessing is the delightful prospect that the Sound affords, I have
counted (every day) from five to Eighteen sail of various
kinds of vessels constantly sailing up and down, which gives
one agreeable reflections. As to the common inhabitance
I can say but little about them not as yet having an opportunity to see for myself. . . . I was deverted yesterday by
asking a Blacksmith to mend my carrage told him by way
of indeucement that I could not stir out until it was done
he answered for that very reason he should delay it for
home was the proper place for women—that he thought
I had better be spinning than rideing about,—people would
think me as mad as Col Babcock if I did you may be sure.
I was much pleased with the old mans advice. Some ladies
have just sent their compliments intend visiting me therefore I am obliged to conclude abruptly which I hope you
will pardon. Remember your promis, and present me kindly
to Mrs. Turner and the dear children My pen is very Bad
I have no Doctor or Mr. G to mend for me—My complements to all friends which I fear are but few.

> Your sincear friend Caty Greene
I repeat again and again how happy I would be to see
Mrs. T and you here—[3]

Caty got the joyous news of the evacuation of Philadelphia
by the British, who could not afford to remain in the capital and
wage a war on several fronts on the continent at the same time.
Nathanael wrote that he had left Valley Forge with his soldiers
on the trail of the enemy troops, who were marching toward
the British haven of New York. "You cannot conceive how the
[Moore] family were distrest at my leaving them," he wrote. "They
expected every kind of insult and abuse after I was gone. You
are their favorite; they pray for you night and day. Mrs. Knox
has been in Philadelphia and is now gone to Morristown. She is
fatter than ever, which is a great mortification to her. The General
is equally fat, and therefore one cannot laugh at the other."[4]

In early July Caty read that the Continentals had attacked the
retiring enemy column at Monmouth, New Jersey. After a drawn
battle, the British had proceeded on to New York City. Caty felt
that the Continental troops in New Jersey should now be free
for a strike at the foe elsewhere, and could not understand why
the army did not march to Rhode Island to drive the enemy out

of Newport. In a letter to Nathanael she asked why he did not now return with his troops to protect his own people. As she pressed her point she thought of more and more reasons why her husband should come home. With the exception of a single night he had not been home in three years while she had ridden all over the country to be near him; moreover, she was carrying his third child and he had scarcely even seen his second. Then when an opportunity presented itself for him to come home, he did not seem anxious to take advantage of it. She felt that her own situation compared poorly with that of the other generals' wives and, in her black mood, hinted that there must be personal reasons why Nathanael wanted to remain in camp.

Her husband was gentle in his response, explaining that the Continentals must stay in the neighborhood of New York City to keep the main enemy force bottled up on Manhattan Island. As for her personal reasons for wanting him in Rhode Island he fully understood, and explained that her desire to have him home was no greater than his own. But the state of the war had obliged him to sacrifice many family pleasures. "This I am sure has done violence to your feelings . . ," he wrote, "but I trust . . . that I shall meet with no difficulty in obtaining your forgiveness hereafter. At the close of the war I flatter myself I shall be able to return to your arms with the same unspotted love and affection as when I took the field. Altho I have been absent from you, I have not been inconstant in love, unfaithful to my vows, or unjust to your bed." He added that he felt himself equally secure in her affection and fidelity.[5]

Caty soon learned that her arguments in favor of Nathanael's coming to Rhode Island had been valid after all, and that they had carried more weight than Nathanael had admitted. General Washington was sending an expeditionary force to Rhode Island to drive out the enemy and Nathanael had been given command of one of the divisions. This meant that he was on his way home at last, and Caty and the children hurried from Westerly to meet him. They reached Coventry a day before Nathanael's arrival, and found the countryside in a state of excitement over reports from Newport.

The British garrison was under attack by a French fleet commanded by Admiral Charles-Henri, the Count d'Estaing, who was cooperating with American land forces preparing to attack Newport from the north. Explosions rocked the countryside. As the French vessels shelled the town, fires broke out and spread rapidly through the wooden buildings. The British scuttled their ships in the harbor and the soldiers fled in confusion through the country to the north, destroying everything in their path, cutting down orchards, burning houses, and collecting everything from the inhabitants that could be carried away.

Nathanael's arrival in Coventry marked his second visit home since the Battle of Bunker Hill more than three years before. Unawed by the reports of the fight raging in Newport Harbor, he set aside a day to spend in peace with his family. He had his first real visit with his daughter Martha, and his first chance to play with his son in many, many months. Caty, now far along in her third pregnancy, had never before had her husband and both children together in their own house. For a brief span of time she found contentment. Still she had to share Nathanael with his family who streamed in from the countryside.

Leaving George at home with a nurse, Caty, Nathanael, and little Martha set out the next day for East Greenwich, visiting the general's family at Potowomut and Caty's aunt and uncle, the William Greenes, at her childhood home. Caty noted that Aunt Catharine made an effort to be cordial to her in Nathanael's presence. Uncle Greene was now governor of Rhode Island and Nathanael spent most of two days with him discussing the prosecution of the war in their state. The general then rejoined his division encamped at Tiverton. Situated on the eastern side of Narragansett Bay north of Newport, it was chosen as the site for the offensive against that British-occupied city.

Caty remained in East Greenwich for a time, but her brief glow of happiness and security had vanished. Most Rhode Island troops were now on the far side of Narragansett Bay, and East Greenwich once again lay unprotected. Moreover, Nathanael had taken the carriage horse with him to camp, and Caty felt marooned with her baby in East Greenwich, separated from George at Coventry. She was utterly miserable and once more her heart gave way to fear. She sent word to Nathanael that she was ill and must go home.

"Would to God," Nathanael wrote back, "that it was in my power to give peace to your bosom, which, I fear, is like a troubled ocean."[6] He agreed that her situation was critical and that she should get back at once to Coventry. He sent the horse with a servant to help her get home safely.

Back in Coventry Caty was still sick with anxiety, but at least she was back in her own house with both children, and on this occasion the remoteness of their dwelling offered some security. She tried to piece together the often conflicting news drifting in from the battle area. The initial reports were encouraging. An American force, 10,000 strong, had landed on Aquidneck Island, above Newport, and had advanced to within two miles of the city. The British appeared to be trapped between the army attacking from the north and the French fleet lying in the harbor to the south. The Tories of Newport were beside themselves with gloom, and the patriots with joy, for surely the city must fall.

Suddenly, following a severe storm, Caty heard that the French fleet had been scattered, and that sails later seen in the harbor belonged to British ships. Her earlier elation turned to despair. Nathanael's brother Jacob told her that the game was up. The Americans were doomed without the support of the French navy. Caty appealed to her husband to let her know the worst so that she could make plans for herself and the children.

Nathanael sent an aide to Coventry with a note to Caty assuring her that all was not lost and that the battle on the northern part of the island might still end in victory for the Americans. He criticized Jacob for his pessimism. "He is always looking over the black page of human life," Nathanael wrote, "never content with fortunes decrees. . . . I write upon my horse and have not slept any for two nights, therefore you'll excuse my not writing very legible."[7]

Day after day passed without further word. Finally a report came, and it was appalling: The defeated Americans were withdrawing to the mainland and Newport was still in British hands. Nathanael returned to Coventry and Caty had never seen him so dejected before.

He told her the story of the French fleet's withdrawal at the critical moment of the campaign; how he himself in company with Lafayette, had been rowed out to d'Estaing's dismasted flagship, wallowing off the coast, to beg the admiral to renew his attack on Newport. He had looked forward to his first good meal in days aboard the ship, but he was so seasick he could not go near the table. He had to present his arguments between paroxysms of nausea. The French admiral refused his entreaties on grounds that the fleet had been disabled by the recent storm. It was then, Nathanael told Caty, that he realized the campaign was doomed.

At Coventry he gathered his troops around him and set up division headquarters in his own home. The house overflowed with his army family. Caty, feeling uncomfortable and unwieldly in her advanced state of pregnancy, could do little to try to cheer the long faces that turned to her, half expecting her to work some bit of magic to chase away the gloom. The barren yard was filled with rows of tents. Soldiers huddled in silent groups, or sat staring down at the river below the house. At night their campfires threw strange, grotesque shadows and flickering ghosts against the ceiling. Caty listened to the soldiers' muffled talk as she lay wearily beside Nathanael.

After a few days that seemed like weeks to Caty, the soldiers were ordered back to New York state by General Washington. The military operations in Rhode Island were abandoned. Caty, nearing the date of her delivery and remembering the horror of her last confinement, begged her husband not to leave her. "She is very desirous of my stay[ing] until that event," Nathanael wrote General Washington in applying for leave, "and since she has her heart set upon it, I could wish to gratify her, for fear of some disagreeable consequences, as women sometimes under such circumstances receive great injury from being disappointed."[8]

Nathanael's request was granted. Their baby girl arrived safely and was named for Cornelia Lott, daughter of Caty's former hosts during her visit to New Jersey in the summer and fall of 1777. Conceived at Valley Forge and born of a distraught mother whose home so recently had been turned into an army headquarters, Cornelia was a frail, sickly infant. She was so small and fragile that her father never expected her to live. She would, however, grow up to become a talented writer and raconteur, leaving behind delightful accounts of her childhood and family life, and outliving her brothers and sisters by many years.

When the new baby showed signs that she would survive, Nathanael persuaded Caty that he must return to Continental headquarters. Feeling reassured about herself and her baby, she was complacent. As she told Nathanael good-bye she never guessed that he had spent his last night in their Coventry home.

7 Merriment at Middlebrook

To the relief of Rhode Islanders the British did not venture forth from their battered Newport garrison, and a measure of peace returned to the countryside. The calm was an uneasy one, however. No one knew what to expect from the enemy, whose arrogance had become more insufferable following their successful defense of Newport. For Caty the tensions of earlier weeks gave way to monotony. With one more child to demand her attention and care, without the help of her husband, life at Coventry became more confining than ever. As cold weather came on she began to sound out Nathanael about the likelihood of her coming to the winter camp that had been established in New Jersey's Middlebrook Valley.

Unknown to her at the time, she had a powerful ally in camp who favored her coming and presented arguments in her behalf. It was General Washington himself, who had felt very much in Caty's debt since the previous winter. The terrible months at Valley Forge were permanently etched in his memory. He never ceased to wonder at the fortitude of his own Martha and the ladies of the other generals who shared with their husbands the privations of the war. He gave them a share of the credit for the miracle of the army's survival. There had been few sounds of gaiety during the bleak early days of Valley Forge but there was one he would always be thankful for: the ringing laughter of Caty Greene, whose infectious good cheer constantly transcended the wretched circumstances of the encampment.

In November, 1778, Caty received a gratifying letter from her husband, who told of General Washington's high regard for her. "He renewed his charge to have you at camp very soon," wrote Nathanael. "Your last letter contained expressions of doubts and fears about the matter. To be candid with you I don't believe half a kingdom would hire you to stay away. But at the same time, I as candidly confess, I most earnestly wish it, as it will greatly contribute to my happiness to have you with me. . . . Bring [George] with you if the weather is not too cold."[1]

Caty drove to Middlebrook, not just with her son, but with all three children. The four-day trip with a driver and her little ones, all packed in a carriage among trunks full of belongings, was an exhausting ordeal. Warned by Nathanael of robberies committed in "The Clove" near Fishkill, the little party crossed the Hudson at King's Ferry south of Peekskill, several miles below the crossing Caty normally used. Here she discovered that her old friend, General Putnam, was in command. He provided her with a small guard of light-horse that escorted the carriage through the worst of Tory country.

Arriving at the Continental camp Caty found rewards that made the long journey seem worthwhile. Situated snugly near the village of Bound Brook, along the banks of the Raritan River and under cover of a mountain range, Middlebrook was a paradise compared to the encampment of a year before. The soldiers lived in log huts that reminded Caty of those at Valley Forge, but the similarity between the two camps ended there. She found the men in good spirits, well-fed and well-clothed, and Nathanael's handsome headquarters dwelling, constructed of Holland brick and situated near the river, made a comfortable home.

Many of Caty's old friends among the generals and their wives welcomed her to camp. Nathanael's aides, particularly the quartermaster assistants, Cox, Pettit, and Wadsworth, could not do enough for her. She could scarcely recall when she had felt so secure. Protected on all sides by a formidable army, with the enemy far away, and her husband close at hand to help with the children, she found herself in a world apart from the one she knew in Coventry.

Lodged in bachelors' quarters a short distance away were other army friends she had met at Valley Forge, among them General Wayne, wifeless as usual, General Steuben, and the polished young Virginian, Major Henry Lee. Bearing no relationship or earthly resemblance to the controversial Charles Lee, "Lighthorse Harry" was a man of such dash and verve, and so splendidly uniformed under all circumstances, that Caty had picked him out as the kind of soldier little girls dream of.

Caty was drawn to the white clapboard house near her own dwelling not only because the Washingtons lived there, but because the immensely handsome Alexander Hamilton was a member of General Washington's staff. Although Hamilton was on hand at all the social functions, Caty saw little of him. She only caught glimpses of him above the heads of the ladies who flocked around him, and he smiled back at her where she stood in the adjoining room surrounded by men. When Caty heard that Lady Washington, in all innocence, had named a headquarters tomcat after Hamilton she giggled delightedly, much to the pleasure of her male companions.

In February the Greenes were hosts at a dance in their living room. Caty, who had just turned twenty-five, wore a lovely gown. As she moved gracefully over the floor, dancing to the strains of lively music played by fiddlers stationed in the hall, Martha Washington remarked how trim her figure looked so soon after the birth of Cornelia. Nathanael had never seen her look more beautiful. She carried a fan and wore a golden locket, containing his picture, that had been presented to her by his aides. While their respective mates sat out most of the evening, General Washington danced with Caty again and again, teasing her all the while about having stolen her from her "Quaker preacher" and betting her that he could outlast her on the floor. "[They] danced upwards of three hours without once sitting down," Nathanael wrote a friend.[2]

Caty was often conscious of the gentle eyes of Martha Washington upon her. Sometimes she wished she could read their look more clearly. Always she felt a bond between her heart and that of her friend, but now she wondered if there weren't some message in Lady Washington's gaze that eluded her. Caty put the fleeting feeling aside and set about to enjoy the new freedom she felt.

The absence of the enemy in the vicinity gave the officers' wives an opportunity to travel about the countryside. During April, while Nathanael remained behind, attending business, Caty left her children with an attendant and drove to a "tea frolick" in Trenton. She was glad to get away because the public hanging of deserters scheduled at Middlebrook was certain to cast a pall of gloom over the camp. Escorted by Bill Blodgett and Ichabod Burnet of the headquarters family, and accompanied by Abraham Lott and his daughter Cornelia, her close friends from Basking Ridge, she set off in a gay mood. The party, hosted by Betsy Pettit, was attended by several members of Congress and a number of fashionable Philadelphia ladies whose critical attention, Caty felt, was often directed toward her. Holding her head high, no longer awed by such society, she accepted another glass of wine and moved confidently among the company, exchanging repartee and easily holding her own in the discussions of the day.

At headquarters, however, when Nathanael accompanied her to soirees, she had begun to feel less comfortable. She was aware that her husband's usual smiles of admiration were ever more frequently giving way to frowns of disapproval. When she later demanded to know why, Nathanael sat down with her for a long talk. He did not accuse, scold, make demands, or raise his voice. He simply told her that she had become too fond of wine. He wanted her to enjoy herself, he said, but too much spirits could lead to coarseness in women and hamper the development of those softer qualities that marked the polished lady. Overindulgence in pleasure could dull wits and ruin health. Nathanael suggested that cultural pursuits, which he felt Caty was neglecting that season, would help mould the type of character to be admired.

Caty placed her own interpretation upon her husband's remarks. His high standing in the army, second only to that of General Washington, commanded respect in every quarter, and she was well aware that his stature as a person was easily equivalent to his military rank. But wasn't she now being told that she had not kept pace, that she did not quite measure up to the image of a high-ranking general's wife?

Nathanael tried to persuade her that he meant no such thing, that he was interested only in her health and happiness, but he repeated his admonitions many times as she listened in uncomfortable silence—a silence that transformed itself into an adamant refusal to change her ways. If her pride was hurt, or if she felt guilt or shame, she hid it well behind that particular veil that Nathanael despised the most. But to her friends she was as charming and talkative as ever.

A defiant Caty continued to enjoy the merriment at Middle-brook. She knew, though, that it must come to an end. In May Nathanael was transferred to a camp on the Hudson, but Caty did not want to go home to Coventry. She made every excuse to stay on but Nathanael thought that the time had come for her to return home. Finally, in June, prodded by a letter from Nathanael who pointedly outlined the arrangements for her trip, she prepared to leave her cozy quarters. She packed up her belongings and got the children ready for the road. Then she paid a farewell call on Martha Washington.

Her heart was heavy as she entered the familiar door of the white clapboard house. She felt she had never needed her friend as much as she did at that minute. When Lady Washington came into the room, Caty could no longer contain herself and she burst into tears. In the comfort of Martha's arms, Caty sobbed out her fear that she was pregnant again. She knew that, if it were true, she might not be able to go to camp the following winter. Lady Washington did her best to console her.

The journey home with the children, in company with Major Burnet, was a grueling one. Caty arrived in Rhode Island exhausted, only to be greeted by an unpleasant situation. There had been an argument among Nathanael's brothers about financial affairs, and Caty was made to feel that she was in the middle of it. Her relations with Aunt Catharine had undergone no change and when she called on her in East Greenwich she was received coldly. Few of the other Rhode Island ladies she knew were cordial, either. There seemed to be nowhere to turn. Peggy and Jacob Greene, upset by the family squabble, did little to raise her spirits.

Her days were long. She was lonely and unhappy. She found no relief, no friendship, and she thought longingly of the camp in Middlebrook. At night when the children were finally bedded down, she escaped to her room where she could be away from her in-laws, and she discovered that wine helped her to relax and sleep.

She kept up with the war news through Jacob and the *Providence Gazette*. Letters from Nathanael continued to arrive. She knew that except for the troops still based in Newport and New York City the British had cleared out of New England and the middle states, shifting their major operations to the South. One word of encouragement would have sent her scurrying westward to New Windsor, on the Hudson, where Nathanael was quartered comfortably with General Knox, Colonel Biddle, and her great favorite among his aides, the wealthy and handsome Colonel Wadsworth. Her brother Billy, who had distinguished himself the previous fall at the Battle of Red Bank, was also a member of the household. (The dwelling, called General Knox's Headquarters, is preserved as a national monument.) "I can assure [you] everybody [at headquarters] is charmed with Billy's behaviour," Nathanael wrote her. "General Knox says he has a great deal of the pure milk of nature. Col Wadsworth says he is a sweet tempered young fellow and will shine by & by to great advantage."[3]

But no invitation came for Caty. Instead, Nathanael told her repeatedly that he would come home for a visit, a promise he would not be able to fulfill. His letters offered advice on every subject: how to handle her dispute with Aunt Catharine without losing the friendship of Uncle Greene; which of his brothers and cousins she could count on for help; which of her friends he wanted her to be particularly polite to; and even how to take care of the horses. He was particularly outspoken in advising Caty how to deal with a recent snub by General Gates: "Don't be mortified, my dear, at the neglect he shows you. Remember it is a greater reproach to his politeness and want of breeding than it is to your want of merit. . . . When you reflect on this I am persuaded you will rather pity than resent his pitiful behavior, which marks him as a little dirty genius that can enjoy a malicious triumph over a female—who never did him injury—because he dont like her husband. I always knew him to be a little-minded wretch but he now appears less than little."[4]

His letters often contained words that gnawed deeply within her, of concern and admonition over her personal behavior. When she finally wrote back that his constant criticism had undermined her self-respect, she received a long letter of apology: "I did not mean to humble you in your own opinion. . . . You must be sensible how capable the most finished characters are of improvement, and how subject human nature is to err. My love for you, the respect with which I wish you to be treated, make me anxious to have you appear to advantage in all circumstances. It is from this principle that I hold out a clue to direct your steps, not from a want of being sensible how happy I am in the real jewel I possess."[5] Along with the letter came a book of English grammar, which he asked Caty to study carefully.

Caty's anxieties were increased by her children's poor health.

Cornelia had fever, George a lump in his breast, and Martha, or "Patty," failed to show improvement from the deformities of rickets in spite of being immersed in cold water every day. Since the nearest doctor was a long ride away, Caty asked Nathanael to consult Dr. William Shippen, Jr., who frequently visited his headquarters, as to the best remedies. But her letters had to be taken to Providence before they could be picked up by courier and forwarded to New Windsor, and Nathanael's response required the same route in reverse. Thus many days passed between question and answer.

In addition to nausea, Caty began to experience upper abdominal pain, climaxed by the vomiting of blood. She hesitated to inform Nathanael, knowing the interpretation he was sure to place on the disorder and its cause. He would not consider her pregnancy as a factor since he was not yet sure of it, and would not understand the tensions she endured. Finally, becoming truly alarmed over the hemorrhage, she wrote for his advice, at the same time attempting to minimize her own fears.

Nathanael placed the blame exactly where she had expected him to—on wine—but censured himself as well for not having been more firm. "My resolution . . . failed me," he wrote. "I have queried with myself frequently in this way: If I do bar her [from] the pleasures she so much admires, will she not think it unkind? Verily. Will she not think it arbitrary? Certainly. Will she not think me more the tyrant than the husband? Undoubtedly. Will it not lessen her affection? Most certainly. Will it not mortify . . . me to have her affection diminished? Indeed it will. . . . Don't I love her most dearly? Inexpressibly so."

Nathanael went on to explain to Caty that he "knew the value of health and was exceedingly hurt to see it bartered away for a few moments of fleeting pleasures. My affection, my present pleasures, and future hopes all served to render me miserable on the occasion, after I found you so wedded to the pleasures. . . . I had spoke to you so many times to so little purpose . . . that I was ashamed to repeat the subject. I knew your health was in danger, indeed I foresaw its downfall and consequently my own misfortune and your distress. . . . I am going up to [Washington's headquarters] this afternoon to consult Dr. Shippen on your case."[6]

Caty suddenly felt better, so much so that she began to doubt that she was pregnant. "Methinks that you can determine from a number of female circumstances," Nathanael, who was now on the march, wrote back. "Should you find you are not, and your other complaint continues, I strongly recommend you going into salt water, not once or twice, but every day or two, for a month to come. I would advise you to stay down at Greenwich for the purpose, in order to be convenient to salt water. This mode was strongly recommended by Dr. Shippen. . . ."

In the same letter Nathanael told of his visit to Kitty Stirling, now Mrs. William Duer, at West Point. "[She] looks charmingly," he wrote, "much handsomer than ever I saw her, and appears infinitely more happy. See the happy effect of a good bedfellow; but this you know by experience."[7] Caty sat with the letter a long time. His words saying how much he missed her did little to ease her hurt.

She depended on messages from friends at headquarters to lift her mood. A package of stockings and gloves came for her from Colonel Cox, assistant quartermaster, and the accompanying note made her smile. The colonel's wife was not good-looking, and had once described herself to Caty as a "plain, old fashioned woman, marked with age and rusticity among the pines."[8] Now she had presented her husband with a baby girl. "[This] you will say is a little mortifying," Colonel Cox wrote Caty. "However, I have the pleasing consolation that if she copies after her mother she will in due time *turn* to a son. . . . Best wishes for your Health and Happiness, and anxious desires for the return of Winter Quarters, for reasons I leave you to guess."[9]

Caty no longer had doubts about her pregnancy and gave up her hopes of soon rejoining Nathanael. She heard of the British raids on New Haven, Fairfield, and Norwalk, but her own neighborhood was quiet. Then in October the countryside was thrown into a fit of expectancy by signs that the British were about to evacuate Newport, a move induced by the shifting of the war to the Carolinas and Georgia. Forty-two transports arrived, and the troops made ready to embark, but not before committing their final acts of destruction. The city's inhabitants were warned to keep indoors, on pain of death, until the ships moved away from the docks. As the last vessel sailed out of the harbor, American soldiers poured over from the mainland, and Newport at last was free of the enemy.

8 A Time of Despair

The winter of 1779-80 arrived, and with it came weather of such severity that for many years it would remain the standard of misery in the East. Newport Bay was frozen solid for six weeks and ice formed in the ocean as far as the eye could see. When Caty, only a few weeks from term in her fourth pregnancy, spoke of joining her husband in New Jersey her friends and in-laws were aghast. Nathanael discouraged her leaving home, but in the same letter he mentioned the attractiveness of the young girls of the countryside who were constantly in and out of his changing headquarters. He might as well have begged her to come.

Caty drove to Morristown in a howling snowstorm, accompanied by a driver and her son, George, but without the little girls. Nathanael received his wife and son warmly in the comfortable headquarters dwelling three miles from the village, and Colonel Cox and aides in the quartermaster department brought them fruits and other delicacies. Caty checked in with the camp doctors and in January little "Nat"—Nathanael Ray Greene—was born. The camp buzzed with excitement and from all quarters came presents crudely, but proudly, made by the soldiers.

By the time Caty regained her strength the camp had taken

on an air of gaiety reminiscent of Middlebrook the winter before. Unfortunately there was one memorable social event that everyone would have preferred to forget. Clement Biddle, Nathanael's commissary general of forage, along with his wife, gave a large party at which the Washingtons and Greenes were present. George and Deborah Olney, relatives of Nathanael's, were the guests of honor. Olney, a Providence auditor, had recently been hired by Nathanael to methodize the books of the quartermaster department. A teetotaler, the auditor became disgusted with the men at the party who had a little too much to drink. Rather pointedly, he left the officers and joined the group of ladies in another room.

The deserted men, feeling rebuffed, held a "council of war" and decided to spirit Olney away from his female companions and make him take a drink. When the ladies refused to yield up their captive, General Washington himself led an expedition into the room. Olney was piously indignant, as was his wife, and suddenly the sham took a nasty turn. As Deborah Olney held onto her husband, Washington playfully seized her wrist. Then, according to Caty's version of the event, Mrs. Olney, in a violent rage, screamed at Washington: "Let go of my hand or I'll pull every hair out of your head! Even if you are a general you are still just a man!"[1] The Greenes were thunderstruck. Caty gave vent to her indignation at Deborah's bad taste, then Nathanael took Olney aside and lectured him sternly about his blunt way of refusing to drink. The party ended on this unhappy note, and Caty was still fuming when she went home.

In March, Caty left her two sons with a nurse at camp and accompanied Nathanael on a business trip to Philadelphia. It was her first view of the city she had heard so much about, one sadly divided in political sentiment but as gay and brilliant as ever. With its population of 40,000 it was the country's largest city. Caty walked with Nathanael along the narrow, crowded streets bordered by rows of red brick buildings. On Chestnut Street he pointed out the Carpenters' Hall where Sammy Ward's father had met with the First Continental Congress before contracting a fatal case of smallpox, and the State House, where the Declaration of Independence had been signed less than four years before.

In the evening they drove down High Street and called on General Benedict Arnold, commandant of the American forces in Philadelphia. His headquarters building was the same that had lodged British General Howe during the recent occupation. Here they met Arnold's bride of less than a year, the former Peggy Shippen, a beautiful girl of twenty who was the talk of Philadelphia society. The daughter of a Loyalist judge, she had Tory leanings herself and had consorted with British officers during their residence in the city. After the British evacuation and the arrival of General Arnold, she had married the controversial officer almost immediately.

When Nathanael's meetings with various Congressional committees commenced, they quickly transformed Caty's visit to Philadelphia into a nightmare. The quartermaster department was under fire by Congress because debts incurred by the office under the country's inflationary economy had piled up to an alarming degree. When Congress attempted to hold Nathanael personally responsible for the debts, he offered his resignation, but the governing body would not accept it until the accounts had been satisfactorily settled.

Nathanael then gave final notice of his refusal to serve the department further, and several infuriated members of Congress, learning of his private speculations in league with army subordinates, offered a resolution that he be dismissed from the service. General Washington was shocked when he learned of it. He sent an urgent note to a member of Congress, explaining that it was impossible for army officers to support themselves and their families on their military pay, and that many who could not supplement their incomes had been forced to resign. As for Nathanael's dismissal, Washington was blunt. Never let such a tragic event take place, he warned the congressman, "if it is within your abilities to prevent it."[2]

The letter saved the army from the loss of one of its ablest generals. Congress dropped the resolution concerning Nathanael's discharge from service in the line, and much to his and Caty's joy, accepted his resignation as quartermaster general. Nathanael was free at last to concentrate on being a soldier again.

When the Greenes got back to Morristown, word awaited them in a letter from Jacob Greene that Caty's older brother, Simon Littlefield, had died at his home at the age of twenty-nine. But news of the little girls was good. Patty was at Block Island visiting her grandfather, while Cornelia was with Nathanael's family in Potowomut. "[She] is very well," wrote Jacob, "and is a charming girl."[3]

During the summer of 1780 Caty was again home in Coventry with her four children and faced her immediate future with more than her usual misgivings. She had heard rumors that Nathanael would be transferred to the South, and such a distant move would give her little hope of joining him at headquarters. It would also mean no more visits to the merry camps of New Jersey. "[Keep] a cheerful heart, and if possible make yourself happy," Nathanael urged, but he knew the chances were slim.[4]

In July Caty sailed to Block Island for the first time since the war began, to pick up Patty and to visit her brother's grave. She felt safe enough in making the trip, with the British fleet no longer based at Newport, but just as her vessel entered the Block Island harbor two enemy men-of-war bore down on the craft. The frightened captain, made more uneasy by having the wife of a rebel general on board, had Caty rowed ashore while he turned his ship around and sailed hastily back to the safety of Newport. Caty was to have gone back on the same vessel, but now she found herself stranded on the island for several days. This gave her the opportunity of having an extended visit with her father and his family, and a chance to renew acquaintances with some of her old friends there. She found the islanders as indifferent as ever, undisturbed by the war and its politics. A detachment of British had garrisoned the island during the occupation of Newport, but the farmers and fishermen hardly noticed the change in government.

Caty visited her brother's grave and stood silently, alone and melancholy. Nineteen years had passed since her mother had been buried on the same hillside, but there had been little change in the scenery. Within her view were the same stone fences, paths, ponds, and distant sea. But while time had stood still on the island, her own world had been altered beyond conception. The five years of war had been an eternity. She had endured the rigors of four pregnancies, reared her children under the most trying circumstances, survived a long illness, lived through a bombardment, traveled hundreds of miles through enemy-infested country, agonized when her husband went into battle, and suffered shattering personal disappointments. Though her trials were of a kind to ravish youth and despoil beauty, her friends on the island still found her trim and lovely, full of spunk and good humor.

On her way back to Coventry with Patty she was met at the Newport dock by the Marquis de Lafayette and escorted to the headquarters of the French commanders who were using the port city as base for their expenditionary fleet and army. She was appalled by the scenes of destruction the British had left behind.

Some 500 houses had been torn down to make firewood; gardens and groves were ruined, stores left empty, commerce brought to a stop. The French were bravely trying to set things in order again. Among the officers she met at headquarters were the commandant, the Count de Rochambeau, and a number of his officers bearing such names as the Baron de Viomenil, the Chevalier de Chastellux, the Chevalier d'Olonne, the Marquis de Vauban, the Count de Saint-Maime, and the Viscount de Noailles.

During her visit, Newport was suddenly thrown into confusion by the report that a British fleet had been sighted off the coast. Many of the town's Tory ladies began rejoicing at the prospects, while the long-suffering patriots received the news with anguish. Lafayette wrote Nathanael of the fear that had come over Caty, and of the great haste in which she and Patty had left the city. Not until they arrived in East Greenwich did they learn that the alarm had been false.

Caty's hopes of joining her husband at one of the camps in New York state were repeatedly dashed by his letters. He wrote that nothing had been determined for the coming campaign, and he was still in the dark about whether he would be sent to the South. In September he wrote that he had been given temporary command of the entire army while General Washington was on a trip to Hartford and that every moment was taken up with military duties.

Caty, lapsing into one of her brooding moods, did not correspond with Nathanael for weeks at a time then finally lashed out at him with a question that had bothered her for many months. If he was too busy for his family, how was it that he frequently found time to visit Lady Stirling and Kitty Duer? Was there a particular attraction possessed by them that he found lacking in her? If so, she at least deserved to be told.

Her husband wrote an immediate reply. Not trusting the usual courier service with such a personal message, he sent the letter in the hands of a high French official who was returning to Newport, and who delivered it to Caty's door.

"Let me ask you soberly whether you estimate yourself below either of these ladies," Nathanael wrote. "You will answer me No, if you speak as you think. I declare upon my sacred honor, independent of the partiality that I ought to feel, I think they possess far less accomplishments than you, and as much as I respect them as friends, I should never be happy with them in a more intimate connection. . . . I will venture to say there is no mortal more happy in a wife than myself. . . . Don't then repine, my dear, for though our felicity is not perfect, yet we have a good foundation for solid and lasting happiness. . . . I can assure you with great truth that I never enjoyed a moment's rational and refined happiness until I had the good fortune of being united to you."[5]

A few days later Caty was startled to read Nathanael's description of General Benedict Arnold's treacherous attempt to deliver the fortress of West Point to the British. In making his escape, Arnold left his wife in "the most awful situation that imagination can form," wrote Nathanael. "For two days she was raving distracted. . . ."[6] Caty felt sorry for Peggy Arnold, whom she had met so recently, not suspecting, as many did, that her hysterical outburst—with hair in disarray, blouse parted, and breasts exposed—was only a show, calculated to delay pursuit of her husband.

Caty was acquainted with Joshua Smith, one of Arnold's suspected accomplices, having spent nights at his Hudson River home during trips between Rhode Island and New Jersey. She grieved for his wife, a forlorn English girl who only recently had come to America and married her husband, and who otherwise had not a relative or friend in the land. Caty had also heard of the British adjutant, Major John André, another suspect, who had been a popular member of the garrisons of Block Island and Philadelphia during their occupation and who had left behind a number of civilian friends when the British evacuated those places.

When news came of Smith's acquittal, Caty was greatly relieved, but the description of the hanging of the brave and gifted André left her sad for days.

Caty had never felt so destitute as she did that fall. The devastation of Newport and its commerce and the destruction of countless farms and orchards by the enemy left the Rhode Island countryside in an impoverished state. The inhabitants subsisted on the barest essentials. Currency had depreciated to such an extent that prices were prohibitive, and Caty began to have serious fears about her family's livelihood.

Suddenly her gloom gave way to joy. Since the flight of the traitorous Benedict Arnold the fort at West Point had been left without a commander; Nathanael had applied to General Washington for the position, had been granted it, and was already on his way to his new post. The headquarters, a fine house on the east bank of the Hudson, would make a comfortable winter home for Caty and the children. Nathanael wrote her to begin her preparations for the trip and suggested a route of travel.

Caty examined one sentence in the letter with mixed feelings. "You will make a stop in Hartford if possible," it read, "or Wadsworth will not forgive you."[7] She wanted very much to see Jeremiah again but at the same time she felt a tingle of apprehension. Their attraction to each other was not something to be taken lightly. She would have to think further before making up her mind.

She went to Providence to spend the last of her savings on new clothing for herself and the children. When she returned, crushing news awaited her in a message from Nathanael.

> My dear angel
>
> What I have been dreading has come to pass. His Excellency General Washington by order of Congress has appointed me to the command of the Southern Army, General Gates being recalled to [undergo] an examination into his conduct. This is so foreign from my wishes that I am distressed exceedingly. . . .
>
> The moment I was appointed to the command I sent off Mr. Hubbard to bring you to camp. But alas before we even have the happiness of meeting I am ordered away to another quarter. How unhappy is war to domestic happiness.
>
> I wish it was possible for me to stay until your arrival, but [by] the pressing manner [in] which the general urges my setting out I am afraid you will come too late to see me. . . .
>
> God bless you my love. With the truest love and sincearest affection, I am Yours
>
> N Greene[8]

Caty's brief dream of security and happiness in a home overlooking the Hudson, surrounded by all her family, faded into thin air. There would be no time to talk over plans with Nathanael, not even a chance to kiss him good-bye, before he was whisked off to the deep South. There would be little opportunity for her to follow him that winter and absolutely no hope that the children could make such a trip. She felt that her misfortune was more than she could bear.

Nathanael was unable to send her cash, forwarding only a number of stock certificates which he warned were not negotiable and might well turn out to be worthless. He wrote that the stocks, the farm in Westerly, and one recently purchased in New Jersey were his entire fortune. He advised her to move with the children to Westerly if her discontent at Coventry became too great, but other than this he urged her to make her own decisions. "In a word, choose for yourself and act for yourself," he wrote, "I have full confidence you will do nothing but [what] will be perfectly to my liking."[9]

Caty lapsed into silent despondency. She already felt that her marriage had been a near-casualty of the war. She had four children to show for her union but the more subtle aspects of her relationship with Nathanael had been forced to endure the most trying circumstances. When reunited after long separations there had been days in which they felt as strangers, and no sooner had they recaptured the joy of being in each other's arms than a movement of the army would rip them apart again. She began to wonder if their love could survive another long separation.

She heard later that Nathanael had received a false report that she was already on the way to West Point. He had waited an extra day before his departure and had gone up to Fishkill, on her expected route of travel, in hopes of meeting her. "But alas," he wrote, "I was obliged to return with bitter disappointment. My longing eyes looked for you in all directions, and I felt my heart leap for joy at the sound of every carriage. O Caty, how much I suffer, and how much more will you. . . . How or when I shall return God only knows. . . . God grant you patience and fortitude. . . . I am forever and ever yours."[10]

A message from Trenton told of Nathanael's disappointment in not hearing from her. However, a letter from Caty greeted Nathanael's arrival in Philadelphia, where he had stopped for conferences with members of Congress. She could not be responsible for the consequences of a long separation, she wrote. Whatever the difficulties, she would come to his camp as soon as he sent for her.

But the first word of encouragement was many months in coming.

9 Letters from the South

The presence of the French forces at Newport helped save Caty's reason. With the British gone, she made several visits to the city to enjoy the spectacular new society there. She found that the patriots, long accustomed to the bad manners of the departed Hessians and the overbearing attitude of the British commanders, were delighted with the gentlemanly demeanor of the French troops and the courtliness of the officers.

Caty burst upon the Newport scene as a welcome relief to the French command. They had found the native women good-looking but cold, lacking in the gentle art of flirtation, much different from the women of the French court. Conversation was dull and one-sided, the officers having to carry the burden of small talk. When the Newport ladies were admired and responded with some encouragement, the foreigners were baffled by their sudden retreat behind a chilly barrier if pressed to go further in the relationship. In France the custom was for both sexes to enjoy their drinks and conversations together in a salon, but in Rhode Island the ladies were in the habit of retiring to another room while the gentlemen lingered over a drink and a smoke after dinner. Married women without their husbands were apt to shrink away as if they didn't belong in these circles.

To all of this, Caty was the glittering exception. She visited Count Rochambeau's headquarters where she delighted the French commanders with her conversational efforts in their native tongue. Some of them, who spoke fluent English, were reluctant to disclose the fact to their charming guest. Invited to a dance given in honor of Newport ladies by Baron Viomenil and his strikingly handsome brother, Caty found herself the most sought-after belle at the ball. Among the new friends she made were Claude Blanchard, chief commissary of the Newport garrison, and Captain Haake, of the Royal Deux-Ponts. In an impulsive moment of conviviality, she invited them to visit her in Coventry, never dreaming they would do so.

Caty found in Newport a strange mixture of French soldiers, Tories, Whigs, and Quakers. At night the city was brilliantly lit, by order of town officials, as a sign of welcome to the French. She could read the political sentiments of the occupants by the number of candles that were burned in the windows—thirteen by Whig families, four to six by Tories, and none at all by the Quakers, whose windowpanes were sometimes broken as a consequence.

She loved the pageantry of the French parades. The artillery-men were distinguishable by their iron gray coats and red velvet lapels, while the infantry wore long waistcoats trimmed in their regiments' colors. All wore a panache of white feathers; the grena-diers had red plumes, the chasseurs, white and green. Caty, as far as she could from her dwindling wardrobe, dressed to match their style.

Returning to Coventry from her lively life in Newport, she found the contrast overwhelming. Gone were the companions and witty chatter she had enjoyed, and she settled down once more to the confining life and routine that she had come to loathe. She was surprised by a visit from the French officers, Blanchard and Haake. She was alone with the children when they came, Jacob and Peggy being away. She was shabbily dressed and the pantry was almost empty. But she made a gallant effort to repro-duce the gaiety she had shared with the officers in Newport.

Blanchard wrote of the visit in his journal. He was shocked by the isolation of Caty's existence, and by the drab, cheerless, almost destitute surroundings of the "amiable, genteel, and pretty" lady he had so recently befriended. "As there was no bread in the house," he wrote, "some was hastily made; it was of meal and water mixed together, which was toasted at the fire; small slices were served up to us. It is not much for a Frenchman. . . . Besides, the dinner was long. Mrs. Greene's house is situated upon a barren piece of land. . . . There is not a single fruit-tree, not even a cabbage. Another country house is pretty near, inhabited by two ladies who compose all the society Mrs. Greene has; in the evening she invited them to her house and we danced; I was in boots and rather tired; besides the English dances are rather complicated, so I acquitted myself badly. But these ladies were complaisant."[1]

Caty and Nathanael reestablished communication during the winter, but mail service to and from the South was so irregular and undependable that weeks often elapsed before the messages were delivered. General Washington, in New Windsor, New York, suggested that his headquarters be made a relay station in the dispatching of mail by the Greenes. "If you will entrust your letters to my care," Washington wrote Caty, "they shall have the same attention paid to them as my own, and forwarded with equal dispatch to the Genl. Mrs. Washington, who is just arrived at my Qrs, joins me in most cordial wishes for your every felicity; and regrets the want of your company. Remember us to my name-sake. Nat, I suppose, can handle a musket."[2]

Nathanael's first letter was one of many that were intended to discourage Caty's plans to join him in the South. The roads were almost impassable, he wrote, and the trip fraught with hazard. Bandits often preyed on helpless travelers. "You have no concep-tion of the nature of the journey, circumstances of the country, or manners of the people," he said. "Indeed, you are much better off at home."[3]

The inhabitants of the Carolinas, he told her, were the most unhappy and frustrated he had ever encountered. The bitterness between patriot and Loyalist far exceeded in physical antagonism anything he had ever seen in the eastern or middle states. At home, he wrote, "the difference between Whig and Tory is little more than a division of sentiment, but here they persecute each other with little less than savage fury. . . . The sufferings and distress of the inhabitants beggars all description, and requires the liveliest imagination to conceive the cruelties and devastations which prevail."[4]

The hatred between families of opposite political convictions was so intense that men were often more fearful of the depradations of hostile neighbors than those of foreign troops. Sometimes the raiding bands were mere outlaws without political loyalties, posing as members of either party, assaulting defenseless farmhouses, robbing, burning, and killing indiscriminately. Nathanael told Caty of a captain of militia who, riding to the home of his sister, found her murdered and seven of her children shot and left for dead.

Bit by bit, from Nathanael's letters that often took weeks to arrive, she was able to piece together a picture of her husband's life in the South. The military campaign was unfathomable, and it was not until long after it had ended that Caty had the barest understanding of the type of warfare being waged by Nathanael's army.

To begin with, his entire force—made up of militia, partisans, and Continentals—numbered less than 3,000 men, but in reality the effective strength of his command, after subtractions were made for absences without leave, illness, death, and desertion, was less than half of that total. Caty realized that with such a paltry force Nathanael had not the faintest hope of crushing the British or driving them bodily out of the land. His tactics were strictly those of guerilla warfare, his strategy to keep the enemy on the run and thus neutralize British influence in the Carolinas and Georgia. His philosophy was that the British Crown could never subjugate the people if they were willing to fight as long as was necessary for their freedom.

Caty was not to be discouraged by Nathanael's descriptions of Southern warfare. Her expressed desire to visit his headquarters, however, continued to bring only negative responses. Finally, in February, 1781, she appealed her case to General Washington at New Windsor through a letter to Martha, but the general was then on his way to Newport to confer with commanders of the French fleet and army.

A message came to Coventry from General Washington, inviting Caty to visit him during a stopover in Providence, but she was detained at home because of the illness of little Nat. A short time later she received a letter from the general, written after his return to his camp on the Hudson, telling her of his disappointment in not having seen her, but pleading a neutral position on the subject of her proposed journey to the South. "I can neither advise you to, nor disswade you from the measure," he wrote, "because the true footing (if you will allow me to say so) upon which the journey should depend is, in my opinion, the encouragement given to it by Genl. Greene, who having a view of all circumstances before him, can alone determine the propriety of it."[5]

Meanwhile an old nemesis had returned to haunt Caty. In March a letter had arrived from Providence written by Deborah Olney, who had been involved in the unfortunate party at Clement Biddle's headquarters at Morristown the year before. She accused Caty of "fabrication and misrepresentation" in spreading the story that Deborah had threatened to tear out General Washington's hair and eyes. "I am obliged," wrote Mrs. Olney, ". . . to convince those to whom you told it, with the most agravating circumstances . . . that it is utterly false."[6]

Caty set out immediately for Providence to see Mrs. Olney but found that she was away from home. Returning to Coventry, she took up her pen:

> Coventry, March 18, 1781
>
> Dear Madam
>
> It is with Great pain that I acknowledge receipt of your letter which is as unbecoming as my temper was at Col. Biddles. I thought for some time the letter had been forged as I could have no idea of such a one from a lady of such good Breeding. Surely it is not the same Mrs. Olney that I used to know and love. I knew a lady of that name who posses'd Many vertues and but one fault—that fault I mention'd freely to her, and . . . her vertues I have also spoak of with approveing warmth. I take the liberty always to [express] the foibles of my friends and they Generally do mine with the same freedom, however this is not the subject I intended writing on—I know not what has been told you of my *fabracation* or *misrepresentation* this I know that such an accusation is unworthy of you, and much beneath my notis. . . . What motive could I have to injure the reputation of a woman I sincerely loved. The affair at Col B —— s I did tell to Mrs. Col Bowen of who I knew to be a friend of yours—I did not agravate one tittle of it and if you will divest your self of parciallity and reflect one moment, you cannot deny it. . . . I will not be so impolite as to charge you with telling falshoods but your memory must be very perfidious. . . . As to your tearing out the Genls Eyes I heard nor said nothing . . . but you did say you would tear out his hear [hair]— and I can bring sworn evidence to the truth of it.

. . . I am very willing you should know all I have ever said of you . . . I will at any time say it to your face. . . . I have nothing to hope of or fear from you, so that my friendship is disinterested. . . .

I am with every wish for your felicity, your sincear friend and very Humble servant

C Greene

I understand that Mr. Olney has said something of me which I am sure he would not have said if Genl Greene had been at home and which I shall not mention to him untill I hear again from Providence.

C. Greene[7]

Caty's postscript caused the Olneys some concern. "[Mr. Olney] bids me tell you," Deborah wrote back, "that he has not the least objection to your or General Greene's knowing all he has said on this Disagreeable subject; but as you may have heard something he never did say he wishes to know what you have been told, and pawns his honor, if true, to own it."[8] Caty let the matter stand and did not send another reply.

A few days later a letter from Nathanael, posted at Guilford Court House in North Carolina, arrived. "We had a very severe general action with Lord Cornwallis," he wrote. "Many fell but none of your particular friends. . . . I had not the honor of being wounded, but I was very near being taken, having rode in the heat of the action full tilt into the midst of the enemy; but by Colonel Morris' calling to me and advertising me of the situation I had just time to retire. Our army retired in good order, and the enemy suffered severely. . . . "

Nathanael had received a letter from Caty the evening after the action, "which was some consolation after the misfortune of the day. . . . Our fatigue has been excessive. I have not had my clothes off for upwards of six weeks; but I am generally in pretty good health. Poor Major Burnet is sick and . . . Morris too is not well. Indeed the whole family is just about worn out. . . . I should be extremely happy if the war had an honorable close, and I on a farm with my little family about me. God grant the day may not be far distant when peace, with all her train of blessings, shall diffuse universal joy throughout America."[9]

In late spring Caty got her first encouraging word from her husband. He told her that Cornwallis had withdrawn from the state and that the British troops remaining in the Carolinas were retreating "with precipitation" toward Charlestown. Their influence no longer extended beyond their picket lines, and once they were bottled up within the city the way would be clear for Caty to come to headquarters. The happiness that had eluded them so long was at last in the offing. "My soul embraces you," Nathanael wrote.[10]

Caty, discontented at Coventry, had by this time moved with the children to Nathanael's farm at Westerly. From here she wrote her husband a newsy letter and enclosed her picture along with a miniature heart. She told of a recent trip to Newport, of the respectful attention paid her by members of the French command, and of a little gossip involving a married lady of Newport who had not only "coquetted it" with the French officers but had fallen all over Colonel Williams when he had come for a visit. Caty found herself grasping at straws of gaiety to relieve a lonesome heart, while her only real desire was to join Nathanael. She would be willing to change headquarters every night and to ride from post to post on horseback if he would only invite her to camp. She hinted strongly that their marital happiness depended upon it.

"You press for my consent for your coming Southerly in the fall," Nathanael wrote back. "Most assuredly you have my permission, providing the state of matters here will afford a prospect of comfort and security. . . . My dear you can have no idea of the horrors of the Southern war. . . . I beg you will not entertain a thought . . . that I magnify the evil to discourage your coming. . . . The gentlemen in this quarter think themselves extreme[ly] happy if they can get their wives and families into some place of safety."[11]

Colonel Wadsworth, who had interests in New London, only twenty miles from Westerly, was an occasional visitor at Caty's home, bringing her much-needed provisions from the warehouses of his and Nathanael's private company. It was an activity that Nathanael had requested of the colonel before his own departure for the South that would render him unable to care for his family. But the whisperers of Westerly, knowing nothing of Wadsworth's role, passed the word back to East Greenwich that Caty was using her home as a rendezvous point in her husband's absence. A vicious charge of adultery was placed against her name by a number of her acquaintances.

During her loneliness, Caty corresponded with a number of her friends among the officers and ex-officers. She exchanged letters with Colonel Otho Williams, of Nathanael's command, who complained of her absence at headquarters. "I please myself," he wrote, "with the expectation of retaining and renewing an intimacy with those cheerful spirits which used to render society in the northern army so charming."[12] Caty swapped teasing notes with James Varnum, parts of them written in French. When a British raiding party under the turncoat Benedict Arnold attacked New London, she wrote Colonel Wadsworth that she was "extreemly affected" by the news. "Can Americans ever forgive Barbarians so Barbarious?" she asked. "I hope you have lost nothing in the town. I have not received the wine nor flour that I heard you gave orders to Mr. Wiles to send me. Pardon the trouble I give you for I am in a widowed state far from most all my friends."[13]

On October 27, 1781, Caty read a thrilling piece of news buried among numerous other items on an inside page of the *Providence Gazette.* On the 20th the schooner *Adventure,* commanded by Captain William Lovett, had left Virginia's York peninsula for Newport. Upon landing, the captain broke the news that Lord Cornwallis had surrendered his entire army to the Americans and French at Yorktown.

This, however, was by no means thought of as the end of the war. Caty knew that other British armies infested the land. The garrisons of New York, Charlestown, and Savannah all remained intact, protected by powerful fleets. Until the last British soldier could be driven out of the country, there could be no true peace in the land.

10 The Wedge Removed

In December, 1781, six weeks after news reached Rhode Island of the Yorktown surrender, Caty was on her way to her husband's camp in South Carolina. Leaving her three youngest children behind, she drove off in her sturdy two-horse phaeton. She was accompanied by her son, George, barely six, and Major William Blodgett of Providence, Nathanael's aide of earlier years.

The four-day ride to Philadelphia on the first leg of the journey was a pleasure trip compared to previous drives through the same country. Caty found that the temper of the inhabitants had undergone a complete change. Even in Loyalist areas of New York state, where she had once been exposed to threatening stares and insults, she looked out upon friendly faces along the way. Arriving in Philadelphia she and her son were put up at the home of the Clement Biddles, anticipating a rest of only a few days before beginning the second stage of their trip.

The Washingtons were in Philadelphia, and Caty's first visit was to Martha, who was in a heartbroken state over the death of Jack Custis, her son by her previous marriage. Caty's presence, with her warm smile and cheerfulness, was a godsend to Lady

Washington, who was glad that a snowstorm kept her friend in the city longer than her intended stay.

General Washington took Caty under his wing. "[She] is in perfect health and in good spirits," he wrote Nathanael, "and thinking no difficulties too great not to be surmounted in the performance of this visit [to South Carolina] it shall be my endeavor to strew the way over with flowers."[1] He and Martha invited her to stop at their Virginia home, Mount Vernon, on the second leg of her trip but advised her not to set out until the weather improved.

In the strongest terms, the general disagreed with Caty's plan to take little George to the South. Leave him behind, Washington urged her, and let him begin his formal training in Philadelphia or in Princeton. Caty was torn. He was not just her oldest child; he had been a close companion to her through some of her bleakest moments. Looking at him she could see reflected in his clear eyes the same dreams she had experienced as a child on Block Island. She recognized in him the same spirit and the same eagerness to learn that she had felt. Should she now take him to a part of the country she knew nothing about and deny him this opportunity for a proper education? She knew at last that she should not. She would leave George behind in the home of Charles Pettit, who had graciously offered to make the necessary arrangements for his schooling.

During Caty's previous visit to Philadelphia Nathanael had been under fire by Congress and she had felt like an outcast. Now, as the wife of a national hero, she found herself the guest-of-honor at one fete after another. Basking in her new glory, she was persuaded to remain in the city until late January. With little time to write, Caty forwarded verbal messages to Nathanael through friends who were on their way to camp from Philadelphia. She sent word by John Mathews, governor-elect of South Carolina, that she would soon resume her journey. "Tell General Greene," she instructed Mathews, "that I claim the privilege of being met by him personally at least five miles from headquarters."[2]

Saying good-bye to her young son was not easy. He seemed so small and yet so grown up and promising that it was all she could do to leave him behind. She had no idea when she would see him again and she had hoped to be the part of his life she was now assigning to someone else. Charles Pettit gently told her that her son would be in good hands. As she left she was grateful that she could take along with her the image of George standing alongside her friend.

Caty and a lady companion were escorted to Mount Vernon by Captain Ichabod Burnet, who was returning to camp in South Carolina after a short sick leave. A notorious grouch, Burnet was irritated over the long delay in Philadelphia, and Caty was hard-pressed to keep him cheerful during the journey. Arriving at the Washington plantation, the travelers were met by Lucy Knox, who had been a fixture there since the beginning of the Yorktown operations and who served as hostess during the absence of Martha Washington.

Lucy and Caty still bore the scars of their old differences, but they began to warm up to each other as they visited on the terrace, with its breath-taking view of the Potomac, and talked of future plans. During a party Caty received a message from Jeremiah Wadsworth who had arrived in Philadelphia and had been disappointed to find that she had departed the day before. She left the gathering to pen a note to him. "I am trembling for fear I shall not have the pleasure of seeing you before I go to the South," she wrote, "[but] I know your time is intirely taken up. Be assured if I can not see you I shall go Mourning all the way. The Company is in a high Romp which I hope will excuse me to my Dear Friend. . . . Burnet has wrote to you but is in an ill Humor therefore I dont chuse to ask him what he has wrote."[3]

The traveling party spent more than a month at the delightful Washington estate before the weather was considered good enough to resume the journey. They found the roads and taverns of Virginia tolerably good, and Caty was cordially received during stopovers in several towns. South of the Dan River, however, she and her company entered the world of devastation that Nathanael had so frequently written about from the Carolinas. Farmhouses that had not been burned down stood rotting in the fields, deserted by tenants who had fled at the sight of the armed soldiers and marauders that stalked the countryside. Carcasses of starved animals were marked by buzzards that hovered overhead or fed by the roadside, and Caty was sure that human bones were among the carnage.

Most of the inhabitants skulked out of the way of her phaeton bearing the uniformed Major Burnet. Those she saw at close hand had dull eyes and expressionless faces as if they expected little more than another day's survival. Occasionally a cheerful smile or gesture of friendship would brighten a long day and restore her faith in human nature.

At Salisbury the travelers rested for several days while Caty recovered from an intestinal complaint, then they resumed the tedious journey to the Continental camp on the High Hills of the Santee. Here, during a stopover at the post where Nathanael previously had headquarters, Major Burnet sent news ahead to the general. "We arrived at this place after a most disagreeable ride indeed," he wrote. "The difficulties and hardships arising from the badness of the accommodations and the excessive deep roads exceed anything I had an idea of. Everything has been undergone with cheerfulness and fortitude by Mrs. Greene who appears to be much less affected than could be expected."[4]

In early April, more than three months after Caty had left Rhode Island, the travelers approached Nathanael's South Carolina camp above Charlestown. On the road ahead a group of horsemen appeared, and as one of them spurred his mount and rushed on in front of his companions, she could see that it was her husband. Within moments she was in his arms for the first time in twenty-three months.

Nathanael turned his horse over to Major Burnet and rode back to camp in the phaeton, escorted by the horsemen, with his wife at his side. Caty's joy at being reunited with Nathanael was tempered by her distress over his appearance. She was aghast that he could have aged so much in two years. Bronzed by long exposure to the southern sun and much thinner than she had ever seen him, he appeared considerably older than his thirty-nine years. The merry twinkle in his eye was gone and his face in repose wore the expression of perpetual concern. For the first time Caty understood how much he had suffered during the southern campaign, and suddenly she realized that although he had escaped injury and serious illness he had given the better part of his life to the American cause.

When Caty arrived at camp she found headquarters located in a plantation house overlooking the Ashley River near Bacon's Bridge. The enlisted men barracked in tents and log huts nearby. The soldiers, though tanned and toughened, were as emaciated as those she had seen at Valley Forge. Transfers, resignations, and illnesses had removed many of Nathanael's former officers from the scene, and she found few of her old friends at camp. Of the former aides only Major Burnet and Captain Lewis Morris remained.

Caty was extremely proud of her husband. His officers told her that of all Washington's generals only Nathanael could have accomplished what he did under the circumstances surrounding him. Where else, they asked, could there have been found a patriot of such fierce devotion, rugged enough to stand the hardships, willing to sacrifice the pleasures of home and family until victory was assured, and competent enough to plan the strategy of the campaign and at the same time handle the immense problems of supply? For more than a year of bitter warfare Nathanael had never had a day's leave, and never found an hour when he considered himself off duty.

Nathanael was equally appreciative of Caty. The maturity brought on by long months of hardship had only added to her charm, and her unfailing good humor still exerted its happy influence on the headquarters staff. She had a remarkably rejuvenating effect on her husband. Several of the officers observed that he looked younger the day she arrived, and he wrote to Charles Pettit with contented pride: "She is a great favorite even with the ladies. . . . Her flowing tongue and cheerful countenance quite triumph over my grave face."[5]

Making new friends was never a problem for Caty. She became acquainted with Colonel William Washington, whom she had previously known only briefly, and his lovely young South Carolina bride. The couple was constantly seen holding hands, hugging, kissing, and generally making the bachelor officers miserable with envy. She also struck up an immediate friendship with one of Nathanael's new aides, the gentlemanly and witty Captain Nathaniel Pendleton, Jr., a member of one of Virginia's most notable families, and a fine musician and craftsman in private life.

Caty soon learned the details of his career. At the age of nineteen, near the beginning of the siege of Boston, he had walked from Virginia to Massachusetts to join the command of General Washington, who was well-known to the Pendleton family in Virginia politics. A year later young Pendleton was at Fort Washington, on the Manhattan shore of the Hudson, when that post fell to the British. Taken prisoner, he spent more than four years of idle captivity in New York City as a paroled officer. He told Caty that the only redeeming circumstance was that he had been taken into the home of a New York physician where he had fallen in love with the doctor's daughter.

When exchanged in the fall of 1780, Pendleton was penniless, but he made his way on foot with a group of fellow exchangees to Philadelphia, where General Washington solicited funds for their return home, having excused them from further service. Pendleton, however, choosing to fight again, was assigned to Nathanael Greene's staff in South Carolina. He arrived in time to distinguish himself in the last battle fought by Nathanael's command, at Eutaw Springs near Charlestown, and received a special citation of thanks from Congress for his bravery.

Caty found that there was little to fear from the British at Charlestown, but the American soldiers, ill-paid and ill-fed, were on the verge of open revolt. Nathanael explained how he had been required to guarantee thousands of dollars himself in order to clothe his soldiers during the winter. With the military chest almost bare and the central government on the verge of bankruptcy, he had been forced to buy uniforms on credit from Charlestown merchants under the very noses of the British. He had dealt through a speculator named John Banks whom he later found was not trusted by the merchants. Before delivering the clothing they insisted on Nathanael's personal signature on the promissory notes.

Nathanael told Caty that there was no immediate concern, for he was confident that he would eventually be backed up by the government. Moreover, he now owned large tracts of land that rendered him solvent. In addition to his holdings in Rhode Island and New Jersey, the enterprising general owned 7,000 acres on Cumberland Island, off the coast of Georgia, which he had purchased as an investment. Three more large estates had been granted him by the legislatures of North Carolina, South Carolina, and Georgia as compensation for his services in those states. But he went on to explain to Caty that although this made them land-rich they were money-poor. There was simply no cash to be had.

During the spring Caty was invited, along with Nathanael and a number of aides, to a dinner party given in her honor by a prominent lady whose fine home overlooked the Ashley River between headquarters and Charlestown. Caty was chatting with the other guests prior to entering the dining room when their conversation was interrupted. A woman had appeared at the door saying she had a warning to the officers. She explained that she was the sweetheart of one of the enlisted soldiers at camp and that she had overheard the details of a conspiracy between disgruntled troops there and British officers in Charlestown. They plotted to capture Nathanael and his staff while at dinner. Caty, overhearing the conversation, was thunderstruck. Nathanael

thanked the woman and assured her that he would not betray
her trust, then organized the hasty departure of the company.
An hour after they galloped off, British dragoons encircled the
residence and shouted for the American officers to surrender.
But by that time the visitors were safely back in camp.

A full investigation was carried out and several soldiers were
found with incriminating papers in their possession, proving that
they were in the process of recruiting men from Nathanael's force
for service with the British army in Charlestown. Caty could
scarcely believe that the steward who had served her faithfully
was one of the men caught. His life was spared but he was dismissed from service. However, Sergeant Gornell, who was found
guilty of being the ringleader of the mutineers, was brought to
the parade ground and executed in front of the entire camp. It
was a step that put an immediate halt to the threatened insurrec-
tion, but it sickened Caty.

Gornell proved that even a turncoat could die bravely. He
walked calmly and firmly to the execution site, distributing to
his fellow soldiers his coat, hat, sleeve-buttons, and other articles
much needed by the threadbare men. He made a public statement
that his trial had been fair and advised all who harbored thoughts
of going over to the enemy to forever discard them. The firing
squad consisted of men from his own company, and Gornell himself gave the signal to fire.

Among the new friends Caty made at headquarters were the
Rutledge brothers, John and Edward. Political refugees from
Charlestown who had played mighty roles in South Carolina's
revolutionary fortunes, they now camped in the vicinity of the
army. They were separated from their families, who remained
virtual prisoners in British-held Charlestown. John, now in his
early forties, had been chosen the state's first governor in 1776.
He had escaped from Charlestown during the British siege of
that city in 1780 and had attached himself to the army for protection. For almost two years he had been constantly on the march,
often sharing with Nathanael whatever shelter could be converted
into a headquarters. During this time he was the only remnant
of the state's civil government, which except for him, had virtually
ceased to exist. Now, with the British driven back to the gates
of Charlestown, he was able to organize a new assembly which
sat at Jacksonborough, a few miles from camp.

Edward, younger than John by ten years, immediately captured
Caty's heart. Although she saw that his health was broken, she

recognized the depth and gentleness of the suffering man's character. Like his brother, he had represented his colony in the first two continental congresses. Returning to the third session in 1776, he became the youngest signer of the Declaration of Independence. Seized by the British after the fall of Charlestown, he had been paroled in his own home for a time but was later sent as a political prisoner to St. Augustine, where he contracted an agonizing case of arthritis. Barely able to walk, he had only recently returned to his state following a general exchange, but he was forbidden by the terms of the agreement to return to his home in Charlestown.

The coming of hot weather brought the usual summer illnesses so disastrous to people living in the South. When several of Nathanael's aides became sick he arranged to send them to the beach at Kiawah Island, near Charlestown, for recuperation. At the suggestion of her husband, Caty agreed to go along as companion and nurse. Since the island was controlled by the enemy, Nathanael sent a request under a flag of truce to General Alexander Leslie, commander of the British garrison, to provide passes for the group. The general, his forces now seriously threatened by the American army, was glad to oblige.

The party that traveled with Caty consisted of Dr. Johnson, a camp surgeon, Colonel Washington and his young wife, and four of Nathanael's aides including Nat Pendleton who brought along his brother, a South Carolina judge. Cooks and servants had been sent ahead to the island and a royal welcome awaited the company. Appetites that were previously lost were regained at the sight of the first dinner; the menu included duck, chicken, beef, crab, fish, prawn and potatoes. "An elegant glass of wine washed it down," Major Pierce reported to Nathanael by letter, "and the whole was settled by a Dish of Coffee *allamode de France.*"

During the day Caty and her rapidly recovering companions rode horses, swam in the surf, and ran races on the beach. The evening's entertainment included cardplaying, backgammon, and games of wit. "[Colonel] Washington and Johnson, like two grumbling old women, sat over the backgammon table and railed at fortune for the whims of the Dice," wrote Pierce. "Mrs. Greene, who is the very picture of health, sets, observes, and laughs at all about her."[6] A week later Nat Pendleton reported to Nathanael: "Mrs. Greene preserves her health and her cheerfulness but our last bottle of wine expired this day in our presence. Never was people merrier at a burying, tho I fear the time of mourning is yet to come."[7]

When the company returned to camp, now located at the "Ashley Hill" plantation, Caty found the army preparing to march into Charlestown. The enemy garrison, completely at the mercy of the besieging Americans, was preparing to evacuate. The British authorities in the city had reached an agreement with Nathanael's command that would allow the withdrawal to be accomplished without molestation by his troops. No time limit had been set, and the British delayed final action for several weeks.

In October, 1782 came definite indications that the departure was at last at hand, and Caty began to prepare for the event. "Mrs. Greene has so much the spirit of the military about her," wrote Captain Morris, of the headquarters family, to his sweetheart, "that she is determined to be in uniform with her husband, and therefore prefers deep blue with yellow buttons and buff facings. . . .She begs that you will be so obliging as to procure a very small pair of gold epaulets for her." Later he added: "Mrs. Greene will be quite militaire with her fine epaulets, and you must not be surprised if she should mount her Bucephalus and enter the town at the head of the army."[8]

For Caty, the long days of waiting for the evacuation of Charlestown were brightened by the arrival of General Anthony Wayne. After Yorktown he had been transferred to the Southern army. Nathanael, who now recognized him as one of the ablest commanders of the Revolution, put him in charge of the Georgia campaign. After its successful conclusion, he had joined Nathanael's staff near Charlestown.

Caty was well aware of Wayne's personal weaknesses. Jealous and rank-conscious, the Pennsylvanian had let few things or few people stand in the way of his ambitions. He had found a deep need for life away from the army, a need that his superiors had recognized and catered to in order to keep the peace when Wayne's moods grew most difficult. He was never able to be away from his sweethearts for long periods of time, and he collected them in every quarter.

Wayne's love of theater showed itself in a dramatic awareness of costume as a part of the panorama of war. He had insisted on uniforms made to his own specifications—of a dashing if impractical design—that made him a spectacular figure. But with all his eccentricities he was a fearless soldier and an innovative, imaginative leader. After his unstable early days, when he won the nickname of "Mad Anthony," he had settled down to become a fine strategist, and his suggestions and recommendations revealed his study and grasp of great campaigns of the past.

On the morning of December 14, General Wayne, selected by Nathanael for the honor, led a vanguard of American troops into Charlestown, as the British completed the final stage of their evacuation. At three in the afternoon Nathanael, on horseback, rode into town with Governor John Mathews at his side, followed by a long procession. Second in line rode a number of officers and other notables. Caty, dressed in blue and gold, and accompanied by prominent ladies of the state, came next in her phaeton. A great throng of citizens trailed behind.

Caty found the streets half-deserted, the British ships having evacuated 10,000 inhabitants and slaves in addition to making off with countless treasures. Some of the balconies were lined with well-wishers, mostly older citizens, who waved quietly, but in many of the best homes doors were closed and blinds drawn. The owners of these houses, many of them in the upper brackets of Charlestown society, had either departed town or were unwilling to participate in the day's festivities. The city had too long been associated with Great Britain in customs and commerce for its more prosperous merchants to be overjoyed when the ragged army of Nathanael Greene marched in.

Five years before, Charlestown had been a thriving city, with business houses and handsome homes extending from South Bay to Boundary Street, and from the Cooper River on one side to the Ashley on the other, almost every home having its own court and garden. Now, as Caty rode in with the victory procession, the town she saw was largely in ruins, the results of a disastrous fire, constant siege operations by one army and then the other, and a long occupation by the British. The whole scene was dismal; even the bells of St. Michael's Church, which Caty had hoped might be ringing in welcome to the victorious army, had been carried off by the enemy.

She and Nathanael moved into the fine stone residence of John Rutledge on Broad Street, which became army headquarters. The Rutledge family, happily reunited after two years of separation, were glad to share their home with the Greenes and Nathanael's staff. Just across the street lived the Edward Rutledges. Caty, referred to now as Lady Greene, became an official hostess along with the Rutledge wives, who were well-established in Charlestown circles. In the evenings, around a fireplace, Caty's laughter often rang out as the men swapped stories of days spent in Nathanael's camp and of nights shared in barnyards and other incommodious lodgings.

Caty collected the stories and wrote them to her friends. In a letter to Sammy Ward she told of one of Nathanael's experiences during the campaign. "While he and his army were wandering like lost Jews in the state of North Carolina," she wrote, "the Govnr of South Carolina [John Rutledge] was obliged to seek protection in the army. After a defeat the Genl, Govnr, and other officers of rank being much fatigued went into the best quarters they could find which was little better than a hovel. Some time after the Genl and govnr who both occupied one bed got into it the Genl complained that the Govnr was a very restless bedfellow. Yes Genl—says the govnr—you have much reason to complain who has been kicking me around this hour. They both denyd the charges which put them upon examining who was at fault and behold the Genl of the southern department, the Govnr of the rich state of South Carolina and—how shall I write it—*a Hog*— (who perhaps thought he had a right to take a place with a defeated General) had all crept into one bed together."[9]

Nathanael wrote Sammy that Caty was "much esteemed by both the Army and the people, as well as loved and admired by her husband. In this situation one would suppose she ought to be happy, but her absent children are a great deduction. A divided family leaves a blank in the heart that often causes a flowing tear, and yet she cannot think of returning without her husband."[10]

As throngs of rural South Carolina families moved into Charlestown to establish their homes in the residences of departed Tories, a new society sprang up in the city. For the moment, Caty found herself, along with the Rutledge ladies, in its higher echelon. Socially, however, the city bore little resemblance to the old town of glittering pre-Revolutionary days, and its name was changed to Charleston to give it less of a British ring.

Caty thought the city should give a ball in honor of the victorious army and, over Nathanael's objections, helped draw up plans for the occasion herself. "You know I am not much in this way," her husband wrote a friend, "but Mrs. Greene has her heart set on it."[11] She decorated a great hall with the help of Colonel Kosciusko and his staff, placing festoons of magnolia leaves around the ballroom and hanging large paper flowers on the walls. On the night of the Victory Ball, Charleston ladies danced minuets with the officers to music played by the army band. After the opening number, Nathanael turned Caty over to Anthony Wayne, and she danced with him through most of the night.

For her, it was the crowning hour of the Revolution.

General Nathanael Greene. *Courtesy, Providence Public Library.*

ABOVE: William Greene home in East Greenwich, R.I., where Caty Greene was reared and married. *Photograph by Janet Stegeman.*

BELOW: A nineteenth-century view of the Greene home in Potowomut, R.I. *Courtesy, Rhode Island Historical Society.*

ABOVE: The rear of the Nathanael Greene homestead in Coventry, R.I., before restoration. *Courtesy, Rhode Island Historical Society.*

BELOW: The front of the Nathanael Greene homestead, Coventry, R.I., as it appears today. *Photograph by Chester Browning. Courtesy, Rhode Island Department of Economic Development.*

ABOVE: George Washington. Engraving by J. C. Buttre after a portrait by Gilbert Stuart. *Courtesy, Rhode Island Historical Society.*

LEFT: Martha Washington. Engraving by J. C. Buttre after a portrait by Gilbert Stuart. *Courtesy, Rhode Island Historical Society.*

ABOVE: General Henry Knox. Engraving by R. Whitechurch. *Courtesy, Providence Public Library.*

LEFT: Marquis de Lafayette. *From John Fiske, The American Revolution (Boston and New York, 1891), II.*

BELOW: General Anthony Wayne. *Courtesy, New York Public Library, Prints Division.*

ABOVE: Jeremiah Wadsworth and his son, Daniel, from a painting by John Trumbull. *Courtesy, Wadsworth Atheneum, Hartford, Conn.*

RIGHT: Eli Whitney. *Courtesy, Providence Public Library.*

ABOVE: John Rutledge home, Charleston, S.C., where Caty Greene served as hostess at Nathanael's headquarters following the British evacuation. *Photograph by Herman Stegeman.*

RIGHT: Ruins of a later mansion at the site of Caty's residence at "Dungeness," Cumberland Island, Ga. *Photograph by Janet Stegeman.*

BELOW: Ruins at the site of the Greene house at Mulberry Grove. *From an old postcard in the authors' possession.*

Caty Greene in later life. *Courtesy, Telfair Academy of Arts and Sciences, Savannah, Ga.*

11 Postwar Newport Days

During the second week of January, 1783, Caty accompanied Nathanael on a triumphant journey to Savannah, which like Charleston was celebrating its recent liberation from British rule. The trip was made in the company of the headquarters staff and a guard-of-honor which traveled down swampy coastal roads in a train of wagons and carriages. Reaching Savannah, the honorees were received with high esteem by officials of the state of Georgia. The visit of several days was climaxed by a huge testimonial banquet, punctuated by the proposing and answering of dozens of toasts to guests, hosts, notables of the recent campaign, and any other hero or event that could be brought to mind.

Before returning to Charleston the Greenes were taken to inspect a rice plantation, fourteen miles north of Savannah, that had been awarded to Nathanael by the Georgia legislature in appreciation for his services in the South. The vast estate, "Mulberry Grove," previously owned by a Savannah Tory whose lands had now been confiscated, was largely in ruins. Although suffering from neglect, the plantation's beautiful dwelling, located on the west bank of the Savannah River, captured the imagination of

Caty and Nathanael. It would make a fine home, they thought, if they ever decided to live in the South.

Unhappy days followed the Greenes' return to Charleston. Although hostilities had ceased, formal peace with Great Britain had not been declared, and there was no assurance that the enemy would not return in a grand invasion to win back the land so recently lost. The fledgling nation, war-sick and poverty-stricken, might not be able to raise another army to prosecute a full-scale war. Nathanael had no choice but to keep his troops together—troops that daily grew more weary of the prolonged military life and whose only desire was to go home. The men were constantly on the brink of mutiny and some left camp without orders, never to return.

Caty could see the strain on her husband's face. He was now being pressed by Charleston merchants for the payment of notes signed by him the previous winter for the purchase of clothing for his soldiers. His agent John Banks had proven dishonest, investing money that was not his own in ill-conceived speculations that had gone sour. Judgements against Nathanael were being handed down in the South Carolina courts, and in order to satisfy them, he was forced to borrow heavily from three wealthy friends, Robert Morris, the Marquis de Lafayette, and his own business partner, Jeremiah Wadsworth.

Nathanael therefore found himself not only without sufficient funds, but heavily in debt. The situation caused a serious misunderstanding between him and Caty. She, having just had her first taste of affluence since the war began, was not willing to start pinching pennies again. She could not comprehend why Nathanael's enormous land holdings did not represent a substantial fortune, and he had difficulty in explaining to her that their property could not be immediately converted into spending money. To produce income, land had to be sold or cultivated but at that time there was no real estate market in the impoverished country, and Nathanael had no capital or time to put farms into operation. To support his family he would have to borrow money until he was free to attend to his estates. Meanwhile he was obliged to remain with the army.

Besides the financial restrictions Caty resented, she began to sense a change in the attitude of the people toward her, toward Nathanael, and toward the presence of the army in general. Where she had seen adulation of her husband before, she now felt a growing resentment on the part of South Carolinians over the power of his position. Because he insisted upon the support of the state in maintaining the Continental army until the war was formally at an end, he was called a military dictator. Caty also found his stand brought him into political conflict with a number of his former militia officers, now mustered out of the army and serving in the legislature. Some were already nursing grudges, born of inevitable command jealousies, for imagined slights during the recent campaign to rid the state of the enemy.

Caty had never been aware of this side of affairs before and now she found it hard to understand. Most Carolinians, backing their local heroes, were willing now to discredit her husband. There was even a rumor afloat that he had been in partnership, for his own gain, with the dishonest agent, John Banks, and this Caty found the hardest rub of all. She was made very conscious of this change in the air and came to know the chill of a Charleston snub.

She took comfort, however, from the good news of the children whom she constantly worried about. The family in Rhode Island was healthy, and she was delighted with reports of how well George was doing in Princeton, where he had been placed under the tutelage of a noted educator, John Witherspoon. George Washington, in a letter congratulating Nathanael for "the glorious end" he had put to hostilities in the South, added: "I cannot omit informing you . . . that I let no opportunity slip to enquire after your son George at Princeton, and that it is with pleasure I hear he injoys good health, and is a fine promising boy."[1]

On April 16, 1783, word was received that preliminary articles of peace had been signed by representatives of the United States and Great Britain in Paris, putting the war to an end at last. Caty noted that it had been eight years, almost to the day, since the opening shot of the Revolution had been fired on Lexington Green, and since Nathanael had galloped off from their Coventry home, leaving her standing at the doorstep. Now the elation she expected to feel at the happy news of peace was tempered by her unsettled personal situation. Though the victory had been won she found little to show for it and felt a share of the bitterness being loudly expressed by the soldiers.

The troops clamored to break camp, but there were insufficient funds to give them more than partial pay. For weeks no transports appeared to bear the weary men home. Many of the soldiers, not waiting to be paid off or dismissed, set off on foot along the dusty roads.

During the summer troopships finally began to arrive and the bone-weary men embarked for the return voyage to their homes north and east. Caty watched the proceedings numbly. She had begun to experience the familiar symptoms of early pregnancy. She was depressed, angry, and frustrated. She wanted only to get away from where she was, hoping somewhere to find the peace of mind she longed for. She confided in Nathanael her feelings, as well as her fears, and he was sympathetic. Although he was forced to remain behind until the last man had departed, he put his wife aboard the first transport sailing to Philadelphia.

Caty had as traveling companions a lady chaperone and Colonel Kosciusko, whose departure broke many a heart in South Carolina. One of the women seeing the colonel off at the dock received a promise that he would return as soon as her husband died. At any other time Caty might have been amused. This time she was not. Terrified of the sea and already feeling sick, she went to her cabin to endure the torture of the long voyage. Throughout the passage every groan of the ship's timbers added to her fear that the vessel would be dashed to pieces against an Atlantic reef.

Arriving in Philadelphia at last, Caty found herself in the midst of a city on a spree. Congress had fled to Princeton because of a shameful mutiny of soldiers of the Pennsylvania line, but the parties and victory celebrations went merrily on. In the middle of it all Caty was delighted to find her old friend Anthony Wayne. She was also pleased to find that Philadelphia society had opened its doors to him and now honored him as Pennsylvania's foremost war hero. He greeted Caty with extreme cordiality and enthusiasm. Since his wife was absent, as usual, he invited Caty to accompany him to state occasions.

She could not resist the opportunity. Rebelling against her pregnancy, she went on a wild spending lark, purchasing a stylish wardrobe chosen from Philadelphia fashions that reflected the boldness of the postwar era. Petticoats were shortened to expose silk garters and gold tassels, and hoops were arranged to bounce up and down when a lady walked, provoking pleasing responses from male observers. Caty and Wayne made a dazzling couple, she in her new gowns and the general impeccably dressed in uniforms he had designed himself.

Caty found, to her mock dismay, that she must share her escort with a number of others. Wayne had won the hearts of the young belles of the city and had made countless conquests among them.

Some of his coterie, whom he referred to jokingly as his "daughters," fluttered around him, flattered him, and brought him little presents. He responded warmly to their attentions, but Caty thought him incapable of having any lasting friendships with any of them.

However, there was one durable attachment in Wayne's life that she could not ignore. Meeting Mary Vining in Philadelphia, she found her to be a redoubtable rival. The sister of a Pennsylvania congressman, beautiful, dark-eyed, and young, she could have won the hearts of any number of eligible men. Wooed by all, she captured the affections, too, of the Marquis de Lafayette, with whom she conversed in perfect French. Nonetheless, it was obvious to Caty that she had chosen to give her heart to Anthony Wayne. He still wore the handsome inlaid sword Mary had sent him years earlier, feigning anonymity, a coy but open invitation to his further attentions.

Caty threw herself into the fast-paced life. In her exuberant mood she bought a phaeton and a pair of horses and placed an order for a chariot. The total bill came to $1,400 which was charged to the company Nathanael owned with Charles Pettit, a company Caty did not know was on the brink of insolvency. Pettit wrote Nathanael that he had paid the bill but would expect reimbursement at an early date.

Caty received and accepted with pleasure an invitation to a gala house party on the bank of the Schuylkill River. Taking with her the most attractive of her new purchases, she went with a number of officers and their ladies, fully expecting to have, and indeed having, a wonderful time. Dining and dancing, frolicking to all hours, she felt a light-heartedness she had not experienced for years. Determined to rise above the unpleasant effects of pregnancy, she ate what she pleased, drank what she pleased, and enjoyed herself to the fullest. With her condition cleverly concealed under high fashion, she felt herself once more as free as a girl and as popular and sought after as ever. In Charleston she had almost forgotten what fun could be.

Returning to Philadelphia refreshed and in good humor, Caty was stunned to find a sharp note of criticism from Nathanael. Alone in Charleston, ill with fever, and almost in despair over his financial affairs, he reprimanded his wife sternly about her spending spree. Caty was hurt and angered by the reproof. She tore the letter up and refused to answer it. Almost on the heels of that letter came another, apologizing for the first. "Notwithstanding all I wrote you the other day," Nathanael said, "I love you most affectionately. . . . I have not been pleased with myself since I wrote that letter and you know self reproach is a painful companion." Financial affairs still disturbed him deeply. He explained that he could only think of the future security of his family and that was his reason for wanting Caty to be as economical as possible. "But at the same time," he added, "I have no desire to deprive you of one rational amusement. My letter I am afraid was both indelicate and severe. . . . You have naturally a generous disposition and perhaps a little vanity at being thought so, which renders you a prey to the artful and designing."[2]

The letter did not mollify Caty and she did not answer it. A few days later another message came from Nathanael saying he "was disappointed and not a little hurt" at receiving no mail from her. He had been presented a final bill by Charles Pettit for her expenditures and was agonized over not being able to pay it. He was already indebted to Pettit for taking care of little George in Philadelphia and arranging for his education. "How or where to get the money god knows," he wrote, "for I don't."[3]

Longing to be reunited with her children in Rhode Island, Caty drove to Princeton to withdraw George from his school. She did not know how much she had missed her son until she saw his manly yet childish face when he greeted her. He was a joy to her. But she found to her disgust that Dr. Witherspoon had taken little interest in the boy's education and she was infuriated at the size of the bill presented. She could not bring herself to write Nathanael about it but sent word through Charles Pettit about the problem and of her own travel plans.

She and George drove to Rhode Island. As they stopped to visit friends in New York City, Caty had her first view of Manhattan since her precipitous departure in 1776. Driving on with her son over familiar roads to Coventry, she was welcomed happily by the younger children, but a sad note was added to the homecoming. A financial settlement had caused the Coventry house to pass out of the family's hands into those of Nathanael's brother, Jacob. It was hard for Caty to think that the home was no longer hers and that her sister-in-law was now mistress there. She was grateful to Jacob and Peggy for all they had done for the children, but after collecting them she felt that the door that closed behind them was another reminder of the insecurity of her family's affairs. She set about finding a home in Newport, purchasing on credit a renovated house on Mill Street near the old stone tower that had long been a landmark in the city.

In late fall Nathanael joined the family in Newport. Caty had been apprehensive about their reunion, but the moment they greeted each other their differences dissolved. Caty watched her husband closely examine his family that he had never seen all together before. The children were shy with him at first, and he with them, but soon their relationship was completely free and they delighted in one another. George was now seven, Martha six, Cornelia five, and Nat three. All were hearty and healthy.

When he could finally be torn away from the children, Nathanael told Caty of his triumphant journey through the country with two of his aides, and how he had been welcomed in town after town as a conquering hero. Stopping at a friends's house in Trenton, he had been surprised to see General Washington standing on the doorstep. They had not seen each other in three years. Neither could conceal the solemn depths of the feeling that existed between them, and for a few moments neither could speak. Later they rode on together to New York where Washington bade his generals farewell.

As happy as their early moments together were, Caty felt the specter of their financial straits hovering over them and knew the subject would have to come up. She could tell that Nathanael was as loathe to mention it as she was to hear it. He told her the situation was bleak; all of his investments had gone bad and he had lost a fortune. Stocks that had been put in Jeremiah Wadsworth's hands—originally worth £1,000—could not be redeemed for more than fifty. The shipping concern with his brothers, in the name of Jacob Greene, had lost heavily, and his various partnerships with Wadsworth, John Cox, and Charles Pettit had lost many thousands of pounds. Only the land grants provided by Georgia and the Carolinas stood between his family and utter ruin. And much of this acreage had been pledged as security for huge sums Nathanael had been forced to borrow to reduce his indebtedness to Charleston merchants.

In spite of material adversity, Caty found contentment in her family. For her, Nathanael's presence at home, with the war at an end, brought a peace of mind unknown to her since the conflict began. The sudden disaffection that had seized her at Philadelphia, after the critical letters from Nathanael, had completely disappeared. Times were hard, but the incredible tensions of the Revolution were over. She now had a husband at home to share the responsibility of rearing the children and to be on hand when household crises arose, a luxury she had never enjoyed before.

Caty knew that the children stood in awe of their exacting mother, a role she had been forced to play in Nathanael's absence. But they were not afraid of their father. "On the contrary," Cornelia wrote in later years, "he was our boon companion and playfellow who winked at every atrocity we perpetrated."[4] Caty was happy watching her children in their new pleasure. Unused to having two parents in the household, they reveled in the joy of their father's company. They began truly to know him for the first time and to gather memories the three oldest would keep for the rest of their lives.

A visitor from Providence, passing by the Greenes' Newport home, found Nathanael, the pregnant Caty, and their four children in the yard, engaged in a vigorous game of "Puss in the Corner." On another occasion Caty dressed herself as a beggar-woman and her disguise was so successful in fooling her family that she tried it on her neighbors. "She went around to the houses of her friends to ask charity," said an eye-witness, "telling a piteous tale. . . . At one house they were at the card-table; and one of her most intimate friends, as she ordered her off, desired the servant to look well as she went out and see that she did not steal something from the entry. At another, the master of the house was just sitting down to supper, and though an old acquaintance and a shrewd man, he was not only deceived, but so moved by her story, that he gave her the loaf that he was on the point of cutting himself. When she had sufficiently amused herself with this practical test of her friends's charity, she took off her disguise, and indulged her merriment at their expense, reminding them that, with the exception of the loaf, she had been turned away without any experience of their liberality."[5]

Many of Nathanael's and Caty's army friends visited them in Newport. The foreign officers, particularly Lafayette, Steuben, and Kosciusko, often stopped at the Greene home during various state occasions honoring the war heroes. Little Cornelia would never forget the impressions she formed of Lafayette during those visits to the household. "He became the idol of our affections," she recalled long afterward. "He had a gentleness of bearing and a benevolence of expression that won all hearts, especially the hearts of children. Partly because the sight of young things, so far from France, had a special charm for him, a warm attachment sprang up between us, and he taught us to call him 'our dear marquis', with an evident enjoyment of the loving sound."[6]

As time approached for the birth of Caty's baby, Nathanael "farmed out" the children in order to give his wife some extra rest. Caty's brother, Billy Littlefield, took Nat to Block Island for a visit with his grandfather. "I hope before this Mrs. Greene is safe in bed with a fine son," Billy wrote Nathanael in March. "I was afraid she wou'd be troubled about our passage upon the Island but with pleasure can inform her we arrived safe. . . . Nat is the greatest Pet in the world—he is in perfect health, as ragged as is necessary and Master of the whole House. He drinks his dram every morng. with his Grand Papa & when I attempt to hinder him he says he wishes uncle Bill was gone home he dont love him."[7]

The baby arrived safely and was a girl. Although her sex was a disappointment, little Louisa became the light of her mother's eye. Caty sailed through the delivery with no problems and she rapidly recovered her strength. It was not long afterward that she and Nathanael found themselves caught up in the brilliant life of fashionable Newport which had regained the social eminence of pre-war days. Nathanael was a reluctant participant in such activities but Caty was in her glory. "One of my great delights as a child," Cornelia later recalled, "was to steal into her dressing-room and watch the arraying of my beautiful mother for some brilliant function. Her blue-black hair, drifting from the poised head over alabaster shoulders, her tiny shoes aglint with diamond buckles, and the delicate laces enmeshing her in filmy glory, contributed to the make-up of a vision which centered the gaze of all eyes."[8]

There was no possibility of Nathanael recouping his fortune or even paying his debts as long as he remained in Rhode Island. To attend to his holdings in the South, he took an extended trip to his estates in 1784. Mulberry Grove, in Georgia, was principally a rice plantation that could be maintained only by the use of slave labor. One of the purposes of Nathanael's journey was to purchase Negroes, a business that was repugnant to him, but which he now found himself dependent upon as a prospective Georgia planter.

While Nathanael was away, Caty sailed to Block Island with her children for a few weeks and her communication with her husband was interrupted. When she got home there was a letter and a cask of rum from Nathanael awaiting her. He said that he had attempted without success to get in touch with John Banks, who had cheated him out of thousands of dollars. "I verily believe if I was to meet him I should put him to death," Nathanael wrote. "He is the most finished villain that this age has produced. There is no crime but murder that he has not committed."

In the same letter Caty was advised about family problems. "I begin to feel anxious about the little girls," her husband said. "Desire Billy [Littlefield] to write to Doctor [Ezra] Stiles [president of Yale College] to recommend a good young Man and get his terms. Me thinks this mode will be little more expensive than boarding the Girls abroad or sending them to school and they may be better taught at home, than from home, and their morals and manners much more attended to. What think you my dear?"

He promised Caty that upon his return he would give her an exact account of the family's financial status but advised her not to be too hopeful. "I am not anxious to be rich," the letter said, "but wish to be independent. (For I agree perfectly with Lord Littleton that he that cannot pay his Taylor bill is a dependent character even tho a Lord). To have a decent income is much to be wished; but to be free from debt more so. I never owned so much property as now, and yet never felt so poor. . . ."9

After Nathanael's return to Newport, he and Caty discussed their bleak economic outlook and the possibility of moving their family to the South to develop one of their estates. They realized the futility of overseeing a plantation without being on the spot to supervise labor and manage business affairs. Sometime during the fall they came to a final decision. If, after one final effort, they were unable to recover a substantial part of the fortune lost in the John Banks fiasco, they would establish their home in Georgia on the rice plantation of Mulberry Grove.

12 Tragedy in Georgia

Seeing Nathanael off at the Newport dock for another trip to inspect his lands, Caty found herself husbandless again in early 1785. As she drove home to her houseful of children, up the steep incline of Mill Street, she had a frightening future to contemplate. At last she realized that she was poor. Her dream of wealth and leisure, once the war was over, had been shattered; she could no longer count on even the most basic security. The family was living entirely on credit, with debts mounting daily, while only the slightest beginning had been made toward developing their Southern property. To further complicate the outlook there were definite signs that she was carrying her sixth child.

The children were now Caty's responsibility alone. There was no longer a winter camp to run off to, with in-laws willing to look after the small ones while she was in the company of her husband and army friends. There was no quartermaster to turn to when her supplies ran low. And financial relief was out of the question until Nathanael could turn a profit from working their land, a circumstance that would surely require the family to leave Rhode Island. Caty faced the prospect of living the rest of her days in the rural South as a farmer's wife.

Nathanael's first letter from Georgia told of walking over his land with Anthony Wayne who, like Nathanael himself, had been awarded a Savannah River plantation by a grateful legislature. Wayne's estate, "Richmond," lay along the river bank adjacent to the Greenes' acreage. The two former generals, now novice rice-planters, were helping each other get crops underway. The fields were in poor condition, not having been worked since early in the war, but the overseers were optimistic over prospects of a good harvest.

Caty was upset about an incident Nathanael tried to make light of. While inspecting his plantation he had received a challenge to a duel by one of his former militia captains, a James Gunn, who was still seething over a reprimand he had received from his commander three years before. Nathanael turned down the challenge on the advice of Wayne, who recognized Gunn as a local political aspirant merely trying to attract attention, but the ex-captain had then threatened to shoot Nathanael on sight. There was nothing to fear from a man of Gunn's character, Nathanael assured Caty, but to play it safe he promised always to wear sidearms.

During the spring Caty received a description of the family's vast holdings on Cumberland Island, which Nathanael visited with a friend, Colonel Hawkins. "I find it a valuable property," he wrote, "and had I funds to improve it to advantage it might be one of the first commercial objects on the Continent. The island is twenty miles long and a large part of it excellent for Indigo. The situation is favorable for trade, the place healthy and the prospets delightful. On the seaside there is a beach eighteen miles long, as level as a floor. . . . It is the pleasantest ride I ever saw."

The same letter told of a voyage to St. Augustine, in Spanish East Florida, taken for the purpose of recruiting families to colonize and develop the Cumberland Island property. Traveling down the inland passage in a canoe equipped with a sail, awning, and sleeping mattress, he and Colonel Hawkins were met and royally entertained by the Spanish governor. "We were introduced to his Lady and daughters," he wrote, "and compliments flew from side to side like a shuttlecock in the hand of good players. You know I am not very excellent at fine speeches. My stock was soon exhausted; but what I lacked in conversation I made up in bowing."

Caty got a full description of the daughters of the governor.

"They are not handsome and their complexions are rather tawny," Nathanael wrote, "but they have got sweet languishing eyes. They look as if they could love with great violence. They sang and played upon the Harpsichord and did everything to please if not to inspire softer emotions. Hawkins professed himself smitten. The old lady unluckily asked if I was married and in so unexpected a manner that I had no chance to evade the enquiry. This limited my gallantry or perhaps I might have got in love too. . . . The Spanish ladies are very free and it is said will admit more freedoms than most Ladies think either decent or reputable. Our stay was too short to try experiments."

Caty knew that Nathanael was teasing her with lighthearted remarks intended to dull the pain of dismal news in store for her. His attempts to interest the Spaniards in settling Cumberland Island were unsuccessful, and his tedious voyage to Florida had been in vain. "I tremble at my own situation," he concluded, "when I think of the enormous sums I owe and the great difficulty of obtaining money. I seem to be doomed to a life of slavery and anxiety; but if I can render you happy it will console me."[1]

When Nathanael returned to Newport in late spring he told Caty of his final disappointment. On the way home he had stopped in Virginia to seek out John Banks and found the speculator had died and left behind no assets. This meant Nathanael would be unable to collect any of the funds Banks had misapplied, and had no hopes of getting out from under his Charleston indebtedness. There was nothing left to do but move his family to the South where they could make their living by cultivating rice at Mulberry Grove, and pay off their debts by selling their other lands when a favorable market emerged.

Under a pall of depression, Caty approached her confinement with misgivings. She was desperately tired. When at last she was delivered, she slept with the new baby girl curled in her arms. Nathanael wanted her named Catharine for her mother, and soon little Caty captured the hearts of the family. The children received her as if she were a present made especially for them, and Nathanael was her captive. Her mother was concerned by a cough the older girls had developed and kept the baby apart. Caty was distraught when she learned that they had whooping cough, and soon, in spite of her efforts, she found little Caty also seized with fits of coughing.

After long illnesses the older girls began to recover, but little Catharine grew worse. Caty and Nathanael took turns caring for the now desperately ill baby. At last her throat closed, and she could no longer breathe. Caty could not believe her child was dead. She collapsed as she watched the body borne away in its tiny coffin.

For weeks she lay ill and despondent, her arms empty and aching. She could not sleep, but stared at the ceiling, feeling nothing but deep loss. No one and nothing could reach her. She did not even want to get better. It was August, and through the hot days she scarcely ate. Nathanael was gentle with her, holding her, comforting her, trying to hide his own despair, wanting only to cheer her. They were alone together much of the time, although he gave the children a great deal of his attention.

As Caty's melancholy lingered on, Nathanael planned with her their move to Georgia. Again and again he described Mulberry Grove in an attempt to get Caty's mind off the haunting vision of her dead baby being carried away. With his love and persuasion, she slowly began to recover.

During autumn, while the family was making preparations for their permanent move to Georgia, Caty was only beginning to regain her strength. At first she thought her illness had made her miss her "complaint" but she soon after discovered that she was pregnant again. Her nervous system gave way completely and she had to be placed under the care of a nurse.

Nathanael now saw that the children would be more than he could handle alone. He was concerned about their education, and with Caty ill and unable to attend to instructing them, and knowing there would be no schools for them in Georgia, he hired the tutor that Caty had inquired about earlier. He was Phineas Miller, a twenty-one-year-old graduate of Yale who had been recommended by Dr. Ezra Stiles, the college president. The teacher, a cultured man of gentle manners and fine intellect, after turning down a more lucrative offer from another source, accepted the Greenes' terms of three pounds per month and board. He agreed to accompany the family to Georgia when Caty was well enough to travel. There he would continue the education of the children and, Nathanael hoped, help assemble his official war papers.

When Caty was introduced to Mr. Miller for the first time, she knew, even in her distressed state, that she was meeting a man she would like. His kindness, his obvious concern for her well-being, and the interest he took in the children comforted her. He was reserved, yet responsive, well-versed in the classics, and an avid conversationalist. In his quiet way he reached through

Caty's depression and offered her friendship and companionship, and most of all, reassurance about the pending trip to the South. His visits to her room, ostensibly to ask some point concerning the children, turned into chats that did more than anything else to revive her.

In October, although Caty was still far from well, the Greenes bid their relatives and friends farewell and, accompanied by the schoolmaster, embarked on their new adventure. They boarded a vessel for Savannah, storing most of their household belongings and two carriages on deck. Caty remained under the care of her nurse while Nathanael assumed charge of the children. During the voyage he took them to the quarterdeck and pointed out a whale that passed near the ship, but this was the sole pleasant experience of the trip.

The passage was a long and disagreeable one. Caty, in the tiny cabin with the nurse, found her fear of the sea to be overwhelming. The creaking of the ship, the closeness, the pitching made her violently ill, and the nurse felt little better. Caty's reason nearly left her when the ship passed through two severe gales which pounded against the hull until the occupants of the cabin were tossed about like baggage. The seas grew so high that a man was lost overboard and Caty's extreme fear caused Nathanael to worry for her sanity. The children were a little sick at first, but cheerful the rest of the voyage and far less trouble than Nathanael could have hoped for. Writing to a friend of the terrible journey, Nathanael said, "It was truly distressing to see Caty's distress. . . . It was happy for us we had not our horses as we must have thrown them overboard to have quieted Caty's fears if not from actual stress of weather."[2]

The vessel finally reached the safety of the Savannah River, upon whose bank, a number of miles upstream, the Greenes' new home stood. The ship sailed up the waterway, past the river forts, to the docks of Savannah. Nathanael helped the children and his pale, badly shaken wife down the gangplank, and the family stepped out upon the soil of their new state.

Before moving on to their plantation at Mulberry Grove, fourteen miles up-river, the Greenes remained in Savannah for several weeks while Caty recuperated. Meanwhile, the dwelling house was cleaned and set in order by servants who had been sent ahead. During this time the family and the tutor, Mr. Miller, were the guests of Nathanael's former aide, Nat Pendleton, the accomplished Virginian—now a Savannah attorney—whom Caty had helped nurse back to health at the beach near Charleston. Pendleton was married to the former Susan Bard, member of the prominent New York City family that had befriended him during the four years he had spent in captivity as a paroled prisoner of war on Manhattan Island.

While at the Pendletons' Caty and Nathanael had ample opportunity to walk along the sandy streets and to become acquainted with their new home town, the bustling, sprawling, bawdy seaport of Savannah. Their host's home stood at the corner of Bay and Barnard Streets, on Yamacraw Bluff, overlooking the river harbor with its docks and warehouses. A two-block walk down Bay Street, along the bluff paralleling the river, brought them to the Coffee House, near the heart of town. Beyond this point the street was a perpetual haunt of seafaring men of varied reputations who frequented the taverns and saloons that lined the thoroughfare. Between Bay Street and the edge of the bluff, high above the river, was a grassy terrace known as the Strand, a favorite duelling ground.

The center of commerce was a short walk from the Pendleton home. Here, surrounding one of the city's numerous parks, was Christ Church, a counting house, and an assortment of public stores and small shops. The town theater was nearby and tickets for the performances (which, that fall, included such fare as *The Tragedy of the Orphan* and *The Fair Penitent*, each production followed by a farce) could be bought for four shillings each.

The more fashionable shops were on Broughton Street, two blocks away, where an importer named Ann Taylor advertised for sale such items as petticoats, lutestrings, Irish linen, diapers, men's silk hose, girls' morocco pumps, spangled fans, and Anderson's pills. On the same street *The Gazette of the State of Georgia* was published by one of the South's earliest presses. At the time of the Greenes' arrival Nat Pendleton had an ad in the paper: "Run away . . . a negro fellow named Tom. . . . He is a young fellow, talks plausibly, and lets his beard grow, which is short and thin. He has a wife or two in or near Savannah, where it is probable he lurks. Whoever secures him, so he is delivered to me, shall receive five guineas reward."[3]

Caty mended well in the Pendleton household, and her stay was so pleasant that she induced Nathanael to delay their final move to Mulberry Grove. She found Susan Pendleton to be a polished, thoroughly educated New Yorker. As her own vitality flowed back within her, Caty's witty responses and unique expressions, so particularly enjoyed by Susan's husband, allowed her to carry points over her more knowledgeable hostess. Susan became her closest female companion in Georgia, but an air of rivalry was already beginning to hover over their friendship.

It was November before the Greenes left the city for their plantation home. Having sent most of their belongings ahead by water, Caty, Nathanael, Mr. Miller, and the five children entered the two family carriages and proceeded several miles up the Augusta Road. Driving through a gate, they turned down a lane surrounded by a vast forest of spreading live-oak, laden with moss. Its dense network formed a shadowy arch above the carriage trail. Wild vines, shrubs, and masses of yellow jasmine made the woods almost impenetrable on either side of the lane. As the river was approached the forest ended and Caty and her family looked out upon a great marshy wilderness, checkered by dikes and levees of the rice fields.

The carriages came to rest at the estate's large main house, which stood in a grove of mulberry trees, the vestige of bygone days of a silkworm farm. The brick residence, of two stories, with a tall chimney at each end, lay a hundred yards from the water's edge on the western bank of the river.[4] In the living room, wide glass panels flanking the central double door offered a fine view of the Savannah River with its bluff covered by enormous trees, and in the distance, the midstream islands and South Carolina shore.

The house had been unused for years, and it took the family weeks to settle in. Behind the dwelling were several outbuildings, including the kitchen, smokehouse, coach house and stables, poultry barn, and pigeon house. The garden, though largely in ruins, contained a great variety of shrubs and flowers. "[Here] Caty promises herself no small amusements," Nathanael wrote a friend. "Mr. Miller has begun his school, and the children improve very fast. He is an exceeding clever lad."[5]

Caty had long before found Miller to be a delightful companion. Inspired by the children's affable teacher, she read by the hour during her advancing pregnancy while Nathanael superintended the fields and Miller gave his lessons. During the evening she matched wits with her husband, the tutor, and other gentlemen who gathered at the dinner table.

One of the earliest callers to the Greene home was Isaac Briggs, a Georgia politician. Nathanael was out, but Briggs was entertained by Caty and Mr. Miller, whom the visitor found to be "a young gentleman of amiable qualities." The level of Caty's discourse was a pleasant surprise to Briggs and he was gratified to find that she was a student of the writings of Laurence Stern. When mention was made of a passage from *Tristram Shandy* that touched on slavery, a lively discussion followed.

"I am not determined in my own mind yet," said Mr. Miller, "whether enslaving the Negroes is right or not."

"Then by all means set about it and determine," said Briggs, leaning back in his chair and folding his arms. "If you mean to reside in Georgia, there is no point on which it is more necessary that you should be determined than that. I have but one argument against slavery, and that is I would not be a slave myself, if I could avoid it; and was it to be my hard fortune to be made a slave of, I would make use of the first means in my power to liberate myself."

"So would I," said Caty, smiling. "But would not your reason operate as strongly with respect to riding your horse, whereas you would not be willing to be ridden yourself?"

"There is a wide difference," responded Briggs. "A Negro has a soul as much as any of us; a horse has not."

"Will you undertake to prove," asked Caty, "that a horse or any other animal has not a soul?"

"Nothing more easy," answered Briggs.

"Then I would thank you, sir, for your proof."

"I believe," Briggs began, then paused, biting his lip, looking first at Mr. Miller and then at Caty. "I believe it is not quite so easy as I expected."

The visitor was glad to change the subject to a well-known scandal of the times, and Briggs found Caty perfectly willing to pursue a sexual topic without the slightest hesitation or hint of uneasiness. The fallen girl under discussion had been dismissed by most of Briggs's female friends as "an impudent, vile hussy, strumpet, whore!" Caty's estimation of the same person was a revelation to Briggs. "God forgive her, poor soul!" she said. " 'Tis as likely as not that her philanthropy and unsuspecting goodness of heart have paved the way for her falling into this snare."

In a letter to a friend, in which he told of his visit to Caty, Briggs wrote:

When I was in New England I was told that General Greene had made application for a divorce from his wife, because she had been unfaithful to his bed in his absence. In Newport, where the General resided, I made enquiry concerning this report and found 'twas all a lie. They had said also that she had no more gravity than an air Balloon, in her acting and thinking, that she had no more affection or regard for her children than if they were no human creatures & consequently paid no manner of attention to their education; that she cared for nothing but flirting, rattling and riding about.

A lady who is superior to the little foibles of her sex, who disdains affectations, who thinks & acts as she pleases, within the limits of virtue and good sense, without consulting the world about it, is generally an object of envy and distraction.—Such is Lady Greene.—She confesses she has passions & propensities & that if she has any virtue 'tis in resisting and keeping them within due bounds. . . . She has an infinite fund of vivacity, the world calls it levity. She possesses an unbounded benevolence . . . , the world calls it imprudence. In short she is honest & unaffected enough to confess that she is a woman, & it seems to me the world dislikes her for nothing else. As for the report that she was destitute of maternal feelings & paid no attention to the education of her children, I cannot for my life see what foundation there is for it; I am perfectly convinced that she has a very great share of maternal affection, & I never met a woman in my life who . . . had formed a system of education so much to my mind as Lady Greene.[6]

In early April, 1786, Caty, in the last stages of her pregnancy, suffered a severe fall in the kitchen, injuring her ankle and hip. "This misfortune," wrote Nathanael to Sammy Ward, "is the greater from her particular situation, being under hourly apprehension of an event which her hopes and fears are constantly struggling with."[7] The accident brought on premature labor, and Caty's baby lived only briefly.

The tragedy aggravated Caty's loneliness and her growing discontent with plantation life. Social custom in rural Georgia called for incessant visits back and forth among one's neighbors, a system Caty disapproved of since it did not allow her to choose her own company. The conversation of the country people reflected their woefully poor educations, and their discourse seldom amounted to an exchange of ideas above the level of chatty small-talk.

Caty's breeding required her always to return the first call, but beyond that she let her visits lapse except for those to her closest friends. She enjoyed her frequent trips with Nathanael into Savannah to call on the Nat Pendletons and other acquaintances there, and often received them in return at Mulberry Grove.

Caty still felt weak from her many ordeals and found that she had to stop to rest far more often than was her habit. Once when she felt the need of Nathanael's comfort, she could not find him. She was told that he had gone out; he had not said where he was going, but he was on foot. From the window she could see him sitting by himself by the river, his head in his hands. She went out to him, standing beside him for some minutes before he looked up, and when he did, she saw that he had been weeping.

How long ago those days at Uncle Greene's seemed when Nathanael had appeared to her a dashing man with twinkling eyes who loved to dance. The face he turned up to her now was that of a tired, haggard ex-soldier who had given himself to a belief, had signed away his future life, in fact, for that cause. Her heart ached. She made up her mind then that they would make Mulberry Grove a success. What they did not know about rice, they would learn. She would do everything in her power to help. She knew that they both would carry, in their own way, the ugly scars of their life during the war. Each had endured. And in some way, they would survive this, too.

Caty settled down to the life of arduous domesticity required by the demands of the plantation. Her duties were no longer limited to her own household but extended also to the cabins of the slaves, whose health problems required daily ministrations. Her new role brought responsibilities she dreaded to assume—unrewarding, exhausting, often depressing—but which she doggedly pursued.

Sitting down for brief rests by the window overlooking the Savannah, she could watch the children at play, making sure they did not wander too close to the river's edge, yet not wanting to imbue them with her own pathological fear of drowning. Ten-year-old George, particularly, liked to play at the side of the river. He would launch rafts with the eager help of laughing black boys, poling them along the near shallows, fishing gear in hand, during afternoons of delight.

Like the other children, George was responding well to the tutelage of Mr. Miller, and often, when lessons were done, Caty would watch him set out with his father walking the fields of the plantation. Some day, she hoped, he would take a full share of the responsibility of running the estate, thus helping and sparing a weary Nathanael.

The Greenes' most frequent visitor was Anthony Wayne, Nathanael's old companion-in-arms, who often rode over from his neighboring plantation. Wayne, whose wife never came to Georgia, courted a local girl named Mary Maxwell whom he had met during the campaign to drive the British out of the state, but his heart's true companion was Caty Greene. Like her, he was a volatile, social soul, often lonely and in need of stimulating companionship, feeling lost to society for weeks at a time in the marshy wilderness of coastal Georgia. The two often rode together after the day's chores were through, and planted and fussed over their flower gardens. In the evenings Wayne was often on hand at the supper table to join his hosts and Mr. Miller in animated discussions over politics, literature, and religion.

Nathanael, who had often seen his wife's gloom disappear in the presence of Wayne, heartily approved of their relationship. The whisperers of Savannah, however, were busily exchanging accounts of Wayne's nocturnal visits to Mulberry Grove which, they noted, occurred even when Nathanael was away on business. A love affair between an ex-general and the wife of his former superior, under the very roof of the latter, made interesting speculation. When one Savannah lady took it upon herself to warn Nathanael of the unfolding scandal, he thanked her politely but told her that Wayne had been a welcome visitor in many of his residences since the beginning of the war. He added that the lady could reassure her friends that Caty was never alone at home, there being five children, several servants, and a tutor as constant residents of the household. Nathanael told Caty and Wayne of the remarks of his informant but required no explanations and never mentioned the subject again.

By spring of 1786, about 200 acres at Mulberry Grove were planted with rice and corn. "The garden is delightful," Nathanael wrote a friend. "The fruit trees and flowering shrubs form a pleasing variety. We have green peas . . . and as fine lettuce as you ever saw. The mocking birds surround us evening and morning. The weather is mild, and the vegetable kingdom progressing to perfection. . . . We have in the same orchard apples, pears, peaches, apricots, nectarines, plums of different kinds, figs, pomegranates, and oranges. And we have strawberries which measure three inches round."[8]

On June 11, Nathanael and Caty drove to Savannah where they spent the evening and night with the Nat Pendletons. On the following day they started home, stopping off at a neighboring plantation for their mid-day meal as guests of a William Gibbons. Before leaving, Nathanael walked over the rice-fields with his host and though the day was exceedingly hot he wore no hat.

On the way home in the carriage, Nathanael suddenly complained of a severe headache, and upon arriving at Mulberry Grove he immediately went to bed. The headache continued all through the next day and became intense the following morning. Alarmed, Caty summoned Dr. John Brickel, a Savannah physician, who drew off a measure of blood. That night Nat Pendleton came for a visit and was shocked at Nathanael's disinclination to talk. When he became worse and lapsed into a semi-stupor, a second doctor named McCloud was called in as a consultant. He made a diagnosis of sunstroke, applied blisters, and drew more blood.

To keep the house perfectly quiet, the children were sent to a neighboring plantation. They were not told the cause of their being hurried away, but the older children never forgot the stricken countenances of their mother and other members of the household. Anthony Wayne came and sat up all night with his former commander.

At dawn on June 19, 1786 Caty sat in a chair, weeping silently. On the bed nearby lay the body of her husband, her greatest admirer, her staunchest friend. Anthony Wayne sent the word to Savannah. His hand trembled as he wrote, "I have just seen a great and good man die. . . ."[9]

13 Miseries of Widowhood

Nathanael Greene was dead at the age of forty-four. Caty brought her children home from the neighbors and, together with Phineas Miller, broke the news to them. Explaining the death of their beloved father, trying to make them understand and accept the finality of what had happened, was a heart-rending task.

The young nation Nathanael had helped preserve mourned its loss. Friends came to Mulberry Grove and dressed his body in the uniform he had worn on formal occasions as major general of the Continental army and placed his hands in gloves that had been a present of the Marquis de Lafayette. On the following day his body was put in a coffin, carried to a boat at the plantation landing, and transported down the river to Savannah. As the vessel approached the harbor, ships anchored there lowered their colors to half-mast. Business in town was suspended for the day. A large crowd gathered at the dock in front of the Nat Pendleton home and watched silently as the casket was brought ashore. While a military guard of honor stood at attention, the coffin was borne up the steps of the bluff to the Pendleton home, where Caty waited with her children.

The body lay in state in the parlor until five in the afternoon when the funeral party proceeded to the old colonial cemetery belonging to Christ Church. As the procession moved through the streets, a band played the solemn "Death March of Saul" while artillerists at Fort Wayne, on the bluff, fired their minute guns. A simple service was read, followed by thirteen rounds of musketry, after which the casket was locked in a vault.[1] As the guard of honor stood with trailed arms the mourners slowly and silently withdrew.

Returning to Mulberry Grove with her children, Caty began to prepare for the grim task of facing the future without her husband. What would Nathanael have advised her to do? His fatal illness had come so suddenly that there had been no opportunity to discuss the eventuality of her widowhood. Her own first impulse was to leave Georgia forever and return to Rhode Island, but there were at least three persons who advised her not to act hastily. One was Phineas Miller, whom Caty now placed in charge of the plantation's management; another was Nat Pendleton whom she retained as her attorney; and the third was Anthony Wayne, her friend and confidant since the days of the Revolution. Their counsel was well-meaning, but there was one burning prejudice common to them all: they adored Caty and did not wish her to leave.

Aggrieved over the loss of his former commander and the prospect of losing Caty, Wayne was the most outspoken of her advisers. His spirits crushed, he called on her again and again, walking with her in her garden, admitting that his arguments were selfish ones, but begging her not to leave. When she prepared to sail to Rhode Island during the summer to discuss her future plans with the executors of Nathanael's estate, Wayne was almost ill with fear she would not return. He drove her and the five children to the Savannah dock and waved a desolate good-bye as the vessel departed.

Caty had scarcely arrived in Newport before she had a letter from Wayne:

> I endeavored to restrain every tender emotion until you descended into the wretched cabin of a more wretched vessel. The effort was too great—for when I saw the Schooner under way, I experienced a sensation more force-ably felt than I had power to describe. Turning from that prospect and attempting to ascend the stairs at that hour thro which we had just passed, I sunk upon the arm of a

kind protector who supported me to my chamber where
I instantly fell into a state of torpidity. . . . I was aroused
by the keenest anxiety for the state of you and your little
family, occasioned by a most tremendous storm resembling
a tornado making its approach as dark as night about four
I think in the afternoon. . . . My feelings were tremen-
dously alive for the safety of an object never absent from
my mind. . . . An involuntary petition to the supreme governor of the universe flowed warm from my heart, for her
alone from whom I had so recently departed perhaps
forever.[2]

Caty met in Newport with the estate's co-executors, two of
her closest friends and admirers. They were Jeremiah Wadsworth
of Hartford, Nathanael's former commissary general, and Edward
Rutledge of Charleston, who had counseled her during her residence in South Carolina. She soon learned the worst. Her husband
had died before he had made the barest beginning toward paying
off the huge debts he owed to his three principal creditors, one
of whom was Wadsworth himself. Though Nathanael had left behind a potential fortune in real estate, he had pledged much of
it as security against his indebtedness. And land values were so
low at the time that the property left over, if sold immediately,
could not possibly provide Caty and her family with permanent
security. Unless Nathanael's estate was reimbursed by the government for the money he had borrowed to equip his Southern army,
there was a grave possibility that its assets would fall short of
its liabilities.

At best it would take years to settle the estate, and meanwhile
Caty and her children could only be supported by the proceeds
from the Mulberry Grove plantation. Sadly she made plans to
return to Georgia. Boarding a schooner with her children, she
sailed first to New York then to Philadelphia to visit old friends,
receive their blessings, and talk over with them her future prospects, especially as concerned the education of her children.

From Philadelphia she went by stage to Mount Vernon, accompanied by eight-year-old Cornelia, to visit the Washingtons. Many
years later Cornelia recounted the story of her introduction:

My mother had deeply imbued me with the honor in store
and had drilled my behavior to meet all the probable requirements for the occasion. I was, for example, to rise

from my seat for presentation to General Washington, and after tendering him my profoundest courtesy, stand at ease, and modestly answer all his possible questions, but at the same time keep religiously in the background, where all the good little girls of that day were socially referred.

The eventful day came. . . . We were graciously welcomed by Mrs. Washington; but my heart was so thick with fluttering, and my tongue so tied, that I made but a stuttering semblance of response to her kindly questions. At length the door opened, and General Washington entered the room. I felt my mother's critical eyes, and advanced with the intention of making a courtesy and declaiming the little address previously taught me; instead of which, I dropped on my knees at Washington's feet, and burst into tears.

All the resources of dramatic art could hardly have devised a more effective coup. Washington stooped and tenderly raised me, saying with a smile, "Why, what is the matter with this foolish child?" The words do not have a tender sound, but language may not convey the gentleness of his manner and the winning softness of his voice, as he wiped away my tears with his own handkerchief, kissed my forehead, and led me to a seat as he might a young princess. He sat beside me, and with laughing jests, brought down to the plane of my appreciation, banished my sins from my eyes, rescued me from humiliation, and brought me back to composure. He guarded me from my mother's outraged eyes, kept me with him while in the drawing room, had me placed beside him at the dinner-table, and with his own hands heaped all of the good things on my plate. After dinner he took me to walk in the garden, and with an intelligent stooping to my intellectual stature, and a sympathetic understanding of my emotional state and need, he drew me into talks on the themes of my daily life, and won me into revelations of my hopes and fears. . . .[3]

After a long discussion with the Washingtons over the schooling of her children, Caty returned with Cornelia to Philadelphia, gathered up her other children, and sailed for Georgia. The family was welcomed at the dock by Anthony Wayne and the Nat Pendletons, and was received warmly by Phineas Miller at Mulberry Grove. Caty found that the plantation had been administered admirably by Miller; the crops of rice and corn were in good condition, and a fine harvest was expected that year.

Caty renewed the role that had been so familiar to her during the war, that of rearing her children without the benefit of their father. She was a stern disciplinarian. One day little Nat begged once too often for some sugar out of a big silver bowl and was compelled to eat it all, sustaining a stomach ache and distaste for sugar that he never forgot. Cornelia told, too, of an unforgettable encounter. She had been given a lovely gown as a present, the first dressy frock she had ever owned, gossamer in texture and covered with delicate embroidery and trimmed with rare lace. Her mother permitted her to wear it only on extraordinary occasions. In later years, Cornelia recalled:

> Once—It is vivid as yesterday—I was invited to spend a long day in the country with a party of fellow-madcaps. I secretly determined to wear my beautiful frock. Knowing that permission to do so would be denied, I arrayed myself in solitude, and waited alone in my room until the moment that the carriage was ready. . . . Then I ran with the speed of a frightened lapwing and took my place in the carriage where the others were already seated, and escaped detection. The day in the country was a poem. We plucked flowers and devoured fruit, ran races in the meadows, rode on horses that were without saddles or bridles, and climbed trees. In the intoxication of the romp my frock was soiled, stained, and rent.
>
> Reaching home, I hurried, with gathering tears and fluttering heart, to my mother's room. To my amazement she showed no trace of anger. After a calm and judicial examination, she said, "Well, my daughter, it must be mended." "But mama," I retorted, "that is impossible; it is torn to pieces." "Nothing is impossible, dear, to patience and perseverance; the frock must be mended." And it was mended. For the next three weeks I invested two hours of each day threading dwarf-eyed needles, setting invisible stitches, and darning up to the exactions of pattern, until at last the impossible was accomplished.[4]

Caty prepared a claim of indemnity in behalf of her husband's estate against the Federal government for recovery of funds Nathanael had paid Charleston merchants to clothe his soldiers. In the summer of 1787 she and her family sailed back to Newport, and while the children visited relatives in Rhode Island she was a guest at the Jeremiah Wadsworth home in Hartford. Wadsworth had financed her voyage to New England for the purpose of talking over estate affairs; moreover, he was a congressional candidate and, if elected, planned to present her indemnity claim to the national body then meeting in New York City. There is no record of how Caty was received by Jeremiah's wife, twenty years her senior and nine years older than her husband, but it is clear from letters that followed that his youngest child, Harriet, perhaps sensing her father's regard for the youthful, vivacious widow from the South, developed a genuine dislike for the family visitor.

Because of the unsettled nature of the estate, the formal education of George Greene, now almost twelve, was an issue of immediate concern. In a letter to Wadsworth, General Washington offered to bear the expense of the boy's schooling. "Should Mrs. Greene, yourself, and Mr. Rutledge . . . think proper to entrust my namesake, G. W. Greene, to my care," he wrote, "I will give him as good an education as this country . . . will afford . . . at my own cost and charge."[5]

A second offer had come from another quarter. The Marquis de Lafayette, who also had a son named for George Washington, suggested in a letter to Caty that her George be educated in France as the guest of the Lafayette household. Caty hesitated, for her position was an embarrassing one; the estate was already heavily in debt to the marquis. But Lafayette insisted, saying that he had promised Nathanael that he would have George educated in France at his own expense. Getting no immediate answer from Caty, Lafayette asked Henry Knox to help persuade her. "Whatever she and you bid me to do shall be done," he wrote.[6]

Knox urged Caty to send George to Lafayette. The academies in France, he wrote, were established on the most healthy principles. "There is no assumed superiority arising from the accidental distinctions of birth—everybody is equal—talents only acquire eminence. Dancing fencing riding and other graceful exercises are taught as well as the mental accomplishments. The son of General Greene ought to have all possible advantages. The Marquis de Lafayette is perfectly ready to perform the offices of a kind parent."[7]

The thought of sending young George across the sea to a country in the throes of political upheaval was difficult to entertain. Caty knew a separation from this promising child would compound her already deep sense of loss. But after much deliberation she decided to accept Lafayette's offer. George was sent to the home of the Knoxes in New York where arrangements were made for his passage. He would travel in the company of Joel Barlow, a diplomat on his way to France. In May, with fifty dollars in his pocket given him by Henry Knox who saw him off at the dock, George began his voyage. "Your lovely son embarks with all the intrepidity of an hero," Knox wrote Caty, who was then back in Georgia. "I have watched the emotions of his mind on various occasions and the result is that he possessed certain traits of greatness which will anon be the pride and solace of your life."[8]

Caty continued to divide her time almost equally between Georgia and the East. Mulberry Grove was flourishing, and in the summer of 1788, leaving the plantation in the hands of an overseer, Caty returned to Connecticut with Phineas Miller, who accompanied her as a business adviser, and her four youngest children. She had come to consult Jeremiah Wadsworth once more regarding her various estate matters but found him to be detained in New York attending a session of Congress, of which he was now a member. Caty's security was vested almost entirely in Wadsworth, who was her only source of ready income until crops at Mulberry Grove could be harvested in the fall. Moreover, as co-executor of Nathanael's estate, of which he himself was the principal creditor, he held a position of incredible power over Caty and her children. Finally, it was he to whom she turned for the presentation of her indemnity petition to Congress. Whether she and her children were to live comfortably or, in her terms, "like common beggars" depended largely on the exertions, the generosity, and the devotion of this one man.

Caty had taken a cottage in Wethersfield, Connecticut, near Hartford. From here she poured out her woes in a letter to Wadsworth in New York. She had been forced to sell her phaeton for spending money and most of her household belongings at Mulberry Grove had been carted away by creditors. "The furniture is gone," she wrote, "some people would say to the dogs—but I say to the Devil." She had been so imposed upon by "every creature almost" that she had lost heart. She told Wadsworth that Mr. Miller had gone to Hartford to "endeavor to procure a bill to send to New York—if he dose not I will thank you to send me 2 or 300 dollars by some safe conveyance. There is left . . . Certificates god knows how much the amount is—for I have not the papers which were to have been here before this—

but it is however what I got for my Phaeton—I wish to have that money to get me a little furniture. . . . Will you be so good as to see a little to it—and one more favor, I must beg you to Procure me a caske of wine such as you think I can afford to drink—dont laugh for I am cerious. . . . The children are delighted with the books you had the goodness to send. I have thought it best to set them up one by one as a prize in the Schools in hope it will have a better effect than acquiring what they want Easily—Nat says if he had a bag of Marbles he would study hard for them. . . . I suppose you will hear from your own family what a delightful time we had on the Mountain the other day."[9]

Caty had not heard from her son since he sailed and she was worried. She asked Wadsworth to write her when he knew of Mr. Barlow's arrival in France. Meanwhile she planned a party in the grove with Wadsworth's children and told him how much she hoped to make them happy. But she was disappointed that he did not return home to meet her in Connecticut. "I cannot help running out to the Stage every time it passes in hopes of seeing you," she wrote, ". . . which god knows I have done in too many instances in my life but I have almost done with hope now."[10] Later, in answer to a letter from him, she wrote: "You did not mention the wine. You would smile at the manner in which I construed your silence on that subject—but shall make no observations than I have not had a bottle in the house for these six weeks."[11]

Caty told Wadsworth she had thoughts of going to New York herself to argue her case before Congress, and added that if she did go she would meet him there. Her eloquence in the letter suggested the form her appeal to the governing body would take. She told of how Nathanael, finding his soldiers without proper protection from the winter, had risked his fortune and future and the happiness of his family to relieve them. "Can Congress hear and know this—and be deaf to the Miseries of the widow and fatherless—No—I will not yet believe mankind so ungrateful, so unjust—I ask no favors but justice—and . . . then it would not be necessary for me to ask favors of anybody. . . . It shall never be told me, that I set myself down quietly and waited for my Ruin— No—I am a woman—unaccustomed to any thing but the trifling business of a family. Yet my exertions may effect something—if they do not—and if I sacrifice my life in the cause of my children, I shall but do my Duty—and follow the example of my illustrious husband."[12]

Wadsworth welcomed Caty to New York but discouraged her plan of appearing personally before Congress. He did not feel it politically expedient from his own standpoint to be publicly identified with her. There had been scandal enough already, not only over his earlier connection with Caty, but more recently because of his involvement in the Elizabeth Whitman case. Only shortly before, the body of the socially prominent young Connecticut woman had been found in a hotel room, with her dead baby, a pair of forceps and a probe lying near her bed. Wadsworth and several others, including one of his agents and a Yale theologian, had all been suspected of being lovers of Miss Whitman, but it was not known which of them had fathered the dead infant.

Caty accepted Wadsworth's proposal to meet him secretly at his New York quarters to discuss her business affairs. After the conferences were over there was ample opportunity for her to remain the night with the man who had loved her for years and who now held such extraordinary control over her welfare. To say that Caty succumbed to his advances would be to use the improper verb; she was not a woman to be dominated by any person or any situation. Her own passions were involved, her own feelings for Jeremiah, her own need to be cherished by this protector who was in such a commanding position to care for her and her family. She contributed a full share in the promotion of the liaison, and letters that followed leave little doubt as to the nature of their relationship.

14 A New Life Unfolds

The course of their love affair was a stormy one. Wadsworth, unwilling to accept anything less than sole possession of Caty, began to question her relationship with Phineas Miller. He knew that Miller, as plantation manager of Mulberry Grove, lived in the same house with her in Georgia but now he was infuriated that he had traveled with her to New England. In a jealous outburst Wadsworth even accused Caty of intimacy with Miller prior to Nathanael's death, stating that he still had a letter from the general expressing concern over the attachment. Caty angrily denied that her husband had ever thought such a thing, and refused to look at the letter.

Some of their differences were settled before they parted. Caty, returning to Connecticut to collect her three daughters and Mr. Miller, left little Nat in the Wadsworth household with the understanding that Jeremiah would oversee his education. Stopping off in Philadelphia on the way home, Caty enrolled Patty and Cornelia in a fashionable school in Bethlehem, administered by Moravian nuns, paying their fees with funds advanced by Wadsworth. Then she, Miller, the baby, and a nurse boarded a coastal schooner and sailed for the South.

Caty debarked at Charleston to attend to estate business while her traveling companions continued on to Savannah. She became a guest in the Edward Rutledge home, just across Broad Street from the house of Edward's brother John, where she and Nathanael had lived during the army's occupation of Charleston. (Both Rutledge homes are still standing.) For three weeks she held daily conferences with Edward, the estate's co-executor. She had once met with him briefly in Newport and had known him and his wife in earlier South Carolina days, but only now did she become truly acquainted with his character. "Mr. Rutledge is all goodness," she wrote Wadsworth, "and I begin to be in better humor with mankind."[1]

Edward, like his brother John, was a political figure of eminence. As a young lawyer of twenty-four, he had stood before the first Continental Congress in 1774 to pledge the allegiance of the South. He had been no brash revolutionary, however, and fought hard against those radicals who wanted to sever all of America's ties with England, the country in which he had received his legal education. He had become the most trusted spokesman for the more conservative members of Congress, but at the last moment, when he saw that the course of his country was irrevocably headed in the direction of open rebellion, he changed his position and voted for resolutions favoring the Declaration of Independence. He signed the document, the youngest man to do so, affixing his name just below the flourishing "J" of John Hancock.

Rutledge was anything but the dashing, pretentious, eloquent orator-statesman that legend has painted. There was nothing striking about his appearance, and unlike many of his fellow congressional delegates, he dressed himself indifferently in untailored clothing. He laughed as he told of how in the early days of his career he had sometimes become entangled in long phrases from which he had trouble extricating himself, often disguising his inarticulateness by muffled but vehement utterances.

The Rutledge that Caty now saw on her visit to Charleston was not yet forty but appeared considerably older. He was middle-sized, a little heavy, and partially bald. The snow-white hair that remained was curled over his neck. Afflicted with gout, which had been aggravated during a year's captivity by the British in East Florida following the fall of Charleston, he limped painfully during relapses of the disease and often used a cane. Even when he suffered, his expression was perfectly composed, pleasant, serene. "His heart was so well expressed in his fine countenance," it was said of him, "that [one] could scarcely mistake the delineation of its feelings, and a stranger in distress might have singled him from a crowd, as the man most likely to bestow sympathy and relief."[2]

Of Caty's closest male acquaintances Rutledge was the one least swayed by her power of fascination. He was entirely absorbed in his own family and, although charmed by Caty's personality, was never awed by it. He assumed complete charge of the friendship, which progressed entirely on his terms, and his objective viewpoint made him Caty's most trustworthy adviser. He was well aware of Wadsworth's conflicting interests in regard to Caty and her circumstances, and often disagreed with his counsel.

While in Charleston Caty counted fifty-one carriages containing "ladies of rank" who came to visit her. She noted with satisfaction, in a letter to Wadsworth, that most of them belonged to the city's tight society whose members seldom paid visits to anyone outside their own "noble families" and who had snubbed Lucy Knox during her visit to the city. Caty again tried to soothe Wadsworth's feelings about Phineas Miller. "Don't be unhappy," she wrote, "Pray do not. You have not the reasons you suppose. I wish you a Merry Christmas and send you a kiss to convince you of it. Kiss the dear children for me whom I love much better since I left them than I did when I was there. God bless you again and again."[3]

Caty was back at Mulberry Grove by the first of the year, having spent a wintry Christmas Day aboard a schooner. Soon after her arrival she had a message from Rutledge who was disgusted over a letter from Wadsworth. "He is very anxious about the estate," Rutledge told Caty, "and not a little about his own situation. He requests a payment for what he advanced. . . . We shall prevent his being called on in the future, to advance any more for the children."[4] A copy of Jeremiah's letter was enclosed.

A little later a confidential message from Wadsworth told Caty of his wife's having questioned his correspondence with her. After a rather feeble explanation to Mrs. Wadsworth that barely averted disaster, he had decided to burn all of Caty's letters, as well as the one from Nathanael written shortly before his death three years previously, which Wadsworth said had expressed alarm over her affection for Phineas Miller.

Caty answered in a private letter of her own that began in newsy fashion:

Jany 31, 1789

My Dear Friend

Mrs. Pendleton and myself are at Mulberry Grove, where we are to await the return of Major Pendleton who is now Chief Justice of this state and has been gone three weeks to the assembly. The Senators are chosen and *behold* they are Col Few, and a Captain Gun[n] of the Lighthorse [who had challenged Nathanael to a duel in 1785] the most ignorant and infamous fellow in the whole army. He was disgraced—ran away to Georgia, married a pretty fortune here, found means to purchase the voats of the common people (which the assembly is composed of) and which have made him senator. . . .

I have just received a letter from Mr. Rutledge inclosing your letter, and a statement of your account with me and the Estate—I am grieved to find you are so distressed in your circumstances—and hope by the time this reaches you, you will receive such remittances as will relieve you. I have sent you the very first of the crop as you desired. I hope you have nothing to fear from the advances made for the children—for while I live you can not possibly suffer. I will take care that you are paid every farthing due you. I have property, and power, sufficient to secure you—and you know my pride (if I had no better motive) would not permit me to suffer you or your children to be wronged for mine. . . .

You say in your private letter, that you were nearly involved in a cerious misfortune. . . . I thought my letters were burnt long since. . . . But why did you burn *that unfortunate letter which you once mentioned to me.* It is true I did not call on you for it—because I was vexed that you should torture the G[eneral]s letter into meanings which he never thought of—and which nothing but his spirit descending from heaven would ever make me believe. You say an explanation of that letter would have made you happy or miserable—This is all mistory to me, I cannot solve it.

You say you are unhappy because you never expected to see me again. I told you before I left you, that it depended on yourself alone. I still consider myself as a kind of ambassador—liable to be recalled by my sovereign—but tell me ceriously—did you for one moment of your life think of coming to Georgia to see me—if you do . . . I should, I believe, submit to be a [illegible]. . . . Tell Natty his Mama will write to him as soon as he can read her letter—and tell him also that his Heffer has had 3 calves which are all marked for him as shall be all the increase. You have no reason for the jealousy you mention—I give you my word—

C G[5]

Caty felt that she was losing her hold on Jeremiah. Their deep attachment had begun years before, during Caty's desolate months in New England when Nathanael was fighting in the South and she considered herself to be in a "widowed state." It was this early connection that had inspired Rhode Island gossips to place the charge of adultery against her, a rumor Isaac Briggs had investigated, finally satisfying himself that "'twas all a lie." If Caty's own basic honesty and frankness are taken into account as they were by Briggs, then it becomes decidedly believable that during Nathanael's lifetime she had remained faithful "to his bed." In her discussion with Briggs shortly before her husband died, she had readily admitted her "passions and propensities" but stated just as candidly that her one redeeming virtue was keeping them "within due bounds."[6]

After the loss of Nathanael, however, when her perpetual desire to dominate the men in her life became accentuated by fears for her family's security, she found little reason to exert her prior restraint. In many of her connections she made use only of the more subtle chemical forces that had always been at work in her relationships, but in others she applied the full power of her sex. Of the four men closest to her, three were married, but in the case of two of them she could easily ignore the fact; Jeremiah Wadsworth and Anthony Wayne seldom mentioned their wives and never brought them out into society. In the case of Nat Pendleton, however, she found his charming Susan to be a formidable rival. Caty was often seized with fits of envy over the special attentions Nat paid to his wife in her presence.

Caty's one serious relationship that did not involve a married man was with Phineas Miller. Ten years younger than she, he had fallen in love with her almost at first sight, and was now in a position to ask for her hand. But he knew the time had not yet come. He recognized her need for other men, endured the pain of bearing witness to her compelling infatuations, and when they were over, tenderly welcomed her back into his arms.

Miller's youth and special eligibility were particular curses to Jeremiah Wadsworth, who as long as his aging wife still lived was in no position to pursue an open, competitive courtship. Wadsworth knew that he might be able safely to enjoy Caty's company in New York for a week or two each year, but Miller, young and free, would always be in the background, awaiting her return to Mulberry Grove. For Wadsworth the situation was intolerable enough to make him want to release himself from his involvement.

His resentment toward his rival boiled to the surface in the spring of 1789. He wrote Miller an angry letter accusing him, as Caty's manager, of holding up repayment of monies borrowed by Caty. Miller showed her the letter. "[He] was very much hirt," she wrote Wadsworth, "and I confess I think he had some reason for it. He is young—without friends and without fortune—he has an honest heart and a proud one— . . . and I suppose that his inferior situation in life made him magnify the slightest reproof from you into the most [illegible] insult."[7]

A self-righteous former army captain named Jack Webb, who had been defeated in the recent elections, spent his spare time in Savannah informing his friends of Caty's various activities. On a trip to New York he had heard of her visits to Jeremiah Wadsworth's quarters and could hardly wait to get home to broadcast an account of them. After his return to Savannah, he kept a close eye on her relationship with Phineas Miller.

Meeting Caty on the street, Webb infuriated her by making remarks about her to two men. "He told the gentlemen that I had Mr. Miller and Mr. Wadsworth in keeping and said things too shocking to think of," Caty wrote Wadsworth. She had then rushed to Phineas Miller who sought out Webb and "cained him without mercy." Miller challenged Webb to a duel, but the latter "sneaked off like the coward and villian that he is." When Webb was safely aboard a vessel in Savannah Harbor he shouted to those on shore that he was going to "publish" Caty as soon as he got to New York. "If he dose I beg you to write to my Brother immediately," Caty said in her letter to Wadsworth. Then she apologized for her penmanship: "I have just been in the garden and have eat so many strawberries that I can with difficulty write."[8]

A new suitor appeared briefly at Mulberry Grove to pay court to Caty. He was a French planter of aristocratic background, the Marquis de Montalet, who, having moved to the Georgia coast from Santa Domingo, now lived on a nearby Savannah River plantation. He had recently lost his young and beautiful marquise and was looking for another wife; quite likely too, thought Caty, he was seeking another fortune. She was not impressed by the man or his title. "I believe," she wrote Wadsworth, "I forgot to mention my noble lover to you, the Marquis of _____, (I forget what) but he made very cerious propositions."

In the same letter Caty told Wadsworth of her intention of returning to New York to press her claim to Congress. "I have a thousand things to communicate," she wrote, "but my little secret hope of seeing you makes me forego my propensity. Perhaps in a month from this time you will see me in New York. Nothing will [then] prevent me from declaring in person how much affection I feel for you."[9]

Again Wadsworth was cool to the idea of Caty's appearing personally before Congress, and suggested that she present her claim by letter. Edward Rutledge disagreed firmly. "Wadsworth may think the business can be done as well by a petition whilst the humble petitioner is a thousand miles off," he wrote Caty, "but he is mistaken. The effects of personal application, with justice, humanity, and gratitude on your side are wonderful. They ought to be irresistible."[10] Rutledge suggested that Caty ask Alexander Hamilton to help draw up her petition.

Caty wrote Wadsworth that she definitely planned to come to New York and that her lawyer, Nat Pendleton, might accompany her. "I hope I may find you in New York when I arrive," she added. "I shall be much mortified if I do not. . . . I dare say J Webb has told you a thousand falsehoods which you have not heard. I wonder how he will look when he sees me."[11]

Nat Pendleton's plans to accompany Caty to New York did not materialize, ostensibly because of his preoccupation with political affairs, but more likely the result of objections by his pregnant wife. For some time Caty had noticed a growing coolness toward her on the part of Susan, who could not have been perfectly comfortable over her husband's regard for his charming client, and who certainly was a constant witness to their playful attentions to each other. The Pendletons' dog, named Edmund after Nat's famous uncle in Virginia, was a great favorite of Caty's, and she carried on pretended repartees with him, in affectionate terms, while Pendleton provided the dog's responses, equally affectionately, in the style of a ventriloquist.

Caty sailed in mid-summer, accompanied by little Louisa and a nurse. As she debarked in New York she was met at the dock by her son, Nat, and Jeremiah Wadsworth. She got a warm hug from her little boy but the chilly reception accorded by Wadsworth suddenly confirmed her fears that his friendship was nearing an end.

Caty divided her time between the home of the Henry Knoxes and that of her cousin Sammy Ward, now a Manhattan merchant, who lived a few blocks away on Broadway. One of her first visits was to the Washingtons in their rented house on the corner of Cherry and Franklin Streets. Overlooking the East River, the home was serving as the nation's first presidential mansion. (The site today is occupied by a pillar of the Brooklyn Bridge.) Four months before, George Washington had been inaugurated President of the United States in modest ceremonies in front of Wall Street's Federal Hall.

Caty found the three-story house and grounds swarming with servants, the coachmen and footmen dressed in the brilliant livery of red and white. The dwelling was crowded by streams of visitors. Some were on official missions, but most, including many old soldiers, merely wanted to get a glimpse of the former commander in chief. As the callers were ushered into the living room, to linger as long as they wanted to, they exchanged polite bows with the president and a few chatted with him. Anxious to set a precedent of ceremony for the new office, Washington always wore a black velvet suit, a pair of immaculate white gloves, and had a polished sword at his side. Caty saw that his hair was powdered and gathered in a small silk bag at the back.

Caty received her usual cordial greetings from the Washingtons, and Martha noted that she was as stylishly dressed and as appealing as ever. She was frequently invited to Friday night receptions at the mansion and Martha particularly relished having her on hand for the Thursday evening state dinners. As Caty was escorted into the dining room with the other guests she found the plates already served with fine foods prepared by the steward, olive-skinned Samuel Fraunces, once a tavern keeper. His delicacies included roast beef, veal, lamb, and varieties of game, with jellies, fruits, nuts, and raisins accompanying the main course.

Lady Washington sat at the head of the table, while the president took his seat to her left, near the center of the long table, with guests on each side and facing him. His private secretary, Tobias Lear, sat at the foot. During formal occasions, when the company began eating, Mrs. Washington was sometimes embarrassed by awkward silences that would fall among the guests, emphasizing the sounds of clinking utensils and self-conscious coughs. Such lapses never seemed to occur, however, when Caty was present. Her great storehouse of anecdotes of camp days of the Revolution often kept the dining room rocking with laughter.

After dinner the ladies would retire, unescorted, to the drawing room on the second floor while the president remained at the dinner table with the men. Often, however, by his own special privilege, Washington would make his way upstairs to spend the last part of the evening with the admiring ladies. Since Caty was unattached, the president was tenderly attentive to her, always escorting her to her carriage when the evening was over, handing her in with a sweeping bow.

Henry Knox, now secretary of war, and Alexander Hamilton, secretary of the treasury, gave Caty every form of assistance in her petition to Congress. Knox wrote out, in several pages, a model of the form he thought the appeal should take; it was full of good sense and legal acumen, and stated clearly the issues that had entrapped Nathanael in South Carolina. Edward Rutledge, too, continued to encourage Caty by mail without giving her false hope. "I know," he wrote, "the power of your eloquence & I expect some wonders from its Charms, but I am afraid that you will have a number of deaf Adders to preach to. However, the object is truly important & difficult as it may be, it may be finally attained by perseverance. . . . You see how anxious I am my good Friend—I indeed think of it every day of my life, & have it almost as much at Heart as if it were my own immediate domestic concern."[12]

Caty was reacquainted with many of her old friends while enjoying the society of government circles. Knox and Hamilton were on hand as cabinet members, and William Duer, Kitty Stirling's husband, was a high official in the treasury department. All of their wives entertained frequently and, along with their husbands, often accompanied Caty to the Johns Street Theatre, sitting together in the presidential stage box. Caty made a new friend in Tobias Lear, the president's personal secretary, who, after a long chat with her, found himself captivated by her charm and intellect. Caty was equally impressed with her new acqaintance, and swapped notes with him after their meeting. Lear's message, delivered to Caty at her quarters, was "to pay tribute to one of the best minds I have ever found in my intercourse with humanity."[13]

Lucy Knox, ascending to the top rung of the New York social

ladder as rapidly as possible, usually climaxed the week's activities by giving a huge Saturday night dinner party at her mansion at number four Broadway, where Caty was a guest for several weeks. The four-story dwelling was on the same block as the house General Knox used for his headquarters during the British siege of 1776 when Caty and Lucy first explored the town together, beholding sights that amazed, shocked, and all the while delighted them. Now, thirteen years later, in a time of peace, Caty found no such stimulation. Depressed over her dreadful fear of the future and her difficulty in getting her petition presented, she found that her spirits could no longer be supported by the kind of activities she had once reveled in. She began to tire of the social whirl of the thriving city.

Wadsworth's indifference was a bitter disappointment. Caty had hoped, since he had promised to sponsor her indemnity appeal, that he would be an aggressive champion of her cause. Instead, he not only neglected to take any action whatever on the petition but ignored her personally. While she was fretting over her ill-fortune, a cursory note came from Nat Pendleton, answering a legal question posed by Caty, and at the same time bringing the news that Susan's pregnancy, which had given Caty a pang of jealousy when she first heard of it, had terminated in the birth of a baby boy. The sex of the infant was a source of pride to Pendleton but a disappointment, he wrote, to his wife.

Caty was in a bad mood when she sat down to answer his letter.

> Genl Knoxes, New York, Novbr 22 [1789]
>
> My Dear friend
>
> Were I to follow your example I shoud begin my letter with a formal *Sir* and then hurry on a few lines as fast as possible in order to discharge a *Duty* (which is commonly performed with reluctance) rather than from inclination.— You do not however forget to make your apology—but I cannot help hopeing your terrors will be at an end . . . and that I shall be favored with an oldfashion letter from you.
>
> . . . You take care to Mention [the baby] that is just Born without ever saying a word of Edmond who I am so much interested in—dose he remember Greeney—I long to see the Dear little dog. . . . Give my love to Mrs P and tell her I am sorry she is disappointed in her darling

wish—perhaps the *next time* she may be more fortunate.—
I have never received a line from her or Genl Wayne since
I left you—do be good enough to enquire the cause and
let me know it.

I saw Jack Webb in my excurtion to the Westward [to
visit Patty and Cornelia in Pennsylvania]—our interview
was the most laughable thing in the world—I wish I could
describe it to you—but I dare say he never will wish for
the honor of seeing me again.

What am I to do with myself—I find an invincable reluctance to Society and amusements of every species—Balls
concerts assemblies and even Plays ceise to please me.
When we have company at home (which is at least three
times a week) I am dejected at the very thought—and always
feel inclined to run away—have I grown callous or has
my pleasures heretofore been of that Exquisit kind as to
make all others Pains by a comparison—but such a total
change never took possession of a heart like mine before.

. . . [Nat] is without exception the most sensible child
I ever saw—Even Mrs. Knox says so—but as he is much
inclined to vixy I have placed him at school with his Sisters
or rather in their Neighborhood and feel that I have done
right—I am most affectionately and Most sincerely Your
Real friend

C Greene[14]

Pendleton wrote back, advising Caty not to return to Georgia.
"Tho I can't help wishing to be in the same place with you always,"
he said, "yet I can't in my conscience persuade you to come back
to this vile, corrupt country. Corruption pervades every public
Department and rudeness every private Society. . . . You enquire
after Edmund, and the poor little stranger who is no more. He
was never well from his birth, and died about three weeks ago.
Edmund is in excellent health and a most amusing little dog.
He frequently calls you, particularly when handsome ladies are
in the room. But I asked him if he loved Greenie and he said
'Greenie damn bitch.' "[15]

In December, when Caty sailed to Charleston for another con-
ference with Edward Rutledge, Pendleton was there to meet her,
and as her lawyer to represent her interests in matters of legal-
ity that she did not understand. His counsel often differed from
that of Rutledge, and, when a particular stalemate arose, he

insisted that Caty sail back home with him in time for Christmas.

She found everything "going on well at the plantation," she wrote Wadsworth after her return to Mulberry Grove, but added that she was still hurt by his recent behavior. "It is not all fair play between you and myself," she said, "or you are not the man I have taken you for. Some persons I suspect have poisend your mind against me—pray tell me. . . . Something whispers to me that I shall live to convince you I have acted honestly to you and that you will repent your unkind suspicions of me."[16]

More bills were on hand from Wadsworth. "To describe to you the continued torments I feel on account of my debts is impossible," she wrote him, "and to reflect that my friends are suffering inconveniences on my account makes it doubly cutting."[17]

Early in 1790 Caty was on the high seas once more, sailing to the East to renew her efforts in support of her claim, to visit her children, and to enjoy the society of New York, a city to which, in spite of occasional protestations to the contrary, she was now thoroughly addicted.

15 An Appeal To Congress

Each time Caty left Mulberry Grove, Anthony Wayne, master of the adjoining plantation, was miserable. He could always turn to Mary Maxwell, or to any number of girls in Savannah or the Georgia upcountry, but when his restless adventures were over, he yearned all the more for his heart's true love. He and Caty had been riding, dancing, and conversational partners ever since the days of Valley Forge and had often laughed at the interpretation camp gossips placed upon their affinity for each other.

Now, however, their need was of a deeper nature. During his lifetime, Nathanael's strength had been their strength; when the pillar came down their weaknesses were laid bare. In the weeks following the tragedy they had fallen into each other's arms in an embrace of mutual consolation. Shortly afterward, when Caty sailed to New England for the first time, and Wayne doubted that he would ever see her again, his grief amounted to virtual collapse. Only her love had sustained him. "I pledge the honor of a soldier," he had written her at that time, "that I will repay you with compound interest upon your personal demand, in any Quarter of the Globe."[1]

Following that intimate period Caty's attitude toward Wayne

began to undergo a gradual change. In earlier days she had sympathized with his estrangement from his wife and understood his sudden need to break away from polite society to seek the company of the sweethearts he had acquired at every post. But now she considered such departures as transgressions upon their special friendship and would no longer tolerate them. Her irritation was such by 1790 that when she sailed to the East she did not bother to tell him good-bye.

Wayne felt that a long letter might soothe her feelings and, besides, he had a favor to ask. "I am making my arrangements [to leave the plantation]," he wrote, "from a conviction that we shall have a very serious Indian war soon. I have solicited the President for a commission. I must therefore ask you to become my advocate with the President and your other friends in power when a favorable opening offers, and you well know how to time it."[2]

Caty, though she doubtlessly gave Wayne a high recommendation to her government friends, wrote him that her true personal feelings were those of "impatience, resentment, and entire indifference" as to whether their friendship continued or not. "You are wanting even in the point of Gallantry," she told him, "and incapable of feeling the professions you make, returning indifference and insult to the solicitudes of friendship."

"No, my dear friend," he wrote back, "you wronged me and you wronged yourself by that idea, for I am confident that my lips wou'd not have opened to give utterances to professions which my heart did not assent to—*when made to you.*"[3]

From Sammy Ward's Manhattan residence, where she was again a guest, Caty wrote Nat Pendleton, complaining that she had received only two short notes from him in several weeks. "I could tell you many things," she said, ". . . but not one word shall you [glean] from me—Nor would I write you now but from the Ill-Natured hope that I may interrupt you in some favorite reflection or amusement. . . . I know not whether I ought to send my love to Mrs. Pendleton—she dose not treat me well. . . . The President has given me his Picture. . . with his and Mrs Washington's hair and with it the most flattering proof of their friendship and affection. Oh I forgot I was angry or I would not have told you this—but dont take it as a mark of forgiveness. . . . Give my love to Edmond who I long to see—Tho I care nothing about the rest of you."[4]

During the summer Pendleton's wife Susan, a native New

Yorker, went home for a visit with her father Dr. John Bard. Though he was in his seventies, he was still an active leader in Manhattan professional circles, having organized the city's first medical society. It was Dr. Bard who, as President Washington's personal physician, shortly before had called in his doctor-son as consultant during the chief executive's critical illness, directing the younger, steadier surgeon in the excision of a huge abscess that probably saved the president's life.

Caty was invited to the Bard home for a social evening during which Susan showed her a letter she had just received from her husband in Savannah. His expression of love for Susan made its way like a dagger to Caty's heart. After returning to her quarters late at night she sat down and wrote a letter to Pendleton.

New York July 27th, 1790

My Dear friend

I have just got home from a Musical party at Doctor Bards, in the course of which I wished a thousand times for you to have made one of it—it was heaven which is all I can say of it—but as Most pleasures are accompanied with pain I was obliged to go home in the rain. There is a rhyme for you—.

I have been reflecting some time to determine what I shall write to you or whether I shall write at all—When I tell you that Mrs. Pendleton has shewn me your letter, you will account for this contension of passions—yet what right have I to have any passions about it? Yes I have a right at least in that part of it which relates to me—but alas that part affects me least. . . .

It is now two oclock and I have not been in bed yet—the strongest wish I have at this moment is that you were here in my room—we should have an uninterrupted tate a tate. . . . I should look disdainfully at you—I should quarrel with you—perhaps complain a little—No that I would not do—but where am I rambling—

The papers [containing additional evidence in the claim against Congress] has not arrived and I shall loose every advantage this session—and another evil I shall suffer by it—which is that if you are not here, I shall not see you—the lord knows when—I will write again tomorrow if the vessel dont sail. God bless you—

Cath Greene[5]

In November, while on her way back to Mulberry Grove, Caty paid her usual visit to the Rutledges in Charleston. Edward advised her to extricate herself from all personal obligations by selling the Cumberland Island property, but she disagreed. The South Carolinian never resented her recalcitrance and was always tolerant of her indecisiveness and occasional impatience. "Rest assured of one truth," he had previously told her, "that I shall never forsake you or your children."[6] Now Caty wrote Wadsworth that she could not persuade Rutledge to think as she did, and she was therefore determined to leave Charleston. But she had found the eating delightful while she was there. "I have gained so much flesh," she added, "as to find my clothes pinch me."[7]

When Caty reached home she continued to correspond with Wadsworth, urging him to take action on her claim, but he would not budge. Upon hearing of it Edward Rutledge was furious. He told Caty that Wadsworth's inaction would be a stain on the memory of Nathanael and give a blow to her interests and those of her children "that the presence of your worst enemy could not effect. Curse on this half-faced fellowship."[8] He urged Caty to insist that Wadsworth fix a specific date to open the proceedings.

In March Caty got a letter from Alexander Hamilton stating that he had found one major flaw in her case against the government. Nathanael, he wrote, had evidently not notified Congress at the time he had endorsed the notes of John Banks in South Carolina. This, he thought, might pose a "tremendous bar" to the claim of indemnification. "I love you too well not to be very candid with you," he wrote. "When will we have the pleasure of seeing you this way? I need not tell you the pleasure I should take in it."[9]

In May Mulberry Grove buzzed with excitement. President George Washington was on his way to Savannah, on the last leg of an extended southern tour, and his plans called for a stopover at the plantation for a visit with Caty. On the morning of the twelfth, word came that the president had embarked on the Savannah River at Purysburg, South Carolina, several miles above Mulberry Grove, and would arrive within the hour.

Caty, Phineas Miller, little Louisa, and the house servants hurried to the landing. Presently they saw a barge-like vessel, rowed by nine captains of ships, containing the president and his traveling staff, including Anthony Wayne and other notables, coming down the river. It was a remarkable sight. The oarsmen were dressed in light blue jackets, black satin breeches, white silk stockings, and round hats with black ribbons, bearing the inscription, "Long live the President."

As the boat came to rest at the Mulberry Grove dock, Washington stepped ashore into the welcoming arms of the widow of his sturdiest lieutenant of the Revolution. Herself a valiant comrade since the earliest, darkest days of the war, Caty had first met Washington sixteen years before, at Cambridge, when she told him that her unborn child, if a boy, would become his namesake. In the years that followed, Washington had found comfort and warmth in the indomitable good cheer of the tiny Catharine Greene, and felt he could never repay his debt of gratitude.

As the president lunched and chatted with his hostess, he found welcome respite from his arduous schedule of state dinners and speeches and endless toasts that marked each day of his long southern tour. Although his conversation with Caty was a private one, and the topics never divulged by either of them, the burning issue of common interest was Caty's indemnity claim. Washington, who was in no position to counsel her about the matter except in strictest confidence, at last had the opportunity to present his views without even his wife being present.

The visit ended all too soon, but before departing, the president accepted Caty's invitation to dine with her again when he left Savannah on the trip home. Entering his boat near dusk, he and his party were rowed down the river toward the brilliantly illuminated city where three days of incessant activities awaited them. At their conclusion on Sunday, Washington returned to Mulberry Grove for a partial day of rest. This time the party came to the plantation by land as the inhabitants along the Augusta Road watched in awe. The lead chariot of the cavalcade, pulled by four horses, contained the president, his valet de chambre, two footmen, a coachman and postillion. Following was a two-horse baggage wagon, flanked by four outriders in their gay livery of red and white.

The equipage turned into the Mulberry Grove gate, rode down the drive under the long arch of moss-covered trees, and came to rest at the dwelling house where Caty greeted the company once again. After a mid-day dinner and "a delightful sojourn here of a few hours,"[10] Washington and his entourage departed in the direction of Augusta. Caty and the members of the household waved good-bye, and as the carriages and horsemen disappeared in the dusk, the silent loneliness of the wilderness descended once more upon the plantation.

By the time Caty left home again, the seat of government had been transferred to Philadelphia and she sailed there in December, 1791, to resume her campaign to induce Congress to square accounts with her late husband's estate. Going straight to the Washingtons' on High Street, she recognized their home as the same one—though restored after partial destruction by fire—in which she and Nathanael had once called on the Benedict Arnolds.

Now fully determined to stand before the Treasury Department personally to make her appeal, Caty was driven to the State House for the presentation of her multipaged indemnity claim to Secretary Alexander Hamilton and his subordinates. She was on the floor for several hours; the petition contained dozens of documents and affidavits, including a sworn statement by John Banks himself, written in a Charleston courthouse many years before, after Nathanael had collared him and marched him there to certify that he had never been in partnership with the general. Several of Nathanael's old letters were in the file, as well as statements signed by such men as Henry Knox, former South Carolina Governor John Mathews, Generals Anthony Wayne and Benjamin Lincoln, Colonel William Washington, and some of Nathanael's former aides-de-camp, many of the certifications being witnessed by Nat Pendleton, all in support of Caty.

Approving the memorial, Hamilton added his own endorsement, stating that although Nathanael technically had erred in signing his promissory notes without the government's authority, his family must never be allowed to suffer poverty in consequence. Hamilton then forwarded the petition to the House of Representatives, meeting in the building next door, for congressional action.

Within the House, Caty had the help of an ardent confederate. It was her long-time and often out-of-favor friend, Anthony Wayne, who was now a member of Congress as a representative from the first Georgia district. Wayne's election, although still regarded as one of the most fraudulent in history, was probably the event that saved the reason of the ex-soldier who, since the death of Nathanael Greene, followed by the long absences of Caty from Mulberry Grove, had drawn in on himself—a lonely, unhappy man.

He had not been able to rise above the morbid pessimism that had fallen upon his spirit. No one could arouse him, not even his children who had remained close to him at heart even though he had long been separated from them and their mother. He did not attend his daughter's wedding in Philadelphia nor did he show the slightest interest in the event. He stopped calling at the post office for his mail and left bills and taxes unpaid. Only on a single occasion did he assert himself, severely criticizing his son for not finishing his education; otherwise the fire was gone. He lacked the initiative to take any course whatever.

And then in 1791 Wayne, at the insistence of friends and office seekers, had stood against the incumbent, James Jackson, for his seat in the national Congress. In an election as rigged and crooked as any that ever took place in America, Wayne's henchmen, acting on their own, had "won" the post for him, and in July he had sailed for Philadelphia.

As yet unaware of the deceit connected with the election, Caty immediately appealed to Wayne to aid her in her petition, and it was this appeal that broke his apathy. He proposed a resolution in her behalf, spoke in favor of her claim time and time again, and spent days rounding up votes in support of her cause. His work for this measure was the one distinguishing feature of his short career as congressman. He performed all the duties Caty and her friends had hoped Jeremiah Wadsworth might have accomplished many months before.

Caty knew, however, that most Southern congressmen, influenced by South Carolina's Thomas Sumter, were prejudiced against her, reflecting the sentiment of former militia officers, some of them now in politics, who still bore old command grudges against Nathanael. Sumter's opposition was obviously personal. He inflamed his colleagues against Caty's cause by introducing a number of her late husband's letters, made public after the war, in which the general severely criticized his militia officers.

It seemed to Caty that the hopes and fears of half a lifetime were at stake that spring. An event of promise would present itself only to be followed by one of crushing disappointment. No sooner had she rejoiced over Wayne's efforts in her behalf than she got news of a movement in Georgia, largely instigated by her own lawyer and friend, Nat Pendleton, to unseat Wayne in the House of Representatives because of the fraudulent nature of his election.

James Jackson, the peppery Georgian who had lost his post in Congress by the infamous election in his state, appeared on the floor of the House to plead his own case and to lead impeachment proceedings against Wayne. His fiery eloquence excited such noisy approval among spectators that a resolution had to be passed by Congress giving the Speaker authority to clear the gallery during future disturbances. Jackson was known to oppose Caty's appeal and should his influence be brought to bear on the question, supplanting Wayne's, her cause was certainly doomed.

A week passed without further action, then in mid-March, Caty heard devastating news. The resolution to unseat Wayne was brought to a vote, and by unanimous acclaim of all fifty-eight members present, was passed. Caty felt the tragedy was as much her own as Wayne's for she had lost her one trusted ally within the House. Moreover, a resolution was offered that, if passed, would give Wayne's vacated seat immediately to Jackson, who would now be free to vent his opposition to her claim.

For five days, while arguments were heard as to whether Congress had the right to seat Jackson, Caty barely ate or slept. She held little hope of Jackson's being turned away. On March 21 word came that the House was deadlocked, twenty-nine to twenty-nine, and that the tie would have to be broken by the Speaker's vote. Caty hardly breathed until the final message came that the deciding ballot had gone against Jackson and that the state of Georgia would have to hold a new election to replace the unseated Wayne.

Now there was still hope, for Caty's issue could thus be decided upon without the menacing presence of Jackson. However, when a committee report favoring her claim was read before the House there was no Wayne to seize the advantage and call for action. Nothing whatever was done, and there were more painful days of waiting. During this time Edward Rutledge, heartbroken over the fatal illness of his wife, wrote a pitiful note of encouragement. But he could do nothing more. "My time is much occupied . . . ," he wrote, "for my dear little girl is on the eve of her departure. I must therefore bid you adieu. God grant you success."[11]

Word came at last that a bill for indemnification was before the House. Caty, in her quarters, heard that a roll call vote was being taken, but numbed by crisis after crisis, would not believe that the final hour of her great fight had arrived. When word reached her that her claim had been approved by a margin of nine votes, thirty-three to twenty-four, pent-up anxieties of years were released, and she trembled and sobbed in a paroxysm of joy.

Final victory was several days in coming. The Senate, before passing the measure, sent the bill back to the House with a minor amendment, which was readily agreed upon. Now it only awaited the president's signature, and the jubilant Caty knew that this was only a formality, as no one had congratulated her more heartily than George and Martha Washington.

On April 27, as Caty sat in the gallery of the House, the business of Congress was interrupted by the arrival at the Speaker's rostrum of Tobias Lear, secretary to the president. Lear bore a message from Washington stating that he had "this day approved and signed an act for indemnifying the estate of the late General Nathanael Greene."[12] Caty was awarded the first installment of the approximately $47,000 involved in the South Carolina indebtedness. The remainder was to be paid within three years. No one could have been happier to sign the check and note than Alexander Hamilton.

Caty, in her ecstasy, did not forget Anthony Wayne, who was living now in near-disgrace. Victorious in her own fight, she turned her energies in support of his efforts to obtain a commission in the new army thrown together for the prosecution of the Indian wars. He might have failed in politics, she said to all who would listen, but he was no less a soldier than when he had helped save his country during the Revolution. His successful forays against Indians who fought for the British during the Georgia campaign had proven his ability to deal with savage tactics. His earlier brilliant surprise at Stony Point on the Hudson had been carried off with the stealth and cunning that would have done justice to the Indians themselves.

Wayne not only obtained his commission but was appointed commander in chief of the army. The new assignment, however, marked the end of his long romance with Caty. Their careers assumed widely divergent courses. Sent west with his soldiers, Wayne again became a military hero, defeating the British-inspired Indians in the Great Lakes region and opening up a vast territory for peaceful settlement. He died at his post four years later without having returned to Georgia.

For Nat Pendleton Caty had stinging words, but fortunately for her friendship with her long-time counselor, few of her letters reached him. The *cause celebre* that had made her a national figure had also created for her political and personal enemies who regularly stole her outgoing mail. Finally in the last week in May she got a letter through to Pendleton, and by that time her bitterness had largely subsided:

I believe I ought to be satisfied that *one* of my letters to you did not arrive safe, as I remember to have expressed (perhaps) more resentment in it than you would have pardoned—for your shall I say shabby conduct to my friend Genl W[ayne]. I heard of all the proceedings. . . . I confess I felt your opposition to Genl. W. was personal not only to him—but to me . . . and I can tell you this for a truth— that had your wishes been successful—I [would] at this moment have been with my children an object of charity— and could I have brought my heart to it—a common Beggar.—Thank God Genl W kept his seat long enough to do me the most essential services, and however insignificant you may think him, it is to his exertions . . . that I principally owe my independence—You will therefore forgive the delicasy of my feeling for him.

. . . I can tell you my Dear friend that I am in good health and spirits and feel as saucy as you please—not only because I am independent, but because I have gained a compleet tryumph over some of my friends who did not wish me success—and others who doubted my judgement in managing the business—and constantly tormented me to death to give up my *obstinacy* as it was called—they are now as mute as mice—Not a word dare they utter. . . . O how sweet is revenge![13]

16 A Genius Comes to Mulberry Grove

In the fall of 1792, a sloop from New Haven, sailing westward in Long Island sound, ran aground near Hell Gate at the East River approaches to New York City. Since the tide was ebbing, the vessel could not be freed for many hours. Five men, impatient to get into town, were rowed ashore. Once landed, they hired a wagon to take them the final six miles into New York.

One of the men was Eli Whitney, a twenty-seven-year-old Yale graduate who was on the first leg of his journey to the South to take a teaching position. The opportunity had come when Caty Greene and Phineas Miller, as a favor to a family that lived across the river from Mulberry Grove, had agreed to inquire after a tutor during their trip to the East that year. Caty went to the same source that had recommended Miller to her own family: Ezra Stiles, president of Yale, who thought that Whitney would be an ideal man for the job.

Miller, who in his ever-expanding duties as Caty's manager wrote all of her business letters over his own signature, negotiated with Whitney by mail. After the young man from Connecticut agreed to the terms offered, Miller suggested that he meet the Greene family and himself in New York and sail with them to

Savannah. When Whitney wrote back that he lacked funds to make the voyage, Caty, feeling prosperous for the first time in years, advanced him the money to pay for his passage.

Arriving in New York, Whitney joined Caty and Miller at their quarters, and gave them an account of the discouraging beginning to his adventure. On the way from New Haven he had become violently seasick. After his vessel had struck the rocks at Hell Gate, requiring the uncomfortable wagon-ride into New York, he had met with another misfortune. Meeting an acquaintance from Connecticut on the street, he was chatting with him when he suddenly realized the man was broken out with smallpox.

Caty immediately insisted that he be inoculated, and sent him to the hospital of a Dr. Coggswell for the purpose. Suffering "no inconvenience" from the procedure, Whitney sat out his quarantine period, then began to enjoy himself in the company of Caty and Miller. "My situation is delightful," he wrote a New Haven friend, Josiah Stebbins. "I have spent my time in New York partly in Mrs. Green's family and the rest in viewing the city."[1] In mid-October, his "Pock nearly filled," he set sail for Savannah in company with Caty, three of her children, and Mr. Miller. Cornelia, now fourteen, was left behind, having been invited to spend the winter in Philadelphia with the Washingtons in the presidential mansion.

The voyage required almost eight days, two of them spent in trying to clear the harbor against an unfavorable wind. Caty spent much of the time nursing Whitney, who proved again to be a poor traveler. "I was very seasick indeed," he wrote Stebbins, "—eat nothing but what I puked up immediately. . . ."[2]

The travelers debarked in late October, and Whitney went with his companions to Mulberry Grove where he was to stay a short time prior to taking his teaching position. By this time Caty knew much of her new friend. He was not handsome, but she was impressed by the intelligence of his glowing black eyes. He had a rather long nose, delicate mouth, good chin, and a tall, well-proportioned physique. Born in Westborough, Massachusetts, ten years before the beginning of the war, he was the oldest of five children. Left motherless at an early age, he had been burdened by family responsibilities ever since he could remember, and reared in a most rigid Puritan atmosphere. Caty could see the markings of his hard early life, not only in his conservative, almost threadbare, manner of dress, but in his overly conscientious and meticulous behavior.

During the Revolution, still only a growing boy, he suggested to his father that they add a forge to the family shop in order to make nails which were then in great demand and bringing high prices. This first venture in manufacturing necessitated new tools which he made himself. After the war, with nails being no longer profitable, young Eli turned to producing hatpins for ladies' bonnets, walking sticks, useful products for farms, and even a fiddle for his sister which made "tolerably good music." While not producing, he spent his time in mending and repairing.

This had not been enough for the eager mind of the youthful manufacturer. He wanted a college education, but money was lacking as well as an opportunity for proper preparation for higher learning. When he was twenty, he answered an advertisement for a schoolmaster in a neighboring town, and received the appointment. His salary was board and seven dollars a month, which he scrupulously saved, paying his way for three summer terms at Leicester Academy.

His father was meanwhile remarried to a woman completely unsympathetic to Whitney's ambition to attend Yale. Over her objections, the senior Eli advanced his son $1,000 for his entrance fees and expenses. Before entering college, for which he felt he was not yet prepared, young Eli spent a term under the tutorship of Elizur Goodrich, one of the country's most noted mathematicians. Goodrich realized that Whitney possessed many of the qualities of his own son of the same age, and took Eli under his wing, passing on to him a wealth of knowledge that could not have been gained formally.

Half the year had passed at Yale before Whitney appeared. But Ezra Stiles, the college's president, was impressed by Goodrich's recommendation of the overaged but self-educated and well-tutored student. After performing acceptably on a late entrance examination, Eli convinced Stiles that he was ready for Yale. Here he had many inspirational teachers, but none more so than Stiles himself, a living library. Stiles was well-versed in everything the eighteenth-century scholar might well expect to know. He was an avid reader of books written by all of the best brains of his day, and the information he gathered was measured, sifted, and filtered down to his students.

At the conclusion of his Yale years, his money gone, Whitney somehow made ends meet until he heard of the teaching job open to him in the South. Because of his penniless situation he felt compelled to accept the position. He abhorred teaching, and during one of the winters he spent as schoolmaster to help defray the expenses of his own education he had written in his diary: "Kept school—curst nobody and called the D——l a fool. He that does not shun keeping school will be called both a D——l and a fool. . . . (Never was a pupil more bored, more unwilling than was this teacher!!!)"[3] He detested travel equally as much, and on the eve of his departure to Georgia, he wrote his brother Josiah that he was setting off to the end of the world and might never be seen alive again.

Whitney's teaching position never materialized. He wrote his father two different versions of why the job was not acceptable to him, but never told him the real reasons: his disinclination to teach and the persuasiveness of Caty Greene. She, impressed by his dexterity and cleverness in constructing items useful to the plantation, and marveling at his intellect, urged him to stay. She suggested that in his spare time he study law under Nat Pendleton.

Whitney, though ten years younger than she, had by now come under the spell of the Lady of Mulberry Grove. Heretofore exposed only to the world of men, he found himself admired, for the first time, by a beautiful woman. She opened a new window in his life and filled him with unfamiliar emotions that excited and at the same time tortured him.

Well-read and beautifully mannered, Caty, at thirty-seven, had become the finished lady that Nathanael had wanted her to be at twenty-five. "In conversation she seemed to appreciate everything said on almost any topic," wrote Elizabeth Ellet, "and frequently would astonish others by the ease with which her mind took hold of the ideas presented. . . . Her power of rendering available her intellectual stores, combined with a retentive memory, a lively imagination, and great fluency of speech, rendered her one of the most brilliant and entertaining of women. When to these gifts was added the charm of rare beauty, it cannot excite wonder that the possessor of such attraction should fascinate all who approached her."[4]

Whitney was mystified by her relationship with Phineas Miller, the gentle, fine man who openly lived and traveled with her. Their naturalness together, their tender attentions to each other, and their obvious deep concern for the other's happiness all bespoke of a well-mated man and wife. Why, though, since they both were free, had they not married? Whitney dared not ask the question but he must have wondered about it when he wrote his first letter from Georgia. "I find myself in a new natural world," he told his friend Stebbins, "and as for the moral world I believe it does not extend so far south."[5]

Whitney did not know until later that a year before his arrival Caty and Phineas had drawn up a legal agreement concerning their relationship and prospective marriage. Recorded in the county court house in Savannah, the document stipulated that Phineas would disclaim any property that might be forthcoming from a disposition of the Greene estate. No marriage ceremony had taken place, however, principally because Caty's status as Nathanael's widow had been of vital importance in her petition to Congress.

This objection was no longer present but there were other reasons Caty was not yet ready to be legally bound to Phineas. Married women in that day became essentially the property of their husbands, forfeiting all personal rights, including jurisdiction over their own children by previous marriages. They could not transact business, retain earnings, make property settlements, or take court action. Only widows and spinsters had such rights. In Caty's case there were, as well, more human motives for retaining her unattached status. Not only was she reluctant to relinquish the title of Lady Greene and thus forfeit the honor and esteem accorded to the wife of a fallen hero but she was not yet entirely willing to disqualify herself in the eyes of other male admirers.

"During this time," Whitney wrote later to his father, "I heard much said of the extreme difficulty of ginning Cotton, that is, separating it from its seeds. There were a number of respectable Gentlemen at Mrs. Greene's who all agreed that if a machine could be invented which could clean the cotton with expedition, it would be a great thing both to the Country and to the inventor. I involuntarily happened to be thinking on the Subject, and struck out a plan of a Machine in my mind. . . ."[6]

Whitney showed a drawing of a contemplated model to Phineas Miller, a mechanical expert himself, who was much pleased with it. Caty was then consulted and agreed to furnish all funds for the construction of and experimentation with such a machine. She pledged money from her recently gained fortune in the name of Miller, who managed her financial affairs. Thus was spawned the firm of Miller and Whitney, a partnership soon to be legally formed with Caty's backing. An upstairs room at Mulberry Grove was converted into a laboratory to which only Miller, Whitney, and Caty were admitted.

Whitney constructed his first crude model with materials gathered at the plantation. "One of the Miss Greenes had . . . a coile of iron wire to make a bird cage," he wrote Stebbins, "and being embarrassed for want of sheet iron, and seeing this wire hung in the parlor, it struck me I could make teeth with that."[7]

One evening, as he sat in the parlor with Caty and Miller, as well as several guests of the plantation including Nat and Susan Pendleton, Whitney remarked that he had reached an impasse. The unfinished model was brought downstairs and placed on the dinner table. As the company gathered around, Whitney cranked the wooden cylinder of his new machine, applying raw cotton from the upper side. As the fibers were caught up by the cylinder teeth and carried through a row of narrow slots, the seeds were wrenched free and dropped below. There remained one last problem to be overcome. The fibers, though separated from their seeds, continued to cling to the cylinder teeth, eventually clogging the slots. It was Caty who first perceived a solution. Seizing a hearth brush standing at the nearby fireplace, she applied it to the cylinder. The bristles were too limber to remove the cotton efficiently, but Whitney was impressed. "Thank you for the hint," he said. "I have it now."[8]

Whitney constructed a full-scale model, powered by one man and a horse, that cleaned cotton far better than older machines that required the labor of fifty men. He was offered 100 guineas for title to his gin. "I am now so sure of success," he wrote his father, "that ten thousand dollars, if I saw the money counted out to me, would not tempt me to give up my rights or relinquish the object."[9]

These were happy days for Caty. Mulberry Grove was humming with the excitement of the cotton gin, and there was a constant flow of visitors to the plantation. By the spring of 1793 all five of her children were at home, reunited for the first time since George had sailed to France almost five years before. "He was strong, in full health, thoroughly educated," Cornelia said of her brother, ". . . a young physical and intellectual athlete, so well equipped for the world's work, and on whom so many prayers and ambitious hopes centered."[10]

George was full of his recent adventures in Paris where events of the French Revolution unfolded on all sides during his entire residence. At first he had been a guest in the Lafayette home on the Rue de Bourbon but later was sent along with the Lafayettes' young son to the boarding school administered by Monsieur

Frestel, the marquis' own childhood teacher. Here Madame Lafayette paid a daily visit to the boys until it was no longer safe to
be out among the murderous mobs that surged through the
streets. George Greene began to write his mother to send him
money for his passage home, and it was well that she complied;
by the time of his departure, the Lafayettes were languishing in
separate prisons and M. Frestel had abandoned his school to rush
their son to a mountain hideout.

George Greene returned home and plunged himself happily
into the country life at Mulberry Grove. Of all Caty's children,
he was the one she missed the most during long separations.
They had weathered many trials together, many of which he had
been too young to recall. His mother would always remember the
warmth of his little body against hers during the Boston bombardment of 1776, and the flow of strength and comfort that had
passed between them as they waited out that terrifying night,
he sleeping intermittently, and she keeping vigil over him.

Only a few weeks after George's return from France, tragedy
struck. He and a friend named Stits had launched a canoe for
an outing on the Savannah. The river was swollen by spring rains
and the currents and eddies were more menacing than usual.
The canoe was upset and young Stits, deeply submerged, came
struggling to the surface gasping for air. He was too nearly
drowned to take notice of his companion. Finally, after making
his way to shore, he scrambled to the edge of the bank, exhausted.
When he recovered his senses he looked out toward midstream
and saw no trace of the canoe or George Greene.

Hurrying back to Mulberry Grove, Stits spread the alarm, and
members of the household rushed to the river bank. Caty was
beside herself. A frantic search was launched, but no sign of young
Greene was found. Darkness finally forced the searchers back to
the dwelling. Here George's family and friends spent a tortured
night, holding only a faint hope of hearing his cheerful voice
announce that he was safely back home. But all was silent except
for the rush of the river.

At dawn the search was renewed and the lifeless body of
George Greene was found on the shore's edge near Mulberry
Grove. On the following day his body was taken down the river,
as Nathanael's had been, first to a Savannah dock, then by hearse
to the colonial cemetery. After a solemn funeral, it was placed
in the Graham vault beside that of his father.

Caty and her stricken family made their forlorn, heartbroken way back to their home on the bank of the river that had claimed their adored son and brother. Caty could never look at the beautiful waterway thereafter without a pang of anguish, and her surviving children later recalled that she was never quite the same again.

The plantation's busy life began to stir once more and it was well the inhabitants of Mulberry Grove could again turn their thoughts to the cotton gin. During the summer, when Eli Whitney sailed for New Haven to set up his shop for the manufacture of the new machines, Caty found her forlorn heart fighting another pang. She kept herself busy every minute, making plans with Miller for the future of the new enterprise.

Whitney's reports from New England were anxiously awaited, and each letter brought more encouraging news. On the way east Eli had stopped off at Philadelphia to apply for a patent to Thomas Jefferson, secretary of state. He was assured of success. Sailing on to New Haven he had hired several workmen to manufacture full-scale gins, while he himself superintended every detail of the manufacturing process, designing and making his own tools. Within weeks the unique manufactory had taken shape, and by midwinter gins were already under construction.

During the following spring Caty bought an ad in the *Gazette,* published in Savannah, containing Miller's description of the gins, and announcing that they would soon be available at Mulberry Grove. The proposition offered was that, in lieu of a cash fee, two-fifths of the ginned product would be charged by the company, while the planters retained three-fifths of the yield.

Two weeks later a happy but pale Whitney, who had again become "damned seasick" during his nine-day voyage, arrived at the plantation with his patent secure. He immediately assembled one of his machines which Phineas claimed was even superior to the one he and Caty had described in their advertisement. Cautious and circumspect as always, Eli was caught up, nonetheless, in Caty's and Miller's enthusiasm. Planters came from far and near, eager to see the new invention. Some secrecy yet prevailed, and only friends were actually allowed admission to the outbuilding where the first gin had been installed.

Whitney offered Miller half-interest in his patent for $1,000, but it was a sum Phineas had no access to, except through Caty. When she made the money available in June, partnership papers were signed that officially launched the firm of Miller and Whitney in business. Caty, the company's only immediate source of capital, was unnamed in the legal papers. She wanted it that way; this was man's work. But between her and Miller there was a private understanding, unwritten, unbreakable, bonded only by love, that she would have an equal share in his half of the venture.

Late in the summer Whitney prepared to return to New Haven to continue production of the gins, but on the eve of his departure he developed chills and fever. For a fortnight Caty nursed him through his illness with a tenderness he had not known since babyhood, then sent him on his way with potions and motherly admonitions.

The year 1794 was deceptively happy for the budding enterprise. Credit was available to the partners, largely because Caty was willing to pledge, as collateral, portions of her late husband's estate. Rejoicing in the auspicious start of the undertaking, certain that the firm was on its way to fortune, Caty made money available to buy up sites where water power and favorable terrain would make the cotton-cleaning machines most profitable.

The coming of the first gins to Savannah marked the beginning of a new era in the South, and New England industrialists were already sending their representatives to Georgia to reap the promised harvest. One such agent was John C. Nightingale, twenty-four-year-old heir of a prominent mercantile family of Providence, who entered into a cotton planting enterprise with Phineas Miller. Brought to Mulberry Grove, he promptly fell in love with Martha Greene, known affectionately as "Patty," though she was only seventeen and quite overshadowed by the beauty of her forty-year-old mother.

Caty liked young John from the first and was a pleased although sometimes amused observer of her daughter's shyly eager response to his attentions. The courtship flourished in an atmosphere of encouragement on Caty's part, and in the spring of 1795, Mulberry Grove was bustling with preparations for Patty's marriage to John. The huge parlor was thrown open, windows washed to a sparkle, drapes and furniture aired and brushed, and floors polished. The kitchen rattled with activity as a feast was made ready. Patty stood nervously while her beautiful wedding dress and trousseau were fitted. Caty personally saw to the arrangements of greens and May flowers from the garden. Finally, with Caty the gracious hostess greeting countless guests and friends, the wedding proved to be the plantation's most gala event since colonial days when the wealthy Tory, John Graham, had lavishly entertained his Savannah friends in the same house.

Within a few days Caty and Miller received news of the first disaster suffered by the cotton gin firm. A letter from Whitney told of returning to New Haven from a business trip to find his shop destroyed by fire, along with all his tools, materials, and a number of cotton gins under construction. Caty and Phineas could see through Eli's brave letter and realized that he felt the fire might well put an end to the entire enterprise.

Though Caty had wept when she first read the message, she drew strength from Miller's calm acceptance and helped him compose a reply. They recognized that the fire was a serious setback but were certain it was not a mortal one. They must not be disheartened; they must persevere and not relinquish the pursuit. It would be "very extraordinary if two young men, in the prime of life, with some share of ingenuity, with a little knowledge of the world, a great deal of industry, and a considerable command of property, should not be able to sustain such a stroke of misfortune as this. . . ."[11]

The fire proved Whitney's genius. Weakened by illness, stunned by the misfortune, but encouraged by the letter from Georgia, he set to work rebuilding his factory and hand-making his tools. It had taken him two years to make the first twenty gins. Now, without his precious papers and drawings before him, but with the memory of everything he had done toward their production fresh in his mind, he was able to write, seven months after the fire, that twenty-six machines were ready to be shipped to Georgia.

In the summer of 1795 Miller, Caty, and all three of her daughters sailed to New England to visit young Nat, who was in school in Connecticut, and Caty's father and family at the old home place on Block Island. During the trip the visitors were guests of Eli Whitney in New Haven, where they inspected the gin factory and watched the manufacture of the machines that were already beginning to revolutionize the South's economy.

Caty and Miller believed implicitly in Whitney's ability to produce gins fast enough, in spite of adversity, to relieve the present demand for them. Where they lacked confidence was in the company's capacity to raise sufficient funds to insure the continued manufacture of the machines at the necessary rate. Neither wanted to tax the Greene estate further, but needing capital desperately, they became interested in an investment scheme that promised to pay huge dividends in a matter of months. It was a land development plan, promoted by New Englanders calling themselves the Yazoo Company. Their aim was to buy up cheap land in Georgia to sell later, at great profit, to prospective cotton planters rushing to the state. The conservative Whitney opposed the idea, but Caty and Miller were impatient to sail home to invest in the new company.

Yazoo—it was a name Caty would never forget.

17 Collapse of a Scheme

John Nightingale, Caty's new son-in-law, was an original member of the Yazoo Company. Made up of New England industrialists, they offered to buy from the Georgia legislature some 35,000,000 acres of undeveloped land. This property, claimed by the state, extended as far west as the Yazoo River, a tributary of the Mississippi. For this huge tract of potential farmland the bidding price was a paltry $500,000, amounting to a cost of one and a half cents per acre, or seventy acres per dollar.

Nightingale, who was certain the legislature would sell at this incredible price, presented the plan to Caty and Miller. Envisioning enormous profits that would insure permanent working capital for the cotton gin firm, they invested heavily, buying shares with promissory notes signed by Caty and secured by assets of the Greene estate.

No sooner had the state government agreed to the transaction, and the terms made public, than a great storm of protest descended upon the legislature. The people, not misled as easily as the politicians had expected, clearly sensed that something was amiss. When it was later disclosed that members of the Georgia House and Senate had received free shares in the land company, an angry wave of resentment engulfed the entire state, and citizens denounced the land scheme as the "Great Yazoo Fraud."

Many innocent families in Georgia and New England, unaware that the legislature had been bribed, were caught up in the affair, investing all the money they could scrape together in the Yazoo Company. How much did Caty and Miller know of the conspiracy? Even if Nightingale had concealed information about the bribery, their lawyer, Nat Pendleton, was in a position as the state's chief justice to warn them of the intrigue involved. What was his counsel to them?

Pendleton's own position was a paradox. He had long since come to think of the Georgia legislature as a seat of corruption, and in his private letters wrote of the Yazoo affair with disgust. But publicly he supported the transaction, wrote briefs in its behalf, and staked his reputation and political fortunes in Georgia on the success of the plan. He had either convinced himself that the Yazoo Act, however reprehensible, was legitimate, or was pressured—or even bribed—into upholding it. Later, there was evidence that he bought Yazoo land in partnership with Miller, but even Caty was not made aware of this clandestine agreement.

The Yazoo question tore Georgia asunder. Caty derived no satisfaction from the fact that the land company's political champion was James Gunn. Now a United States Senator, he was the same bellicose, raucous Gunn who had once challenged Nathanael Greene to a duel. Gunn did not bother to resign from the Senate; he simply abandoned his responsibilities at the national level and remained at home to help ram the Yazoo Act through the Georgia legislature. He strode about the streets of Augusta, then the state capital, arrayed in broadcloth, beaver hat, and tan boots, carrying a whip with which he threatened any legislator that voiced disapproval of the Yazoo scheme.

Leading the anti-Yazoo movement was another old nemesis of Caty's, James Jackson, the fiery ex-militia hero who had opposed her indemnification claim and who had led the proceedings to unseat Anthony Wayne in the House of Representatives. But though Jackson was again opposed to Caty's financial interests, she knew by now that his position regarding the Yazoo issue was morally the correct one, and that her own investments in the company were in imminent peril.

It was largely the fierce fight put up by Jackson that brought about the Rescinding Act of the following year, but only after the stormy ex-congressman had fought a number of duels. In one of them he was stabbed in the chest with a knife that missed entering his heart by half an inch. As governor in 1796, his influence led to the voiding of the Yazoo Act. Litigation on the national level continued long afterward, but for practical purposes the matter was settled in Georgia that year before a great crowd in the public square at the new capital of Louisville. Drawing "fire from Heaven" through a magnifying glass, Jackson applied the flame to the Yazoo papers, destroying all state records of the legislation and land sales.

The Yazoo collapse cost Caty and Miller their ready cash, tied up estate property pledged for collateral, and severely compromised the credit of the cotton gin firm. It embarrassed Caty in her relationship with Whitney, who from the beginning had opposed the land scheme as a means of raising capital. Moreover, it cost her the company of several New England friends who, losing their expected fortune in the South, returned to their eastern homes.

Nat Pendleton, his political career in the state ruined by his public support of the Yazoo Act, his heart full of hate for Georgia and Georgians, his relationship with his beloved Caty severely strained, moved with his wife to New York. Here he became a Federal judge and a close friend and associate of Alexander Hamilton, a connection that was destined to have a sad ending.

That John Nightingale, Miller's planting partner, had been an officer in the Yazoo Company now became an inescapable and discomfiting bit of public knowledge. The name of Eli Whitney, attached to that of Miller, was now suspect. Georgia farmers, taking advantage of the gin firm's humiliation, gained sympathy in their efforts to have the company's patent rights set aside. They called the partners greedy monopolists, citing their exclusive control over the machines that cost the growers two-fifths of their crop to have it ginned. It was inevitable that pirating began, and with it rumors spread that cotton ginned by Miller and Whitney was inferior to that processed by other machines. Such gossip was even disseminated in Great Britain, upsetting the company's plans to secure the English trade.

All of their trials served only to bring Caty and Phineas closer together. Referring to him as her "other self," she later confided to a friend that she fully expected their love to be renewed in heaven. While on a visit to the Washingtons in Philadelphia during the spring of 1796, counseled by their hosts, they came to a decision that would bring into their lives a new dimension of happiness they previously had denied themselves.

It had been eleven years since Phineas had joined the family of the Nathanael Greenes as tutor to the children. Struck by Caty's wit and beauty, he had soon found the pleasure of being in her company giving way to agonized longing. It was not until after the death of General Greene, whom he highly respected, that he first felt free to express his feelings to Caty. To his utter amazement and joy, he found that she returned his love. He was compelled to share her with others during the unstable days of her early widowhood. Ultimately she pledged herself, without binding herself legally, to him alone. In spite of their age difference—Miller was the younger by ten years—the two were ideally mated. In the troubled years that followed, however, the fact of their unmarried state, with its attending strains and stares, not only did little to advance their peace of mind but, as pointed out by the Washingtons, became a mark against them in the prosecution of their public affairs.

On the last day of May, in a Philadelphia ceremony witnessed by only the Washingtons and a few other intimate friends, and so private that it did not make the local papers, Caty knelt beside Phineas and heard a clergyman pronounce them man and wife.

For a few blissful days they were able to forget the problems that faced them at home. They sent word of their marriage to Eli Whitney in Connecticut, and when the news reached him it came as a crushing blow. Several months would pass before he could express himself on the subject, and before Caty and Phineas came to know how deeply he had been hurt. Though he had been aware of their relationship at the very beginning of his career in Georgia, his initial shock had given way to tolerant but somewhat painful acceptance, and there had then grown between him and Caty a strong covenant of affection, based on common interests, a subtle understanding of the other's needs, intellectual compatibility, and mutual respect. As long as Caty lived, she would be Eli's only true emotional tie to womanhood. Prior to the wedding in Philadelphia, he had never felt that Phineas stood between his and Caty's special feeling for each other, but rather that the two men were members of a three-way partnership, with Caty as their common joy and inspiration in one of the great adventures of the world. Now, for Whitney, this was all changed, and he suddenly felt very much alone.

When the Millers returned to Mulberry Grove, they found

their ginning company virtually bankrupt and their credit gone. They were reduced to the "cruel and mortifying necessity" of selling more land from the Greene estate to procure cash, and the South Carolina property that had been awarded the general by that state's legislature brought only half its value.

In May, 1797, the first patent suit brought by Miller and Whitney against one of the surreptitious gin manufacturers was heard in Savannah. Phineas, himself despondent for the first time, wrote Eli of the result. "The tide of popular opinion was running in our favor," his letter said; "the Judge was well disposed towards us, and many friends were with us who adhered firmly to our cause. . . . The Judge gave a charge to the jury pointedly in our favor; after which the defendant himself told an acquaintance of his, that he would give two thousand dollars to be free of the verdict—and yet the jury gave it against us after a consultation of about an hour. . . . Thus after four years of assiduous labour, fatigue and difficulty are we again set afloat by a new and unexpected obstacle. . . . The actual crisis has now arrived which I have long mentioned as possible . . . our insolvency as a partnership."[1]

A letter came from Whitney, who had given way under the strain of adversity. "The extreme embarrassments which have been for a long time accumulating upon me are now become so great," he wrote, "that it will be impossible for me to struggle against them many days longer. . . . I have labored hard against the strong current of disappointment, which has been threatening to carry us down the cataract, but I have labored with a shattered oar and struggled in vain, unless some speedy relief is obtained. I am now quite far enough advanced in life to think seriously of marrying. I have ever looked forward with pleasure to an alliance with an amiable and virtuous companion, as a source from whence I have expected one day to derive the greatest happiness. . . . [But] my own unremitted attention has been devoted to our business. . . . It is better not to live than to live as I have for three years past. Toil, anxiety and disappointment have broken me down. My situation makes me perfectly miserable."[2]

"It is very true," Phineas wrote back, "that I have the advantage of you in partaking with a beloved partner of my life the sweets of domestic felicity—but you will remember my dear Whitney that this is not my fault—and that of the burthens occasioned by our failure I have at least borne my proportion. . . . If we have lost money I shall be tolerably well satisfied if by prudence and industry we can be preserved from ruin and preserve our character and integrity."[3]

Word came back from Whitney that, having despaired of making a living solely by the manufacture of cotton gins, he had entered into a contract with the Federal government for the manufacture of firearms. It was a hard decision to make, for it meant he would have to remain for the most part in the East. But he would constantly long for Mulberry Grove, where he had enjoyed a society he had never known before. Above and beyond his attachment to Caty, he would sorely miss the new social freedom he had discovered under her guidance, and the stimulation of his friendships with the eminent gentlemen who flocked to the plantation.

By the fall of 1798, the poverty of Caty and her family having reached alarming proportions, a notice was placed in a Savannah paper advertising the sale of Mulberry Grove. But there were no buyers, and when creditors and tax collectors pressed, twelve slaves from the rice plantation were sold to raise critically needed cash. Miller wrote Whitney in early 1799 that no relief was in sight. "The prospect of making any thing by ginning in this state is at an end," he said. "Surreptitious gins are erected in every part of the country; and the jurymen at Augusta have come to an understanding among themselves that they will never give a verdict in our favor, let the merits of the case be as they may."[4]

In January, 1800, news came to the plantation that added to the gloom of the unhappy household. George Washington was dead. Caty had saved among her priceless possessions her last previous letter from Martha, written three winters before, near the close of the president's second term, telling of the happiness with which he had looked forward to his retirement at Mount Vernon. But poor health had diminished his pleasure, and now a sudden attack of quinsy had carried him away. Caty's grief at losing such a friend at such a critical time in her life was profound. This remarkable man, who had held the country together during its most hopeless days, had never been too busy to listen to her personal problems and to offer counsel and practical help. While she and her family were mourning the news from Mount Vernon, another tragic message arrived. A letter from Edward Rutledge's son told how his father, then governor of South Carolina, having arrived home from a session of the legislature depressed over political misfortune and broken in health, had died a few days later. Thus within three weeks Caty had lost two of her truest friends.

For the Millers, and Caty's children, the new century began under the most ominous circumstances. The economic depression of 1800 gripped the South and precluded all chances of a favorable market for the sale of Mulberry Grove. To satisfy unpaid taxes, county collectors put the plantation on the auction block.

On August 6, 1800, the estate was "knocked down" to a Major Edward Harden for $15,000. Fortunately, Caty, Phineas, and the children were not present for the excruciating event. They had moved earlier in the year, along with John and Patty Nightingale, to Cumberland Island, where they made their home on the property that Nathanael Greene had bought near the close of the Revolution.

18 Life on a Georgia Sea Isle

Lying within easy view of Spanish East Florida, and separated
from the mainland only by marshes and tidal waterways, the Georgia isle of Cumberland presented a balmy refuge for the displaced
family from Mulberry Grove. At the lower end of the island, a
few hundred yards from the foaming surf and hard white beach,
where wind-hollowed sand dunes overlooked the sea, Nathanael
Greene, fourteen years before, had begun the construction of
his family's future home. After his untimely death the same year,
work was discontinued, and only the foundation stones were in
place when Caty and her family sailed to Cumberland in the spring
of 1800.

They moved into a dwelling on the island two miles north
of the home site picked by Nathanael, but Caty and Phineas immediately made plans to renew construction of the house the general
had begun. Manpower was to be furnished by slaves that still
remained from the Mulberry Grove colony. At the same time
they planted vegetable and flower gardens and cleared land for
great sugar cane and cotton fields. To finance the undertaking,
and to help clear up immediate debts, a contract was let for the
cutting of a forest of live oak. (Eli Whitney's brother, Josiah, was

an agent of the Millers in the lumber business, and later helped secure government contracts.) A work gang of 112 men assembled at the house. "All the heads of the different gangs were invited to our table," Cornelia Greene wrote a friend, "so that with the noise without and trouble within doors which lasted 17 days, we were on the verge of distraction. I thought my mother would scarcely keep her reason, particularly as we had all the time either some friend or stranger to visit us."[1]

Cornelia, now twenty-two, and Louisa, seventeen, were still single. Caty, recognizing the hazard of their seclusion on an isolated island, made sure that a sufficient number of eligible males were among the guests invited to Cumberland. One of the first to come was a Savannah physician, Dr. Lemuel Kollock, who had been family doctor to Caty and her children since setting up practice in Georgia the year of the cotton gin invention. A native of Massachusetts, he had entered a medical preceptorship in Newport under Dr. Isaac Senter, Caty's and Nathanael's close friend of Revolutionary days. During one of the numerous trips Phineas Miller and Caty made to Newport, they persuaded Kollock to set up practice in Savannah, where he became immediately successful and helped organize Georgia's first state medical society.

When he arrived in Georgia, Kollock, at twenty-six, was still a bachelor, thirteen years younger than Caty. He was in frail health and had lost the use of one eye, but his intellect and personality made him much sought after by the women of Savannah society. He fell into an age group that had such a strong appeal for Caty as she approached her middle years, and he in turn seems to have preferred her company to that of younger ladies.

Now that she was married, Caty had in mind a connection between Dr. Kollock and one of her daughters, and she persuaded him to buy property near their Cumberland home. Louisa was a bit young for the physician, however, and Cornelia, hearing that he had made a number of romantic conquests in Savannah, was not as tolerant of his penchant for sowing wild oats as was Caty. "When he will consent to leave all vulgar pleasures and Earth-born enjoyments behind him is quite uncertain if ever," Cornelia wrote a friend.[2]

In many ways, Cornelia was more like her mother than any of the other children, being endowed with much of her vivacity and wit. A few years before, Caty had written a friend that none of her girls were pretty. Cornelia was only thirteen at the time, and the wondrous changes of adolescence had not yet taken place.

During her last years at Mulberry Grove she had become a lovely, popular girl. "That she should capture all of Savannah is not surprising," a young friend named John McQueen had written of her,[3] and the youthful admirer's father during an exploration in Florida had named a landmark "Mount Cornelia" in her honor.

From New Haven, a letter came to Caty from a lonesome Eli Whitney. He asked her help and advice in his plan to undertake a serious courtship of Cornelia, enclosing a note to her, to be delivered only with her mother's approval. But Caty refused. "Because," wrote Phineas Miller to Eli, "in the first place, a Person pretending to be your friend has taken the most artful and unwearied pains to impugn a young mind with prejudice against you—and in the second place Mrs. Miller is principled against using her influence in such cases."[4] What Caty meant was that if Eli expected to court a daughter of hers he would have to do it on his own. She suggested, through her husband's letters, that he might consider paying the island a visit.

The man attempting to discredit Whitney in Cornelia's eyes was Ethan Clarke, a Newport importer of wine and spirits, and an old friend of Nathanael's. Clarke was a frequent visitor to Cumberland where he made Caty's and Miller's lives miserable by his exorbitant property claims arising out of a debt owed by Miller, who could not scrape up sufficient cash to repay him.

When Whitney heard of Clarke's attempts to influence Cornelia against him, he referred to him in his next letter as "this infernal fiend of Perdition . . . abominable villain . . . vile hypocrite . . . infernal wretch . . . devil." He said he had it in his mind to visit Cumberland the following winter, as Caty had suggested, but only if he had some hope of success. "If there be no prospect of obtaining the object of my wishes," he wrote, "prudence would perhaps dissuade me from the attempt."[5] Clarke was successful in his endeavor to poison Cornelia's mind and Miller was obliged to write Whitney the sad truth.

In late summer Caty and part of her family, all being ill, moved into a cottage on the isolated south end of the island, more closely exposed to the sea air which they hoped would improve their health. When they recovered they were so well-pleased with their situation that they remained in the small dwelling, which stood near the site of their large house that was in the making. They now had easy access to their flower gardens, orchards, and fields which were yielding a beautiful harvest.

The area was called "Dungeness" after the retreat established there by James Oglethorpe, the founder of Georgia, who named it for the country seat of the Earl of Cumberland. Situated beside a marshy creek, his hunting lodge had occupied a plateau created by a great mound of shells accumulated by the Indians for centuries. Here Caty's family home was now being built, surrounded by the ever-expanding areas under cultivation that were gradually replacing the vast live-oak forests of Oglethorpe's day.

During the fall Caty made her first visit away from her island home. The occasion was a gala houseparty given by James Seagrove, a former New Yorker who now lived at St. Marys, a port on the Georgia mainland opposite Cumberland. Phineas was detained at home on business, but Caty was accompanied by all of her children and a train of visiting young relatives from New England. During a day of fun Caty accepted a dare to walk from one end of a scaffold to the other. As she approached the far end, mischievous members of the company, including her host, would not let her come down until she paid a toll. Giggling, she turned around and began to run the other way, but her foot slipped and she fell to the ground, severely spraining her ankle.

She was carried to her room where she remained for several days, unable to walk. Cornelia wrote to a friend that the accident provided the party with a rare treat: "It was apology for our remaining most of the time in her chamber."[6] Though she often clashed with her mother, Cornelia was always aware of her great attraction and in later life remembered her as "the most remarkable combination of intellectual power and physical beauty I have personally encountered in womanhood."[7]

After returning to Cumberland, Caty and her family did not leave the island again until the Christmas of 1801 when Dr. Kollock influenced them to visit his home in Savannah. While there they took a wistful trip to the old homestead at Mulberry Grove and found it occupied by a family of strangers. When they were back at Dr. Kollock's once more, fiddlers were brought in and the company had a lively dance. One of the reasons for the trip was that Caty's health had been poor, but the carefree fun during this visit restored her vigor.

Early in the following year, Cornelia was introduced to Peyton Skipwith, Jr., a member of a prominent Virginia family, who came to Georgia seeking an opening in the rapidly expanding cotton business. Skipwith invested in land on Cumberland as a planting partner of Phineas Miller and John Nightingale, Patty's husband. Skipwith and Cornelia fell in love and were married in April.

Phineas, as the island's justice of the peace, performed the ceremony. Shortly afterward the newlyweds moved to an estate on the mainland, a few miles from St. Marys.

Phineas was often away from Cumberland, continuing his tenacious fight to save the firm of Miller and Whitney. He continued to bring lawsuits against Georgia businessmen who blatantly infringed upon the patent rights with little fear of the law. Finally he offered to sell the patent to the State of South Carolina, but because of his own connection with the Yazoo scandal he thought it best for Eli to come South to press the transaction.

In the spring of 1802, Caty and Phineas had word that Whitney, having completed negotiations with the South Carolina General Assembly in Columbia, was on his way to Cumberland. Meeting him at the Dungeness dock, they perceived at once that he bore good news. The legislature, he said, had agreed to buy patent rights to the gin for $50,000. As Caty and her husband heard the tidings that the maligned, harrassed partnership was at last solvent, they danced a little jig of happiness on the dock.

Whitney's pride welled up within him as he recounted the story of his recent adventures. Hating water travel and his long sieges of sea sickness, he had come south from Connecticut in a sulky, a single horse employed for the entire journey. Reaching Columbia he had spent two weeks attending the sessions of the legislature, soliciting the support of the lawmakers in his bid to sell the patent rights to the state of South Carolina. It had been a time of anguish, more tedious and frustrating than the clean act of manufacturing gins or muskets. For the first time he appreciated the fatiguing nature of the type of legal work Phineas Miller had been performing for years in behalf of the partnership. An hour after the favorable vote he had set forth to Georgia to give Caty and Miller the news they had so long hungered for.

Whitney's days on the island, with the family he truly loved, were happy ones, and he savored the hours of rest and relaxation. Then setting out for New Haven once more, he returned to Savannah by canoe, and drove off alone in his sulky, pulled all the way again by his unbelievably durable horse.

In 1803 Caty and her family moved into their new Dungeness dwelling, a huge structure that rose four stories above the cellar, with four-foot walls of "tabby," a rock-hard mixture of shells, lime, and broken stone. Above the basement the mansion had twenty rooms, sixteen of which were warmed by fireplaces having access to four enormous chimneys. (The towering, ghostly walls that today mark the site of Dungeness are the ruins of a later nineteenth century dwelling that occupied the same spot as Caty's home.)

Surrounding the structure, the interior of which was still far from finished, were twelve acres of countless varieties of tropical and semi-tropical flowers, shrubs, and fruit trees, divided from the fields of cotton and cane by a high wall of masonry. In the rear of the main house, terraced gardens bordered by silvery olive trees led to the boathouse and landing on a nearby stream. To the front of the house was a tree-lined avenue and on each side of the gate was a noble magnolia, planted years before by Nathanael.

Caty at last had her dream house and she intended to share it with as many of her relatives and friends as possible. In addition to herself, Phineas, Nat, and Louisa, the permanent residents of the mansion included her younger sister and brother-in-law, Phebe and Ray Sands, the Sands children, and several house servants. Patty and her rapidly-growing family, who lived on the island a few miles north of Dungeness, and Cornelia, her husband, and young son, who resided on the mainland, were often present for week-long house parties. Any number of other relatives and visitors were frequently on hand. Few Rhode Islanders ever came to Georgia without a stopover at Dungeness, and old Savannah friends were often house guests, not rarely for a season at a time.

Filling the mansion with friends not only provided her daughters company but was Caty's way of allaying her own loneliness. The constant rush of visitors served to temper the intense feeling of remoteness that pervaded Dungeness. At night, for hours on end, the only sounds were those of the wind and rolling surf.

Cumberland, an island consisting mostly of forests and marshes, had no villages; dwellings and farms scattered here and there were the only signs of civilization. From Dungeness to the north end of the island, a little less than eighteen miles distant, a road, straight as a rod, called "Grand Avenue" by the inhabitants, had been cut through the dense forest that covered the isle's interior. Shaded by intertwining branches of live-oak and their graceful pendants of Spanish moss, the road gave the impression of a fairyland tunnel. ("Grand Avenue" remains today in its haunting, unspoiled state.) It was the line of communication for the island, connecting Caty's plantation near the south end with the homes and farms to the north.

Providing food for the teeming household at Dungeness was

never a problem. The orchards and fields yielded enormous quantities of fruits and vegetables, and fish and game abounded. Giant sea turtles trapped on the beaches provided Caty with the opportunity of making soup that was her own particular delicacy. Deer were so plentiful that venison became a staple. Completely self-supporting and independent of the outside world, the plantation, ably managed by Phineas Miller and Ray Sands, soon began to yield a handsome cash income as well. The sea-island cotton cultivated on Cumberland was considered the best that could be raised, and lumber from the live-oak forests, barged over to the docks of St. Marys, was shipped to ports around the world. A contract for the timber was let by the Federal government for the purpose of building men-of-war. Cumberland oak, used in the famed hull of the U.S.S. *Constitution,* would help win for it the nickname of "Old Ironsides."

The household at Dungeness was a happy one and Caty watched its success with pride. Almost a year had passed, and Caty felt a bit of the peace she had longed for. She and Phineas worked in the garden, planning additional beds and discussing the variety of plants they would like to add. During the fall he went to St. Augustine to procure tropical plants. While in the process he punctured his finger on a thorn. By the time he returned to Dungeness, the finger had become sore and he showed it to Caty. She applied poultices, but the next day the pain and swelling were worse. Alarmed, Caty called in Dr. Kollock who diagnosed blood poisoning and confided to her that the condition was critical.

Giving up her other duties, she nursed her husband by the hour, agonizing with him through each chill and each episode of fevered delirium. Every morning she examined his countenance, hoping against hope to find him looking better, but realizing at length that he was growing weaker. Death came on December 7, ravishing Caty beyond reconciliation and casting a pall of sadness over the entire island.

Thus died the gentlest of men, whose secluded life as a tutor took such an abrupt turn when he fell in love with, and eventually married, the mother of the children he had come to teach. He had participated in the development of a new machine which at the time of his death had brought more grief than reward, but which he knew was well on the way to vitalizing the economy of the South. In a dark hour of the enterprise, when Eli Whitney was prepared to capitulate to adversity, Phineas simply refused to allow his partner to "relinquish the pursuit." In his attempt to raise capital, he had made one terrible mistake, his participation in the Yazoo debacle, which added to the embarrassment of his family as well as the cotton gin firm. But, instead of giving way to a spirit of self-reproach, he had toiled all the harder toward the accomplishment of the success he knew the partnership deserved.

Phineas was dead, at thirty-nine, and his name passed into virtual oblivion. The part he played in the development of the cotton gin was soon forgotten. His grave in a Dungeness garden is today unmarked, and no physical description of him has been set down for history. But a sufficient number of his letters have been preserved to give a glimpse of the traits that endeared him to all and won for him the heart and hand of Caty Greene.

19 Toward a Spring of Hope

At the time of Miller's death Eli Whitney was again in the South, negotiating with the states of North Carolina and Tennessee for the sale of rights to the cotton gin. While in Raleigh he had word that South Carolina had revoked its purchase of the previous year, and he wrote his brother that he had been "Yazooed."[1] Painstakingly he went to work to have the contract renewed, and eventually won his case. Assured of success in North Carolina and Tennessee as well, he turned his attention once more to Georgia where he was determined to triumph over the men who continued to pirate the gins and undermine the reputation of the partnership.

He knew the unpleasantness he must face. Phineas Miller had been threatened with a public stoning if he should continue the prosecution of the law-suits, some sixty of which had been filed in Georgia. "I have a set of the most Depraved villains to combat," Eli wrote his friend, Stebbins, "and I might as well go to *Hell* in search of *Happiness* as apply to a Georgia court for justice."[2]

But now, oblivious to intimidation and driven by fierce resolution, Eli began to assemble a barrage of evidence to fire at his enemies. He expected the help of Phineas in the prosecutions, but when he arrived in Savannah in January, 1804, he was met with the shocking news of his partner's death the month before.

Hurrying to Cumberland, Whitney shared in the grief of Caty and her family. His sense of personal loss and feeling of responsibility, even guilt, weighed heavily upon him, for had not the misfortunes of the cotton gin and the thankless burdens of legal and financial affairs aged Phineas far beyond his years? Eli had noticed for months the tremulousness of Phineas's handwriting, but had been too occupied with other problems to give it much thought. Eli was severely depressed when he told Caty and the children good-bye and set out for the mainland, now to face alone the grim struggles of the cotton gin enterprise.

The gloom of Phineas's death still hung heavily over Dungeness when news of another tragedy arrived: a fatal duel in Savannah between two of Caty's family friends. The antagonists were Dr. Horatio Senter, son of her former physician Dr. Isaac Senter of Newport, and John Rutledge, Jr., nephew of Edward and son of her former hosts in Charleston during the days following the British evacuation. Caty had known both of the young duelists since their boyhoods, and had closely followed their careers.

The wife of the junior Rutledge had come under the care of the youthful Dr. Senter during a trip to Newport, and had fallen in love with him. Senter later set up practice in Savannah as a protégé of Dr. Kollock, perhaps to be closer to Mrs. Rutledge. While on a trip to Charleston during the winter, Senter visited his beloved in her country home and was surprised there by the unexpected arrival of Rutledge. As the physician rushed from his sweetheart's chamber, he was fired at by the husband but received only a flesh wound in the hand.

Following Senter to Savannah, Rutledge issued a challenge, and the two met with pistols at dawn on the Strand above the Savannah River. Senter was hit in his left leg just below the knee, and although the limb was amputated, he died of tetanus a few days later. "This cruel business has been the means of destroying Mr. R[utledge]'s peace of mind," read a newspaper account, "and ruining his wife's character forever."[3]

During the summer of the same year, the code of honor cost the life of another of Caty's intimate friends. News came to Cumberland of the death of Alexander Hamilton following an encounter with Aaron Burr, vice president of the United States, at Weehawken, on the Jersey bank of the Hudson River. Caty and her household were reduced to tears. She recalled her visits with Ham-

ilton dating back to the days of the British siege of New York—
how she had burst into laughter at Middlebrook when Lady Washington named a tomcat in his honor, and how in later years, she
had depended upon his kindness and practical help in her petition
to Congress.

Cornelia was heart-broken, too. Hamilton was the object of
her teenage crush during the two winters she had spent with
the Washingtons in Philadelphia. "He was then in the meridian
of his young manhood," Cornelia recalled, "intellectually as well
as physically, and was not only a model of manly beauty, but
distinguished by a refinement of thought and bearing which made
him easily the most attractive man in the social life of his day.
. . . When he was struck down . . . I was but one of the thousands
who wept over his untimely fate."[4]

Bringing the tragedy even closer home was the knowledge
that Nat Pendleton had been Hamilton's second, and that as liaison between his friend and William Van Ness, Burr's second,
he had been powerless to prevent the fatal meeting. It had been
Pendleton who read the rules to the duelists, who gave the ominous signal to fire, and who supported Hamilton in his arms as
the dying man was rowed back across the river to his New York
home. Pendleton later returned to the spot of the encounter and
brought back a bullet-pierced limb from high in a tree to prove
to the world that Hamilton had fired his pistol in the air.

During the late summer Caty received a note from Burr, written from St. Simon's Island, just up the Georgia coast, where
he was hiding out from Federal authorities bearing warrants for
his arrest. He very much wanted to visit an old friend and asked
her permission to come to Dungeness. Caty's manners were put
to a test; she could scarcely deny such a request from a former
aide on Washington's staff, but she had grown to hate him since
the killing of Hamilton.

She had met Burr early in the war, knew something of his
charm, and was well-acquainted with his reputation as a ladies'
man. After the war his home in New York had become the scene
of brilliant social gatherings where the former colonel, well before
the death of his wife, became involved in love affairs with a number
of ladies of high standing. Now he was alone in a strange part
of the land, far from the arms of his sweethearts, and obviously
in quest of female companionship during his long months as a
fugitive from justice.

Caty's dilemma was laid to rest for the moment by a terrifying natural event. Unusual weather conditions developed. A glaze covered the sky following a hot and breathless day, and at the expected time of low tide it was found that the beach was flooded with rapidly rising water. The winds increased in strength until a full hurricane blew, "the most violent . . . ever experienced since the settling of Georgia."[5] Trees went down before the shrieking gale, and large portions of Cumberland were inundated.

Caty gathered her friends and loved ones around her at Dungeness. Shutters rattled and glass shattered, but the dwelling's four-foot walls were immune to the worst of the storm. Soon the house was packed with whites and blacks of the entire island, and later it served as refuge for passengers and crews of ships driven aground on the beaches and bars.

After the winds subsided the inhabitants set to work clearing debris from the gardens and fields. Although some of the groves were in ruins the plantation had stood up to the gale far better than Caty had anticipated. She had forgotten about Aaron Burr, but within days another note from him arrived, this time from St. Marys just across the marshes, repeating his request for a visit. Caty wrote back perfunctorily that her house belonged to him as long as he cared to stay.

She sent a servant to the Dungeness landing to meet the boat, asking to be informed when it came into sight. She had her carriage ready, and when the message arrived that Burr was on the way she and her family drove rapidly, not to the landing, but to the interior of the island. "She could not receive as a guest one whose hands were crimsoned with [Hamilton's] blood," wrote Elizabeth Ellet.[6] At Dungeness, Burr was met by only the household servants. Thoroughly snubbed, he did not stay long. Caty awaited word of his departure, then she and her family returned home, having repaid a debt to the memory of Alexander Hamilton.

In November, 1804, a boat from the schooner *Rolla* landed at the Dungeness dock, bearing a young man who would become very much a part of the lives of Caty and her family. He was twenty-two-year-old Daniel Turner of East Greenwich, son of Dr. Peter Turner, Caty's friend and physician of Valley Forge and later Rhode Island days. Daniel himself was a practitioner of medicine who, partly because of the influence of Caty, and upon the recommendation of Dr. Lemuel Kollock, had decided to come to Georgia to set up an office at St. Marys. 'I was very cordially received by Mrs. Miller and family," Daniel wrote his parents upon his arrival. "I left them yesterday [for St. Marys] with many assurances of their friendship."[7]

St. Marys being only a short boat-ride from Dungeness, young Dr. Turner became Caty's personal physician, a service relinquished by Dr. Kollock, whose Savannah office was too far removed for him to attend Caty as often as she wished. Turner found Caty active in the affairs of the great plantation during some periods but almost completely indisposed during others. He diagnosed her recurring illness as an emotional affliction aggravated by her grief over the loss of her husband and the insecurity that attended her hopelessly snarled financial affairs.

Phineas Miller had left half of his estate to Caty, dividing the remainder among his seven brothers and sisters. But what were the assets? Much of Caty's money had been turned over to Phineas for investment, in his name, in the ill-fated Yazoo speculation. Although arguments of the land companies were still being heard in Federal courts, there was little hope of recovery. The income of Miller and Whitney up to that time was insufficient to pay off the firm's creditors, and now, just as profits were beginning to be realized, the death of Phineas had dissolved the partnership.

Caty had no idea what returns she could expect from her heavy investments in the gin company. She knew she was at the mercy of the courts and the conscience of Eli Whitney, and while she placed little trust in the former she retained full faith in the integrity of her late husband's partner. She would soon receive $5,000 as Phineas's share of an installment paid by South Carolina for the patent rights in that state; otherwise all settlements at best were in the vague future. She should by now have had two fortunes at her disposal, but found herself still under the necessity of making her living and paying off debts from the proceeds of her plantation.

The appearance of Daniel Turner on the scene was a mutual blessing. The doctor was lonely, often going days in St. Marys without a patient entering his office. He was retained by Caty as physician to her plantation which included a large population of slaves requiring frequent ministrations, and the arrangement was quite a boon to a young physician whose office receipts in the early months of his practice amounted to almost nothing. Turner found that attending the blacks was an "extremely unpleasant business," their illnesses difficult to diagnose, and proper nursing out of the question. Generally a severely ill Negro, surrounded by ignorance and neglect, was doomed to early death.

Otherwise the care of the blacks at Dungeness was better than
that on the mainland. They worked for their overseers from sun-
up to noon, then were allowed the rest of the day to attend to
their own needs. Each slave had his own cornfield, was furnished
meat and potatoes by his master, and given a suit of clothes each
winter and summer. "The house servants live like the family,"
Turner wrote his parents, "are generally well-dressed & much
indulged."[8] He predicted, however, that Georgia slaves would
succeed in emancipating themselves within a few years.

The doctor became the close friend of Caty's children. He
found Nat "an eccentric good-hearted soul," Louisa "agreeably
charming," and had "every reason to be pleased" with Patty,
Cornelia and their husbands, John Nightingale and Peyton Skipwith. "[Skipwith] is a man of understanding and property, affable
in his manners & very friendly to me," he wrote his family. "He
is judge of the County court & much respected. . . . I receive
the most flattering attentions from Mrs. Miller. . . . She agreeably
makes her house a home to me—& if I find myself unwell or
low spirited & at leisure I have orders from her to come immediately to Dungeness . . . there to stay as long as I please and do
as I please."[9]

Caty took frequent trips with Dr. Turner and her young people
in the plantation's ten-oared, thirty-passenger canoe, rowed by
blacks along the inland waterway to points along the Georgia
and Florida coasts. On one occasion she joined the group on a
voyage up the Crooked River to a house party at Cornelia's home
on the mainland. She declined to go along, however, on a trip
to Savannah where Dr. Turner wished to visit the grave of Nathanael and George Greene, and to see the spot on the Strand where
John Rutledge, Jr. had shot down Horatio Senter.

Ethan Clarke, still plying his trade as wine merchant back and
forth between Georgia and Rhode Island, continued to be a frequent visitor to Cumberland. Since Phineas Miller's death, Clarke
now looked to Caty for a settlement of the old debt her late
husband owed him. His intent was obvious; if she would not turn
over a portion of her property to him, he would be content to
possess her instead. Daniel Turner well understood what Clarke
was about. "The old man has little or no prospect of succeeding
with this Widow," he wrote his parents, later adding: "I can't
help saying here that Mr. C——ke is not much admired on Cumberland—his character is fully comprehended & he is as much
despised as is requisite. . . ."[10]

Although the United States maintained an uneasy peace with Great Britain and other European powers, the calm of Caty's isle was broken intermittently by ramifications of the war being fought by England against France and Spain. The waters surrounding Cumberland were frequently scenes of encounters between privateers fitted out in nearby Spanish East Florida and British men-of-war attempting to protect their merchant ships. Occasionally warships of the belligerent nations met head-on, battling furiously within plain view of Cumberland residents watching from the shore.

The hottest part of the arena was the narrow sound separating Cumberland from the Spanish isle of Amelia, off the northeast Florida coast, a favorite haunt of adventurers from all parts of the world. From a vantage point on the southern tip of their own island, only a short ride down the beach from Dungeness, Caty and the members of her household were often spectators of high maritime drama unfolding in Cumberland sound.

In the summer of 1805 a Spanish privateer captured two British merchant vessels and brought them as prizes into the sound, anchoring them off the Florida shore. The intention was to smuggle their cargoes into the United States through St. Marys where higher prices could be obtained than in Spanish Florida. Before the vessel could be unloaded the British gunboat *Matilda*, a former French vessel captured off the Cumberland coast, sailed into the sound and challenged the privateer standing guard. After an hour's cannonading, the British sailors boarded the Spaniard, engaged the adventurers in fierce hand-to-hand fighting, and forced the vessel to surrender. A few months later when a Creole privateer brought a British prize of 400 tons into the Cumberland sound, Caty and her family were shocked to hear that forty British sailors, after surrendering their ship, had been massacred by the boarding Creoles. For a few nights thereafter, the firing of cannon could be heard off the bar, but no harm came to the privateer, whose captain sold his captured vessel and cargo to private citizens of St. Marys, then sailed his ship off on another marauding expedition.

The willingness of St. Marys merchants to deal illicitly with captains of Spanish and French privateers not only outraged Caty and her family but widened the political gulf that already existed between the islanders and the rural Georgians of the mainland. Cumberland was largely populated by conservative former New Englanders of Federalist leanings sympathetic to the British cause, while the "Crackers," who detested "English-lovers," sided openly with the Spanish and French. The feelings of the St. Marys merchants were less inspired by national and international issues than by their concern for their own livelihoods. The proximity of Spanish East Florida offered a special opportunity for them: fortunes could be gained by accepting smuggled goods from across the border.

The antagonism between the merchants engaged in this commerce and those who opposed the practice was so bitter that the citizens began wearing sidearms. Occasionally the conflict carried over to Cumberland. The islanders avoided going into St. Marys but complained to the lawmakers of the illegal activities taking place there. Caty was particularly revolted by the attitude of the Crackers, but declining to be drawn into local politics she simply expressed her resentment by shunning the St. Marys merchants and refusing to trade with them.

Caty, not well, no longer took her annual voyages to the East. Patty Nightingale, although she was pregnant for the third time, sailed to Rhode Island with her two children, leaving her husband at their plantation, "The Springs." When Caty heard that Nightingale was ill with fever, she sent Nat to care for him and asked Dr. Turner to examine him. The physician was not too concerned over his patient's condition at first, but when he returned three days later, after an urgent summons from Nat, he found Nightingale dead. The entire island was shocked, and it was up to Caty to write the crushing news to her daughter in New England.

Patty was in a state of collapse when she returned home with her children, and her grief lingered on without relief. Eight months after Nightingale's death Dr. Turner wrote that she had not yet "got over her dispair for the loss of her husband—generally requests to see me when I go to Dungeness—takes me by the hand, but her tears prevent her saying much. Mrs. Miller is . . . very hysterical."[11]

Not until the early spring of 1808 did Caty's health take a decided turn for the better. She went on an extended visit to Columbia, South Carolina, on plantation business, and her success in negotiations with live-oak contractors rendered her able to pay back to the Greene estate a considerable amount of money borrowed from it during her efforts to salvage the cotton gin company. On her way back to Dungeness she picked up on the road two English boys, ten and thirteen years old, and brought them back to the plantation. "They are sons of a Blacksmith," she wrote Eli Whitney, "who were coaxed away by expectations of picking up a hat full of gold in America. The Embargo induced the Captain to throw them upon the World. I found them starving and brought them home. They are fine boys. . . . One of them can make a good key to any lock now—and both have great ambition to excell in this trade."[12]

A final settlement of Nathanael's estate was now at hand, and Caty hoped soon to conclude the financial affairs of Miller and Whitney as well. "There ought at all events to be a settlement between you and myself," she wrote Whitney. "Say that you will be ready to meet the thing—and that you will come here next winter prepared for this purpose. . . . *My settlement* to *you* will be everything. Old Ethan Clarke is here watching for the moment to administer and *woe* be to you if he should succeed—for he is what he is."[13]

Two weeks later she wrote an ecstatic letter to Whitney:

April 9th 1808
My Dear Friend
This has been a delightful day to me having accomplished one great object of my life—that is a settlement with my children of the estate of Genl Greene. I have had with reason (as you know) great cause to fear how their characters would turn out upon a tryal of Self. My Pride as a Mother is highly gratified—They have done honor to their Birth and Education—I believe there are few instances where (on such an occation) . . . there is a Mother and four Children to divide an estate so large, that every *one* could trust the others to do them justice. I left the four children to themselves, for the division—they have settled in perfect love and *harmony* which I can consider *worth* the forty thousand dollars which each has divided for themselves. They have left me double that amount. I am doomed to go on to the North where I promis Myself no one pleasure greater than that of seeing you—perhaps in *May* you may expect me in New Haven—Louisa and Natty with me. Mrs. Nightingale will leave . . . in a few days to go by land. I shall go to N York by water—where I expect to have some difficulty with Judge P[endleton] but more of that when I see you.
I wish you could dine with us tomorrow as we shall have green turtle and venison & if [it] would suit you better

as it does me . . . you could walk in my garden of sweets—
so brilliant are my flowers—so fragrant . . . but your *Rose*
has not yet arrived to grace it—but you shall pay interest
for keeping me so long out of my Roses—Georgia interest—eight per cent—remember that—My house is full of
Company—all in high spirits and I have retired to scribble
nonsence to my friend. . . . Remember me always as your
old friend for I am so on all occasions—

Cath Miller[14]

During the summer Caty, Nat, and Louisa boarded a vessel
at St. Marys for a voyage to Newport. Cornelia, who did not
make the trip because of her pregnancy, saw them off at the dock.
As Caty stepped aboard and waved good-bye she felt free of the
worst of the burdens that had long weighed heavily upon her.
For the moment, at least, she did not contemplate with great
alarm the problems that faced her in the East.

20 Winter of Frustration

Caty and her family had not been in Rhode Island long before Nat Greene, who was now twenty-eight, married Anna Marie Clarke of Newport. The fact that the bride was a daughter of the much-despised Ethan Clarke must have been a bitter pill for Caty to swallow, but she held no prejudice against her son's wife and accepted her cordially into the family.

Caty was hurt, however, that during her stay in Newport she received no visit from Eli Whitney, whose home was in nearby New Haven. She wrote him of the injury she had felt from his negligence and of a dispute she was having with his brother, Josiah. The younger Whitney, a former agent of Phineas Miller's who had handled the Cumberland Island live-oak contract with the government, claimed that the Miller estate owed him a great deal of money.

"It has been painful to me," wrote Eli in response to Caty's letter, "that you could for a moment suppose it possible I could . . . treat . . . the person for whom I had long cherished the sincearest friendship & esteem 'with marked contempt'—I can however perceive the causes & am fully aware of the innumerable suggestions & exaggerations of a busy imagination. . . . Our mutual friend Kollock who arrived here with his family last evening is extremely solicitous that the Dispute between you & Josiah should be concluded. . . . As to his commencing a suit that's all fudge . . . at any rate you shan't want for Bail in Connecticut. I shall not say you both act like fools about this business—but I think you both exercise less *wisdom* and discretion in this business than you do on most other occasions. . . . You must be friends again & it is to no purpose for either of you to say you *won't*."[1]

Caty went to New Haven to visit Eli and to meet there with his brother in an attempt to settle their differences. Dr. Kollock, as executor to the estate of Phineas Miller, sat in on the business sessions. Also present in Eli's household was Kollock's bride, a circumstance that made Caty uncomfortable as she had voiced strong disapproval of the match. She thought the young woman was too self-centered to make the doctor happy, but her critical appraisal was influenced by the fact that her own daughters had once been the lady's rivals.

Little was accomplished at New Haven and the entire company proceeded on to New York to meet with judges there in an attempt to settle the estate. The issues were complex, involving not only Miller and Whitney cotton gin affairs, but the old Yazoo investments that were being aired by the Federal courts. One of the justices that Caty appeared before was her old friend Nat Pendleton, now a Federal judge. To make matters more complicated, Pendleton himself had entered a personal claim of $10,000 against the Miller estate for legal fees, a matter that awaited arbitration in another court.

Whitney and Kollock could not remain any longer in New York, and the burden of the court procedures fell on Caty's shoulders. While busily engaged, she received in late October a staggering blow—news of the death of Cornelia's husband in Georgia. "Poor Skipwith was one of the untimely victims of the cruel feavor raging at St. Marys," Caty wrote Eli. "The night you left me the sad news Pinned my heart. Too little fortifyed for such an addition to a propensity to Melancholly I have been confined to my room ever since and have really been ill. Louisa too was much shocked—she was taken with a violent puking—and remains much indisposed. . . . [Skipwith] died at Cumberland on the 2nd inst— I can gain no other particulars—all communication is stoped between Savannah and St Marys which increases my anxiety about Cornelia and Ray [Sands] to an intolerable degree."[2]

Dreadful news of entire families being wiped out by the yellow fever epidemic on the Georgia coast continued to reach Caty. (Visitors to the village cemetery at St. Marys today can count dozens of graves of persons of all ages bearing death dates of the summer and fall of 1808.) Among the victims was her young and beloved physician, Daniel Turner, who had attended the sick and dying for many weeks. When he himself had contracted the disease there was no one to care for him. He had sent his pregnant wife, whom he had married only a few months before, to her father's home miles away, while he made his tedious rounds by muleback throughout the countryside. A slave had been left at the doctor's house to cook for him but when the servant became ill Turner had to attend him also. No one knew that the physician himself had contracted the fever. He continued to work until he could no longer stand, then he lay down on his bed and died.

Caty found that she could proceed no further in the settling of Phineas's accounts with the gin firm until Eli came back to New York. She sent letter after letter urging him to return, but he wrote that he was tied up in New Haven with Federal inspectors who were attempting to force cancellation of his musket contract. It was a critical time for Eli, who felt personally responsible for the dozens of young apprentices, including three nephews he had adopted, who lived in his household and whose livelihood depended upon the success of his enterprises. Finally, in his own desperation, he wrote Caty that her continued entreaties to him placed him "on tenterhooks."

Caty apologized for her persistence and for calling him a fool, a term he particularly objected to, and amended it to "blockhead." "I command not regular answers [to my letters]" she wrote, "— only give me my just due—confide in me and love me as well as you can and I will be satisfy[d]."[3]

The torment Eli suffered at this time can scarcely be imagined. He desperately wanted a wife and children of his own, but Caty, the only woman he had ever loved, had slipped past the child-bearing years. To marry her would not only deny him his right to have heirs but involve him in the wretched financial complications that stalked Caty's every step, and very likely compromise his own interests in the settlement of the Miller estate. Such considerations were entirely incompatible with the pursuit of the career he had staked out for himself.

Caty obviously understood the complexities without having to be told. But if she could not marry Eli, she could still love him and mother him. She coddled, flattered, and scolded; when he complained of not feeling well she prescribed cold water applications for his aches and a diet of rare beef for "assed stomach." "If I were with you," she added, "I would *compell* you to [take care of yourself] but I can not compell you to look out for a wife. . . . I am keeping a room for you here. I long to see you and tell you what you already know."[4]

Louisa, her doting mother's constant companion, was herself a candidate to become Mrs. Whitney. Now twenty-four, still single, and free of economic encumbrances, she was a far less complicated marital prospect than was her mother. None too subtly, Caty promoted the match in her correspondence with Eli as an alternative to the one she really longed for. Louisa wrote regularly to Eli, often enclosing her letters with her mother's, but she wistfully noted that most of his responses were addressed to Caty.

The simple truth is that Louisa, although bright and attractive, never possessed the charm and warmth of her mother. In spite of Caty's own broadmindedness in matters of love, she had brought up her youngest daughter under immensely sheltered circumstances, seeing to it that she conformed to the most rigid moral standards. Louisa developed into womanhood with an air of prudishness and was ever ill-at-ease in the presence of men.

Caty, though she herself was dismayed and at the same time amused by her daughter's attitude, felt it might be an advantage from the viewpoint of the staid Whitney. She told of putting Louisa on a stage to Philadelphia in company of a young Frenchman who was to teach her his language during the trip. "Her first lesson was truly laughable," wrote Caty. "The only french words she ever pretended to speak . . . was *in English—dont touch me— dont touch me*—blushing and trembling lest he should put his hands about her. The two young Ladies who took lessons with her laughed ready to die at her fears—and called her country girl."[5]

Upon returning to New York, Louisa was visited by a well-to-do gentleman obviously intent on early matrimony. "He is as sweet upon her as Mapel Sap," Caty told Eli, "[but] as *his* charm advances, *hers* recedes. You would laugh to examine the expression of her countenance on these occasions. It is an assemblage—bashfulness, vexation and benevolence."[6]

Eli had written Caty a poem lamenting his frustrated desire to put his "head in the lap of Venus." "I wish to god my dear friend you were married," Caty wrote back in her next letter, "that you might have some one to love and chear you when alone—to caress and nurse you when you are sick—and in short to charme you away from that incessant occupation which will deprive the world of one of its best subjects—and me also of one of my dearest and beloved friends. I am prepared to love any woman who would make you happy. . . ."[7]

Caty had shown Eli's poem to Louisa with the suggestion that the words were meant for her. "I vow, mama," she exclaimed, "the man is in love!" Louisa wrote immediately to Eli, but days passed without an answer. Each morning she sent a servant to pick up the mail. "Before [her letter] could well have got to your hands," Caty wrote Whitney, "she anticipated the answer. It was (every morning) Billy have you been to the post office?—Yes ma'm—No letters?—No ma'm.—Well Mama I really think my lord and gentleman might have answered my letter—he cannot plead business for there has been two Sundays and six snowstorms—and what else could he do—but wright?"[8]

While in New York Caty frequently visited the home of her cousin, Sammy Ward. His friends flocked in to be entertained by his vivacious guest from Georgia. One young lady, who had heard so much about Caty that she had resolved not to like her, met her for the first time at a tea at the Ward home, and later recalled that Caty "was dressed completely in black, even to the head dress, which was drawn close under the throat. From her seat on the sofa she was holding the whole company in breathless attention to the lively anecdotes of the war. . . . It was impossible not to listen to her. Still my resolution was not shaken . . . and I took a seat at the opposite side of the room. How long I remained there I was never able to tell; but my first consciousness was of being seated on a stool at the lady's feet, leaning upon her knee, and looking up in her face as confidingly as if she had been my own mother."[9]

In February, 1809, Nat Pendleton visited Caty at her lodgings. Their greetings were strained, the warm intimacy of their friendship of earlier days in the South having totally vanished. Pendleton, impatient to be awarded the $10,000 he had claimed against the Miller estate, insisted upon an early meeting with the referees, but little could be done until Eli Whitney came to New York. Finally, in a desperate bid to keep Pendleton's friendship, Caty signed a note to him for the face value of his claim. Shortly afterward, and for similar reasons, she also made a "settlement" with Josiah Whitney for the same amount, satisfying his claim in full. Caty naively believed that neither of her friends would press for payment of the notes until the referees had certified them as valid debts.

It was during this stormy, frustrating winter, while her unhappy business transactions were taking place, that she sat for the portrait by James Frothingham that hangs today in Savannah's Telfair Academy. She posed in a cold room, wearing her black cape and headdress. She was shocked to see the painting upon its completion for the artist had captured nothing of her charm. She looked all of her fifty-four years; she had put on weight and her round face wore an expression of mellowness, fatigue, and resignation.

When February ended without a visit from Whitney, who had promised to come to New York weeks before, Caty lost her forbearance completely and poured out her anger in a letter to him:

> March 1st, 1809
>
> I certainly am endowed with more than a common share of patience my dear Whitney to think of you with any kindness—after the shabby trick you have play^d me. The greater part of last week our Bell never rang but my fancy presented you—as the kind performer of your promis—You may judge therefore how many disappointments I have suffered—and you know . . . that I never was celebrated for bearing disappointments as I ought. You will say its time you learned then—and I will back you—but I say—if I must learn I will not be *taught by you.* . . . Your letter of 25th Feb. came to hand—(filled with many pretty things) a few hours ago—and one of them is that you hope you shall see me before *Many days*—and you might have added—I can flatter her along for a month yet—but I can tell you my Lord that you *must come* immediately. . . . It is my opinion if you were not compelled to come by a sort of duty and honor—that you would feed me upon soft Corn . . . until . . . the time . . . I shall set off for poor dear Dungeness—but come here and let me scold you. . . . I shall expect you by Sunday at farthest—if you delay longer you may have something to answer for—which would give you an uneasy conscience for life and which I will tell you when I see you next *Sunday*—not one days grace after Sunday. . . . God bless you with more Leisure and every other good prays your friend
>
> C Miller[10]

A response from Eli explained that since he had not received her last letter until Saturday he could hardly be expected to be in New York on Sunday. Besides, he was ill in bed with the "March Devil." "I shall allow nothing of my own concern to detain me," he told Caty. "I have been greatly wounded by your suspicions of my sincerety & want of disposition to serve you. I do not believe however that you are in serious earnest in making these accusations."[11]

"I can almost find it in my heart," Caty wrote Eli when he failed to appear by the Sunday deadline, ". . . to wish you were at this moment on Carters Mountain especially if it is very cold, and you could find no better means of warming yourself than by a split wood fire. . . . You will say that I have no right to be vexed with you—but I say I have—and I will be vexed with you—and so good night. I cannot help adding god bless you notwithstanding."[12]

Eli came to New York and for Caty all the doubts, all the bitterness, all the frustrations of the long separation were at once dispelled. Certainly the meeting was not one of perfect joy. Caty found that the legal affairs which stood between her and Eli could not, after all, be soon resolved. And she recognized, too, the final hopelessness of her dream of holy union with this man she badgered, pitied, worried over, and loved with all her heart.

But suddenly she found the pain was gone. Eli had come to her, at last, in her distress, to be at her side. She pressed him to her heart and found contentment in the last weeks she would ever spend in New York.

21 Descending into the Vale of Years

A strange illness suffered by Louisa in the spring of 1809 forced her and Caty to cancel plans to return to Georgia. Instead, after Louisa began to feel better, they booked passage to Rhode Island for a reunion with the other three Greene children, all of whom were then in the neighborhood of East Greenwich.

As their vessel passed between Block Island and the mainland, on its approach to Newport, it was struck by a sudden gale of the type that made Caty tremble with fear. Louisa, though violently seasick, tried to comfort her mother, but found her inconsolable until port was reached. This was Caty's last sea voyage—she vowed never to sail again.

She remained with her children in East Greenwich all summer, nursing Louisa through her illness and helping take care of her two widowed daughters and their children. Patty was her chief concern; her health was miserable and her spirits depressed. She had lost interest in everything but her children, and Caty felt that they were all that sustained her.

Part of Caty's time was spent in Nathanael's old home in Poto-womut where his brothers, some quite elderly, still lived and worked. Though Louisa remained ill, she was the particular pet of her Greene uncles. She would wait at the forge until they finished their work, then rush to their side, throw her arms around them, and kiss their grimy faces. "You would laugh to see her folded in the arms of her old uncles," Caty wrote Eli. "They adore her and she is all gratitude to them. They are plain Country people with very good sense tho but little Education, live in the most plentiful but plain Manner and are celebrated for their Hospitality. They are very Opulent (nay Rich)—but work just as hard as if they were poor and feel a kind of vanity in doing so."[1]

The cause of Louisa's symptoms is not known, but in all likelihood a *mal-de-coeur* contributed to her indisposition. Utterly confused as to her place in the heart of Eli Whitney, she had long complained bitterly that his letters to Caty, even the ones she was permitted to see, were warmer than the ones to herself. As time went on she developed a growing awareness of the depth of her mother's and Whitney's attachment to each other, and during Eli's recent visit to New York the real object of his affection had been painfully revealed.

Louisa began to sense her own part in this strange triangle she shared with her mother. Since the complications that discouraged Whitney from marrying Caty did not apply to her, was she not expected to take her mother's place as Eli's functional wife, to bear his offspring, while his true fulfillment was forever vested in Caty?

When Whitney came to East Greenwich for a visit in the fall, Louisa put his love to a test. She arranged to be alone with him, and during the course of an emotional evening, during which he earnestly wooed her for the first time, she ecstatically gave her promise of marriage. The next day she confided in her mother and received her complete benediction.

But Eli, who was not certain that Louisa was really the woman he wanted for a wife, had second thoughts. Being an honorable man, he felt he could not withdraw his proposal. At the same time he was miserably aware that he had made a mistake. When he returned to New Haven, his letters reflected his grave reservations and he could not bring himself to write to Louisa except in the most perfunctory and businesslike terms. This was worse for Louisa to bear than an abrupt withdrawal. She was hurt to the core.

"He writes with constraint—even pain," Louisa confided to her mother. "Every sentence bears testimony to it." When Caty asked her for details of the proposal, Louisa burst into anguished tears when she described the scene. "When I promised," she blurted, "my every thought, every feeling was for *him*. I forgot myself—forgot my own dignity—and at that moment I would have given my life to him."

Caty was not sure how to counsel the would-be lovers. Finally, realizing that the match she had hoped to promote was ill-fated from the first, she decided to write to Eli telling him that the tone of his letters had confirmed Louisa's fears about his sincerity. "I do not believe [she] will ever perform her promise to you," she said, "tho she continually (when we are alone) speaks on that subject. I think under *present circomstances*—she had better not correspond with you. Both ought to *forget* that which will give more pain than pleasure to remember—There are other reasons too which I could give for this opinion. She knows not that I am writing—nor would I for anything have her know what I have written."[2]

Late in the fall Caty and Louisa were at last on their long-delayed trip back to Georgia, Cornelia and her children having traveled ahead of them by water. Refusing to sail, Caty went with Louisa by stage to Philadelphia, bought a carriage and pair of black horses, hired a driver, and continued southward.

The first part of the trip was delightful. "My carriage is a charming one," wrote Caty to Eli along the way, "light and so easy as hardly to make us sensible of motion—we scarcely know what fatigue is after a days journey. . . . We are up so early in the morning as to ride twelve miles before Breakfast—which we do in three hours—and the afternoon's journey is accomplished with eaquel ease—and we find abundant time to read . . . at the houses we stop at which we find very good."

The travelers spent nights in Baltimore and Washington, and took "a hasty look at the public buildings" in the new capital city. In Raleigh the dearth of rooms caused by the convening of the state legislature forced Caty and her daughter to stay "in a most wretched little Room in a wretched small Out House" belonging to a tavern. "I will pass away the time in writing," Caty told Eli, "especially as Louisa is too sick to chat or read to me—her Bed was on the floor last night—with a space opened at the feet four inches wide. She took cold and has kept *not her bed*—but mine all this dismal day—her ague has gone off and she is now in a quiet sleep—and I trust will be well enough in the morning to persue our yet (until last night) pleasant journey."[3]

After a long delay because of a sudden snow-storm, the travel-

ers set off again for Georgia. Along the way they met a young
lady who had recently been to Cumberland Island and who gave
them the first accounts of Dungeness they had received in two
months. The news was good—everyone was in perfect health—
and when Louisa heard the tidings she burst into tears of relief.
"I am knitting with great delight on the stockings," Caty wrote
Eli from Augusta, "which occasions much speculation and not a
little Laugh among my acquaintances. Some bet a hundred dollars
they never will be finished . . . but no one has found out who
they are for."[4]

Caty and Louisa reached Savannah near Christmas and immediately left on the last leg of their trip, down the wretched "coastal
highway," to St. Marys. Here the weary travelers embarked to
Cumberland in their own canoe, rowed by blacks from their own
plantation who had been sent over to await their arrival. As they
approached the island after their absence of eighteen months
and saw smoke pouring from the chimneys at Dungeness, the
fatigue of the long, long journey gave way to the blessed joy of
being home.

The happy days that Caty spent in her garden of paradise
were all too few, and it soon became evident that she was not
to pass the latter years of her life in peace and serenity. The
possibility of another great war with England loomed on the hori-
zon, and if it came Caty might well have to flee her island home.
Georgia politicians joined "war-hawks" of other states in clamor-
ing for a declaration of hostilities with their own special hope
that in such a war East Florida could be wrested from Spain,
which had now become a British ally. Cumberland, lying on the
frontier, was a prospective battleground, and Georgia militia were
sent over to garrison the island.

In October, 1810, Caty was bitterly disappointed by the elope-
ment of Cornelia with her first cousin Ned Littlefield. Though
he was the son of Billy, Caty's beloved younger brother, Ned
was despised by his new mother-in-law, who called him a fortune-
hunter. "As to Cornelia," she said in a letter to Whitney, "I never
intended to mention her name again. The manner of her Marriage
[aggrieved] *all all.* She went in the canoe to St Marys as she said
upon business—went into the *Post office* without a soul of her own
sex. The only witness to her Marriage was a Cracker Tavern
keeper—the ceremony performed by that cutthroat Ross—This
disgraceful transaction almost drove me to Madness—and will I
doubt not be the Death of me."[5]

While Patty was in Rhode Island she had also married again and now returned to Cumberland with her new husband. He was Dr. Daniel Turner's brother, Henry, of East Greenwich, who joined Ned Littlefield in a concerted campaign to convince Patty and Cornelia that their mother had been unfair to them in the division of the Greene estate. A cash settlement had already been agreed upon, but large tracts of land, notably the Duck River plantation in Tennessee, a gift of the North Carolina legislature before Tennessee gained its statehood, was yet to be divided. The activities of Turner and Littlefield drove a wedge between Caty and her two older daughters, while Nat and Louisa remained loyal to their mother.

The Miller estate also remained unsettled and Caty was denied indefinitely the right to enjoy the fruits of her investment in the cotton gin enterprise. Nothing could be accomplished until Eli Whitney came to Georgia, as he often promised to do, but he always found reasons for delaying his trip. He was not only reluctant to leave his businesses in Connecticut but often blamed poor health for his disinclination to travel.

Dr. Kollock recognized some of Whitney's chronic complaints as being hypochondriacal and often teased him about them. "You cannot die yet," wrote the physician, "unless it is absolutely necessary. . . . We cannot well spare you—there are yet many good & useful things for you to do which no one else can do quite so well. I therefore charge you to come [to] Georgia, and let me assist in taking care of you."[6]

The hostility of Ethan Clarke stood as always between Caty and her quest for happiness and peace of mind. "Such is the determination of Clarke to ruin her family," Kollock wrote Whitney "& such is the feeble resistence they can furnish to his devilish ingenuity . . . that either they must be reduced to indigency . . . or you and I must step in between them and this vampire, who you know would suck the blood of his grandmother for gold."[7]

"I think Mrs. Miller is unnecessarily alarmed by [Clarke's] threats," Eli wrote back. "Let him do his Damnest—it is not in his power to ruin her. . . . [She] has been improperly alarmed about this business. . . . The truth is Cornelia's folly has broken her mother's heart & I sincerely wish you would do all in your power to banish that subject from her mind. That Mrs. M. with all her good sense should suffer that transaction to prey upon her mind to such a degree as wholly to destroy her health, happiness & life is certainly extremely wrong. If she would make a vigorous & determined effort she might by the aid of her friends shake it off."[8]

Years before, Phineas Miller had borrowed $2,000 from Clarke, mortgaging a large tract of property on the mainland. After Phineas died without repaying the debt, Clarke recovered not only the property but won an additional judgment of $13,000 against the Miller estate. Now he was suing for more, and Caty prepared to go to Savannah to fight the litigation. "I will take with me such documents as will skin the old wretch . . . ," she wrote Eli.

She continued to beseech Whitney to come to Georgia, but began to suspect that his refusal was not only because of his fear of legal entanglements but of his reluctance to face up to Louisa. Caty assured him he would have only herself to contend with. "Come here," she implored, "and let me teach you by *my example* how to injoy the fleeting years which any can calculate upon."[9]

Her next letter, posted at Savannah, told Whitney of her severe disappointment in court. Although Clarke's suit was set aside for the time-being, Caty was told that she was personally responsible to the estate for the $20,000 she had left in the hands of Nat Pendleton and Josiah Whitney while in New York, since their claims had not been validated by the referees.

Returning sadly to Dungeness, she found Cumberland occupied by a company of United States Marines as well as state militia. The impressment of former British sailors from American vessels, even though they had become naturalized citizens of the United States, infuriated lawmakers in Washington who retaliated by imposing further embargoes on British goods. This action brought war ever closer.

Caty found pleasure in once again being associated with a military post. "We are gay as Larks," she wrote Whitney, "and pass the time delightfully. Company enough we always have. There are three officers which belong to the Marine Corps stationed at the South point of Cumberland who are very cleaver People, and visit us often. The old Captain Williams is a great favorite with us all—particularly the young ladies. We are all to dine there the fourth of July. We shall drink to your health."[10]

Dr. Kollock was at Cumberland and worked all summer on Caty's affairs. In going over the old papers of Miller and Whitney at Dungeness he made several interesting discoveries. One was in connection with the $10,000 fee Nat Pendleton had charged the Miller estate for the handling of Yazoo affairs. Kollock found papers establishing that Pendleton himself had been in partnership with Miller in these same Yazoo ventures. Moreover, the physician found evidence that Caty had grossly overpaid Josiah Whitney in her private settlement of his claim against the Miller estate. Kollock sent the revealing papers to judges handling the case.

He continued his attempts to persuade Eli to come south. "From the view I have of Mrs. Miller's situation I am extremely apprehensive that she will be absolutely ruined. The debts which have already fallen upon her are accumulating & will shortly be more than her property is worth. . . . Mrs. Miller . . . is enfeebled & is descending into the vale of years."[11]

At length Dr. Kollock lost his patience and complained bitterly to Whitney of his "incorrigible silence & obstinate perseverance in a determination not to come out to us in our distress."[12] Later he added: "I am sickened at the condition & the dreary prospect of our unfortunate friend & am truly astonished at the resolution with which she sustains this pressure of complicated evil & perplexity—but unless we can continue some alleviation, some attenuation of the thick gloom that surrounds her . . , she must inevitably sink & lessen your & my attachment to this miserable world."[13]

But Eli Whitney never returned to Georgia.

22 Finding Peace

Four judgments totalling $60,000 were determined against Caty in the spring of 1812. "She has no means of satisfying [the debt]," wrote Dr. Kollock to Whitney, "but by the sale of her lands and negroes. . . . She is on the eve of being pulled to pieces."[1]

Caty was advised by her lawyer to file a lawsuit against Eli to force him to come to Georgia to settle accounts. "I shrink with horror from such an Idea," she wrote Eli, ". . . for to give you trouble is wounding my own heart. In your last letter to me you lash the villiany and ingratitude of Mankind. I hope you did not mean to include me as I shall not *you* when I tell you that I have more reasons than anybody to distrust and dispise those who I have not only loved but cherished. Never was any one so cheated and ill-used as I have been."[2]

By the summer of 1812 the United States had declared war on Great Britain and once more a home of Caty's was exposed to enemy raids. She was advised to leave Cumberland, but nothing could have been further from the mind of this veteran of eight years of the Revolution. She was much too concerned with her own tribulations that threatened to deprive her of her homestead forever to be overly disturbed by the war.

Not until late in the same year did she make final settlement of Nathanael's landed property with her children. The transaction was agreeably acceptable to Nat and Louisa, but the settlements with Patty and Cornelia were accompanied by distressing scenes. Caty broke off relations with her two older daughters, refused to speak to them, and would not mention them in her letters except to refer to them by their husbands' names. "I would not see them or permit them through my gate," Caty wrote Whitney. "I bore all and so did Louisa pretty well untill L[ittlefield] and T[urner] demanded their proportion as they *Called it* [of] the Honors of Genl Greene—such for instance as two fifths of the Meadles, Cannon &c &c &c—This as you Yankeys would say—so put me out—that I have been ill ever since."[3]

August, 1813, brought an unhappy climax to the long nightmare. Caty had journeyed to Savannah to spend several days with the Kollocks. The tranquility of her vacation was broken by the sight of Cornelia and her husband and children, accompanied by a wagonload of blacks, driving down one of the back streets. She immediately realized what was taking place. The Littlefields were moving to their new home on the Duck River plantation in Tennessee that had been divided among Nathanael's heirs. Taking advantage of Caty's absence from Dungeness, they had hand-picked several of the plantation servants, though they still legally belonged to Caty, and were transporting them to Tennessee. It was by pure accident that Caty saw them as they passed through Savannah.

She was furious but refused to make a scene. Instead she quietly obtained a court order restraining the family from leaving town with the slaves. Then without awaiting further developments she embarked for Cumberland. Cornelia and her traveling party were arrested and detained for several days before bonds were signed by old family friends of Savannah guaranteeing Caty the amount of money at which the Negroes were valued.

Arriving at home, Caty went to her room and remained there, brooding, day after day. Shutting herself off completely from the world she had come to mistrust, she barely touched the food sent in to her. Friends feared that she had lost her mind. She adjusted her will, bequeathing Dungeness to Nat and Louisa, and providing for a large award to Lemuel Kollock—"my best beloved friend."[4] She arranged to leave generous sums to many of her relatives, but practically excluded Patty and Cornelia, making only token bequests to them of a few dollars each.

Gradually Caty began to leave her room for visits downstairs, and the members of her household were glad to see that her spirit had only been stunned, not broken. She had been engaged in another struggle, this time a fight within herself, to cast off the bitterness that had seized her soul. She had found, as Nathanael had once suggested, that self-pity made a sad companion.

In her isolation she had come to accept the fact that her tangled financial affairs would never be settled during her lifetime and resolved that she would no longer allow herself to suffer over material matters, or be the instrument by which any more of her loved ones would suffer. She knew that Patty and Cornelia had gone out of her life forever, as irrevocably lost to her as her dead son George. But other mothers had lost children, and other children had lost mothers, and had recovered. So would she, and so would Patty and Cornelia. Caty had come to grips with herself, and had found her peace.

A letter came from Eli explaining that since Caty intended to sue him, he was afraid a trip to Georgia might land him in jail. "Tho the Idea you suggest of going to Prison gives a shock to my heart," Caty wrote back, "I cannot help smiling at the novelty of the thought."[5] Recalling that Eli had once offered to pay her bail if she were ever arrested in Connecticut, she offered to return the favor in Georgia. But she added that she did not really expect him to come.

In March, 1814, Louisa was married at Dungeness to James Shaw, a Scottish gentleman many years her senior, who had lived at the mansion for two years and who was associated with Louisa in farming enterprises. It was Shaw who had entered into a contract with Caty some time before to complete the interior of the dwelling if funds ever became available. Since they had not, many of the rooms of the mansion remained in an unfinished state.

In view of the war, the fact that Shaw was a British subject was a matter of concern and Caty asked Louisa to make no public announcement of the wedding. "We all respect, honor, and love him," Caty wrote of Shaw to Eli. "He is not only tender and affectionate to her—but *to me* the most dutiful son and excellent friend."[6]

During the spring a bill was placed before Congress that was of immense importance to Caty's welfare. This legislation called for an appropriation of $8,000,000 for the relief of disappointed Yazoo investors of almost twenty years before. Many, like Caty and Phineas Miller, had sunk all the money they could muster into the ill-fated venture. In April Caty saw an announcement in a Savannah paper that the appropriation bill had passed Congress. This notice would ordinarily have brought great joy to her, for it meant that the Miller estate was, at last, on the eve of being relieved of its long distress. But instead she received the news with equanimity; there were other things, now, that seemed more important. "You have seen how Yazoo has terminated thus far," was her only comment in her correspondence with Whitney.[7]

In late spring of 1814, the war with England was almost two years old, and the Georgia seaboard was under imminent threat of invasion. "The enemy is near at hand," read the *Savannah Republican* of May 7. "Letters were received on Thursday last from St Mary's to the Mayor of this city and the officer commanding the United States troops here, stating that a large British force was off St. Mary's bar and that an attack was momentarily expected. Citizens, be on the alert!" From the southern tip of their island, the inhabitants of Dungeness could see the British men-of-war *Majestic* and *Morgiana*, as well as a number of transports loaded with soldiers, lying at anchor in Cumberland sound. But if Caty felt the slightest concern over the proximity of the enemy, her letters never mentioned it.

Later in the month Josiah Whitney, then at Cumberland, wrote his brother Eli: "Mrs. Miller and myself have come to a full and clear and friendly understanding and it is agreed and fully understood that we are to be Friends forever. . . . She *had* quarrelled with me two or three times, but she said she *never* would again, and advised others never to quarrel with me."[8]

Nat Greene was again at Dungeness with his family, and during the summer Caty found her house once more full of relatives and friends. On July 5 she wrote Eli general news of the plantation and said that the crops looked good. "We have a party of Eighteen to eat Turtle with us tomorrow," she added. "I wish you were the nineteenth. Our fruit begins to flow in upon us—to partake of which I long for you. . . . ."[9]

In the last week of August Caty was struck by one of the coastal fevers that regularly haunted Georgians in the summertime. The date of her illness corresponded with a critical time in the history of the United States. During the same week the capital city of Washington lay in ruins, having been burned by British forces under the notorious naval raider, Rear Admiral Sir George Cockburn. But Caty never knew.

The fever mounted. Nat and Louisa watched their mother struggle wearily as they tenderly helped Dr. Kollock care for her. For a week she shook with violent chills as nothing seemed to abate the disease. The alarmed household waited anxiously for some encouraging word, but there was no change.

On September 2, 1814, her long, racking fever finally broke, and Caty drifted off peacefully into a deep and endless sleep.

Chapter Notes

1. *A Colonial Childhood*

1. Benjamin Franklin to Catharine Ray, March 4, 1755, Manuscript Division, New York Public Library, Astor, Lenox and Tilden Foundations.
2. Franklin to Catharine Ray, September 11, 1755, Franklin Papers, American Philosophical Society.
3. Catharine Ray to Franklin, June 28, 1755, Franklin Papers. For a full record of the Franklin-Ray connection, see William Greene Roelker, ed., *Benjamin Franklin and Catharine Ray Greene, Their Correspondence, 1755-1790* (Philadelphia, 1948).
4. George Washington Greene, *The Life of Nathanael Greene*, 3 vols. (Cambridge, 1871), I, 72. The author of this multi-volume work was Nathanael's grandson.
5. See Mary Williams Greely, *The Cambridge of 1776 (The Diary of Dorothy Dudley)* (Cambridge, 1876), 68. Though the diary is undoubtedly fictitious, the text is based upon historic documents.
6. Elizabeth F. Ellet, *The Women of the American Revolution*, 3 vols. (New York, 1849), I, 72. Miss Ellet was a personal friend of some of Caty's younger friends.
7. These descriptions are quoted, respectively, from Roelker, *Benjamin Franklin*, 3, by permission of the publisher, The American Philosophical Society; G. W. Greene, *Nathanael Greene*, I, 72; and Martha Littlefield Phillips, "Recollections . . .," *Century Magazine*, LV (January 1898), 364. All of these authors wrote authoritatively on the subject of Caty from personal recollections or family mementoes. Roelker was a descendant of Governor William Greene, Jr., Caty's "Uncle Greene," and lived in the same East Greenwich house in which Caty had been brought up and married. G. W. Greene was her grandson. Mrs. Phillips quoted her grandmother who was Caty's daughter, Cornelia.
8. Clifford P. Monahan and Clarkson A. Collins, eds., "Nathanael Greene's Letters to 'Friend Sammy Ward,'" *Rhode Island History*, XVII, No. 1 (January 1958), 16. Nathanael's cousin, Christopher, who became a Revolutionary soldier of considerable fame, is not to be confused with Nathanael's brother of the same name, called "Kitt," who did not join the army.

2. *Life with a Besieging Army*

1. General Greene to his wife, June 2, 1775, Greene Papers, William L. Clements Library, University of Michigan, Ann Arbor, Michigan.
2. General Greene to his wife, June 28, 1775, Greene Manuscripts, Rhode Island Historical Society, Providence, Rhode Island.
3. General Greene to his wife, August 27, 1775, Greene Papers.

4. Ellet, *Women of the Revolution,* I, 63.
5. G. W. Greene, *Nathanael Greene,* I, 143-144.
6. General Greene to his wife, September 10, 1775, Andre de Coppet Collection, Princeton University Library, Princeton, New Jersey.

3. *The British Wedge*

1. General Knox to his wife, July 8, 1776, Knox Papers, Massachusetts Historical Society, Boston, Massachusetts.
2. General Greene to his wife, November 2, 1776, Morristown National Historic Park Collection, National Park Service.
3. General Greene to his wife, December 4, 1776, Andre de Coppet Collection.
4. G. W. Greene, *Nathanael Greene,* I, 285.
5. Ibid., 284-286.
6. General Greene to his wife, December 30, 1776, Greene Papers.

4. *A Brief Reunion*

1. General Greene to his wife, April 27, 1777, Andre de Coppet Collection.
2. General Greene to his wife, April 8, 1777, Greene Papers.
3. General Greene to his wife, undated, G. W. Greene, *Nathanael Greene,* I, 373.
4. General Greene to his wife, May 3, 1777, Andre de Coppet Collection.
5. General Greene to his wife, May 20, 1777, Andre de Coppet Collection.
6. Ibid.
7. General Greene to his wife, May 20, 1777, Greene Papers.
8. General Greene to his wife, July 23, 1777, Greene Papers.
9. See General Greene to his wife, September 10, 1777, Andre de Coppet Collection.
10. General Greene to his wife, September 14, 1777, Andre de Coppet Collection.
11. See General Knox to his wife, December 2, 1777, Knox Papers, Massachusetts Historical Society. In his explanation to his wife as to why Caty remained at Morristown, Knox wrote: "Mrs. Greene in a very unpleasant season of the year, with much difficulty, and in an ill state of health, reached Mr. Lott's. General Greene saw her there and was with her for three days—at which time the Army marched Southward and he has never seen her since." A biographer of Knox, misreading his handwriting, confused "season" for "person" and quoted his letter thus: "Mrs. Greene is an unpleasant person and in ill health." (See North Callahan, *Henry Knox, General Washington's General,* 128, quoted by permission of Holt, Rinehart and Winston, Inc.) This distorted version, referred to in other biographies of Caty's acquaintances, offers a good example of why her image has suffered in literature.
12. General Greene to his wife, November 2, 1777, Andre de Coppet Collection.

5. *Valley of Distress—and Hope*

1. See James L. Whitehead, ed., "The Autobiography of Peter Stephen Duponceau," *Pennsylvania Magazine of History and Biography,* LXIII, No. 2 (April 1939), 209.

2. General Greene to William Greene, Jr., undated, G. W. Greene, *Nathanael Greene*, II, 79.
3. Griffin Greene to General and Mrs. Greene, April 12, 1778, Greene Papers.

6. *War Comes to Rhode Island*

1. General Greene to his wife, undated, G. W. Greene, *Nathanael Greene*, II, 93.
2. General Greene to his wife, undated, ibid., 84-85.
3. Caty to Dr. Peter Turner, June 9, 1778, Greene Papers.
4. General Greene to his wife, June 23, 1778, Andre de Coppet Collection.
5. General Greene to his wife, July 17, 1778, Greene Papers.
6. General Greene to his wife, August 16, 1778, Andre de Coppet Collection.
7. General Greene to his wife, undated, G. W. Greene, *Nathanael Greene*, II, 123-124, 129.
8. General Greene to General Washington, undated, ibid., 145.

7. *Merriment at Middlebrook*

1. General Greene to his wife, November 13, 1778, Andre de Coppet Collection.
2. General Greene to Jeremiah Wadsworth, undated, G. W. Greene, *Nathanael Greene*, II, 161-162.
3. General Greene to his wife, July 20, 1779, Andre de Coppet Collection.
4. Ibid.
5. Ibid.
6. General Greene to his wife, August 16, 1779, Andre de Coppet Collection.
7. General Greene to his wife, August 30, 1779, Greene Papers.
8. See G. W. Greene, *Nathanael Greene*, II, 84-85.
9. Colonel John Cox to Caty, August 30, 1779, Greene Papers.

8. *A Time of Despair*

1. George Olney to Tench Tilghman, March 11, 1781, Marian Sadtler Hornor, ed., "A Washington Affair of Honor," *Pennsylvania Magazine of History and Biography*, LXV, No. 3 (July 1941), 364.
2. General Washington to unnamed congressman, undated, G. W. Greene, *Nathanael Greene*, II, 328-330.
3. Jacob Greene to General and Mrs. Greene, April 25, 1780, Greene Papers.
4. General Greene to his wife, June 12, 1780, Andre de Coppet Collection.
5. General Greene to his wife, undated, G. W. Greene, *Nathanael Greene*, II, 383-385.
6. General Greene to his wife, ibid., 231-232.
7. General Greene to his wife, October 7, 1780, Greene Papers.
8. General Greene to his wife, October 14, 1780, Greene Papers. General Gates had fled the field early in the rout of his army at Camden, beating a long personal retreat while his soldiers were left to fend for themselves. The British assumed complete control of South Carolina, exposed to only sporadic raids by partisans.
9. General Greene to his wife, October 21, 1780, ibid.

10. The quotes are from two letters from Gen. Greene to his wife bearing the date of October 21, 1780, ibid.

9. *Letters from the South*

1. See Howard W. Preston, ed., "Rochambeau and the French Troops in Providence in 1780-81-82," *Rhode Island Historical Society Collections*, XVII, No. 1 (January 1924), 9.
2. General Washington to Caty, December 17, 1780, John C. Fitzpatrick, ed., *The Writings of George Washington*, XX, 469-470.
3. General Greene to his wife, December 29, 1780, Greene Papers.
4. General Greene to his wife, January 17, 1781, Andre de Coppet Collection.
5. General Washington to Caty, March 22, 1781, Fitzpatrick, ed., *Writings of Washington*, XXI, 352-353.
6. Deborah Olney to Caty, March 17, 1781, Hornor, ed., "A Washington Affair of Honor," 365-366.
7. Caty to Deborah Olney, ibid., 366-368.
8. Mrs. Olney to Caty, ibid., 370.
9. General Greene to his wife, March 18, 1781, Greene Papers.
10. General Greene to his wife, May 15, 1781, ibid.
11. General Greene to his wife, June 23, 1781, Andre de Coppet Collection.
12. Colonel Otho Williams to Caty, March 19, 1781, "Greene Letters," *Rhode Island Historical Society Collections*, XX, No. 4 (October 1927), 107.
13. Caty to Jeremiah Wadsworth, September 11, 1781, Wadsworth Papers, Connecticut Historical Society, Hartford, Connecticut.

10. *The Wedge Removed*

1. General Washington to General Greene, December 15, 1781, Fitzpatrick, ed., *Writings of Washington*, XXIII, 392.
2. See John Mathews to General Greene, January 24, 1782, Greene Papers.
3. Caty to Wadsworth, January 31, 1782, Wadsworth Papers.
4. Major Ichabod Burnet to General Greene, March 21, 1782, Greene Papers.
5. General Greene to Samuel Ward, Jr., undated, G. W. Greene, *Nathanael Greene*, III, 487.
6. Major Pierce to General Greene, September 14, 1782, Greene Papers.
7. Major Nathaniel Pendleton to General Greene, September 20, 1782, Greene Papers.
8. Lewis Morris to Ann (Nancy) Elliott, in two letters dated October 29, 1782, and November 19, 1782, *South Carolina Historical and Genealogical Magazine*, XLI, No. 1 (January 1940), 5, 8-9.
9. Caty to Samuel Ward, Jr., December 23, 1782, Monahan and Collins, "Nathanael Greene's letters to 'Friend Sammy Ward,'" 19-20.
10. General Greene to Samuel Ward, Jr., December 21, 1782, ibid., 18.
11. General Greene to unnamed friend, undated, G. W. Greene, *Nathanael Greene*, III, 488.

11. *Postwar Newport Days*

1. General Washington to General Greene, February 6, 1783, Fitzpatrick, ed., *Writings of Washington*, XXVI, 103-104.

2. General Greene to his wife, August 1, 1783, Greene Papers.
3. General Greene to his wife, August 4, 1783, Greene Papers.
4. Phillips, "Recollections," 364.
5. Ellet, *Women of the Revolution,* I, 71-72.
6. Phillips, "Recollections," 369.
7. Billy Littlefield to General Greene, March 22, 1784, Greene Papers.
8. Phillips, "Recollections," 364.
9. General Greene to his wife, September 8, 1784, Greene Papers.

12. *Tragedy in Georgia*
1. General Greene to his wife, April 14, 1785, Greene Papers.
2. General Greene to Ethan Clarke, November 23, 1785, George H. Richmond, ed., "Letters by and to General Nathanael Greene," (New York: privately printed, 1906), 22. A copy of this pamphlet was made available through the courtesy of Mr. and Mrs. Malcolm Bell, Jr., Savannah.
3. September 15, 1785.
4. Only a rubble of brick and stone today remains to mark the site of the dwelling. It had been built before the war by John Graham, a wealthy Scotsman and outspoken Tory who, after 1776, was unable to maintain his property in the face of raids by patriots. When Savannah was evacuated in 1782, Graham, then lieutenant governor of the British administration in Georgia, departed with the fleet, leaving a vast fortune behind. His property was confiscated by the state of Georgia.
5. General Greene to Ethan Clarke, November 23, 1785, Greene Papers.
6. Isaac Briggs to Joseph Thomas, November 23, 1785, *The Georgia Historical Quarterly,* XII, No. 2 (June 1928), 180-182. An account of Briggs's conversation with Caty and Miller is contained in this letter.
7. General Greene to Samuel Ward, Jr., April 4, 1786, Monahan and Collins, "Nathanael Greene's Letters to 'Friend Sammy Ward,' " 21.
8. General Greene to Ethan Clarke, undated, G. W. Greene, *Nathanael Greene,* III, 532.
9. Anthony Wayne to James Jackson, June 19, 1786, G. W. Greene, *Nathanael Greene,* III, 534.

13. *Miseries of Widowhood*
1. The vault had been the family property of John Graham, the Tory whose confiscated estate was turned over to the Greenes. In 1901, 115 years after the funeral, Nathanael's remains were reinterred, along with those of his oldest child, beside the Greene monument in Johnson Square.
2. Anthony Wayne to Caty, August 1, 1786, Greene Papers.
3. Phillips, "Recollections," 366-368.
4. Ibid., 365.
5. General Washington to Jeremiah Wadsworth, undated, G. W. Greene, *Nathanael Greene,* III, 529 n.
6. See Henry Knox to Caty, August 31, 1787 (in which Lafayette's remarks are quoted), Greene Papers.
7. Ibid.
8. Henry Knox to Caty, May 18, 1788, Greene Papers.
9. Caty to Wadsworth, August 12, 1788, Wadsworth Papers.
10. Caty to Wadsworth, August 13, 1788, Wadsworth Papers.
11. Caty to Wadsworth, undated, Wadsworth Papers.
12. Caty to Wadsworth, September 19, 1788, Wadsworth Papers.

14. *A New Life Unfolds*

1. Caty to Wadsworth, December 24, 1788, Knollenberg Collection, Yale University Library, New Haven, Connecticut.
2. See John Sanderson, *Biography of the Signers to the Declaration of Independence,* 9 vols. (Philadelphia, 1828), V, 182.
3. Caty to Wadsworth, December 24, 1788, Knollenberg Collection.
4. Edward Rutledge to Caty, January 8, 1789, Greene Papers.
5. Caty to Wadsworth, January 31, 1789, Wadsworth Papers.
6. See Isaac Briggs to Joseph Thomas, November 23, 1785, *The Georgia Historical Quarterly,* XII, No. 2 (June 1928), 180-182.
7. Caty to Wadsworth, April 18, 1789, Wadsworth Papers.
8. Ibid.
9. Caty to Wadsworth, April 19, 1789, Wadsworth Papers.
10. Edward Rutledge to Caty, May 27, 1789, Greene Papers.
11. Caty to Wadsworth, June 9, 1789, Wadsworth Papers.
12. Edward Rutledge to Caty, September 12, 1789, Rutledge Papers, South Caroliniana Library, University of South Carolina, Columbia, South Carolina.
13. Tobias Lear to Caty, undated, Greene Papers.
14. Caty to Nathaniel Pendleton, Jr., November 22, 1789, Pendleton Papers, Yale University Library, New Haven, Connecticut.
15. Pendleton to Caty, November 30, 1789, Greene Papers.
16. Caty to Wadsworth, December 8, 1789, Wadsworth Papers.
17. Caty to Wadsworth, undated, Wadsworth Papers.

15. *An Appeal to Congress*

1. Wayne to Caty, August 1, 1786, Greene Papers.
2. Wayne to Caty, February 4, 1790, Greene Papers.
3. Wayne to Caty, February 21, 1790, Greene Papers. Caty's remarks are quoted in this letter.
4. Caty to Pendleton, May 3, 1790, Pendleton Papers.
5. Caty to Pendleton, July 27, 1790, Pendleton Papers.
6. Edward Rutledge to Caty, April 12, 1790, Greene Papers.
7. Caty to Wadsworth, November 3, 1790, Wadsworth Papers.
8. Edward Rutledge to Caty, January 3, 1791, Greene Papers.
9. Alexander Hamilton to Caty, March 8, 1791, John Church Hamilton Papers, owned by Columbia University Libraries, New York, New York.
10. See Archibald Henderson, *Washington's Southern Tour, 1791,* (Boston, New York, 1923), 233.
11. Edward Rutledge to Caty, April 17, 1792, Greene Papers.
12. *Independent Gazetteer and Agricultural Repository* (Philadelphia), May 5, 1792.
13. Caty to Pendleton, May 25, 1792, Pendleton Papers.

16. *A Genius Comes to Mulberry Grove*

1. Eli Whitney to Josiah Stebbins, October 8, 1792, Whitney Papers, Yale University Library, New Haven, Connecticut.
2. Ibid., November 1, 1792.
3. Eli Whitney, Diary, 10-11, Whitney Papers.
4. Ellet, *Women of the Revolution,* I, 63-64.
5. Whitney to Stebbins, November 1, 1792, Whitney Papers.

6. Whitney to his father, September 11, 1793, Whitney Papers.
7. Whitney to Stebbins, March 7, 1803, M. B. Hammond, ed., "Correspondence of Eli Whitney Relative to the Invention of the Cotton Gin," *American Historical Review*, III, No. 1 (October 1897), 123.
8. See William Scarborough, ed., "Sketch of the Life of the Late Eli Whitney . . . ," *Southern Agriculturist and Register of Rural Affairs*, V, No. 8 (August 1832), 397-398. Caty's remarks to Whitney were never considered by either of them to have played an important part in the invention, but the incident was recorded in a number of early accounts of the development of the original model.
9. Whitney to his father, September 11, 1793, Whitney Papers.
10. Phillips, "Recollections," 369.
11. Phineas Miller to Whitney, undated, see Denison Olmstead, *Memoir of Eli Whitney, Esq.* (New Haven, 1841), 21-22.

17. *Collapse of a Scheme*

1. Miller to Whitney, May 11, 1797, M. B. Hammond, ed., "Correspondence of Eli Whitney," *American Historical Review*, LIII, No. 1 (October 1897), 105-107.
2. Whitney to Miller, October 7, 1797, ibid., 111-112.
3. Miller to Whitney, October 29, 1797, Whitney Papers.
4. Miller to Whitney, undated, Olmstead, *Memoir of Whitney*, 27.

18. *Life on a Georgia Sea Isle*

1. Cornelia Greene to Margaret Cowper, May 3, 1800, Mackay-Stiles Papers, Southern Historical Collection, University of North Carolina Library, Chapel Hill, North Carolina.
2. Ibid.
3. See Walter C. Hartridge, ed., *The Letters of Don Juan McQueen to his Family* (Columbia, South Carolina, 1943), 42.
4. Miller to Whitney, May 26, 1800, Whitney Papers.
5. Whitney to Miller, July (?), 1800, Whitney Papers.
6. Cornelia Greene to Margaret Cowper, October 10, 1800, Mackay-Stiles Papers.
7. Phillips, "Recollections," 364.

19. *Toward a Spring of Hope*

1. Eli Whitney to Josiah Whitney, February 7, 1803, Whitney Papers. "Yazoo" was a despised word for Eli.
2. Eli Whitney to Stebbins, October 15, 1803, Whitney Papers.
3. *Providence Gazette*, February 18, 1804.
4. Phillips, "Recollections," 371.
5. *The Charleston Courier*, September 14, 1804.
6. Ellet, *Women of the Revolution*, I, 71.
7. Daniel Turner to his parents, November 15, 1804, Richard K. Murdoch, ed., "Letters and Papers of Dr. Daniel Turner, a Rhode Islander in South Georgia," *The Georgia Historical Quarterly*, LIII, No. 3 (September 1969), 380.
8. Daniel Turner to his parents, August 13, 1806, Murdoch, ed., "Letters," *The Georgia Historical Quarterly*, LIV, No. 1 (Spring 1970), 102.
9. Daniel Turner to his parents, April 20, 1805, Murdoch, ed., "Letters," *The Georgia Historical Quarterly*, LIII, No. 4 (December 1969), 485.

10. Daniel Turner to his parents, March 25 and April 20, 1805, ibid., 484, 486.
11. Daniel Turner to his parents, May 23, 1807, Murdoch, ed., "Letters," *The Georgia Historical Quarterly*, LIV, No. 1 (Spring 1970), 118.
12. Caty to Eli Whitney, March 23, 1808, Whitney Papers.
13. Ibid.
14. Caty to Eli Whitney, April 9, 1808, Whitney Papers.

20. *Winter of Frustration*
1. Eli Whitney to Caty, September 6, 1808, Whitney Papers.
2. Caty to Eli Whitney, October 31, 1808, Whitney Papers.
3. Caty to Eli Whitney, November 30, 1808, Whitney Papers. Whitney's "on tenterhooks" is quoted in this letter, and Caty's "blockhead" appeared in her letter of the next day.
4. Caty to Eli Whitney, February 2, 1809, Whitney Papers.
5. Caty to Eli Whitney, December 31, 1808, Whitney Papers.
6. Caty to Eli Whitney, February 12, 1809, Whitney Papers.
7. Ibid. Whitney's "lap of Venus" is quoted in this letter.
8. Caty to Eli Whitney, February 16, 1809, Whitney Papers.
9. See Ellet, *Women of the Revolution*, I, 72-73.
10. Caty to Eli Whitney, March 1, 1809, Whitney Papers.
11. Eli Whitney to Caty, March 5, 1809, Whitney Papers.
12. Caty to Eli Whitney, March 7, 1809, Whitney Papers.

21. *Descending into the Vale of Years*
1. Caty to Eli Whitney, July 27, 1809, Whitney Papers.
2. Caty to Eli Whitney, October 29, 1809, Whitney Papers. Louisa's conversation with her mother is quoted in this letter.
3. Caty to Eli Whitney, November 29, 1809, Whitney Papers.
4. Caty to Eli Whitney, December 9, 1809, Whitney Papers.
5. Caty to Eli Whitney, begun October 12, completed October 19, 1810, Whitney Papers.
6. Dr. Lemuel Kollock to Eli Whitney, October 13, 1809, Whitney Papers.
7. Kollock to Eli Whitney, December 17, 1810, Whitney Papers.
8. Eli Whitney to Kollock, December 17, 1810, Whitney Papers.
9. Caty to Eli Whitney, March 20, 1811, Whitney Papers.
10. Caty to Eli Whitney, June 20, 1811, Whitney Papers.
11. Kollock to Eli Whitney, February 12, 1812, Whitney Papers.
12. Kollock to Eli Whitney, April 17, 1812, Whitney Papers.
13. Kollock to Eli Whitney, May 16, 1812, Whitney Papers.

22. *Finding Peace*
1. Kollock to Eli Whitney, May 18, 1812, Whitney Papers.
2. Caty to Eli Whitney, May 18, 1812, Whitney Papers.
3. Caty to Eli Whitney, January 3, 1813, Whitney Papers. Caty misdated the letter "1812."
4. See *Georgia Genealogical Magazine*, I (July 1961), 39-40.
5. Caty to Eli Whitney, October 19, 1813, Whitney Papers.
6. Caty to Eli Whitney, April 16 and July 5, 1814, Whitney Papers.
7. Caty to Eli Whitney, April 16, 1814, Whitney Papers.
8. Josiah Whitney to Eli Whitney, May 26, 1814, Whitney Papers.
9. Caty to Eli Whitney, July 5, 1814, Whitney Papers.

Bibliography

Manuscripts

American Philosophical Society, Philadelphia
 Franklin Papers
Clements Library, University of Michigan
 Greene Papers
Columbia University Libraries
 John C. Hamilton Papers
Connecticut Historical Society
 Jeremiah Wadsworth Papers
Georgia Historical Society
 Kollock Papers
Historical Society of Pennsylvania
 Greene Letters
 Wayne Manuscripts
Massachusetts Historical Society
 Greene Collection
 Knox Papers
Morristown National Historic Park, National Park Service
 Special Collection
New York Public Library (Manuscript Division)
 Astor, Lenox and Tilden Foundations
 Harkness Collection
Princeton University Library
 Andre de Coppet Collection
Rhode Island Historical Society
 Greene Manuscripts
South Caroliniana Library, University of South Carolina
 Rutledge Papers
Southern Historical Collection, University of North Carolina Library
 Mackay-Stiles Papers
University of Georgia Library
 Keith-Read Collection
Yale University Library
 Blake Family Papers
 Knollenberg Collection
 Pendleton Papers
 Washington Family Papers
 Whitney Papers

Books, Pamphlets, Articles

Abbott, Wilbur C. *New York in the American Revolution.* New York, London,
 1929.

Adams, Charles Francis, ed. *Familiar Letters of John Adams and His Wife, Abigail Adams, During the Revolution.* New York, Cambridge, 1876.

Bayles, Richard M., ed. *History of Newport, Rhode Island.* New York, 1888.

Belknap, Jeremy. "Journal of My Tour to the Camp, and the Observations I Made There," *Proceedings of the Massachusetts Historical Society,* V (April 1858), 77–86.

Bill, Alfred Hoyt. *Valley Forge, the Making of an Army.* New York, 1952.

Billias, George A. "Soldier in a Longboat," *American Heritage,* XI, No. 2 (February 1960), 56–59, 89–94.

Boyd, Thomas. *Mad Anthony Wayne.* New York, London, 1929.

Briggs, Isaac. "Three Letters," *Georgia Historical Quarterly,* XII, No. 2 (June 1928), 177–184.

Butterfield, L. H., ed. *Adams Family Correspondence.* 2 vols. Cambridge, 1963.

Callahan, North. *Henry Knox, General Washington's General.* New York, Toronto, 1958.

Chidsey, Donald Barr. *Valley Forge.* New York, 1959.

Coleman, Kenneth. *The American Revolution in Georgia.* Athens, Georgia, 1958.

Collins, Varnum Lansing, ed. *A Brief Narrative of the Ravages of Princeton in 1776–1777.* New York, 1968.

Commager, Henry Steele and Richard B. Morris, eds. *The Spirit of Seventy-Six.* New York, Evanston, San Francisco and London, 1975.

Cutter, William. *The Life of General Putnam.* New York, 1847.

Davis, Matthew L. *Memoirs of Aaron Burr.* 2 vols. New York, 1837.

Dexter, Franklin B. *Biographical Sketches of the Graduates of Yale College.* New York, 1907.

Donovan, Frank. *The George Washington Papers.* New York, 1964.

Downey, Fairfax. "The Girls Behind the Guns," *American Heritage,* VIII, No. 1 (December 1956), 46-48.

Doyle, Joseph B. *Frederick William von Steuben.* Steubenville, Ohio, 1913.

Ellet, Elizabeth. *The Women of the American Revolution.* 3 vols. New York, 1849.

Evans, Elizabeth. *Weathering the Storm: Women of the American Revolution.* New York, 1975.

Faulkner, Leonard. "A Spy for Washington," *American Heritage,* VIII, No. 5 (August 1957), 58-64.

Federal Writers' Project. "Mulberry Grove in Colonial Times," *Georgia Historical Quarterly,* XXIII, No. 3 (September 1939), 236-252.

Fitzpatrick, John C., ed. *The Writings of George Washington, from the Original Manuscript Sources, 1745-1799.* 37 vols. Washington, D.C., 1931-1944.

Fleming, Berry. *Autobiography of a Colony.* Athens, Georgia, 1957.

Flexner, James T. "Benedict Arnold: How the Traitor Was Unmasked," *American Heritage,* XVIII, No. 6 (October 1967), 6-15.

———. *George Washington in the American Revolution, 1775-1783.* Boston, Toronto, 1967-1968.

———. *The Traitor and the Spy.* New York, 1953.

Floyd, Dolores B. "Mulberry Grove Plantation Near Savannah." Pamphlet distributed by the Savannah Chamber of Commerce, 1936.

Foster, William O. *James Jackson, Duelist and Militant Statesman, 1757-1806.* Athens, Georgia, 1960.

Freeman, Douglas S. *George Washington, a Biography.* 7 vols. New York, 1951.

Frey, Carol. *The Independence Square Neighborhood.* Philadelphia, 1926.

Gamble, Thomas. *Savannah Duels and Duellists, 1733-1877.* Savannah, 1923.

Georgia Writers' Project. "Mulberry Grove from the Revolution to the Present Time," *Georgia Historical Quarterly,* XXIII, No. 4 (December 1939), 315-336.

Gottshalk, Louis. *Lafayette and the Close of the American Revolution.* Chicago, 1942.

Greely, Mary Williams. *The Diary of Dorothy Dudley (The Cambridge of 1776).* Cambridge, 1876.

Green, Constance McL. *Eli Whitney and the Birth of American Technology.* Boston, Toronto, 1956.

Greene, D. H. *History of the Town of East Greenwich and Adjacent Territory from 1677 to 1877.* Providence, 1877.

Greene, Francis Vinton. *General Greene.* New York, London, 1913.

Greene, George Washington. *Life of Nathanael Greene, Major-General in the Army of the Revolution.* 3 vols. Cambridge, 1871.

Greene, Nathanael. "A Letter to His Wife," *Pennsylvania Magazine of History and Biography,* XLI, No. 2 (1917), 251.

Greene, Samuel Ward. "Greene Letters," *Rhode Island Historical Society Collections,* XX, No. 4 (October 1927), 103-107.

Hammond, M. B., ed. "Correspondence of Eli Whitney Relative to the Invention of the Cotton Gin," *American Historical Review,* III, No. 1 (October 1897), 90-127.

Hartridge, Walter C., ed. *The Letters of Don Juan McQueen to His Family.* Columbia, South Carolina, 1943.

_____, ed. *The Letters of Robert Mackay to His Wife.* Athens, Georgia, 1949.

Henderson, Archibald. *Washington's Southern Tour, 1791.* Boston, New York, 1923.

Holliday, Carl. *Woman's Life in Colonial Days.* New York, 1960.

Hornor, Marian Sadtler, ed. "A Washington Affair of Honor, 1779," *Pennsylvania Magazine of History and Biography,* LXV (July 1941), 362-370.

Howell, Clark. *History of Georgia.* Chicago, Atlanta, 1926.

Johnson, William. *Sketches of the Life and Correspondence of Nathanael Greene, Major General in the Armies of the United States in the War of the Revolution.* 2 vols. Charleston, 1822.

Jones, Charles C. *Reminiscences of the Last Days, Death, and Burial of General Henry Lee.* Albany, New York, 1870.

Ketchum, Richard M., ed. *The American Heritage Book of the Revolution.* New York, 1958.

Keyes, Nelson Beecher. *Ben Franklin.* Garden City, New York, 1956.

Lawrence, Alexander A. *Storm Over Savannah.* Athens, Georgia, 1951, 1968.

Leiding, Harriette Kershaw. *Charleston, Historic and Romantic.* Philadelphia, 1931.

Lippincott, Horace Mather. *Early Philadelphia, Its People, Life and Progress.* Philadelphia, 1917.

Lundin, Leonard. *Cockpit of the Revolution, The War for Independence in New Jersey.* Princeton, New Jersey, 1940.

McCrady, Edward. *The History of South Carolina in the Revolution, 1775-1780.* New York, 1902.

McCullar, Bernice. *This Is Your Georgia.* Northport, Alabama, 1966.

Mackenzie, Frederick. *Diary.* 2 vols. Cambridge, Massachusetts, 1930.

Miller, Stephen F. *The Bench and Bar of Georgia, Memoirs and Sketches.* Philadelphia, 1858.

Mirsky, Jeannette and Allan Nevins. *The World of Eli Whitney.* New York, 1952.

Monaghan, Frank and Marvin Lowenthal. *This Was New York, the Nation's Capital in 1789.* Garden City, New York, 1943.

Monahan, Clifford P. and Clarkson A. Collins, III, eds. "Nathanael Greene's Letters to 'Friend Sammy Ward,'" *Rhode Island History,* XV, No. 1 (January 1956), 1-10; No. 2 (April 1956), 46-54; XVI, No. 2 (April 1957), 53-57; No. 3 (July 1957), 79-88; No. 4 (October 1957), 119-121; XVII, No. 1 (January 1958), 14-21.

Moriarty, G. A., ed. "Early Block Island Families," *New England Historical and Genealogical Register,* LXXXVI (January 1932), 75-77, 324-330.

Murdoch, Richard K., ed. "Letters and Papers of Dr. Daniel Turner: A Rhode Islander in Georgia," *Georgia Historical Quarterly,* LIII, No. 3 (September 1969), 341-393; No. 4 (December 1969), 476-509; LIV, No. 1 (September 1970), 91-122; No. 2 (December 1970), 244-282.

Niles, Blair. *Martha's Husband.* New York, London, Toronto, 1951.

Ober, Frederick A. "Dungeness, General Greene's Sea Island Plantation," *Lippincott's Magazine,* XXVI (1880), 241-249.

Olmstead, Denison. *Memoir of Eli Whitney, Esq.* New Haven, 1846.

Paine, Thomas. *The American Crisis.* 1776.

Palmer, John McAuley. *General Von Steuben.* Port Washington, New York, 1937, 1966.

Phillips, Martha Littlefield. "Recollections of Washington and His Friends," *Century Magazine,* LV (January 1898), 363-374.

Preston, Howard W., ed. "Rochambeau and the French Troops in Providence in 1780-81-82," *Rhode Island Historical Society Collections,* XVII, No. 1 (January 1924), 1-23.

Ravenel, Mrs. St. Julien. *Charleston, the Place and the People.* New York, 1906.

Repplier, Agnes. *Philadelphia, The Place and the People.* New York, London, 1899.

Rhett, Robert Goodwyn. *Charleston, an Epic of Carolina.* Richmond, Virginia, 1940.

Richmond, George H., ed. "Letters By and To General Nathanael Greene, with Some from His Wife." New York, 1906. A pamphlet privately published. Lent to the authors by Malcolm Bell, Jr., Savannah.

Roberts, Kenneth, ed. *March to Quebec: Journals of the Members of Arnold's Expedition.* New York, 1946.

Roe, Clara G. "Major General Nathanael Greene and the Southern Campaign of the American Revolution, 1780-1783." Doctoral dissertation, University of Michigan, Ann Arbor, Michigan, 1943.

Roelker, William Greene. *Benjamin Franklin and Catharine Ray Greene, Their Correspondence, 1755-1790.* Philadelphia, 1948.

Salley, Alexander S. *Delegates to the Continental Congress from South Carolina, 1774-1789.* Columbia, South Carolina, 1927.

Sanderson, John. *Biography of the Signers to the Declaration of Independence.* 9 vols. Philadelphia, 1828.

Scarborough, William, ed. "Sketch of the Life of the Late Eli Whitney with Some Remarks on the Invention of the Saw Gin," *Southern*

Agriculturist and Register of Rural Affairs, V, No. 8 (August 1832), 393-403.

Scheer, George F., ed. *Private Yankee Doodle, Joseph Plumb Martin's Narrative of Some of the Adventures, Dangers, and Sufferings of a Revolutionary Soldier.* New York, 1962.

_____, and Hugh F. Rankin. *Rebels and Redcoats.* Cleveland, New York, 1957.

Seymour, William. "A Journal of the Southern Expedition, 1780-1783," *Pennsylvania Magazine of History and Biography*, VII, No. 4 (1883), 286-298, 377-394.

Showman, Richard K., ed. *The Papers of General Nathanael Greene.* Volume one. Chapel Hill, North Carolina, 1976.

Special Committee of the General Assembly of Rhode Island. *The Remains of Major General Nathanael Greene.* Providence, 1903.

Smith, D. E. Huger, ed. "Letters from Col. Lewis Morris to Miss Ann Elliott," *South Carolina Historical and Genealogical Magazine*, XLI, No. 1 (January 1940), 1-14.

Stevens, William Oliver. *Charleston.* New York, 1939.

Stoudt, John Joseph. *Ordeal at Valley Forge.* Philadelphia, 1963.

Swiggett, Howard. *The Forgotten Leaders of the Revolution.* Garden City, New York, 1955.

Syrett, Harold C., ed. *The Papers of Alexander Hamilton.* New York, London, 1965.

_____, and Jean G. Cooke, eds. *Interview in Weehawken.* Middletown, Conn., 1960.

Thane, Ellswyth. *Washington's Lady.* New York, 1954, 1959, 1960.

Thayer, Theodore. *Nathanael Greene, Strategist of the American Revolution.* New York, 1960.

Tompkins, D. A., ed. *The Cotton Gin.* Charlotte, North Carolina, 1901.

Tower, Charlemagne, Jr. *The Marquis de LaFayette in the American Revolution.* Philadelphia, 1895.

Van Doren, Carl, ed. *Benjamin Franklin, Autobiographical Writings.* New York, 1945.

Warden, G. B. *Boston 1689-1776.* Boston, Toronto, 1970.

Whitehead, James L., ed. "The Autobiography of Peter Stephen Duponceau," *Pennsylvania Magazine of History and Biography*, LXIII, No. 2 (April 1939), 189-227.

Whitlock, Brand. *LaFayette.* 2 vols. New York, London, 1929.

Whitney, David C., ed. *Founders of Freedom in America.* Chicago, 1964.

Whittemore, Charles P. *A General of the Revolution: John Sullivan of New Hampshire.* New York, London, 1961.

Wilson, Rufus Rockwell. *New York, Old and New, Its Story, Streets, and Landmarks.* 2 vols. Philadelphia, London, 1909.

Wills and Appraisements, Book "A," 1795-1829, Camden County (Georgia) Court of Ordinary, *Georgia Genealogical Magazine*, No. 1 (July 1961).

Winn, William. "Private Fastness," *American Heritage*, XXIII, No. 3 (April 1972), 26-32, 104.

Newspapers

Charleston Courier
Columbian Museum and Savannah Advertiser

226

Federal Gazette and Philadelphia Daily Advertiser
Gazette of the State of Georgia
Independent Gazetteer and Agricultural Repository (Philadelphia)
New Hampshire Gazette
New York Evening Post
Pennsylvania Packet, or the General Advertiser
Pennsylvania Journal, or the Weekly Advertiser
Providence Gazette
Republican and Savannah Evening Ledger
Savannah Republican

Index

9 780820 307923